Baba Yaga's Assistant

Baba Yaga's Assistant

WITHDRAWN

Marika McCoola
illustrated by Emily Carroll

CANDLEWICK PRESS

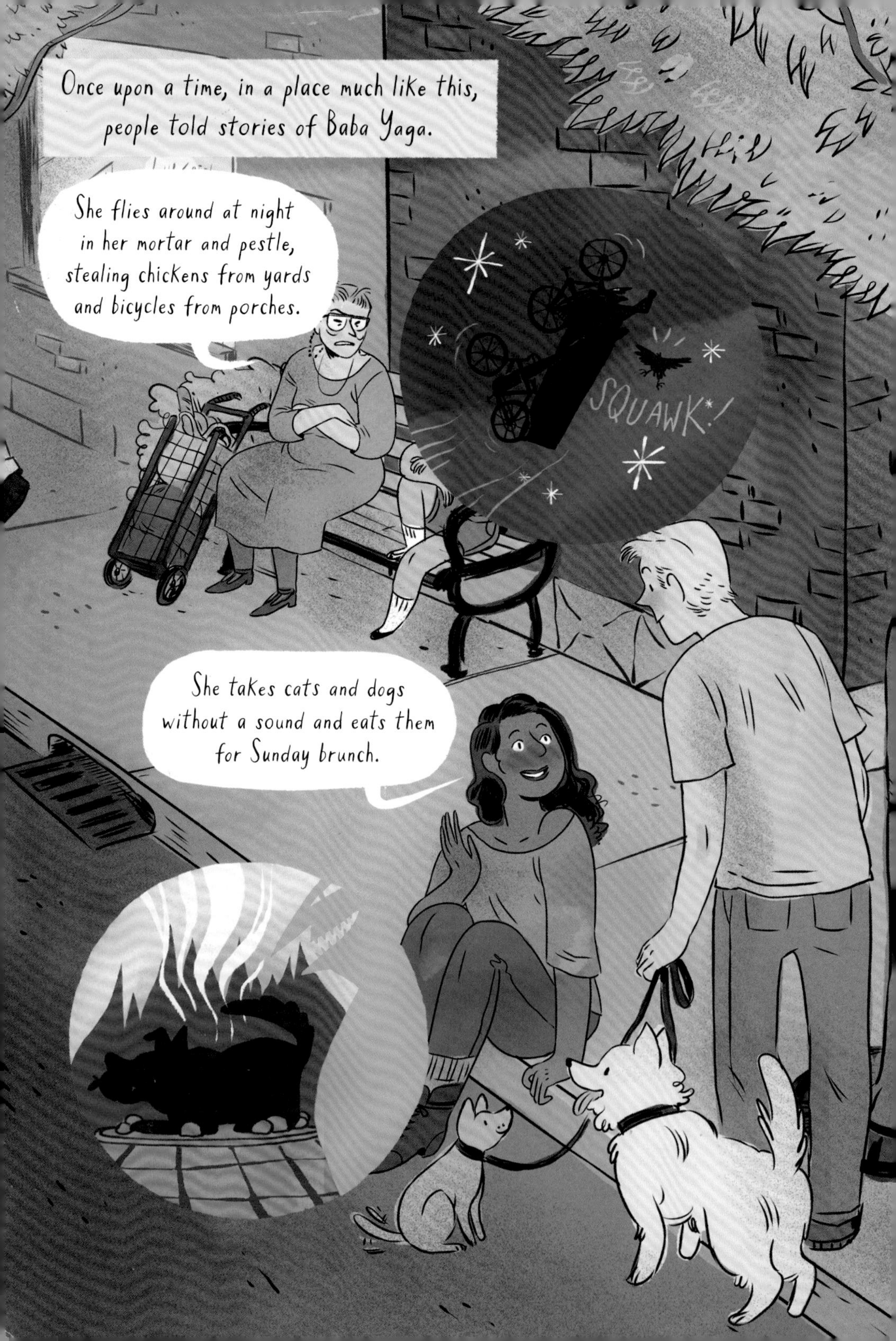
Once upon a time, in a place much like this, people told stories of Baba Yaga.
She flies around at night in her mortar and pestle, stealing chickens from yards and bicycles from porches.
SQUAWK!
She takes cats and dogs without a sound and eats them for Sunday brunch.

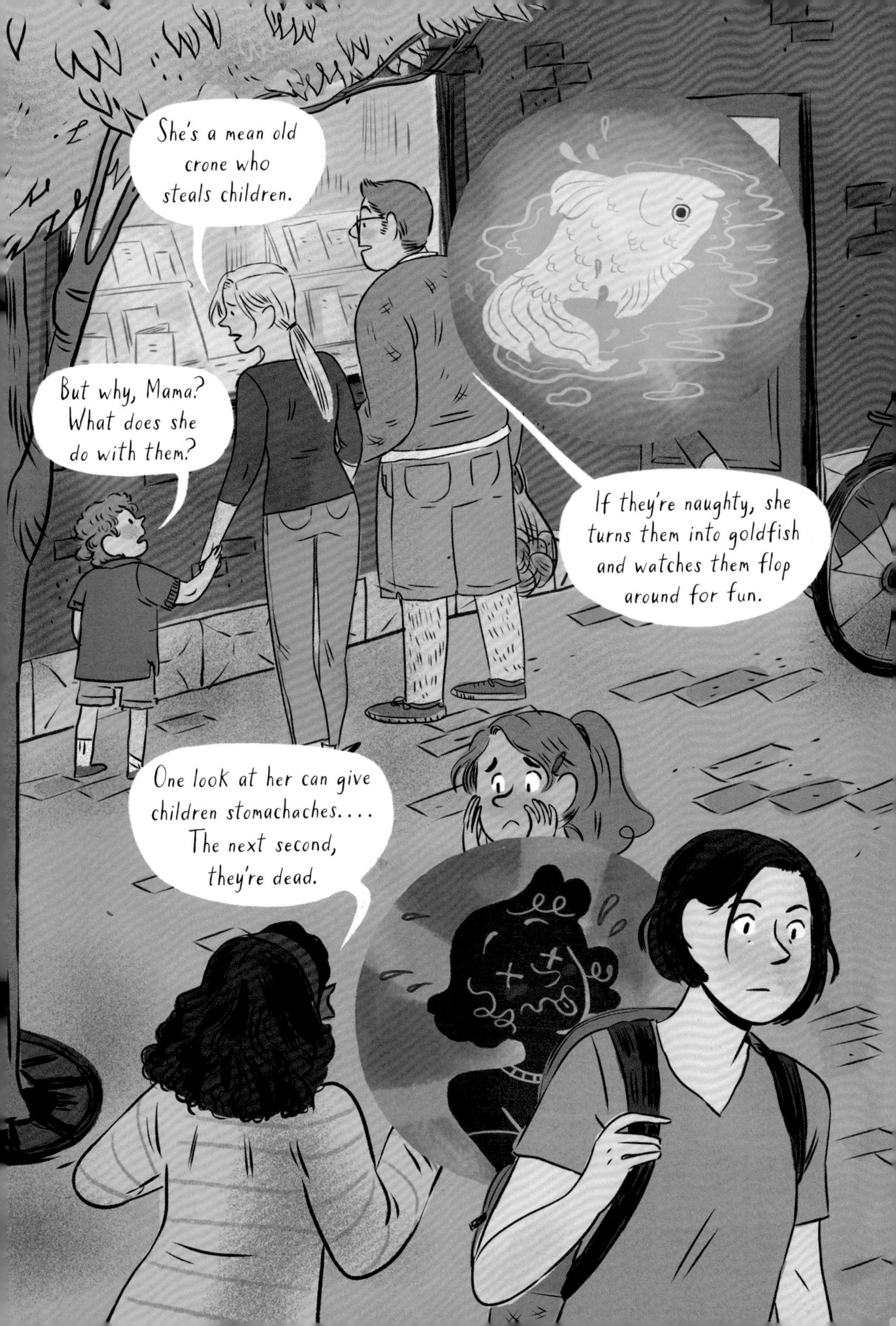
She's a mean old crone who steals children.
But why, Mama? What does she do with them?
If they're naughty, she turns them into goldfish and watches them flop around for fun.
One look at her can give children stomachaches.... The next second, they're dead.

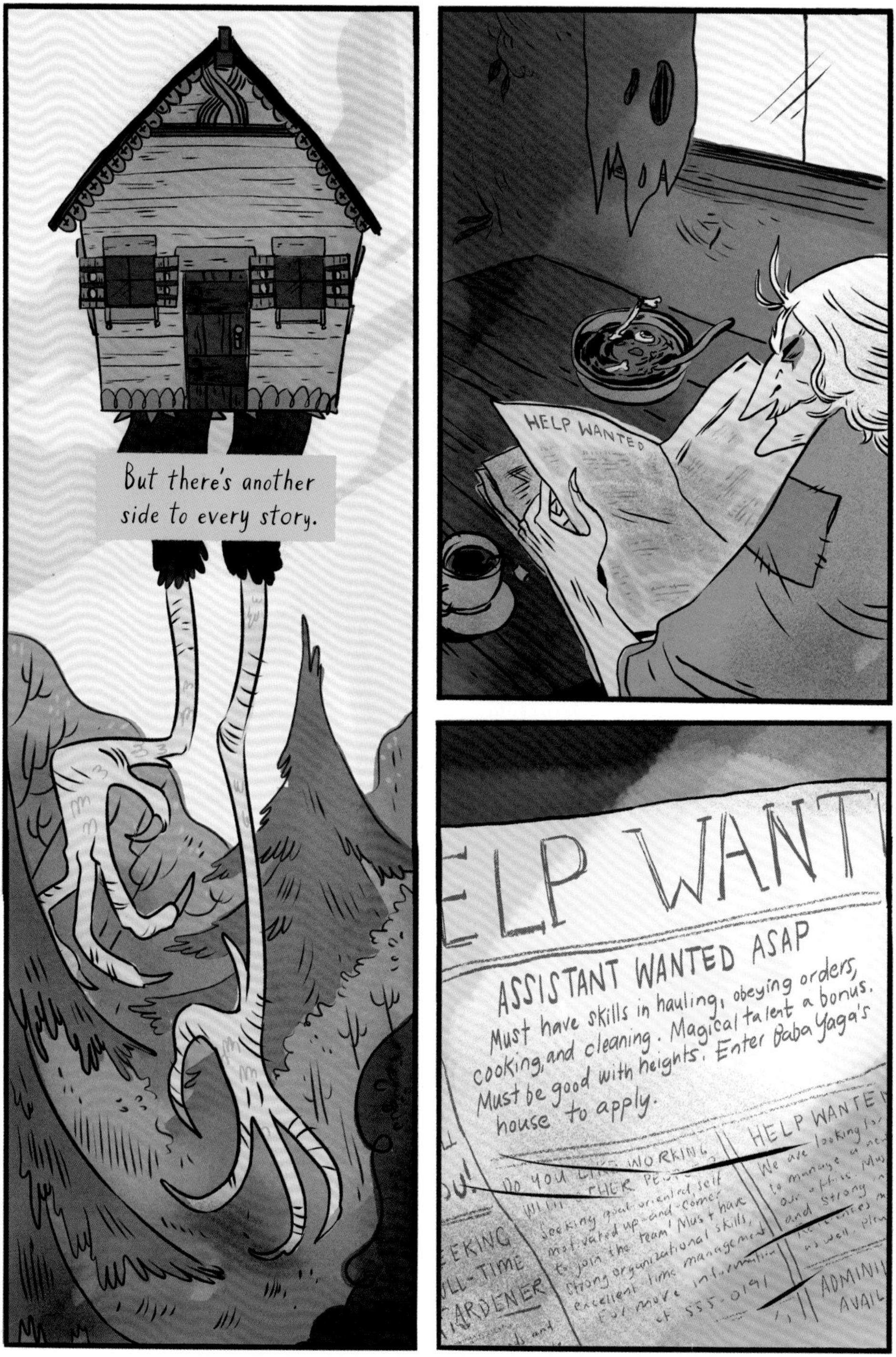
But there's another side to every story.
HELP WANTED
ELP WANT
ASSISTANT WANTED ASAP
Must have skills in hauling, obeying orders, cooking, and cleaning. Magical talent a bonus. Must be good with heights. Enter Baba Yaga's house to apply.

BABA YAGA'S ASSISTANT

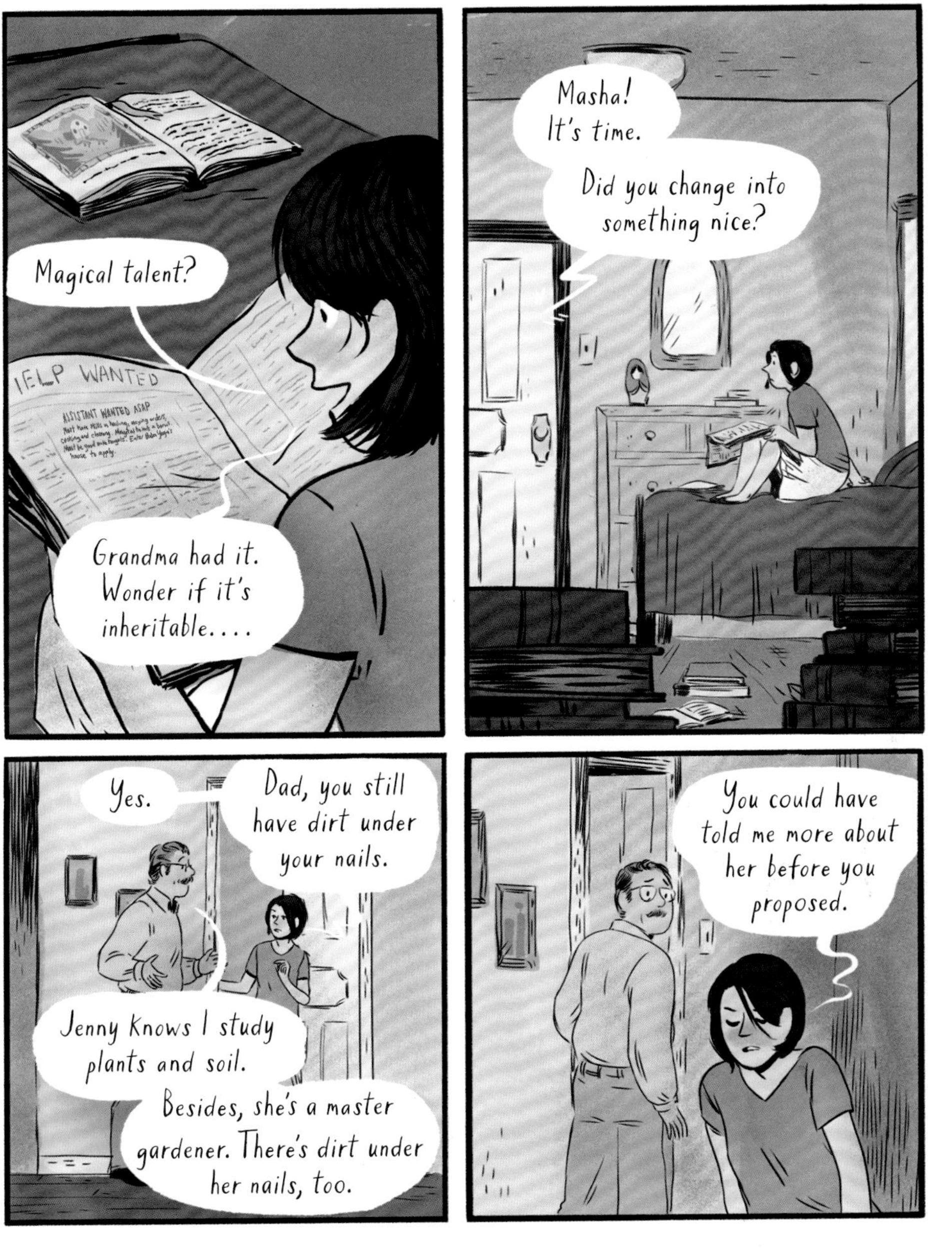

ASSISTANT WANTED ASAP
Magical talent?
Grandma had it. Wonder if it's inheritable....
Masha! It's time.
Did you change into something nice?
Yes.
Dad, you still have dirt under your nails.
Jenny knows I study plants and soil.
Besides, she's a master gardener. There's dirt under her nails, too.
You could have told me more about her before you proposed.

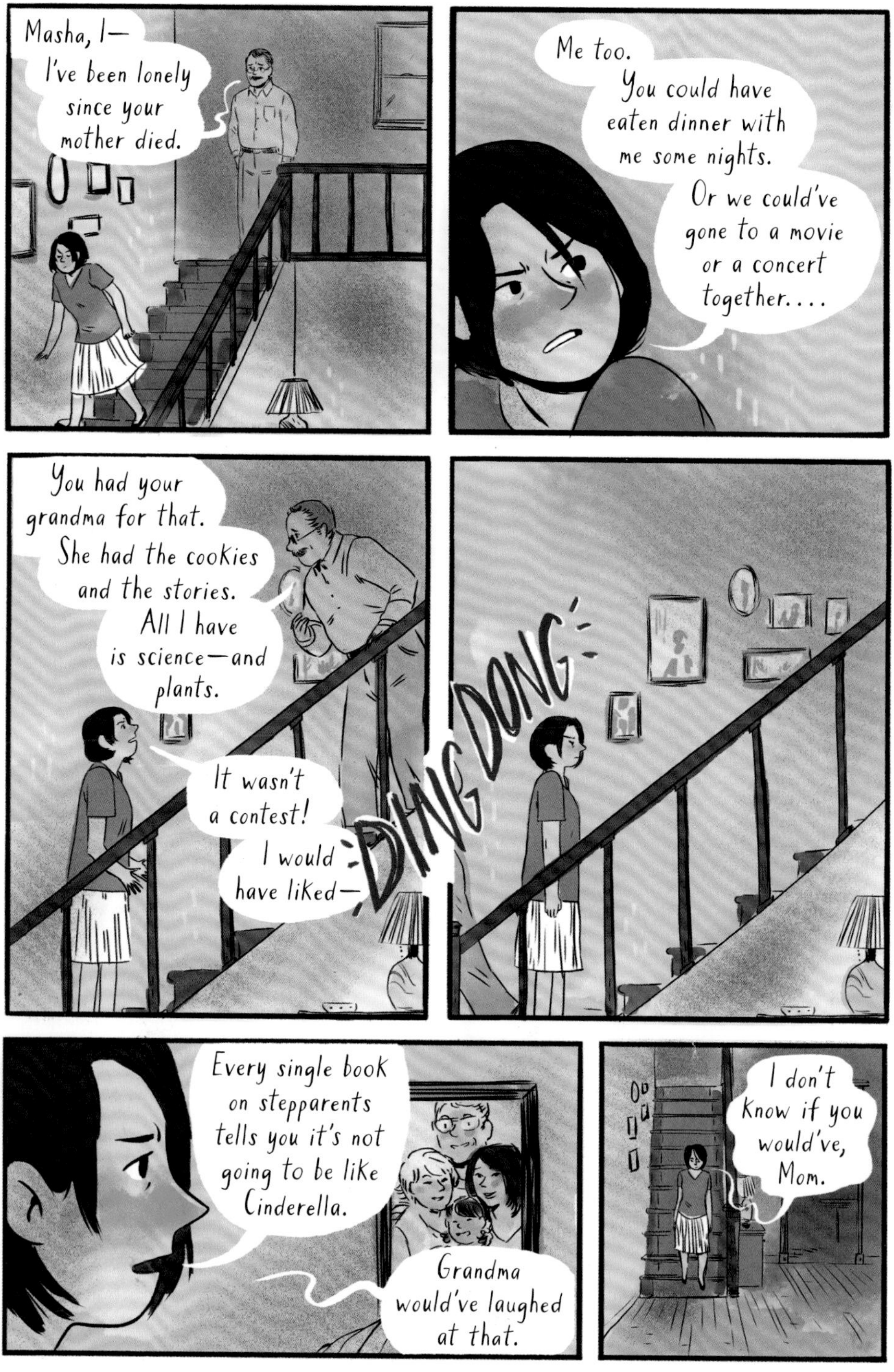
Masha, I—
I've been lonely since your mother died.
Me too.
You could have eaten dinner with me some nights.
Or we could've gone to a movie or a concert together....
You had your grandma for that.
She had the cookies and the stories.
All I have is science—and plants.
It wasn't a contest!
I would have liked—
DING DONG
Every single book on stepparents tells you it's not going to be like Cinderella.
Grandma would've laughed at that.
I don't know if you would've, Mom.

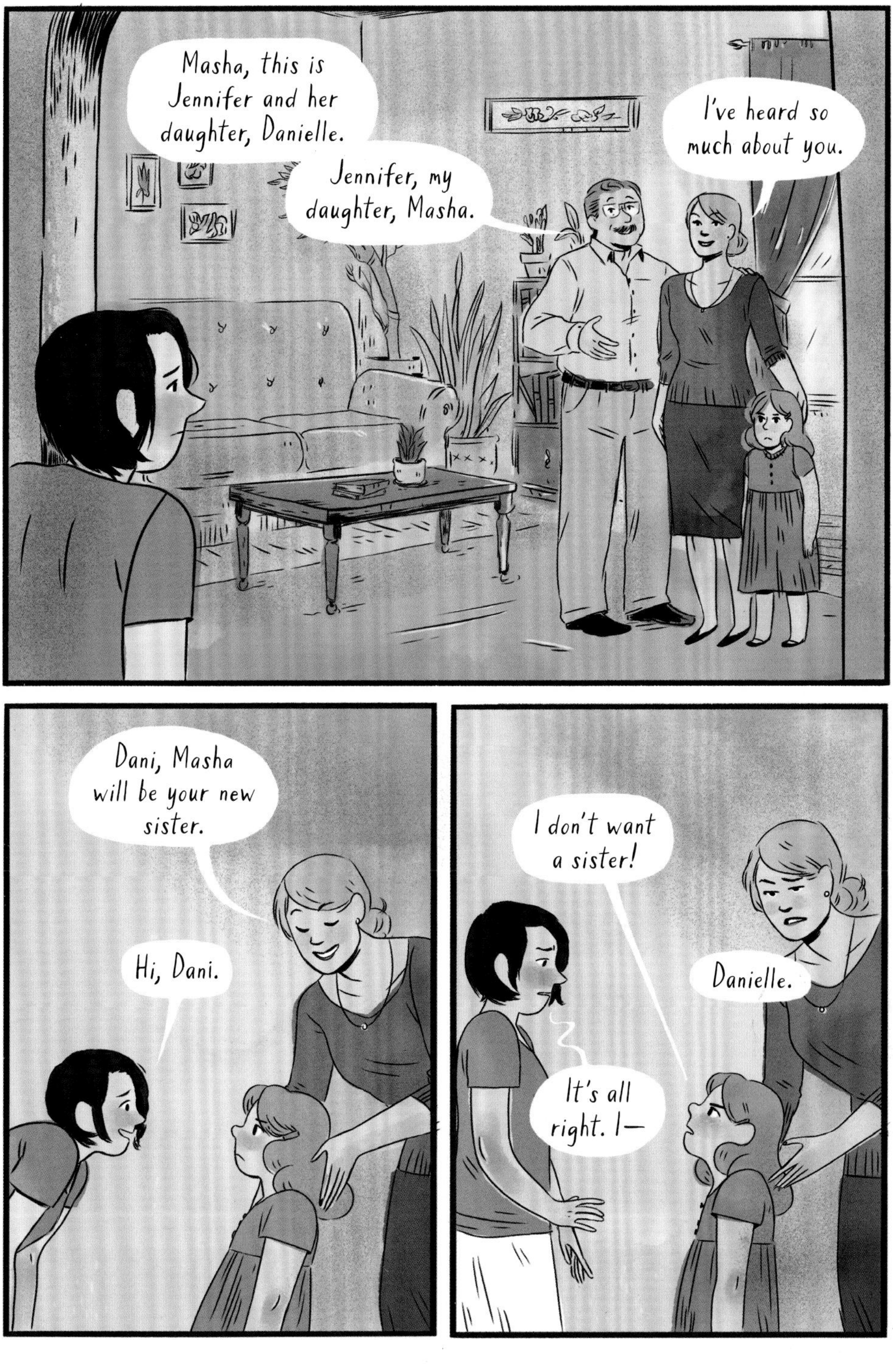
Masha, this is Jennifer and her daughter, Danielle.
Jennifer, my daughter, Masha.
I've heard so much about you.
Dani, Masha will be your new sister.
Hi, Dani.
I don't want a sister!
It's all right. I—
Danielle.

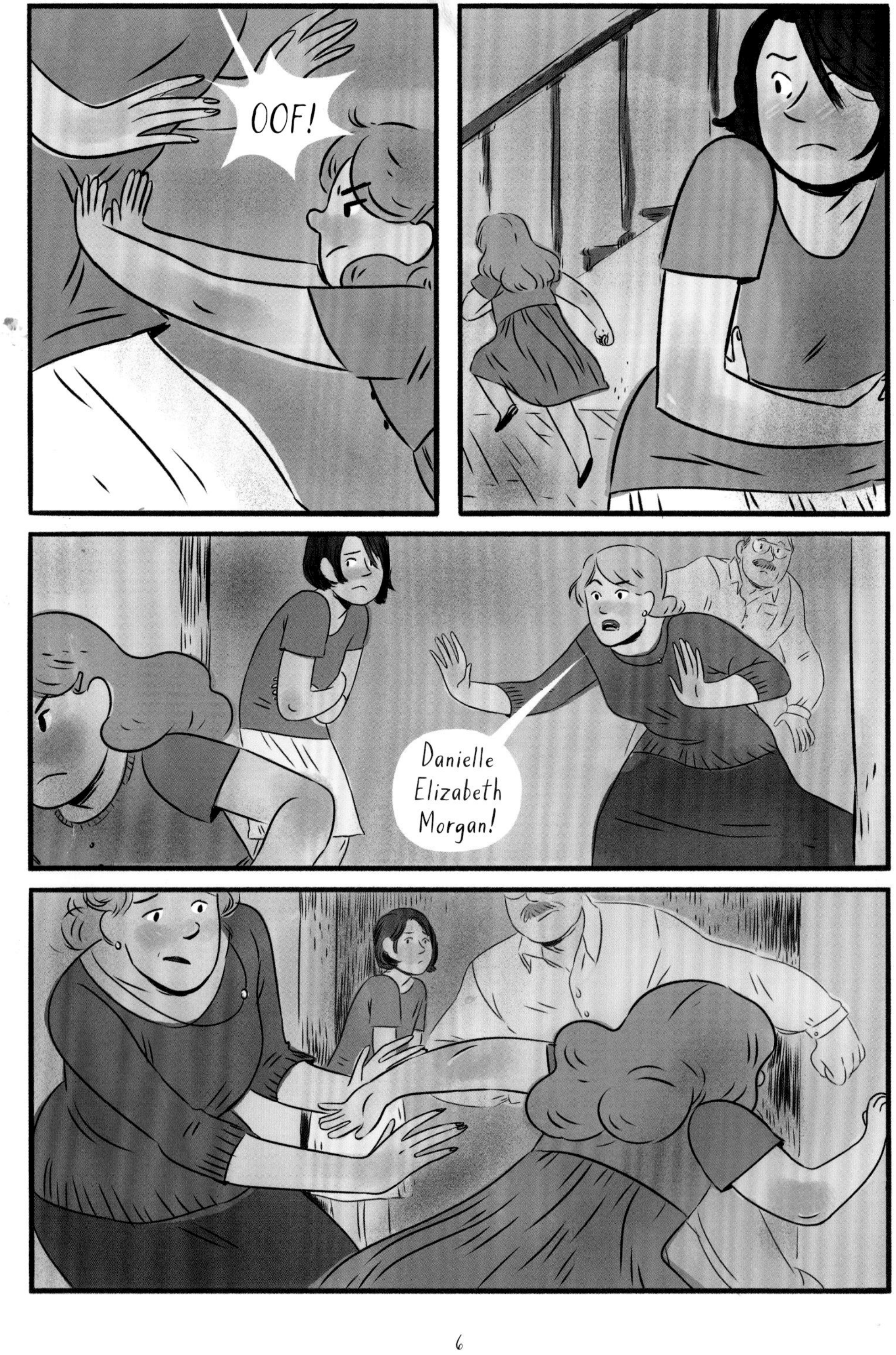
OOF!
Danielle Elizabeth Morgan!

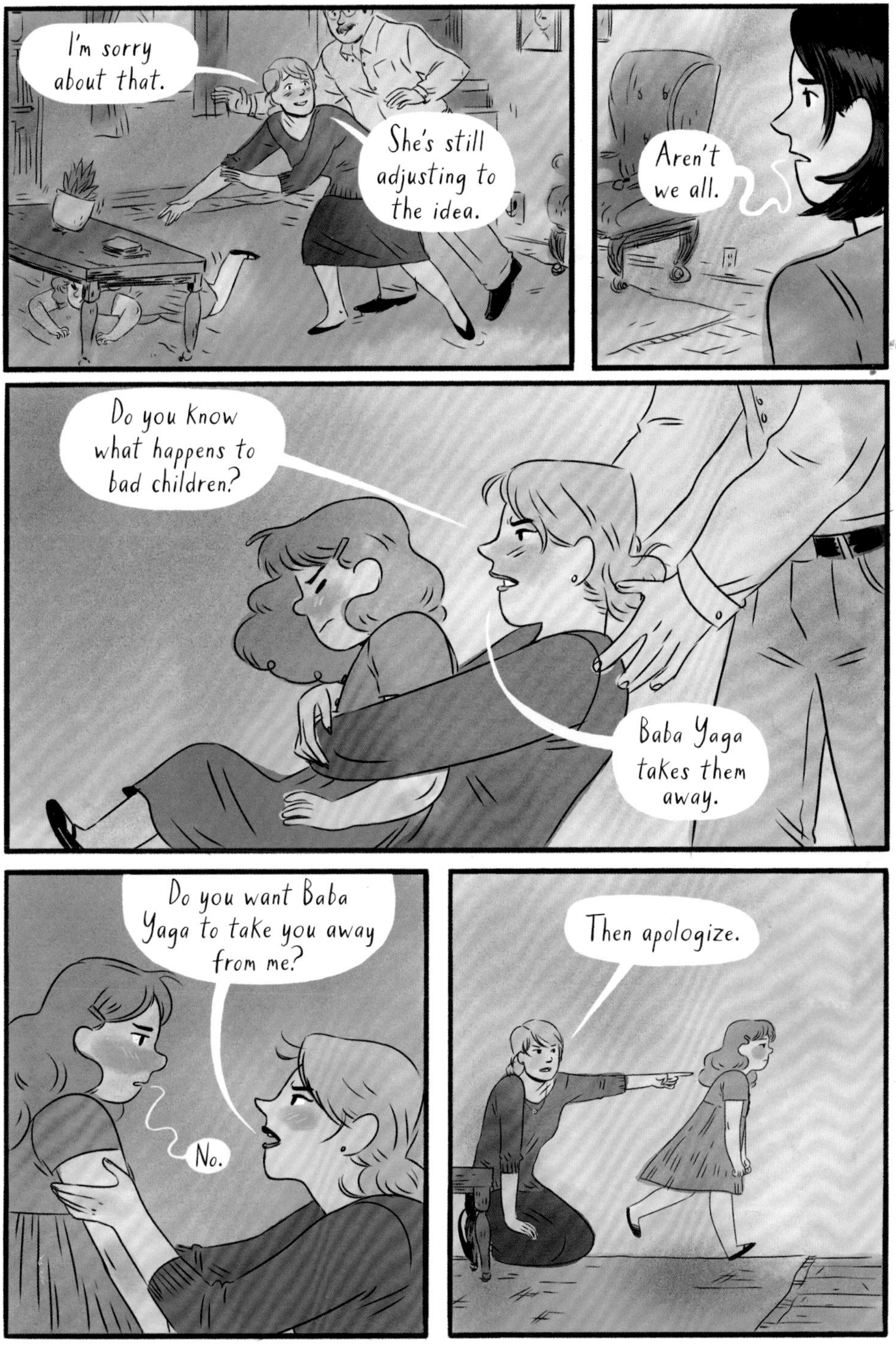
I'm sorry about that.
She's still adjusting to the idea.
Aren't we all.
Do you know what happens to bad children?
Baba Yaga takes them away.
Do you want Baba Yaga to take you away from me?
No.
Then apologize.

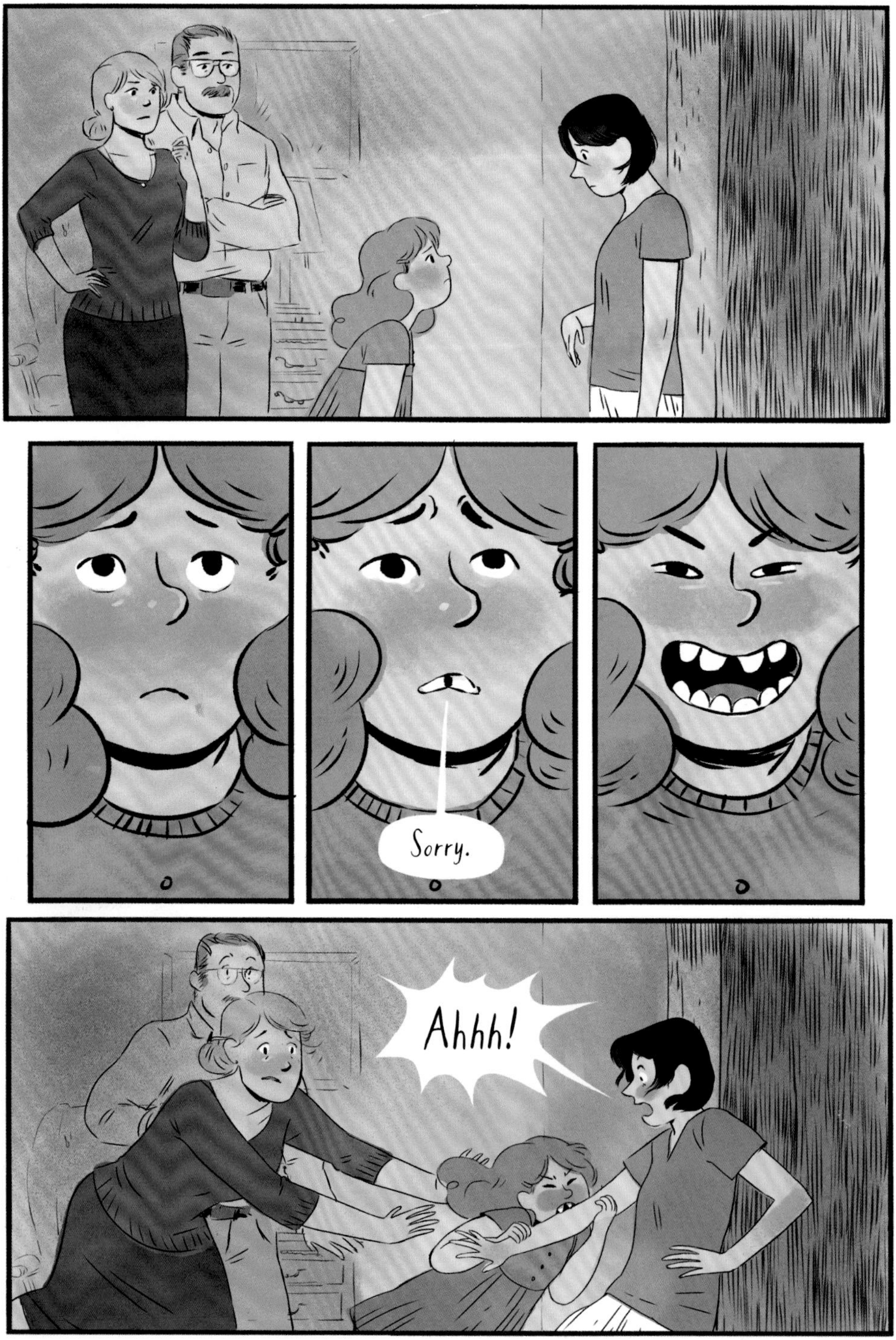
Sorry.
Ahhh!

I'm going for a walk.
Will you join us for dinner?
You won't be having it in your office?
No. Jenny prefers me to eat with her and Dani.
You've been eating with them while I'm here alone?
Well, I'm glad you finally found a family worth your time.

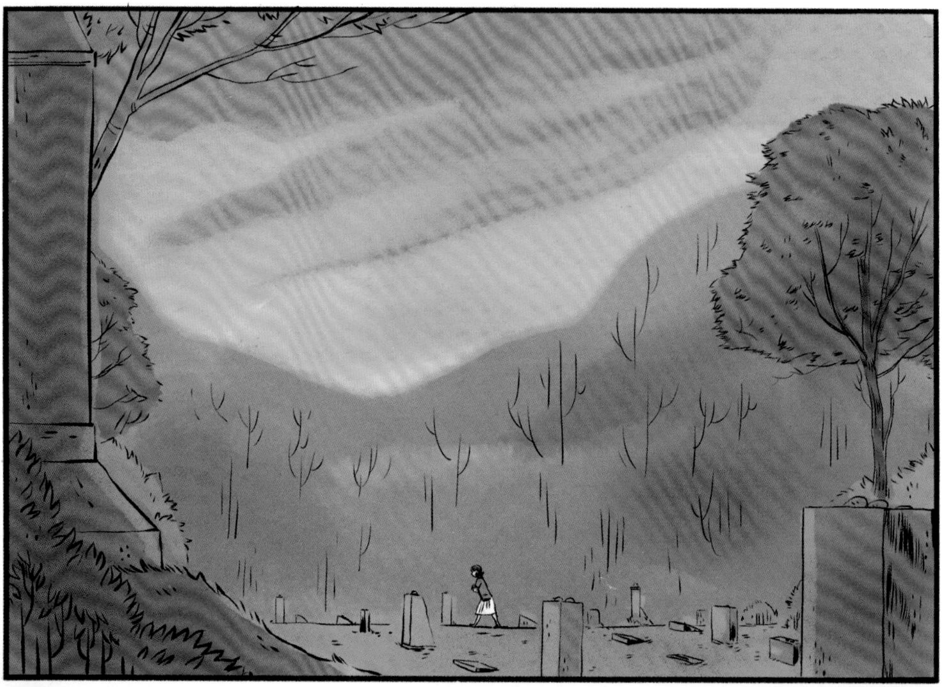

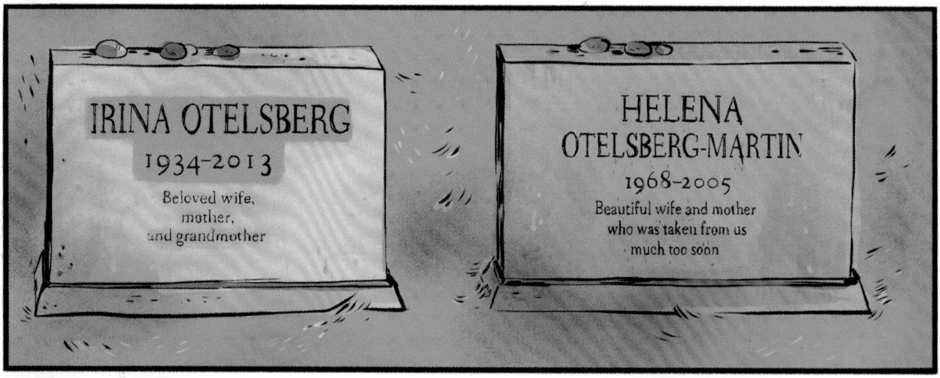
IRINA OTELSBERG
1934-2013
Beloved wife,
mother,
and grandmother
HELENA
OTELSBERG-MARTIN
1968-2005
Beautiful wife and mother
who was taken from us
much too soon

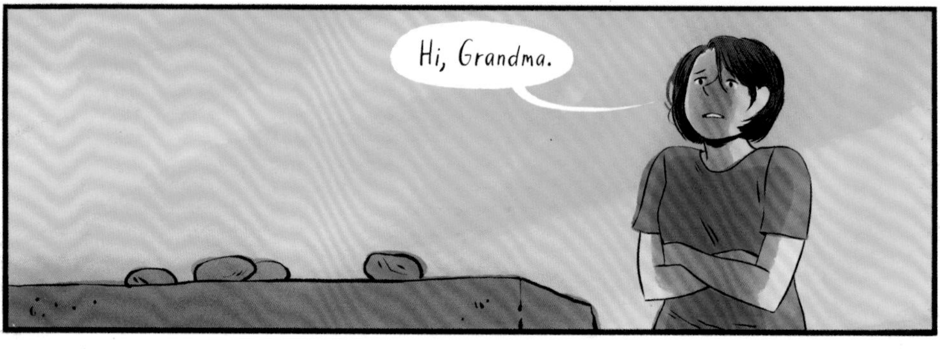
Hi, Grandma.

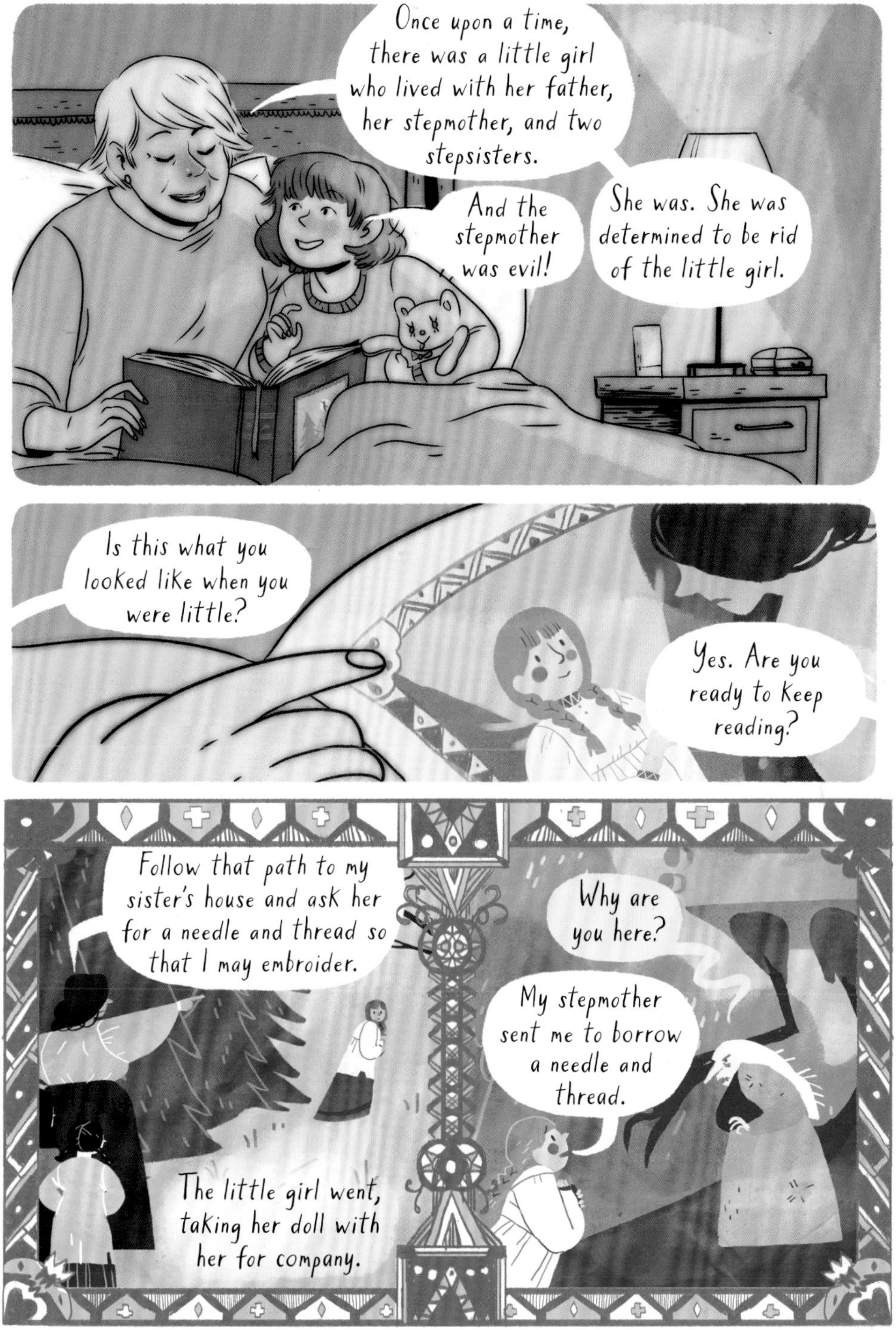
Once upon a time, there was a little girl who lived with her father, her stepmother, and two stepsisters.
And the stepmother was evil!
She was. She was determined to be rid of the little girl.
Is this what you looked like when you were little?
Yes. Are you ready to keep reading?
Follow that path to my sister's house and ask her for a needle and thread so that I may embroider.
The little girl went, taking her doll with her for company.
Why are you here?
My stepmother sent me to borrow a needle and thread.

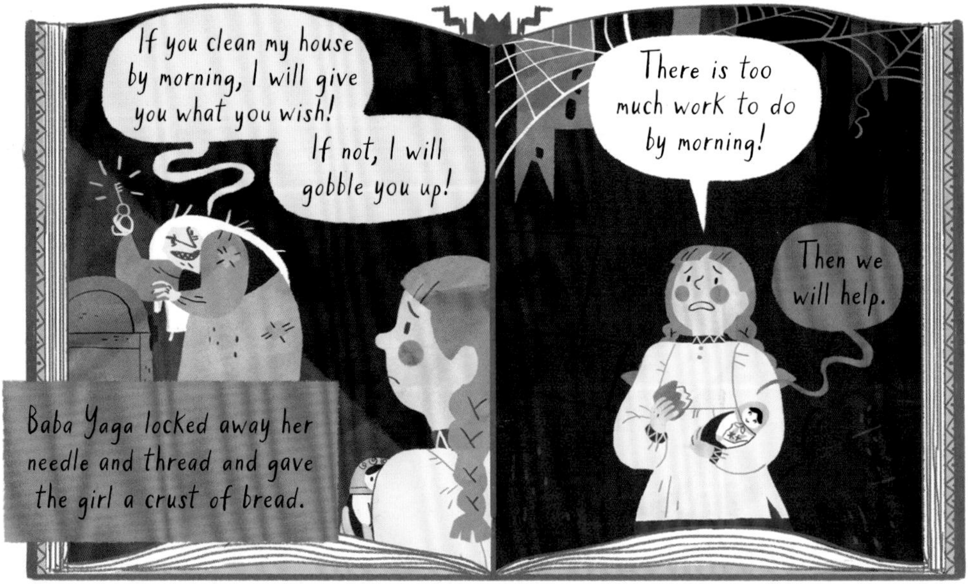
If you clean my house by morning, I will give you what you wish!
If not, I will gobble you up!
Baba Yaga locked away her needle and thread and gave the girl a crust of bread.
There is too much work to do by morning!
Then we will help.

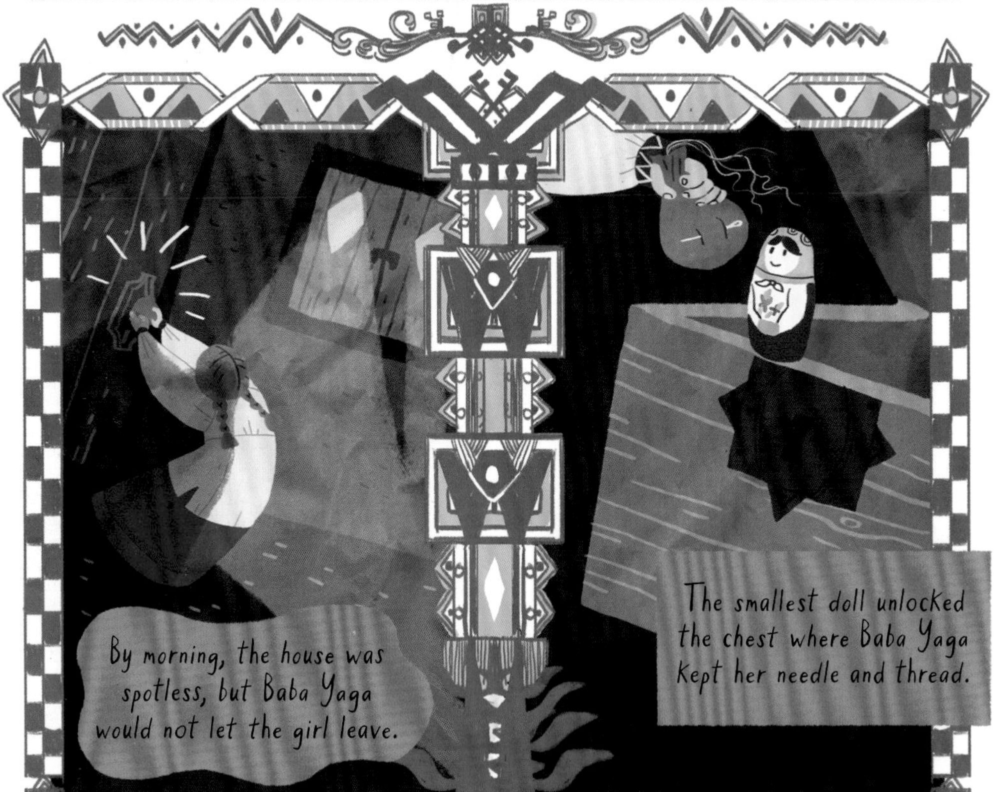
By morning, the house was spotless, but Baba Yaga would not let the girl leave.
The smallest doll unlocked the chest where Baba Yaga kept her needle and thread.

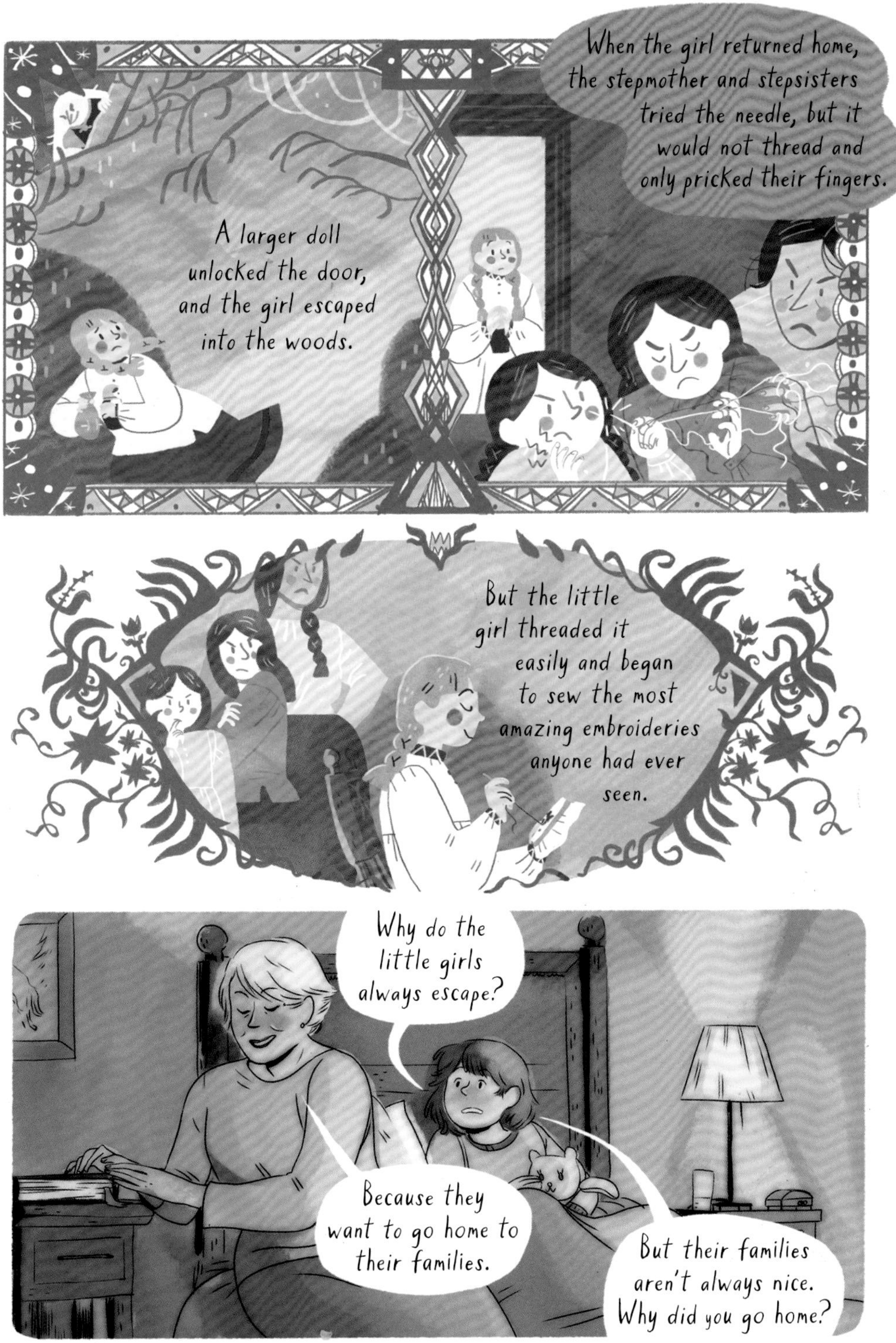
When the girl returned home, the stepmother and stepsisters tried the needle, but it would not thread and only pricked their fingers.
A larger doll unlocked the door, and the girl escaped into the woods.
But the little girl threaded it easily and began to sew the most amazing embroideries anyone had ever seen.
Why do the little girls always escape?
Because they want to go home to their families.
But their families aren't always nice. Why did you go home?

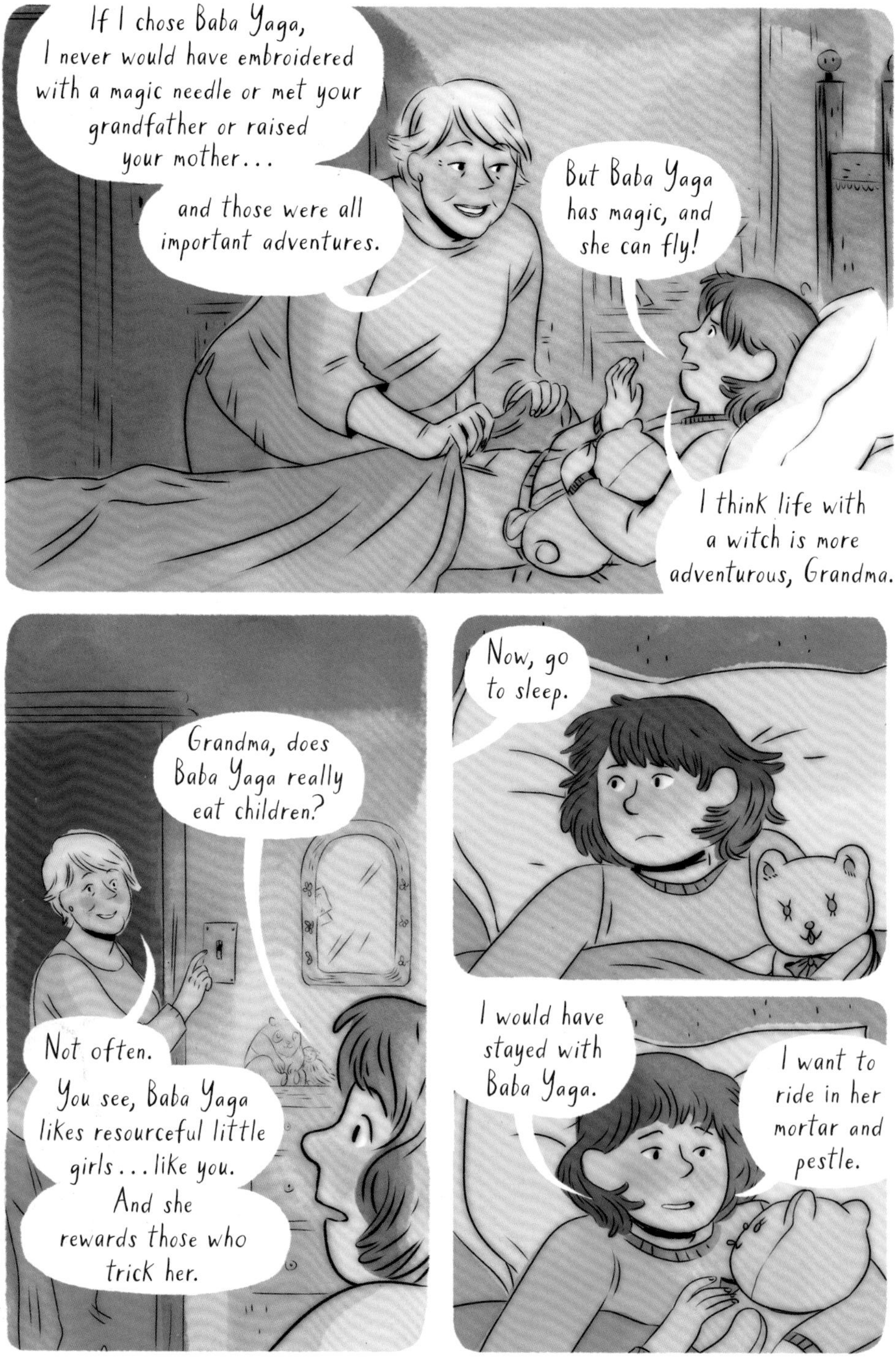
If I chose Baba Yaga, I never would have embroidered with a magic needle or met your grandfather or raised your mother...
and those were all important adventures.
But Baba Yaga has magic, and she can fly!
I think life with a witch is more adventurous, Grandma.
Grandma, does Baba Yaga really eat children?
Not often.
You see, Baba Yaga likes resourceful little girls... like you.
And she rewards those who trick her.
Now, go to sleep.
I would have stayed with Baba Yaga.
I want to ride in her mortar and pestle.

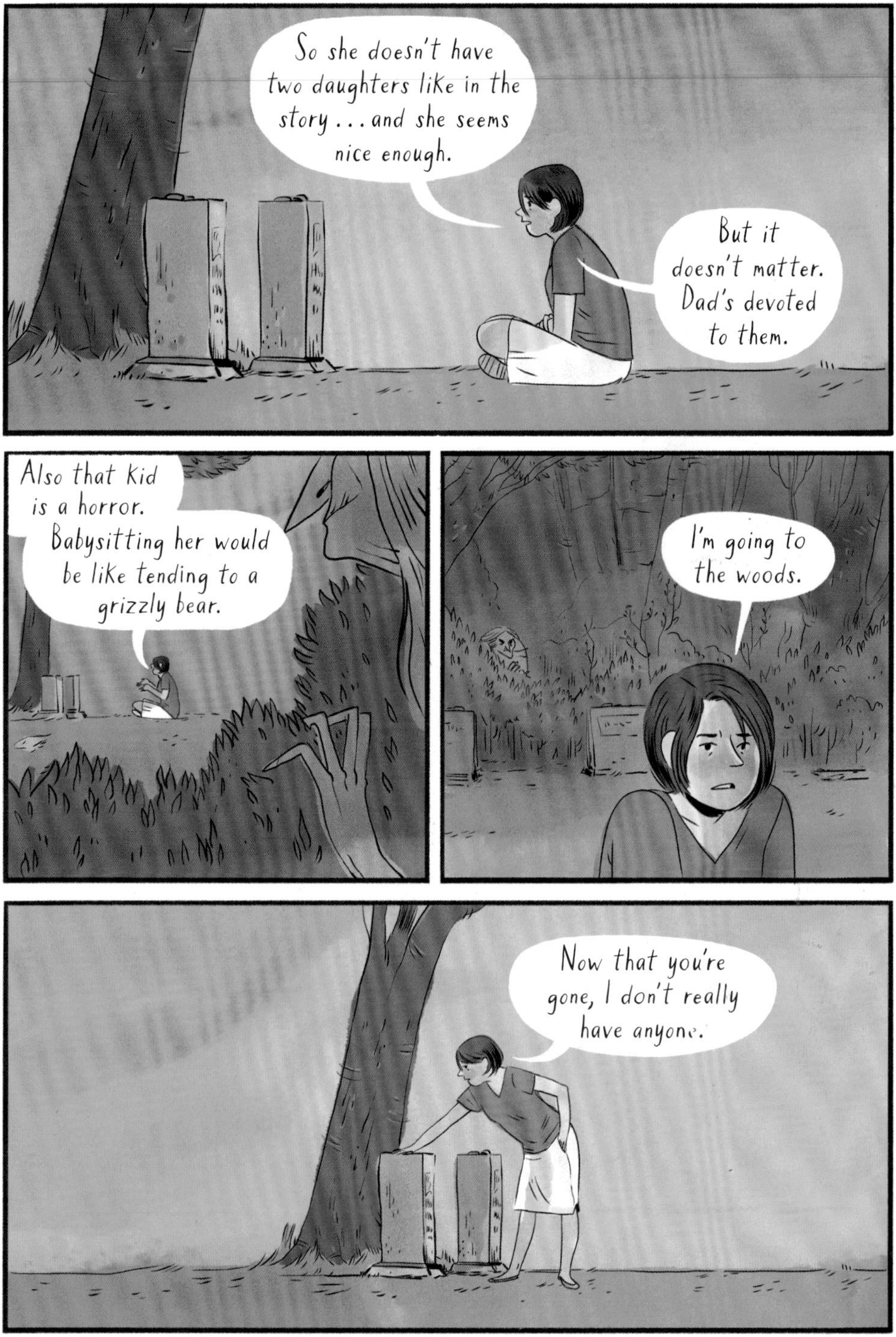
So she doesn't have two daughters like in the story . . . and she seems nice enough.
But it doesn't matter. Dad's devoted to them.
Also that kid is a horror. Babysitting her would be like tending to a grizzly bear.
I'm going to the woods.
Now that you're gone, I don't really have anyone.

Dad's found a new family. Why can't I?
I know Baba Yaga is a witch...
but she's a grandma, too. Right?
But I don't think her grandchildren help her.

I'm tired of being overlooked. I need to do something useful for someone.
You had your adventure with Baba Yaga. . . .
ASSISTANT
Must have skills in
cooking, and cleaning. Magical talent a bonus.
Must be good with heights. Enter Baba Yaga's
house to apply.
It's time for me to have mine.
I love you.

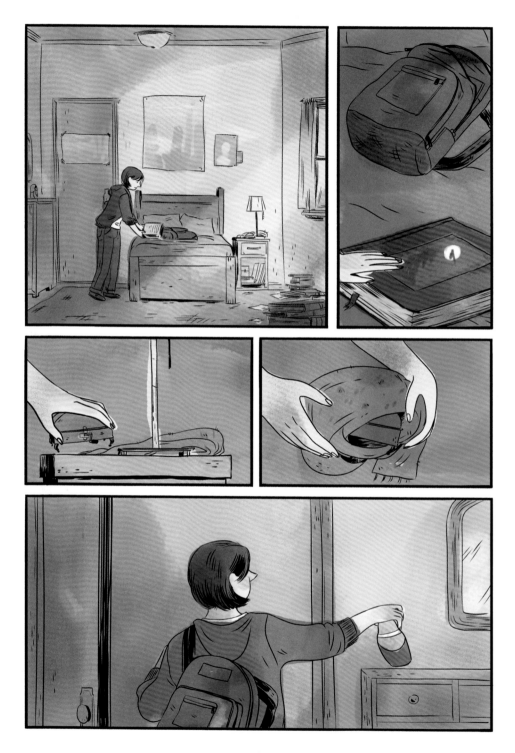

18

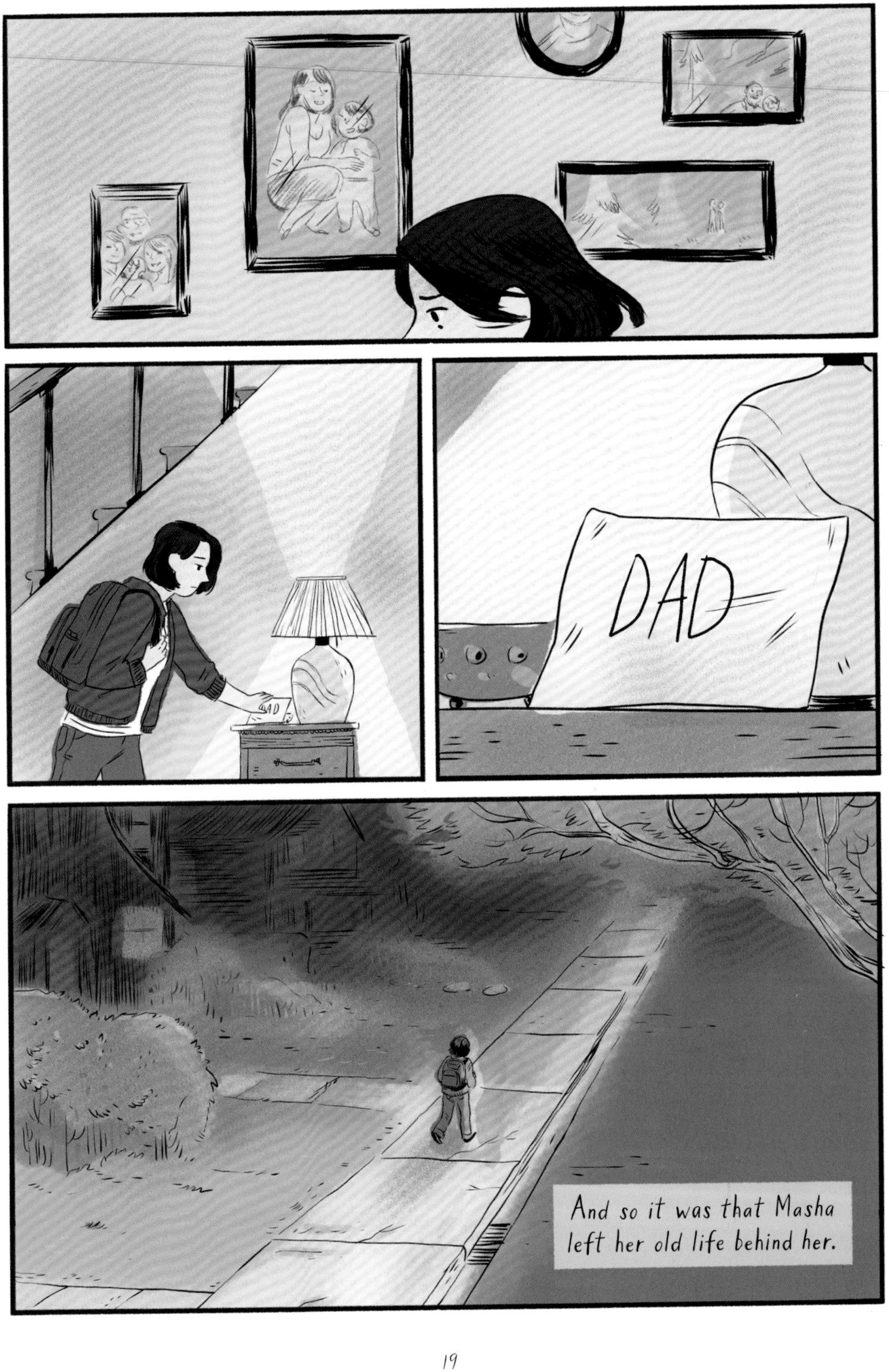
DAD
And so it was that Masha left her old life behind her.

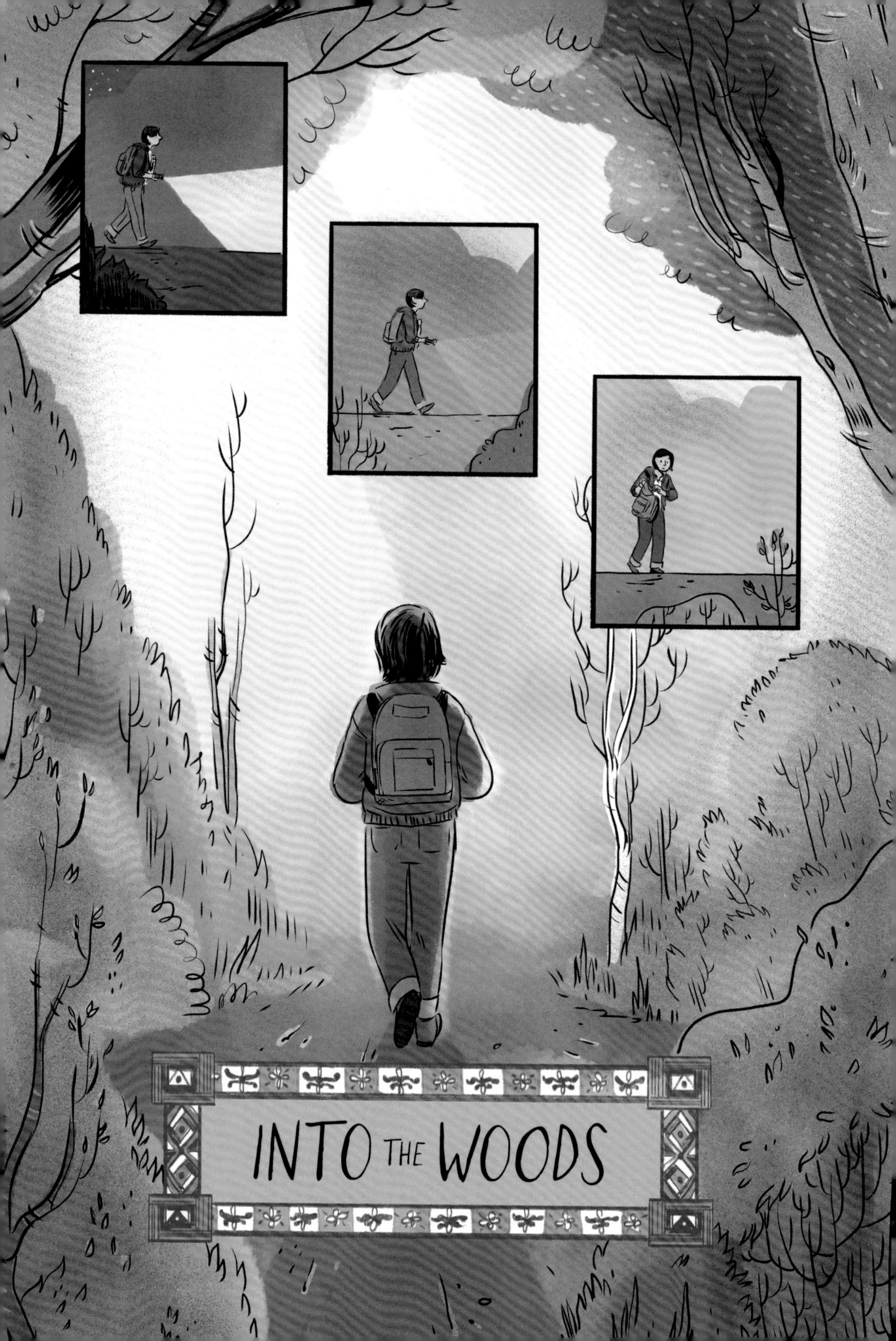
INTO THE WOODS

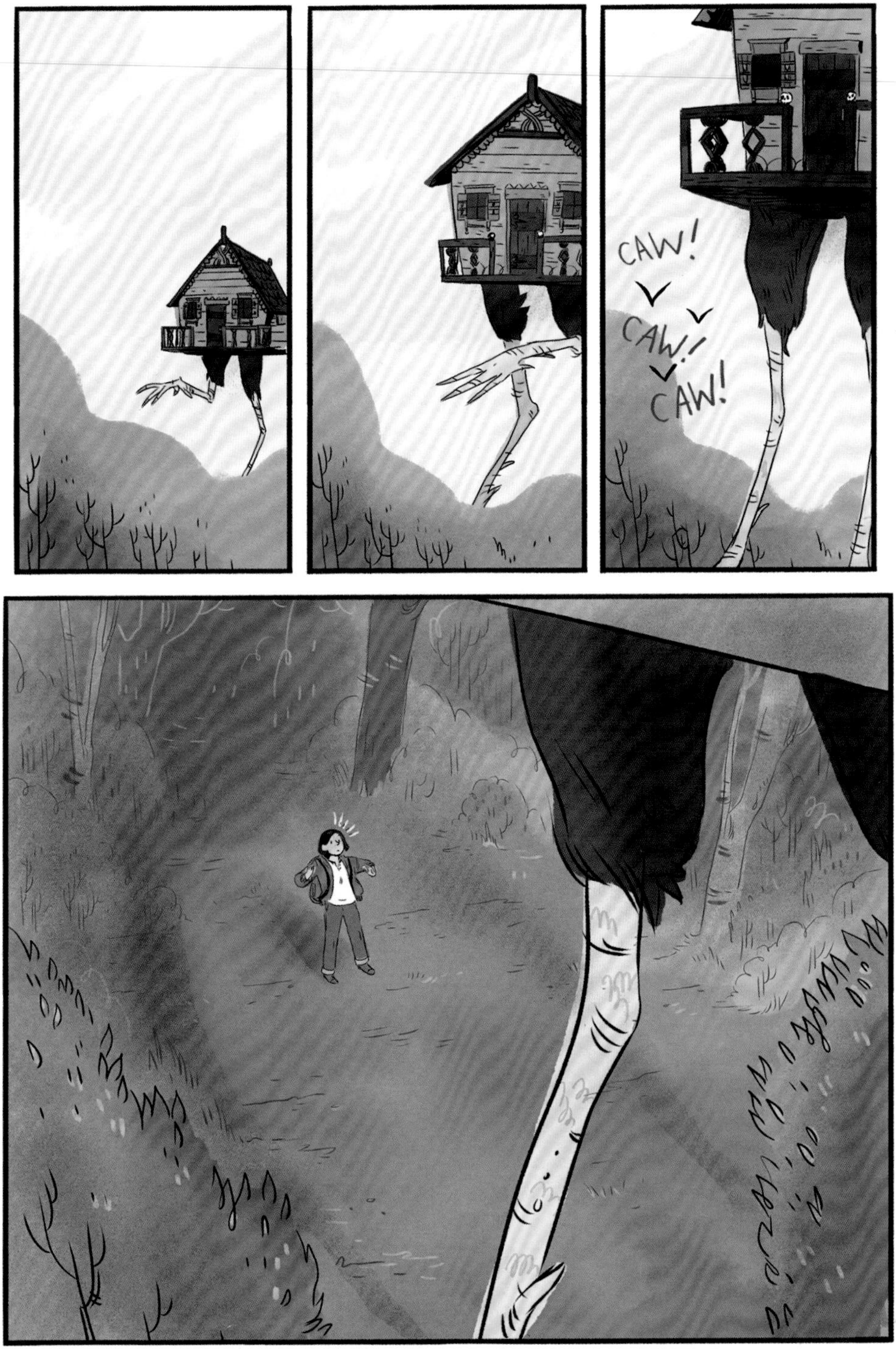
CAW!
CAW!
CAW!

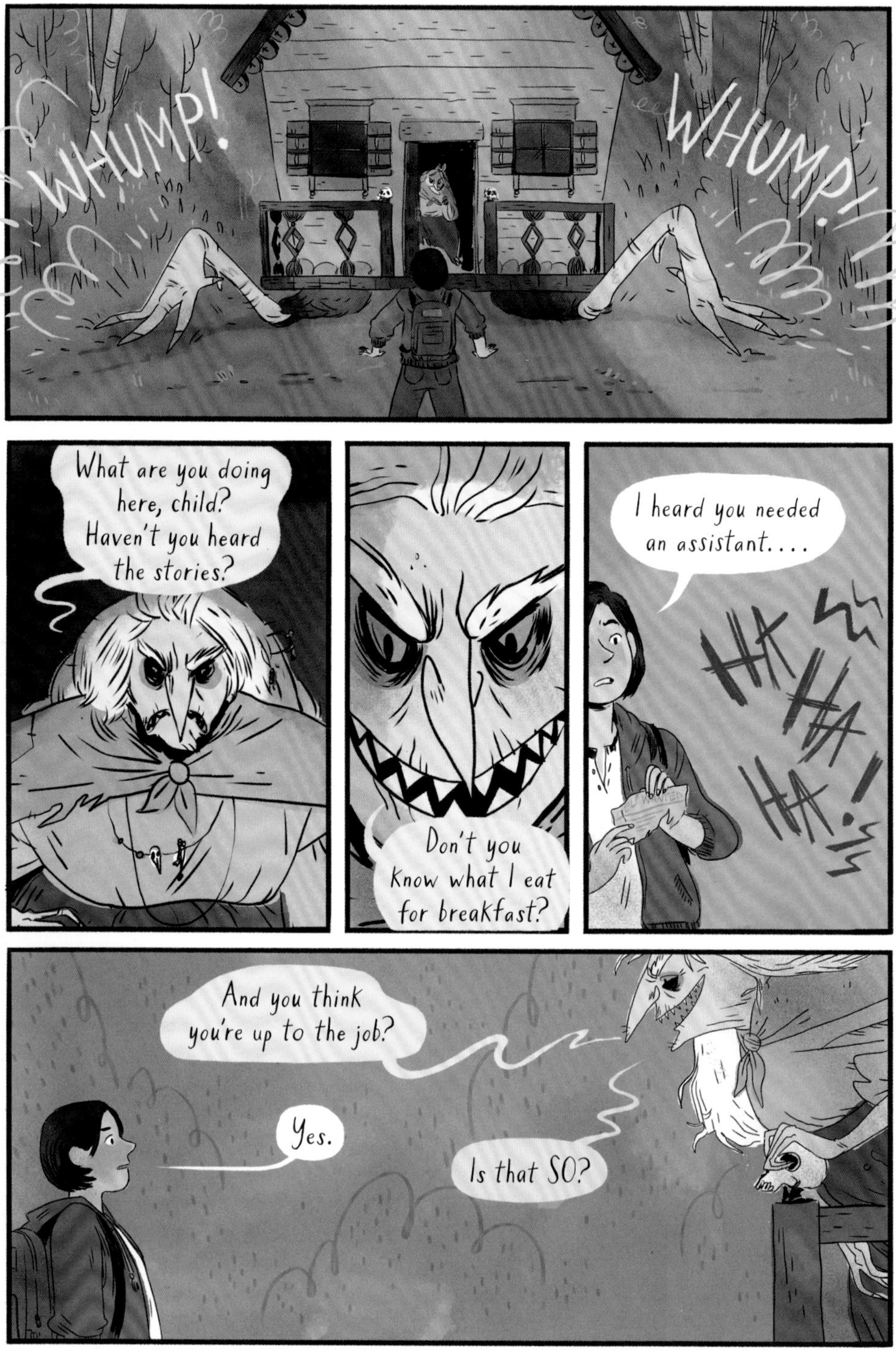
WHUMP!
WHUMP!
What are you doing here, child? Haven't you heard the stories?
Don't you know what I eat for breakfast?
I heard you needed an assistant. . . .
HA HA HA HA!
And you think you're up to the job?
Yes.
Is that SO?

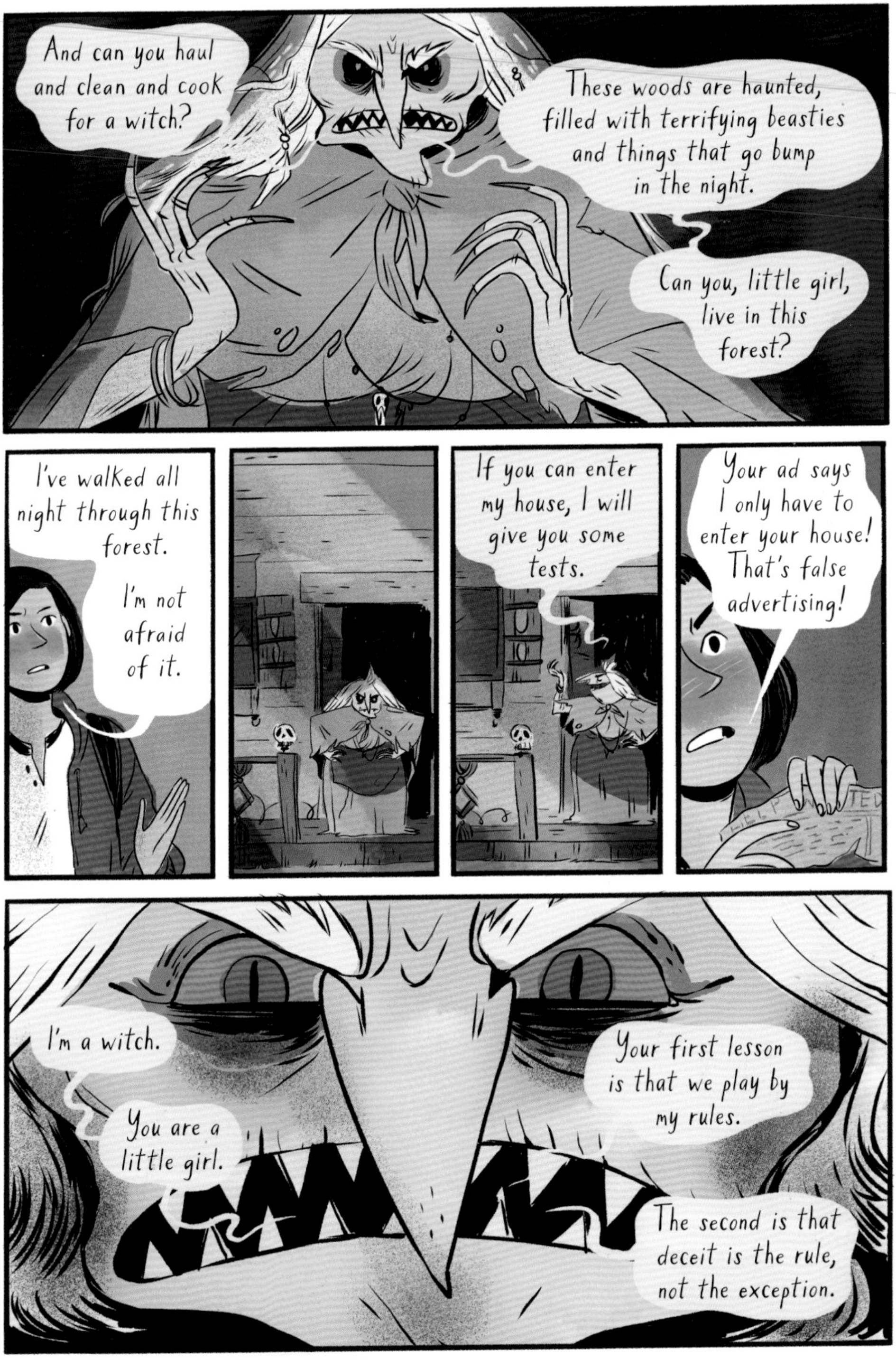
And can you haul and clean and cook for a witch?
These woods are haunted, filled with terrifying beasties and things that go bump in the night.
Can you, little girl, live in this forest?
I've walked all night through this forest.
I'm not afraid of it.
If you can enter my house, I will give you some tests.
Your ad says I only have to enter your house! That's false advertising!
I'm a witch.
You are a little girl.
Your first lesson is that we play by my rules.
The second is that deceit is the rule, not the exception.

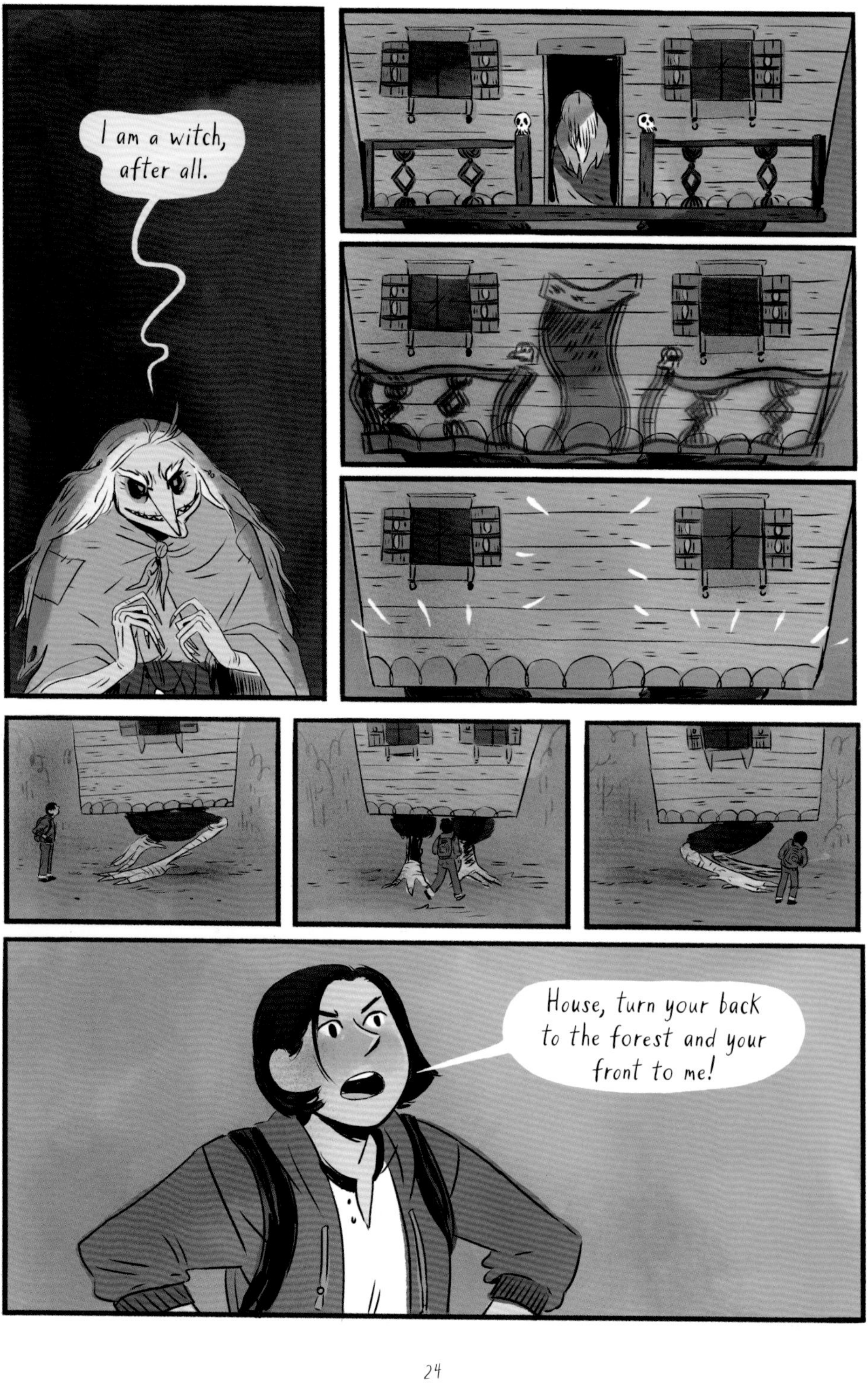
I am a witch, after all.
House, turn your back to the forest and your front to me!

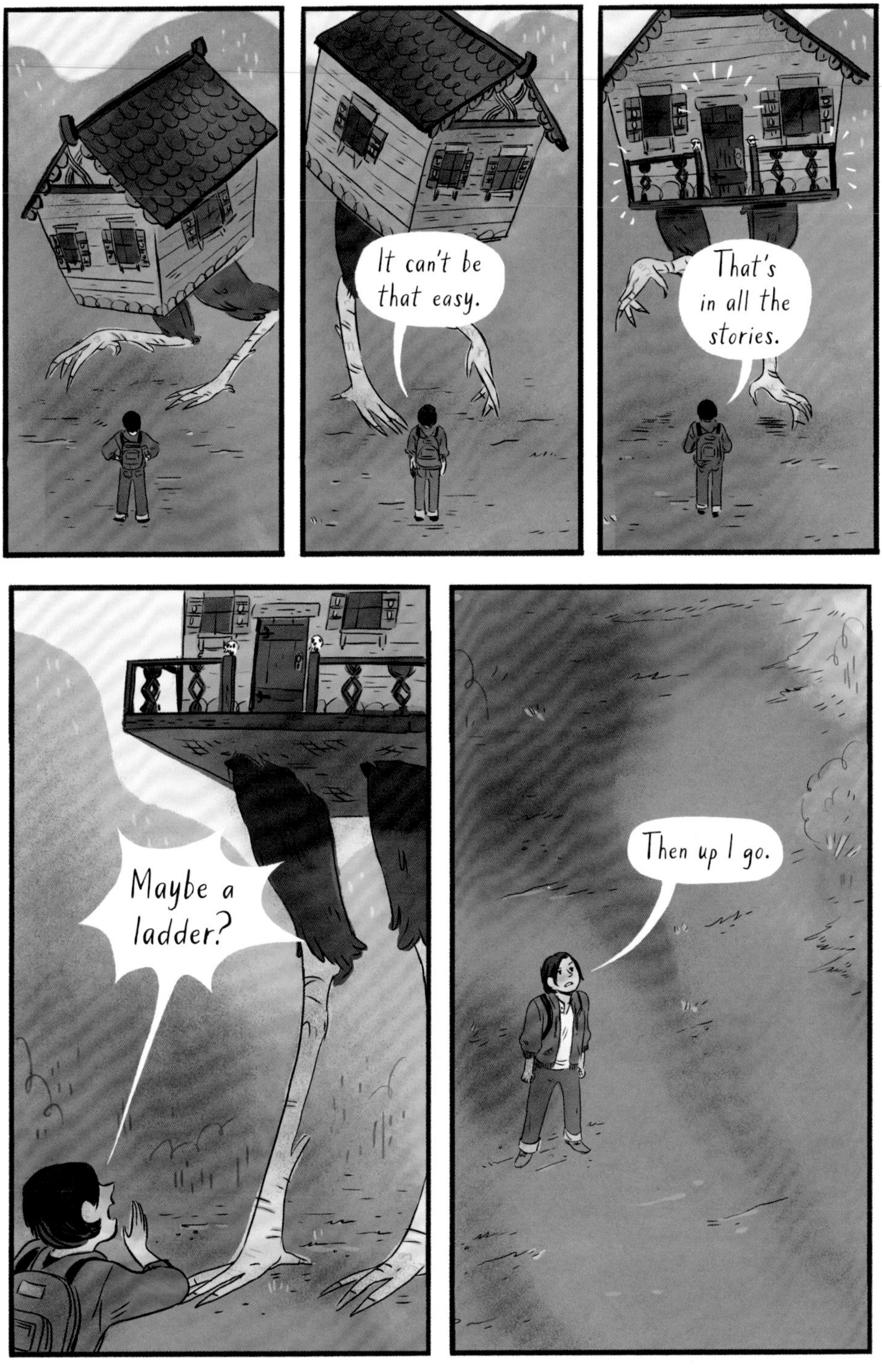
It can't be that easy.
That's in all the stories.
Maybe a ladder?
Then up I go.

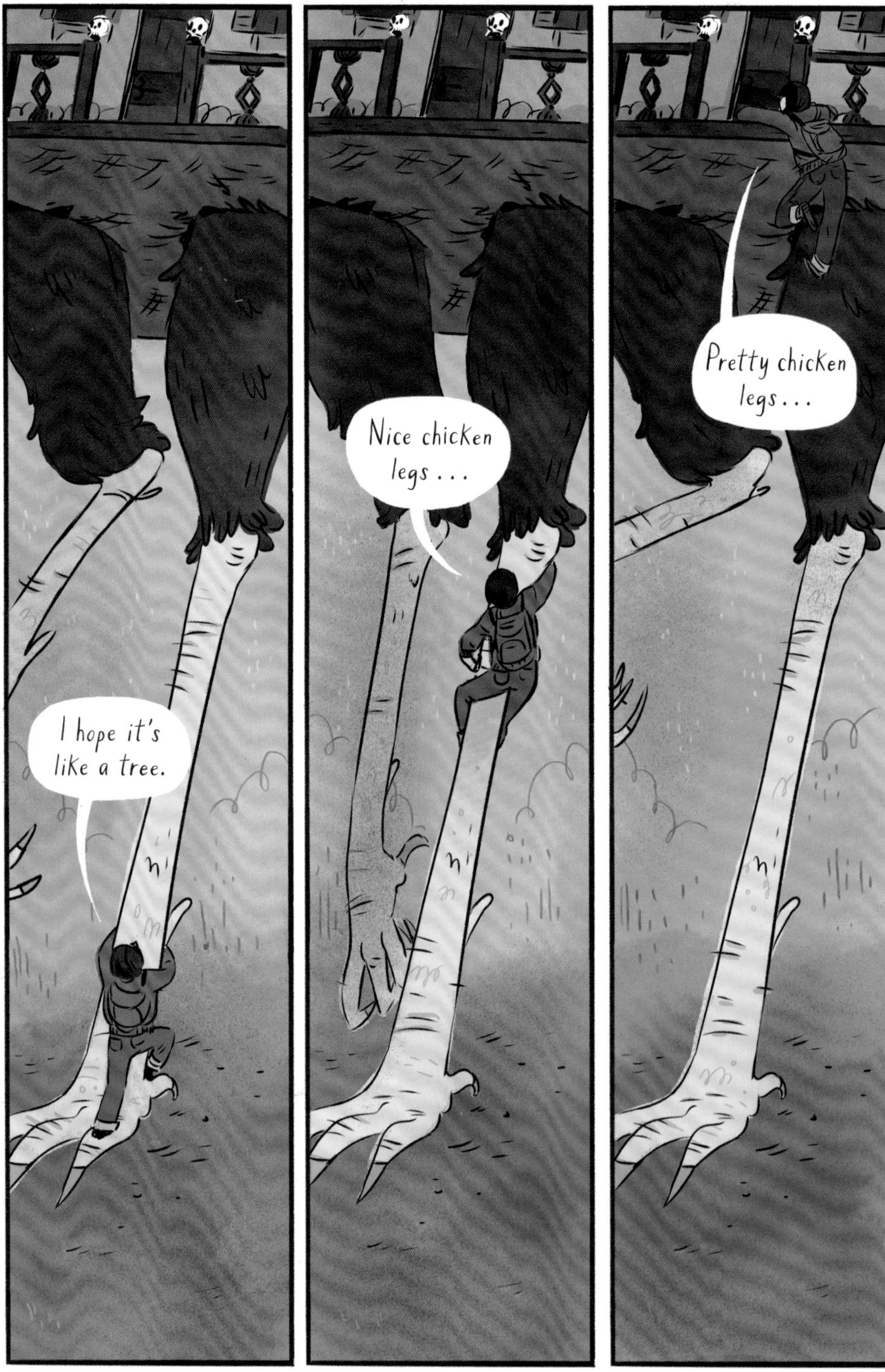
I hope it's like a tree.
Nice chicken legs . . .
Pretty chicken legs . . .

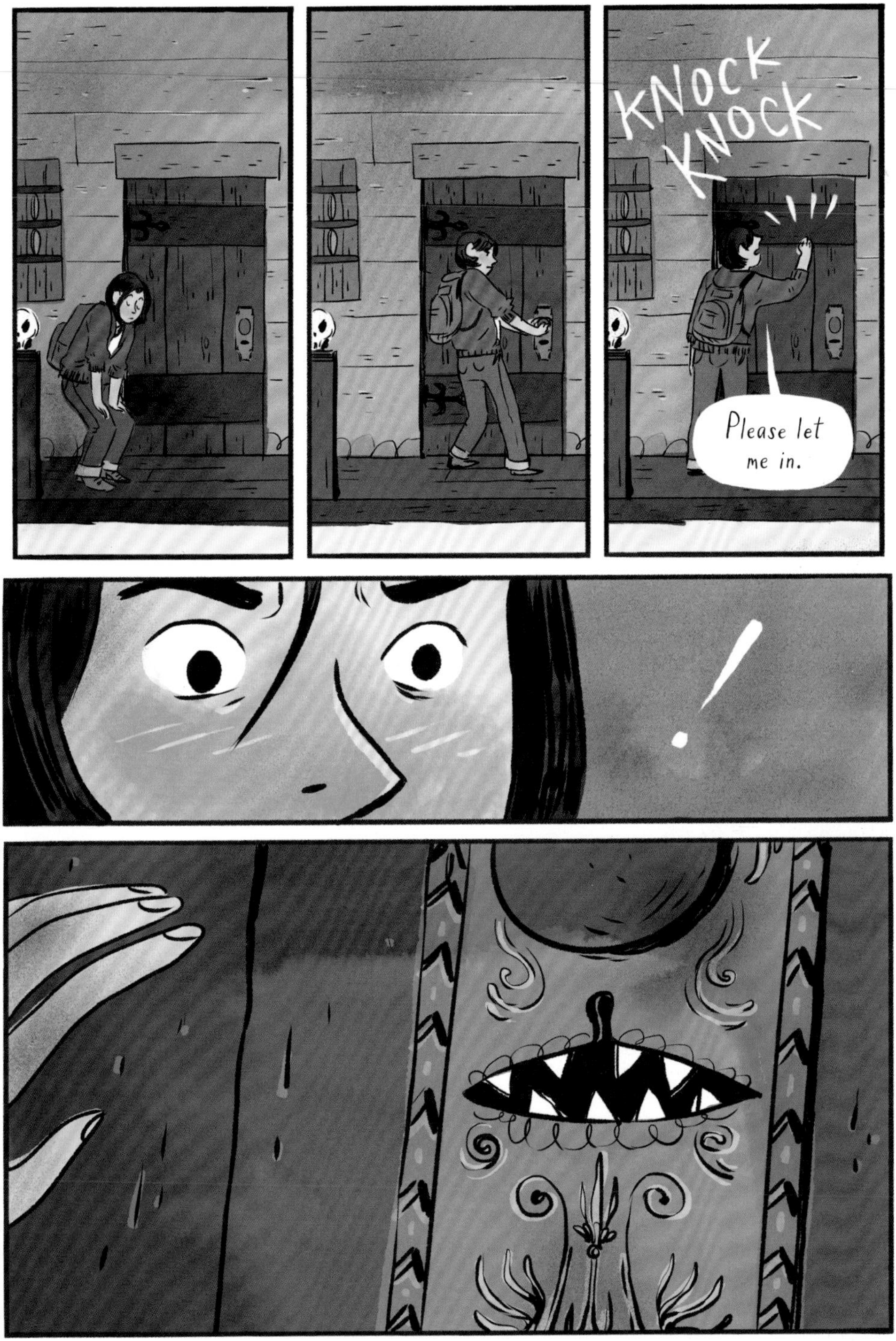
KNOCK
KNOCK
Please let me in.

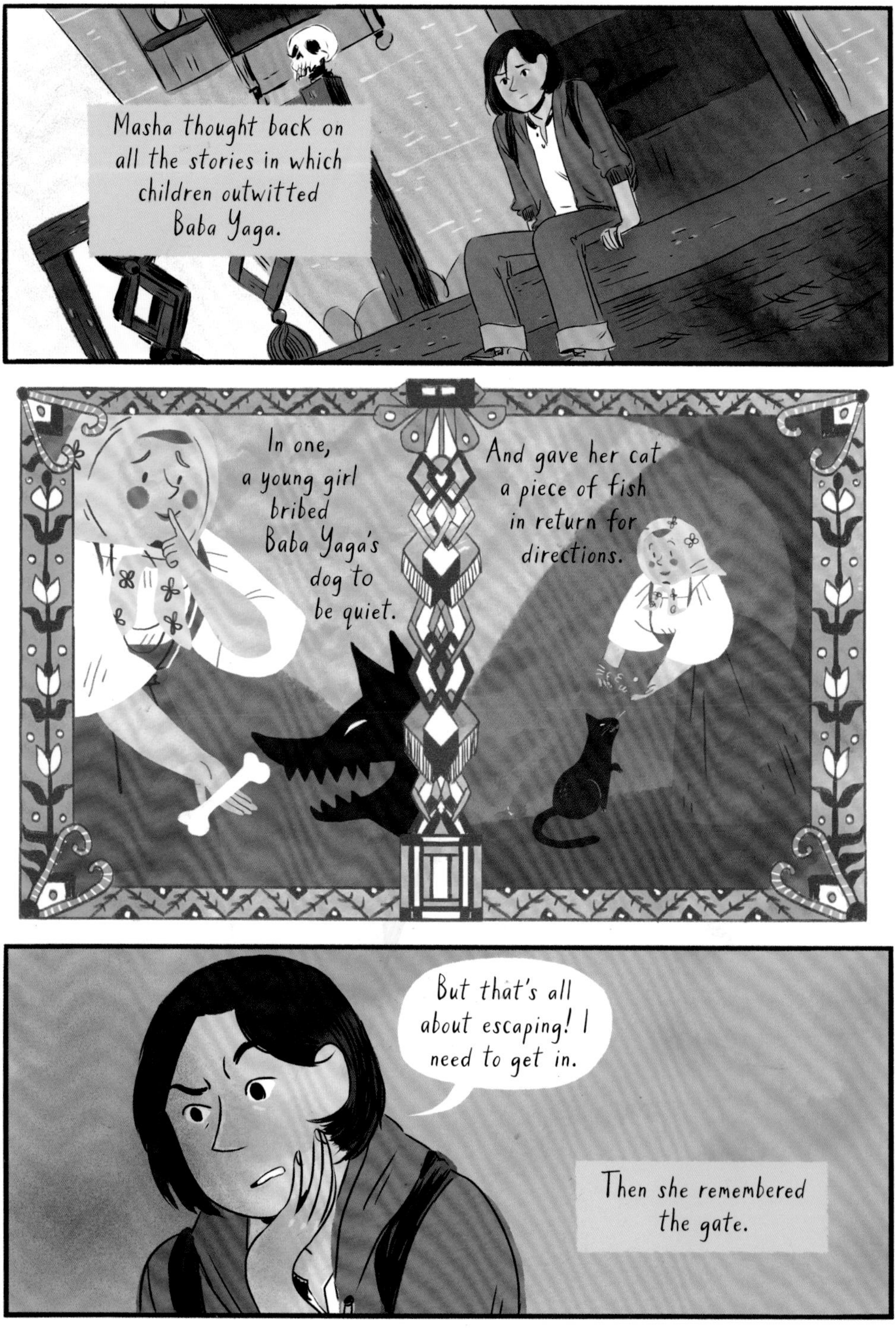
Masha thought back on all the stories in which children outwitted Baba Yaga.
In one, a young girl bribed Baba Yaga's dog to be quiet.
And gave her cat a piece of fish in return for directions.
But that's all about escaping! I need to get in.
Then she remembered the gate.

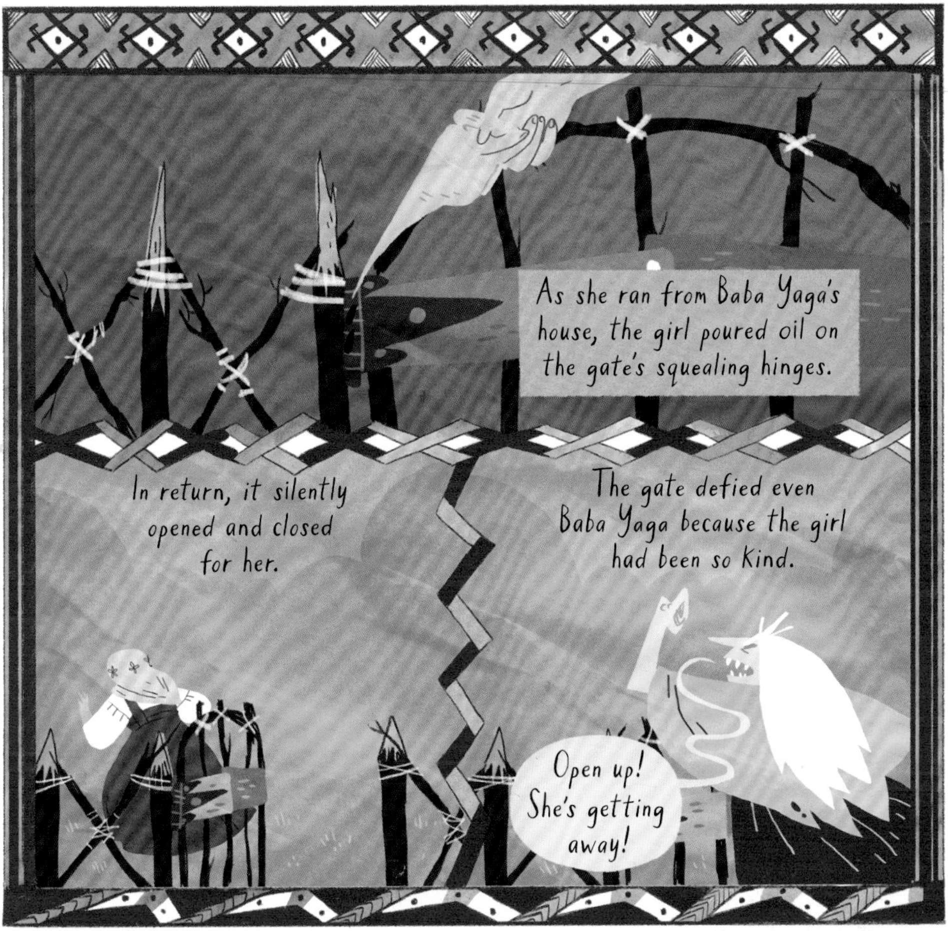
As she ran from Baba Yaga's house, the girl poured oil on the gate's squealing hinges.
In return, it silently opened and closed for her.
The gate defied even Baba Yaga because the girl had been so kind.
Open up! She's getting away!

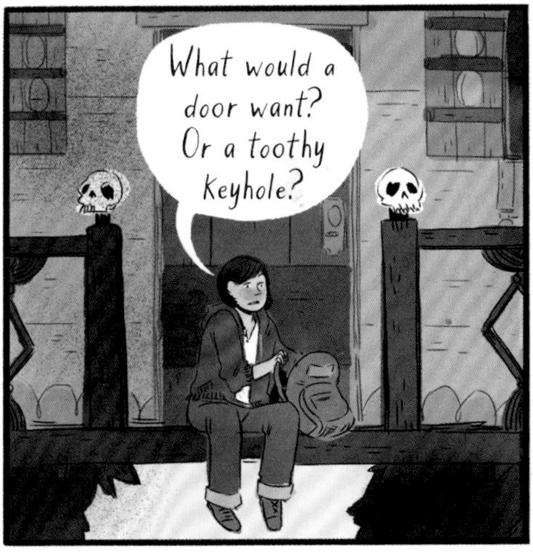
What would a door want? Or a toothy keyhole?

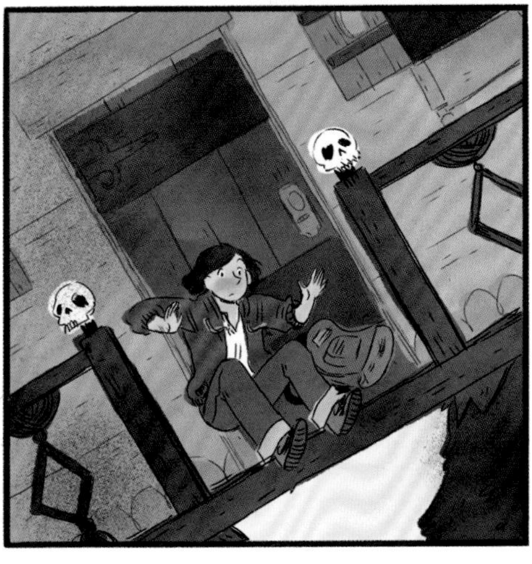

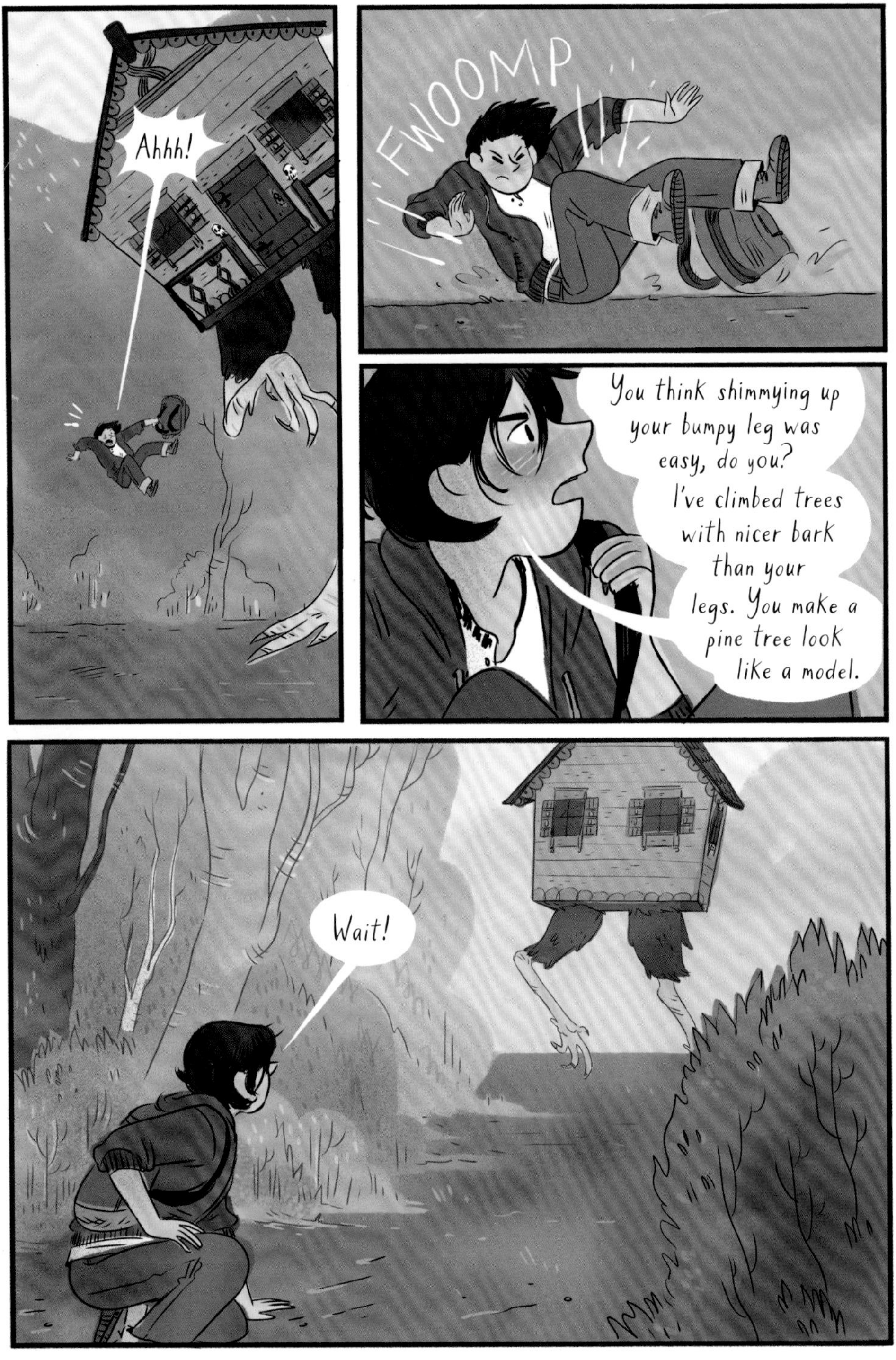
Ahhh!
FWOOMP
You think shimmying up your bumpy leg was easy, do you? I've climbed trees with nicer bark than your legs. You make a pine tree look like a model.
Wait!

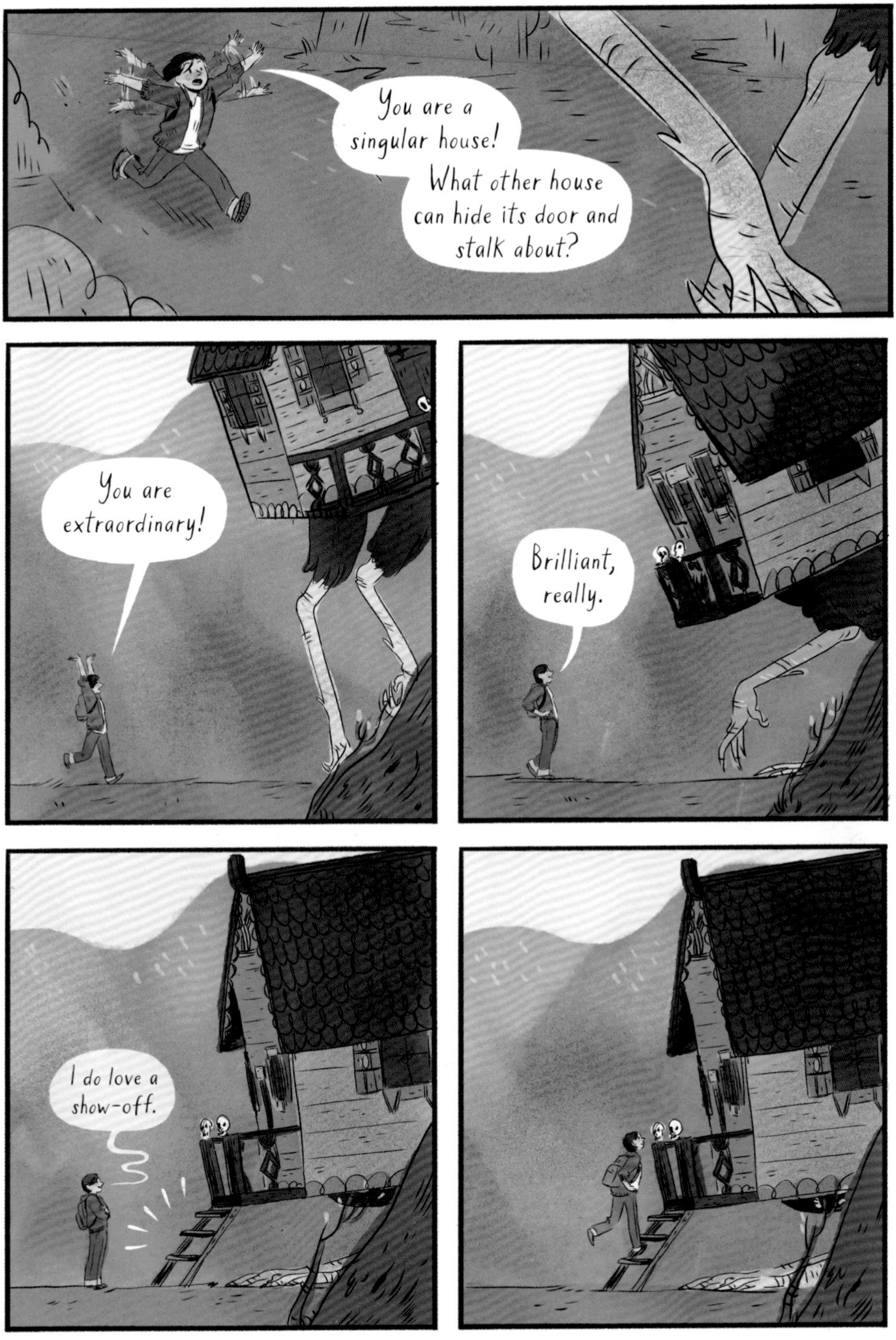
You are a singular house!
What other house can hide its door and stalk about?
You are extraordinary!
Brilliant, really.
I do love a show-off.

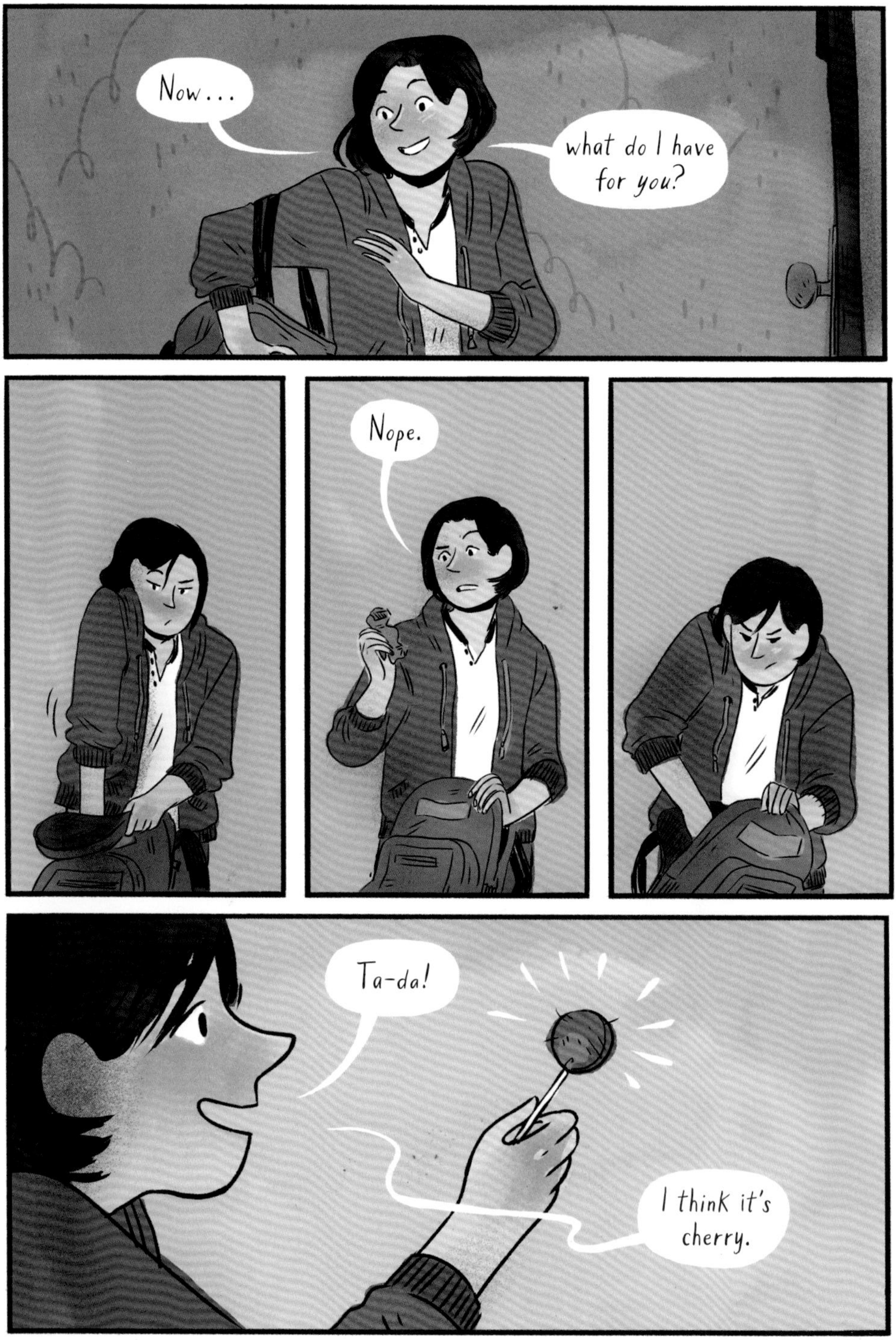
Now...
what do I have for you?
Nope.
Ta-da!
I think it's cherry.

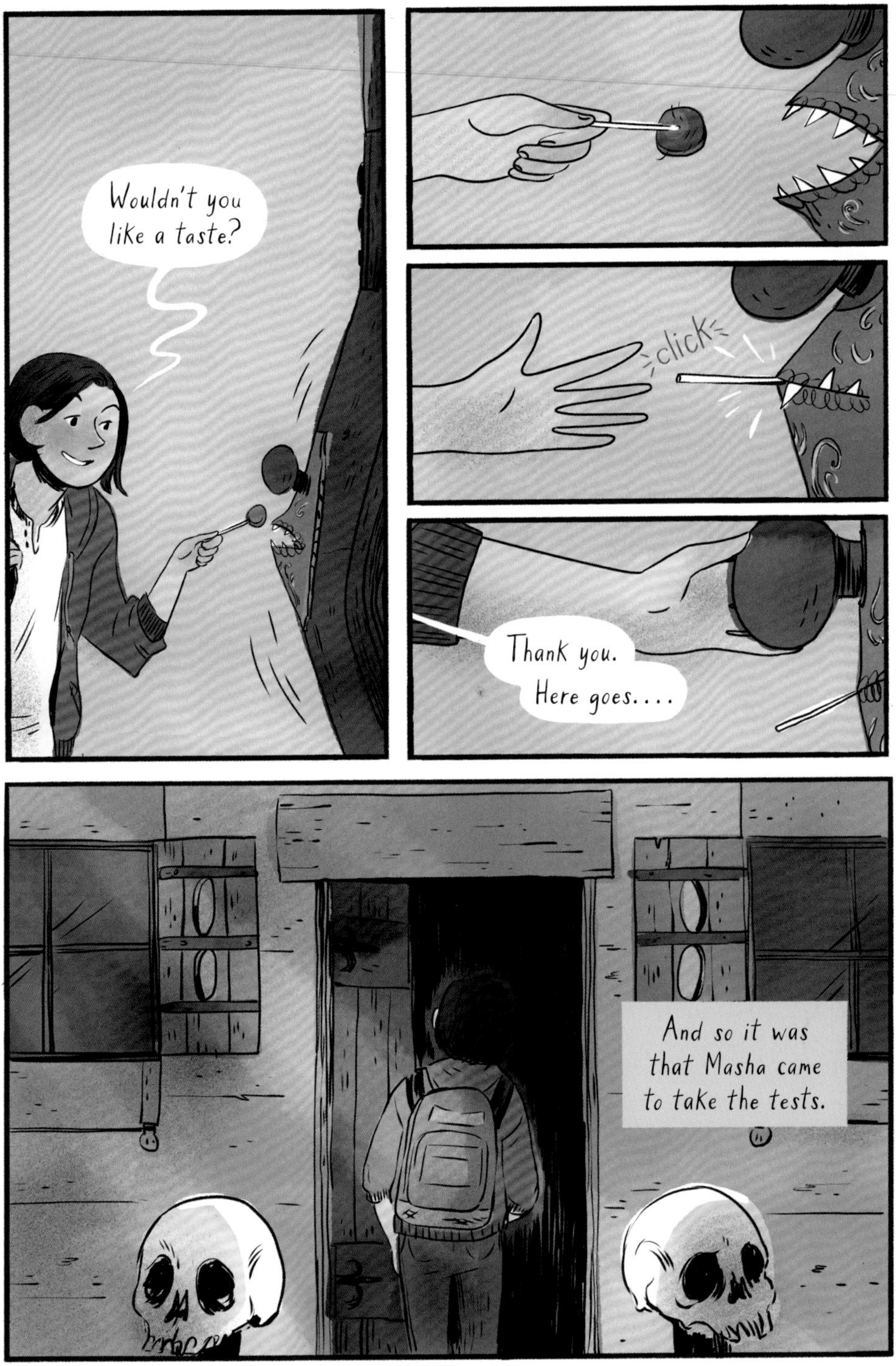
Wouldn't you like a taste?
click
Thank you. Here goes....
And so it was that Masha came to take the tests.

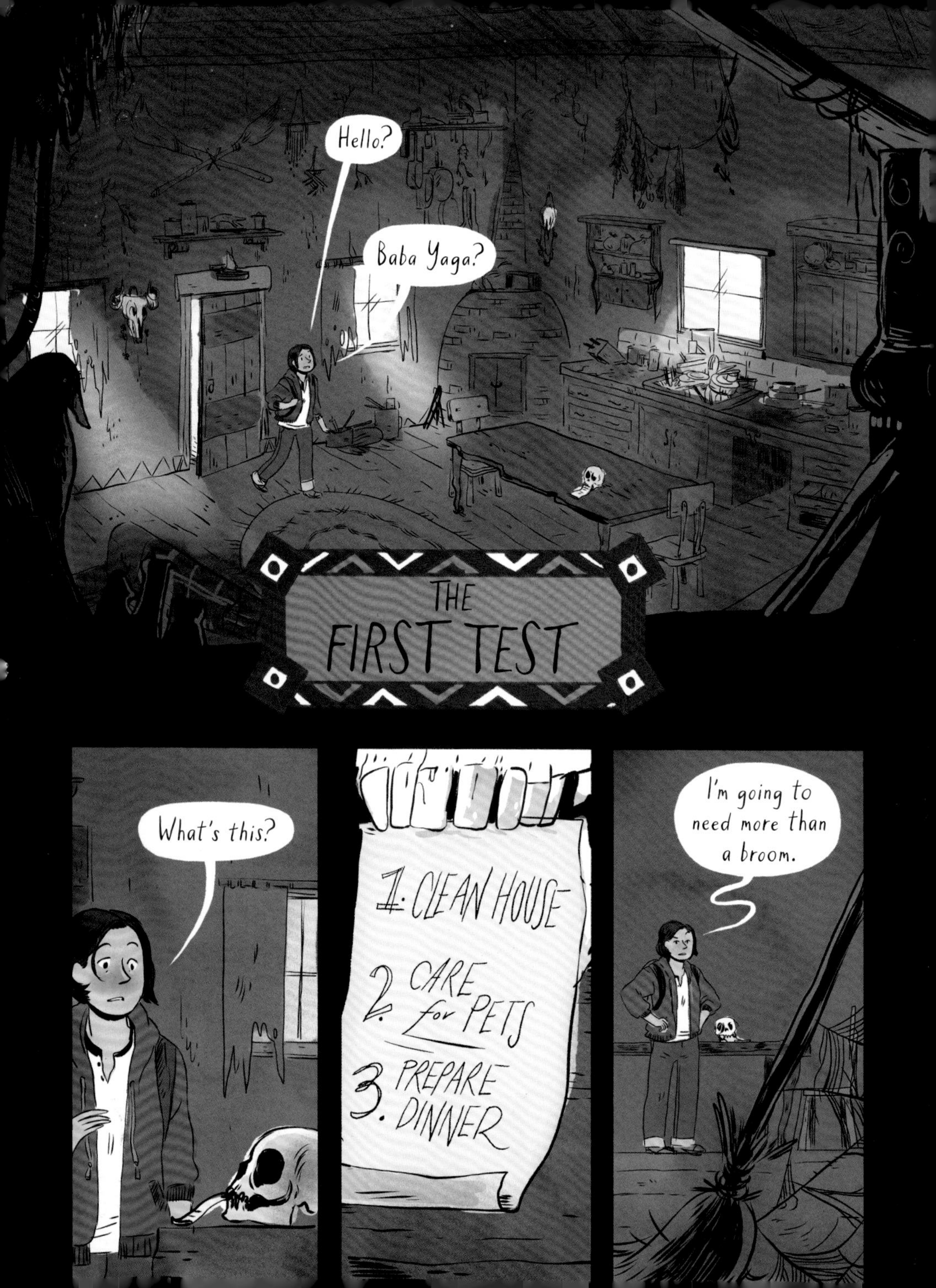
Hello?
Baba Yaga?
THE FIRST TEST
What's this?
1. CLEAN HOUSE
2. CARE for PETS
3. PREPARE DINNER
I'm going to need more than a broom.

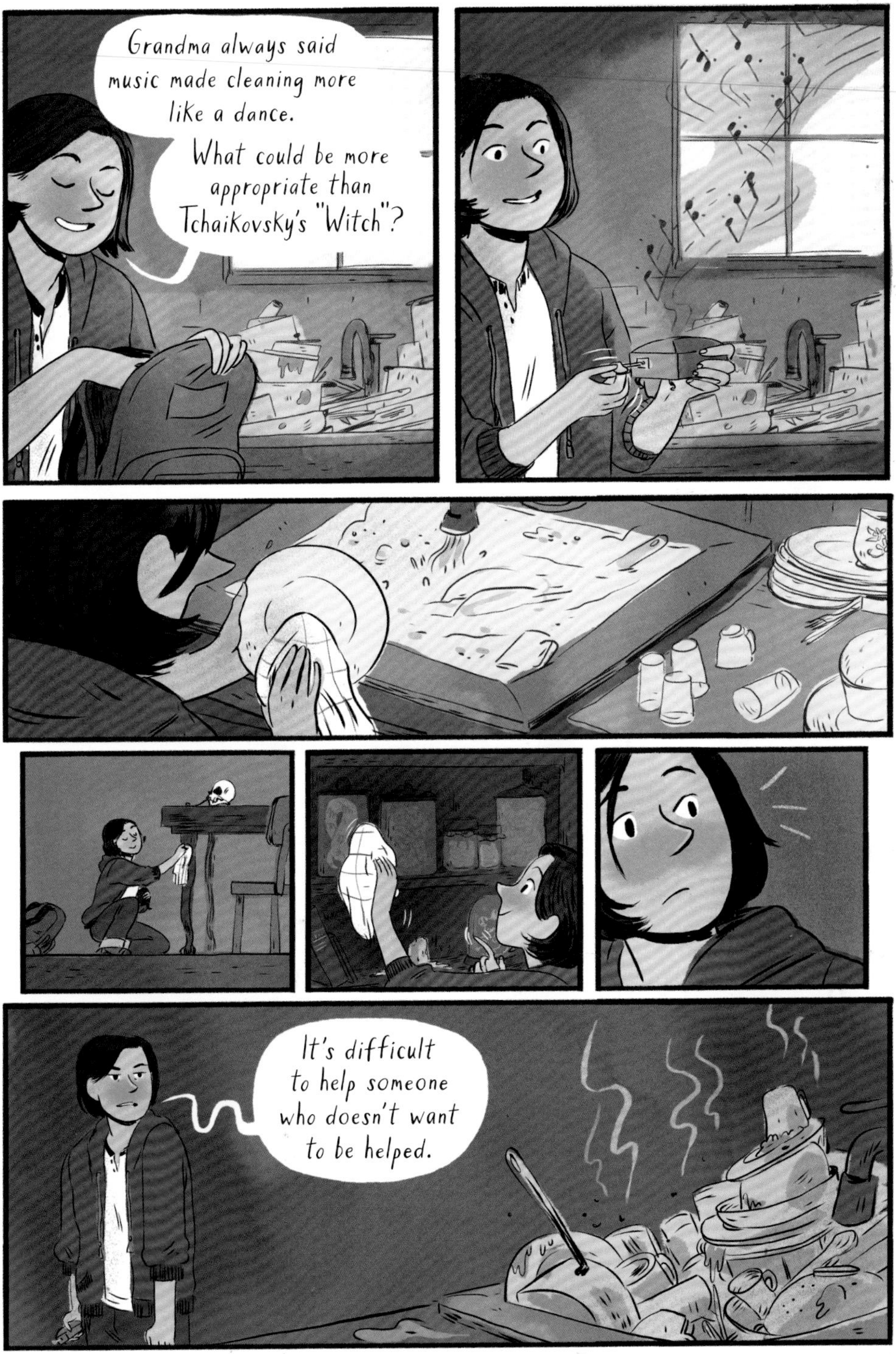
Grandma always said music made cleaning more like a dance.
What could be more appropriate than Tchaikovsky's "Witch"?
It's difficult to help someone who doesn't want to be helped.

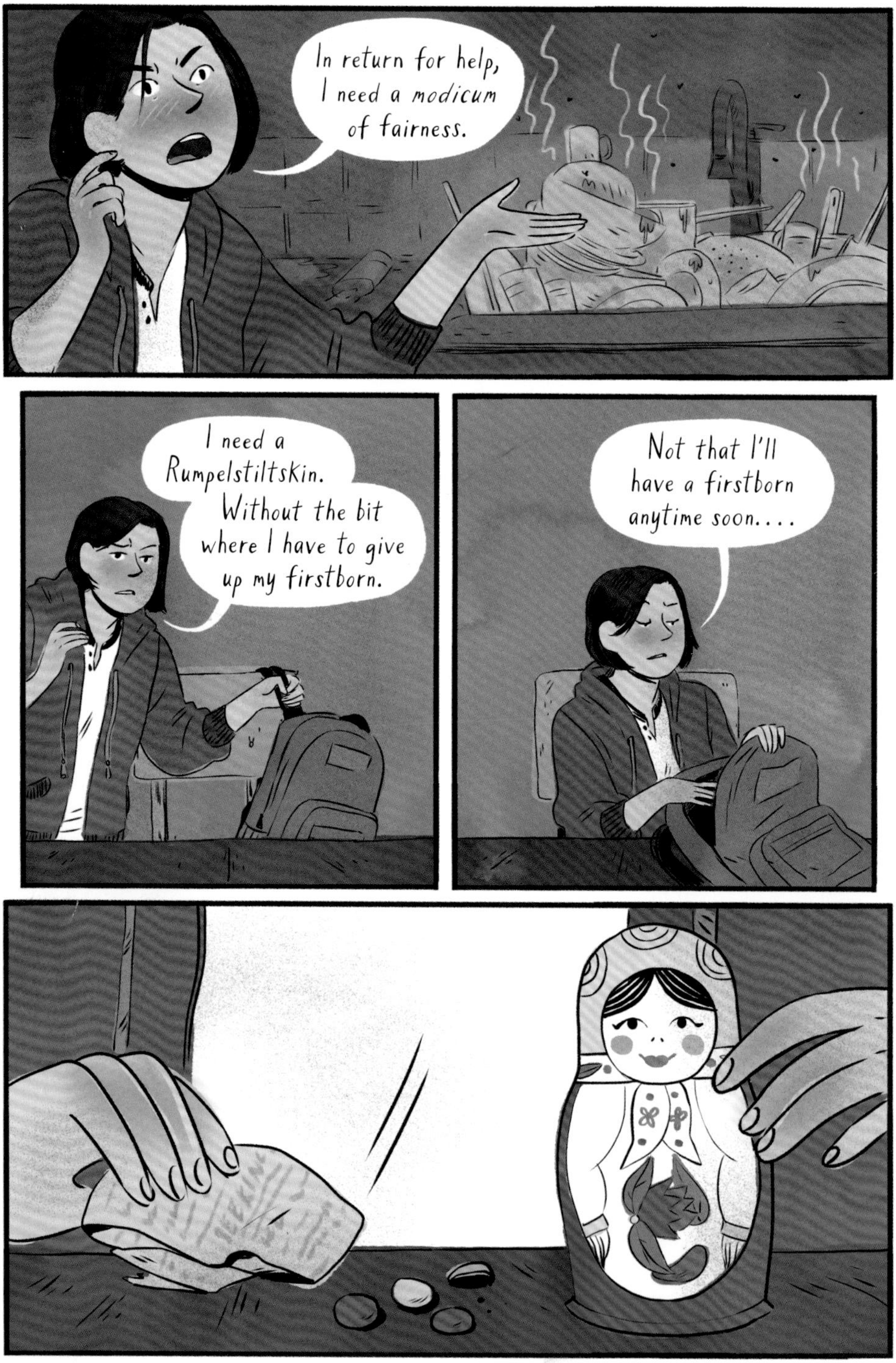
In return for help, I need a *modicum* of fairness.
I need a Rumpelstiltskin.
Without the bit where I have to give up my firstborn.
Not that I'll have a firstborn anytime soon. . . .

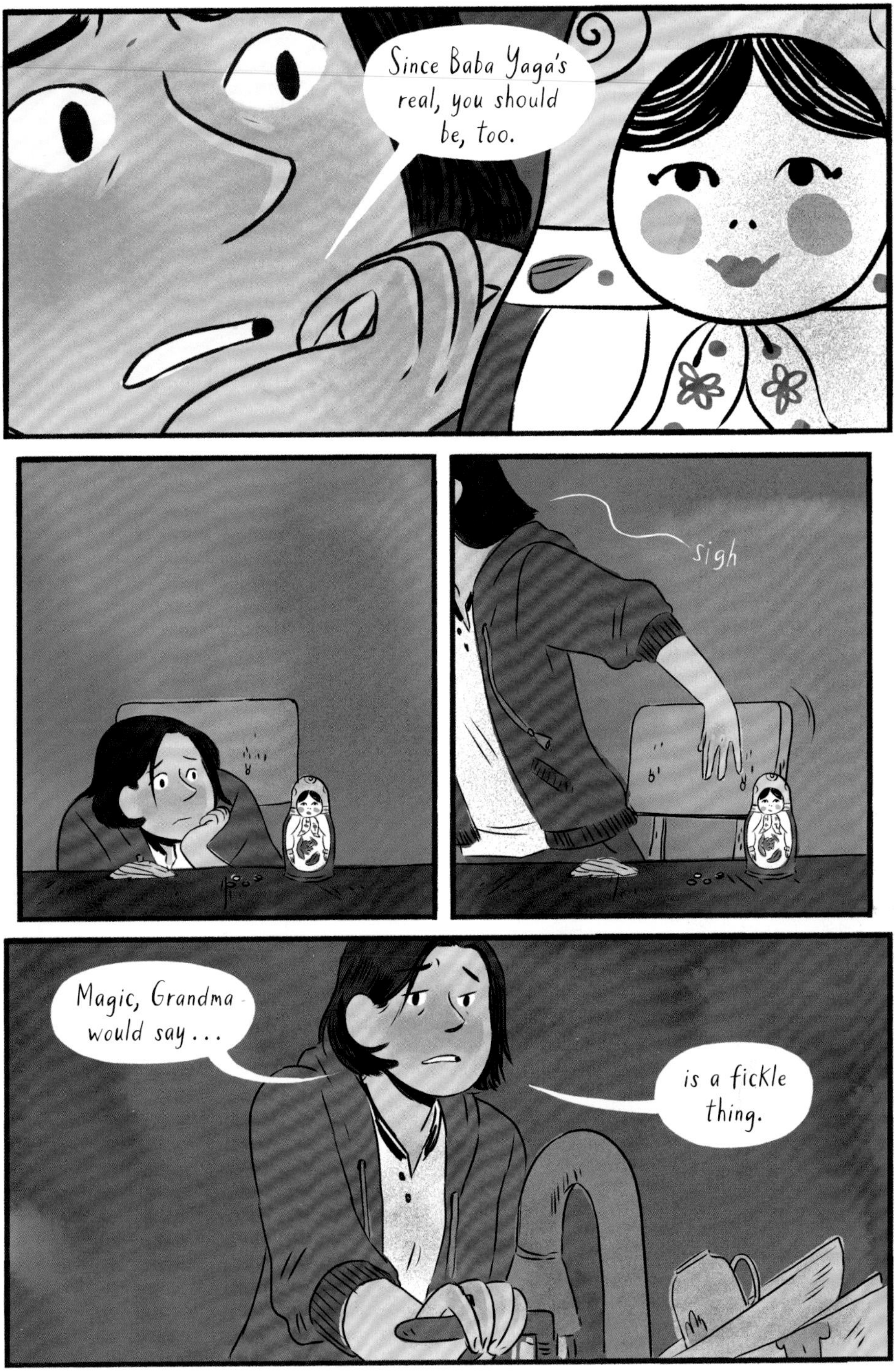

Since Baba Yaga's real, you should be, too.
sigh
Magic, Grandma would say...
is a fickle thing.

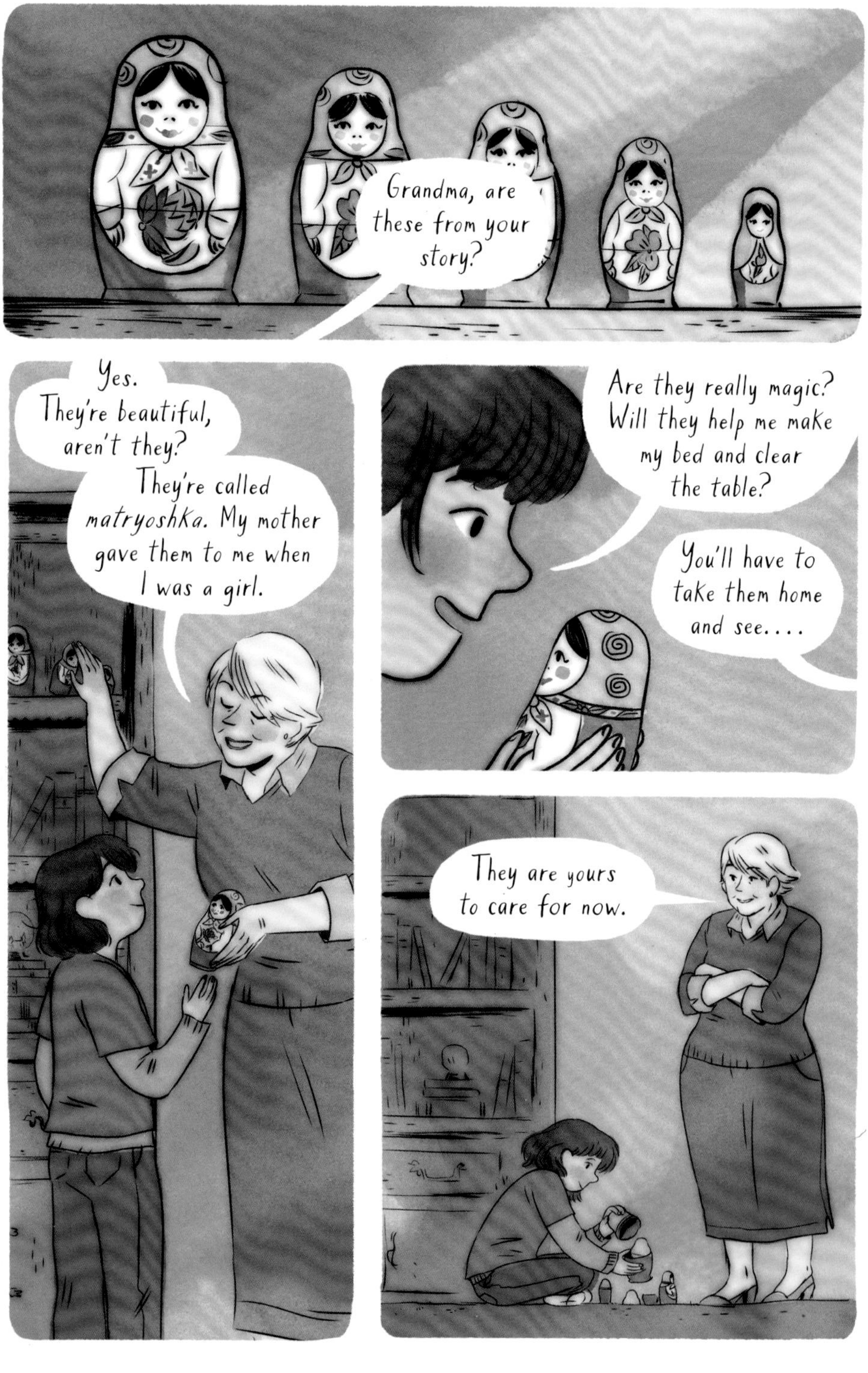
Grandma, are these from your story?
Yes. They're beautiful, aren't they?
They're called matryoshka. My mother gave them to me when I was a girl.
Are they really magic? Will they help me make my bed and clear the table?
You'll have to take them home and see. . . .
They are yours to care for now.

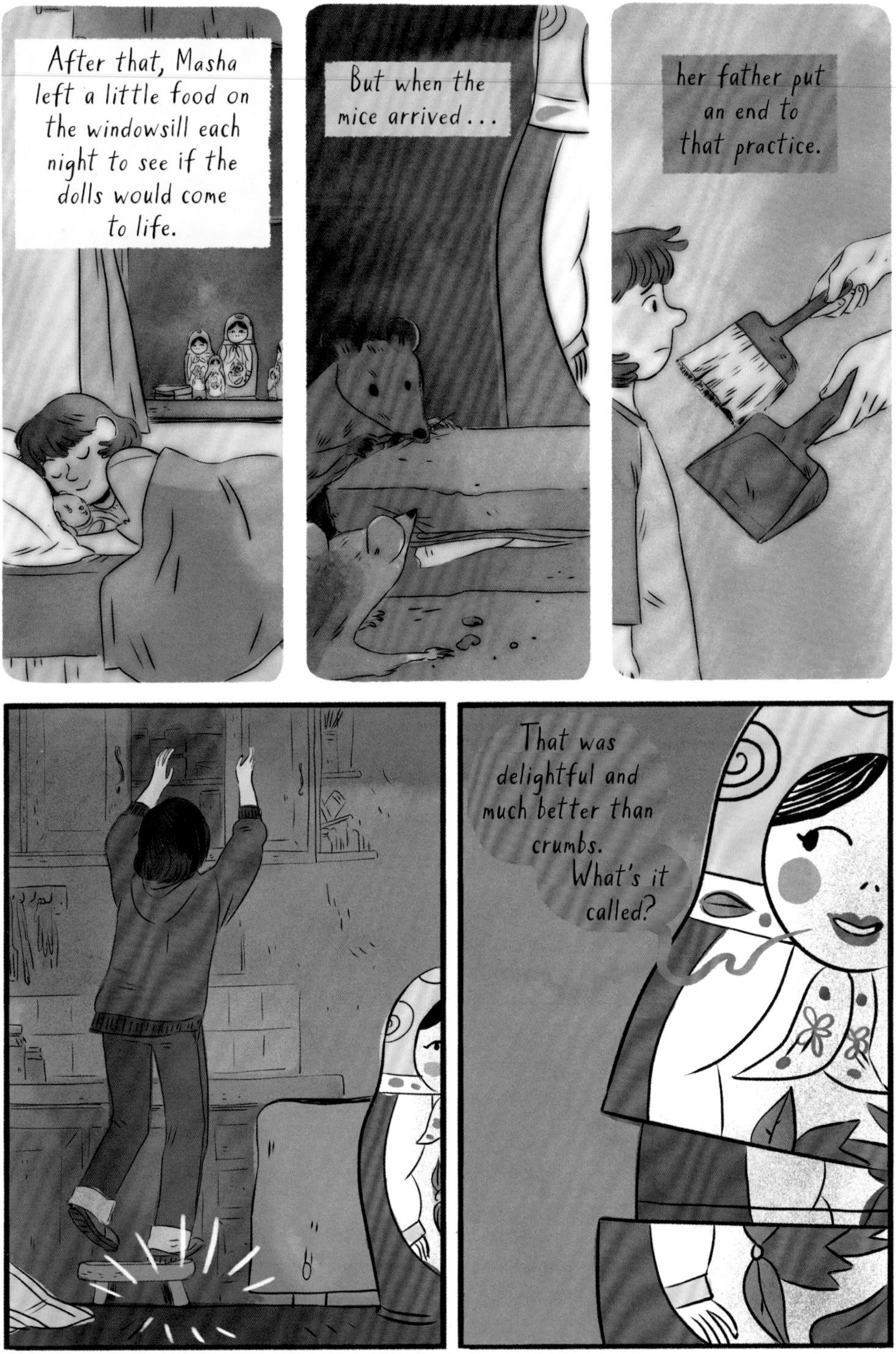
After that, Masha left a little food on the windowsill each night to see if the dolls would come to life.
But when the mice arrived . . .
her father put an end to that practice.
That was delightful and much better than crumbs.
What's it called?

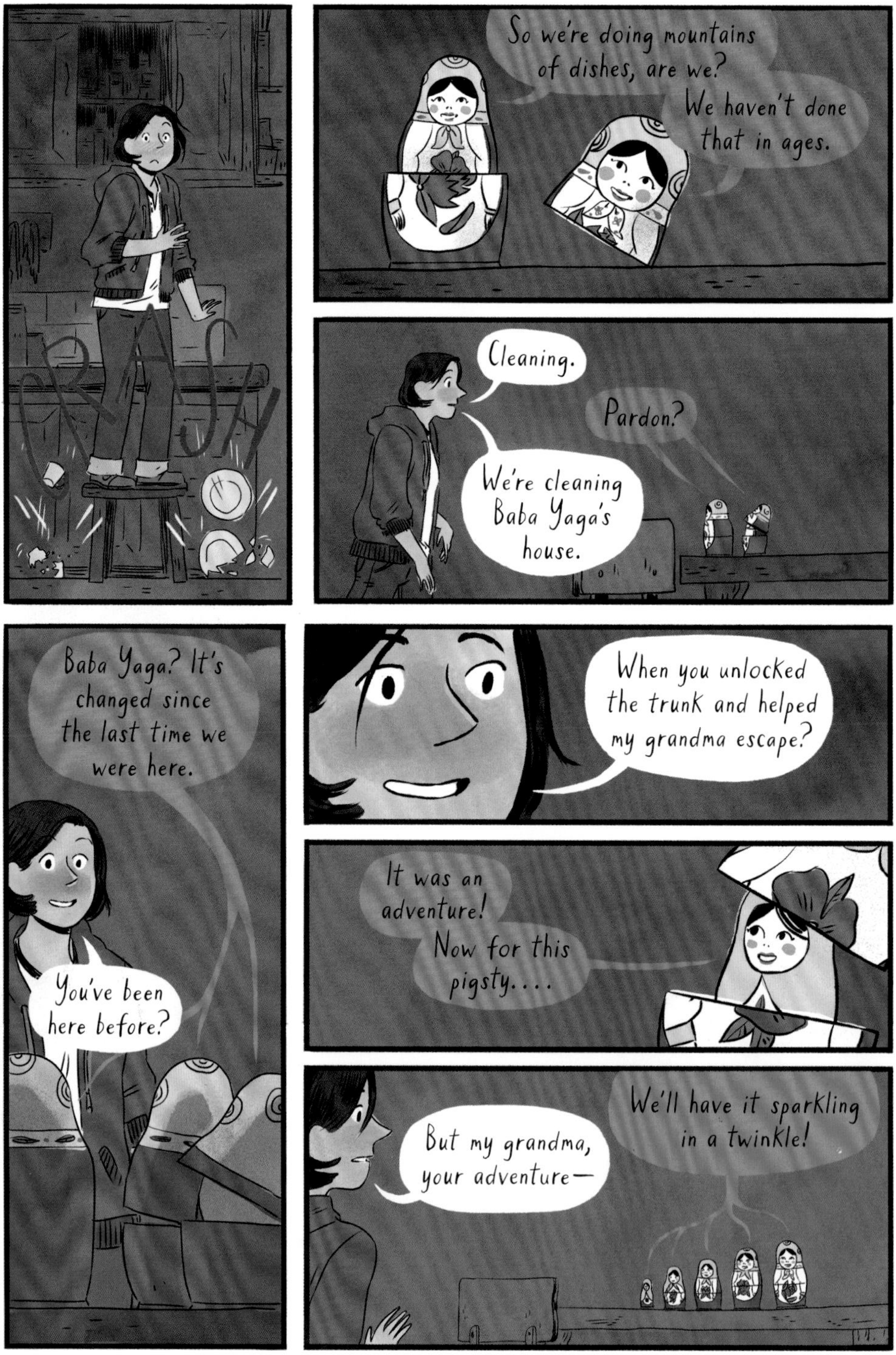
CRASH
So we're doing mountains of dishes, are we?
We haven't done that in ages.
Cleaning.
Pardon?
We're cleaning Baba Yaga's house.
Baba Yaga? It's changed since the last time we were here.
You've been here before?
When you unlocked the trunk and helped my grandma escape?
It was an adventure!
Now for this pigsty....
But my grandma, your adventure—
We'll have it sparkling in a twinkle!

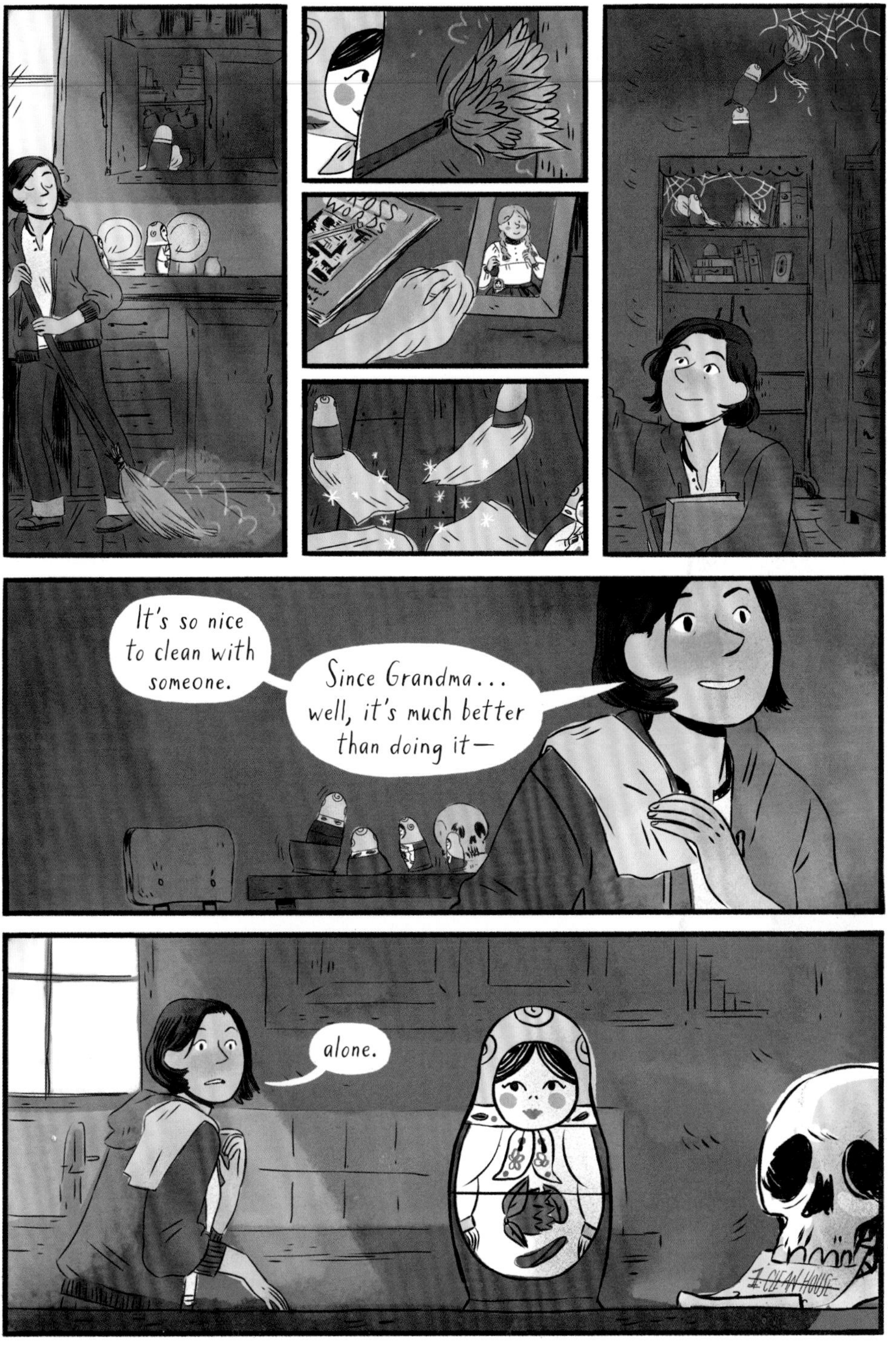
It's so nice to clean with someone.
Since Grandma... well, it's much better than doing it—
alone.

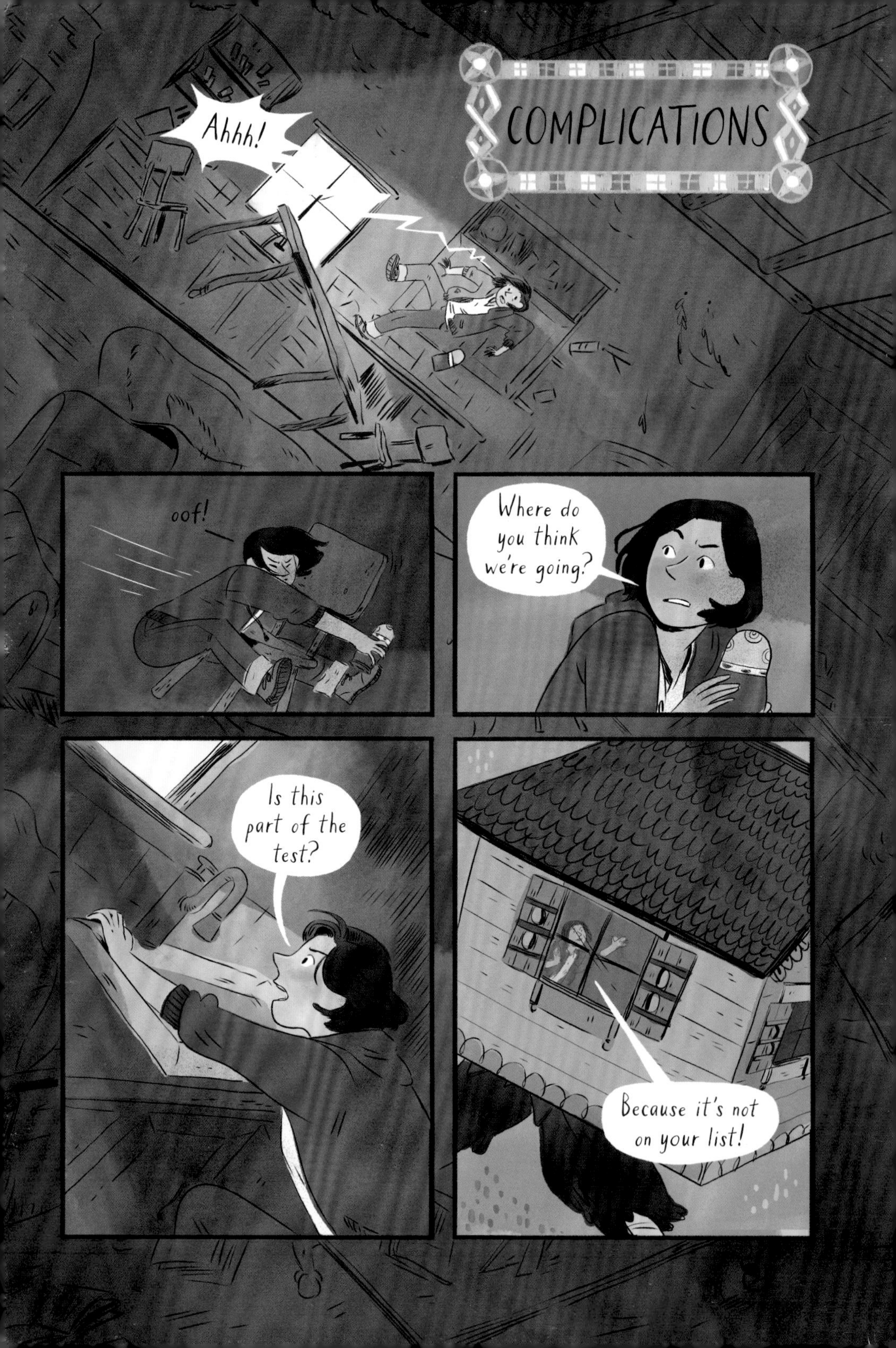
COMPLICATIONS
Ahhh!
oof!
Where do you think we're going?
Is this part of the test?
Because it's not on your list!

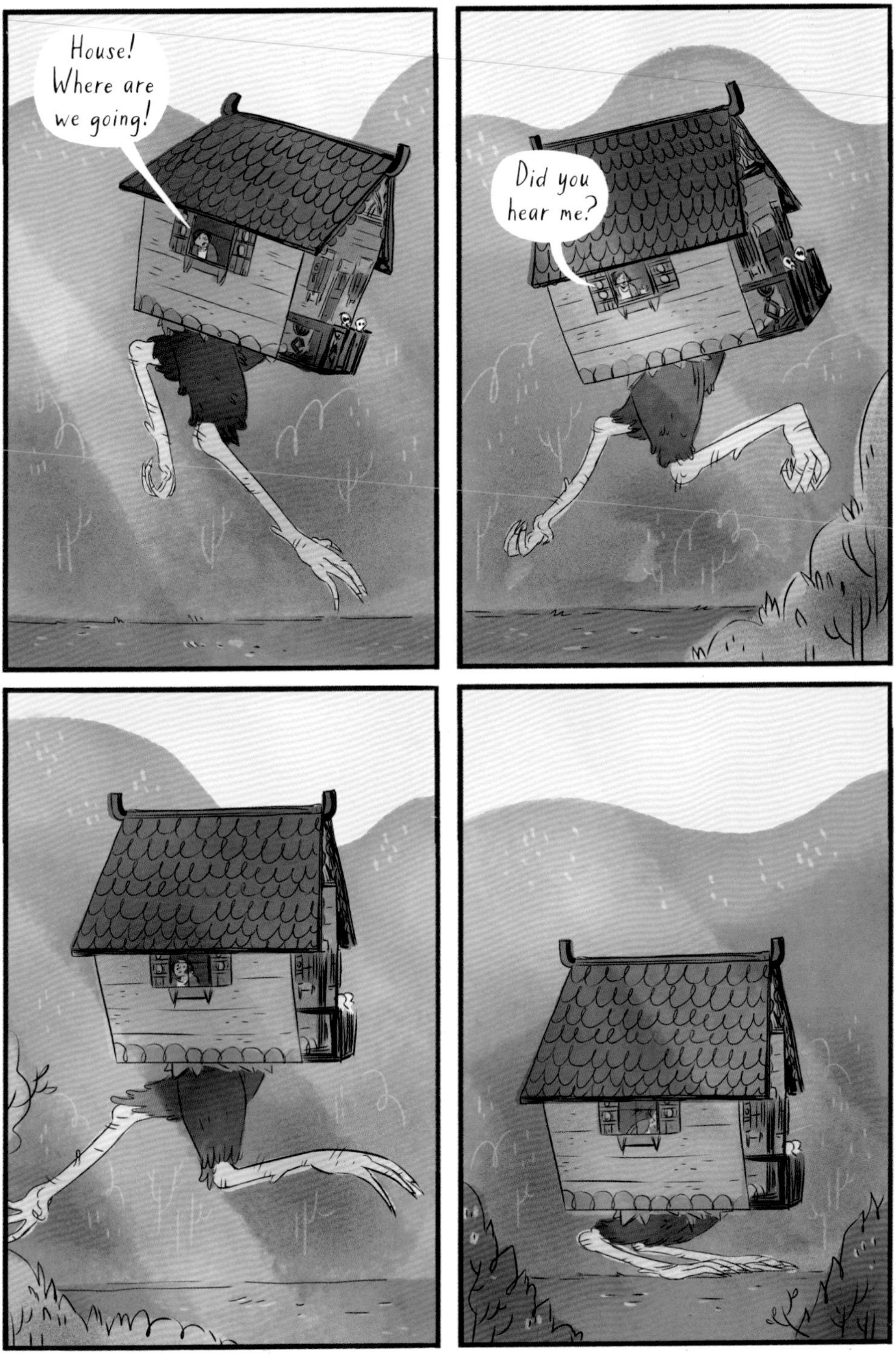
House! Where are we going!
Did you hear me?

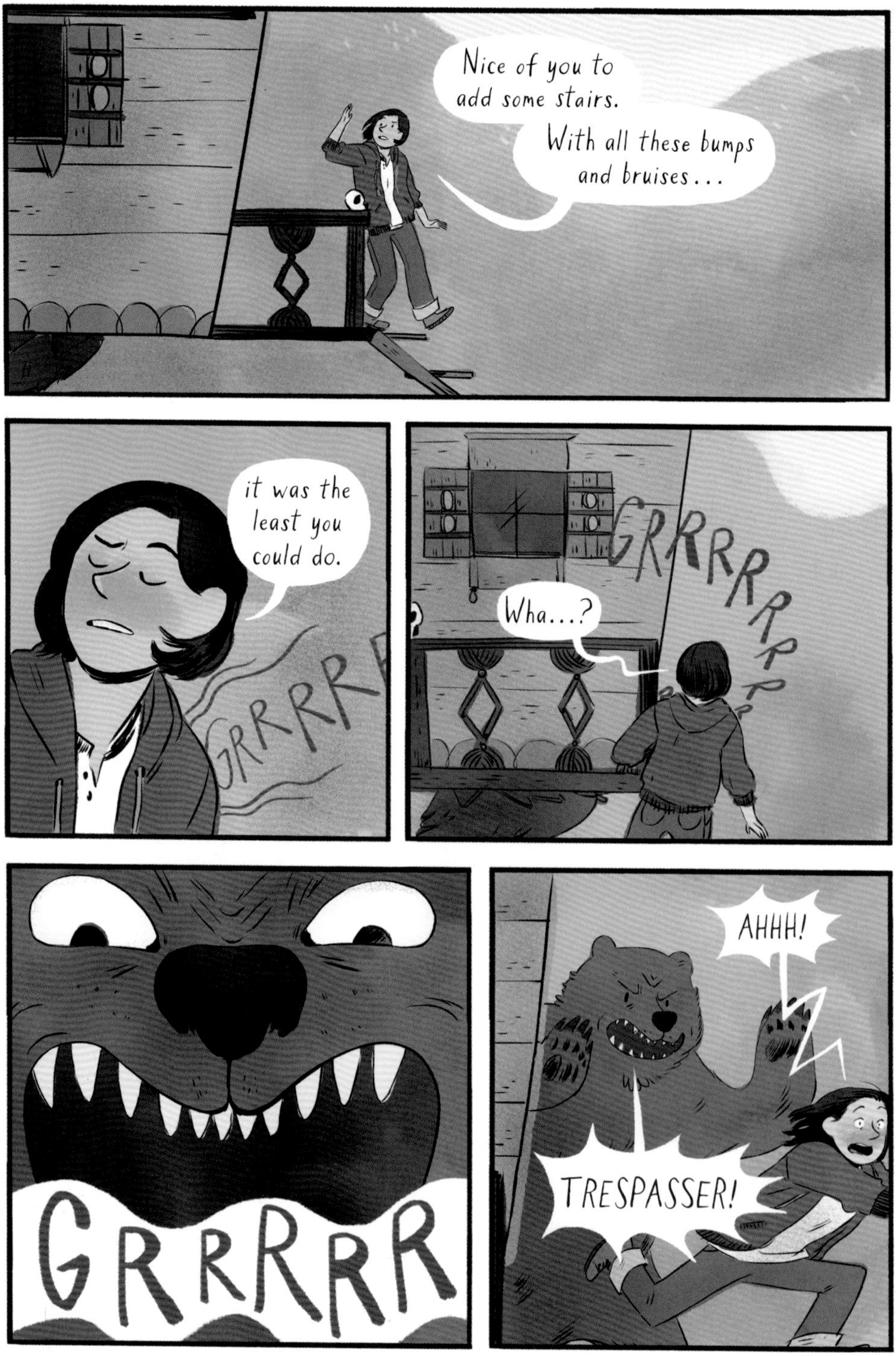
Nice of you to add some stairs.
With all these bumps and bruises...
it was the least you could do.
GRRRRR
Wha...?
GRRRRRRRR
GRRRRR
AHHH!
TRESPASSER!

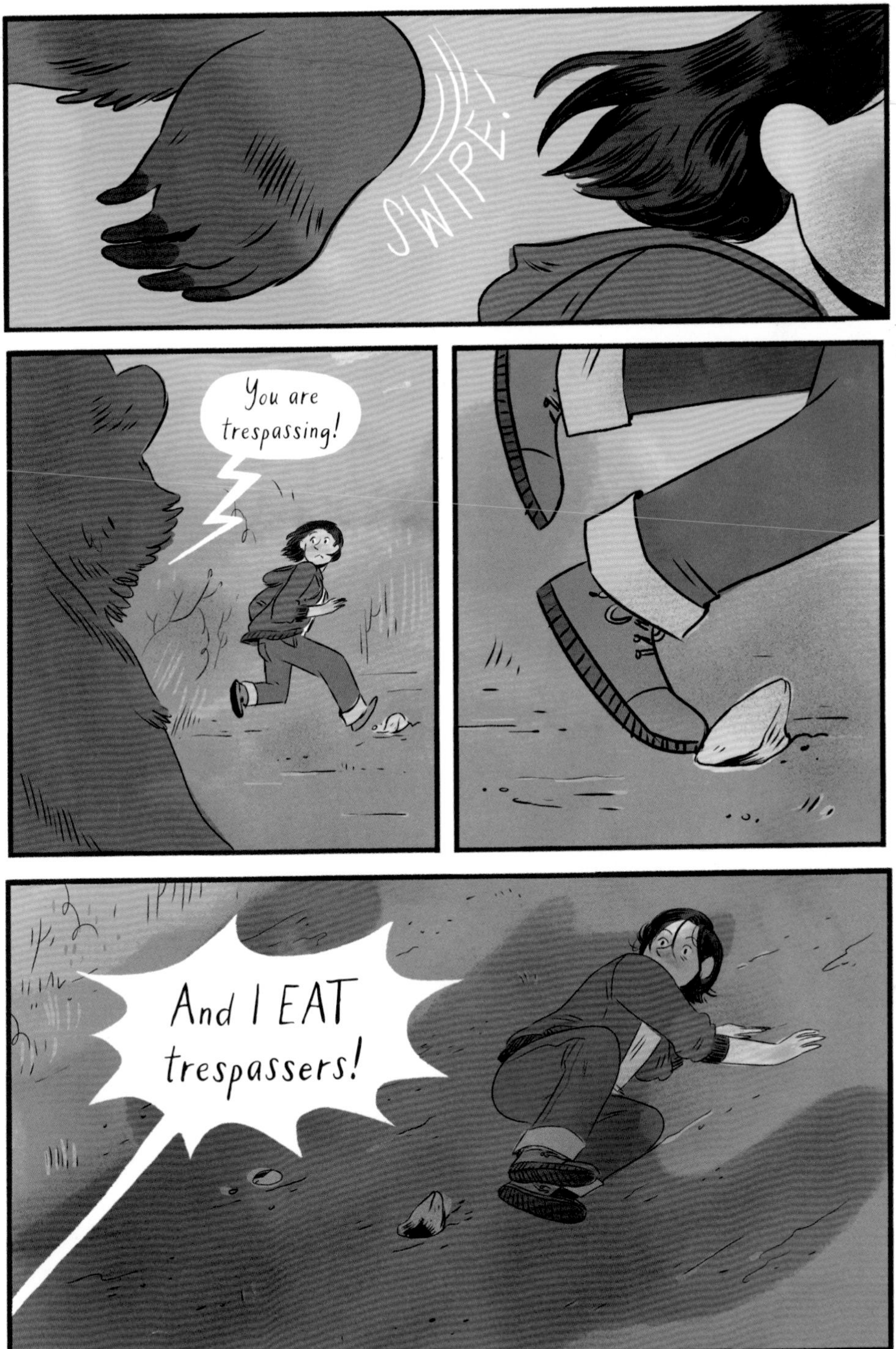
SWIPE!
You are trespassing!
And I EAT trespassers!

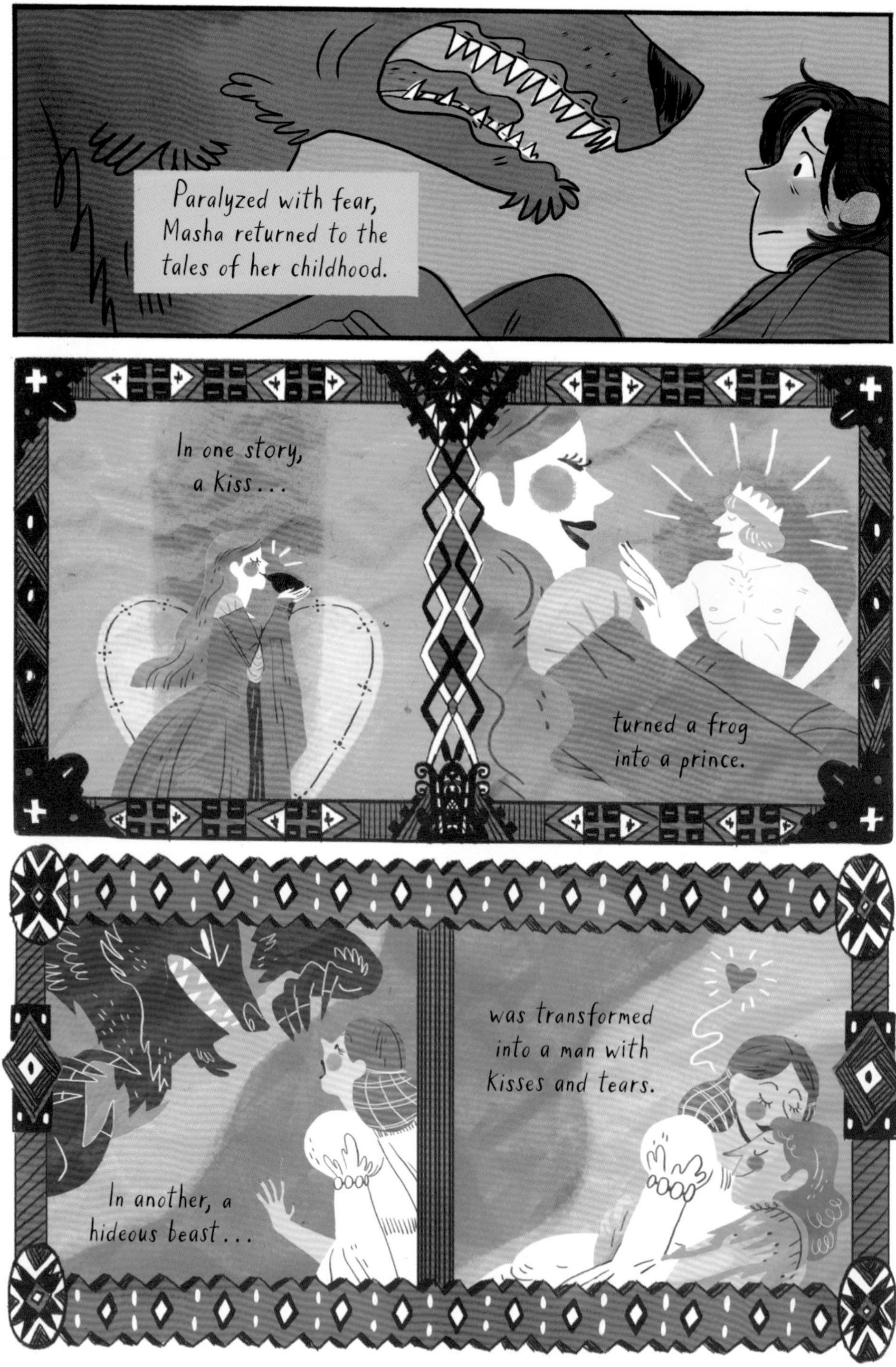
Paralyzed with fear, Masha returned to the tales of her childhood.
In one story, a kiss . . .
turned a frog into a prince.
In another, a hideous beast . . .
was transformed into a man with kisses and tears.

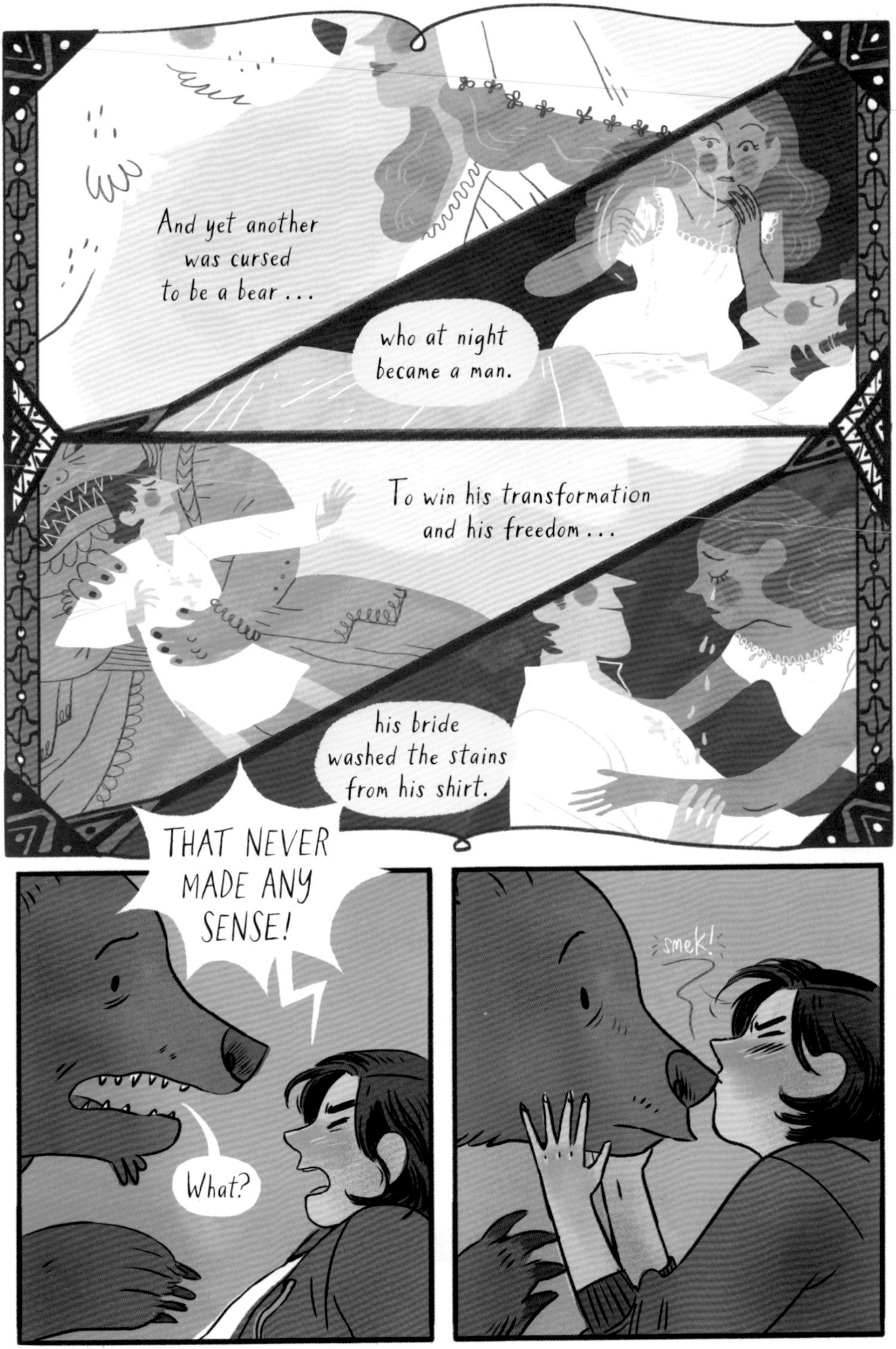
And yet another was cursed to be a bear . . .
who at night became a man.
To win his transformation and his freedom . . .
his bride washed the stains from his shirt.
THAT NEVER MADE ANY SENSE!
What?
smek!

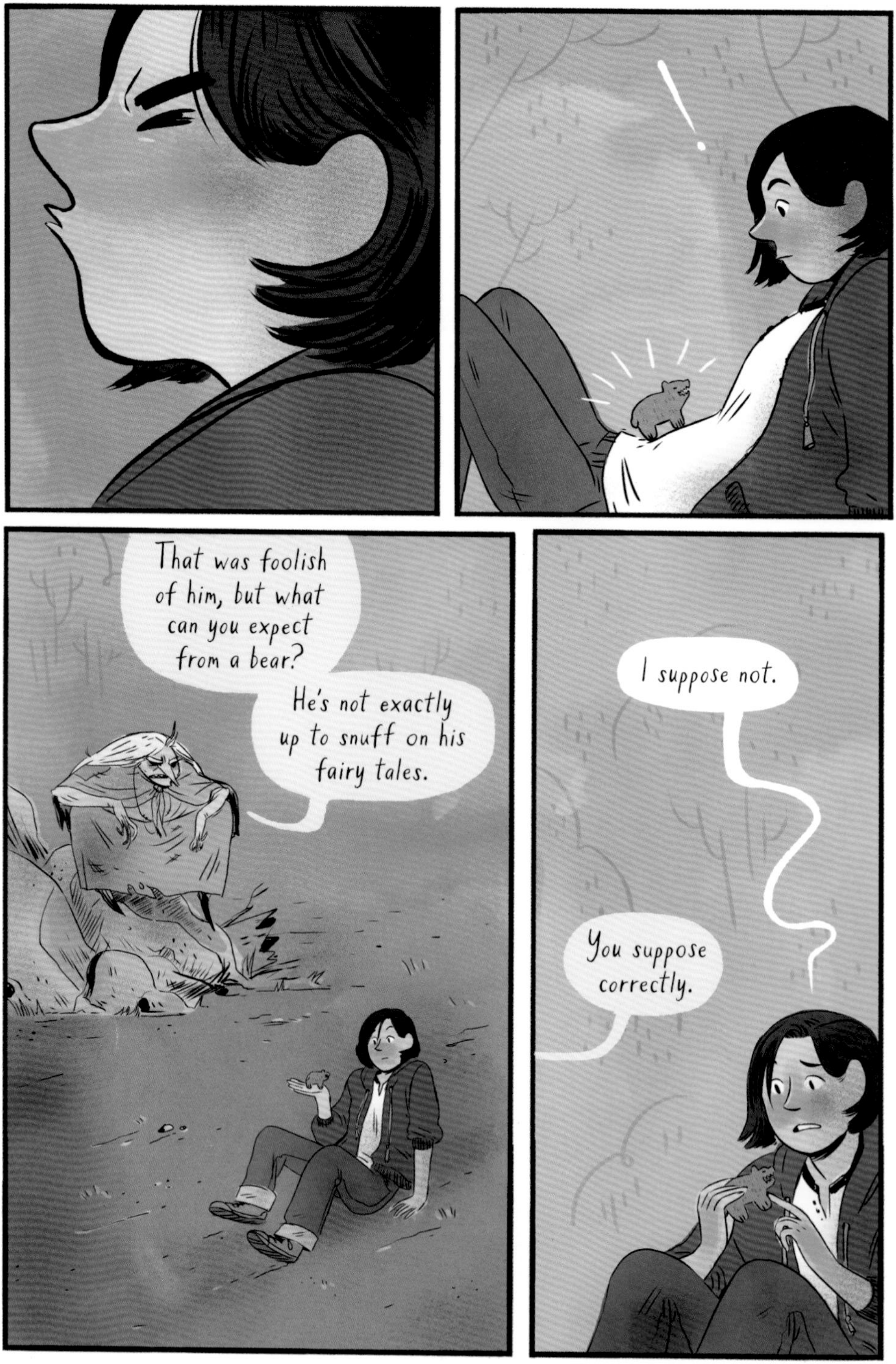
That was foolish of him, but what can you expect from a bear?
He's not exactly up to snuff on his fairy tales.
I suppose not.
You suppose correctly.

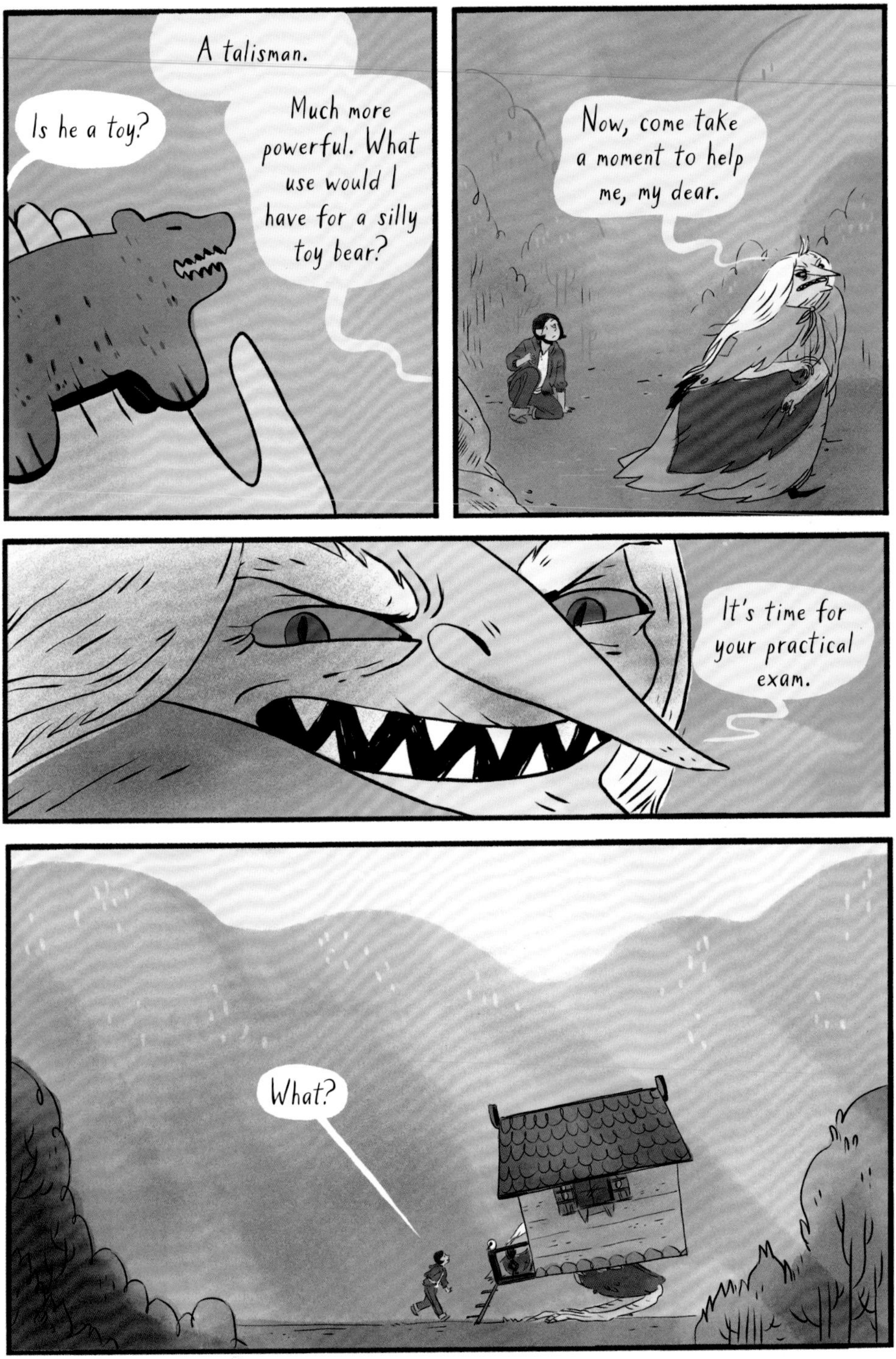
Is he a toy?
A talisman.
Much more powerful. What use would I have for a silly toy bear?
Now, come take a moment to help me, my dear.
It's time for your practical exam.
What?

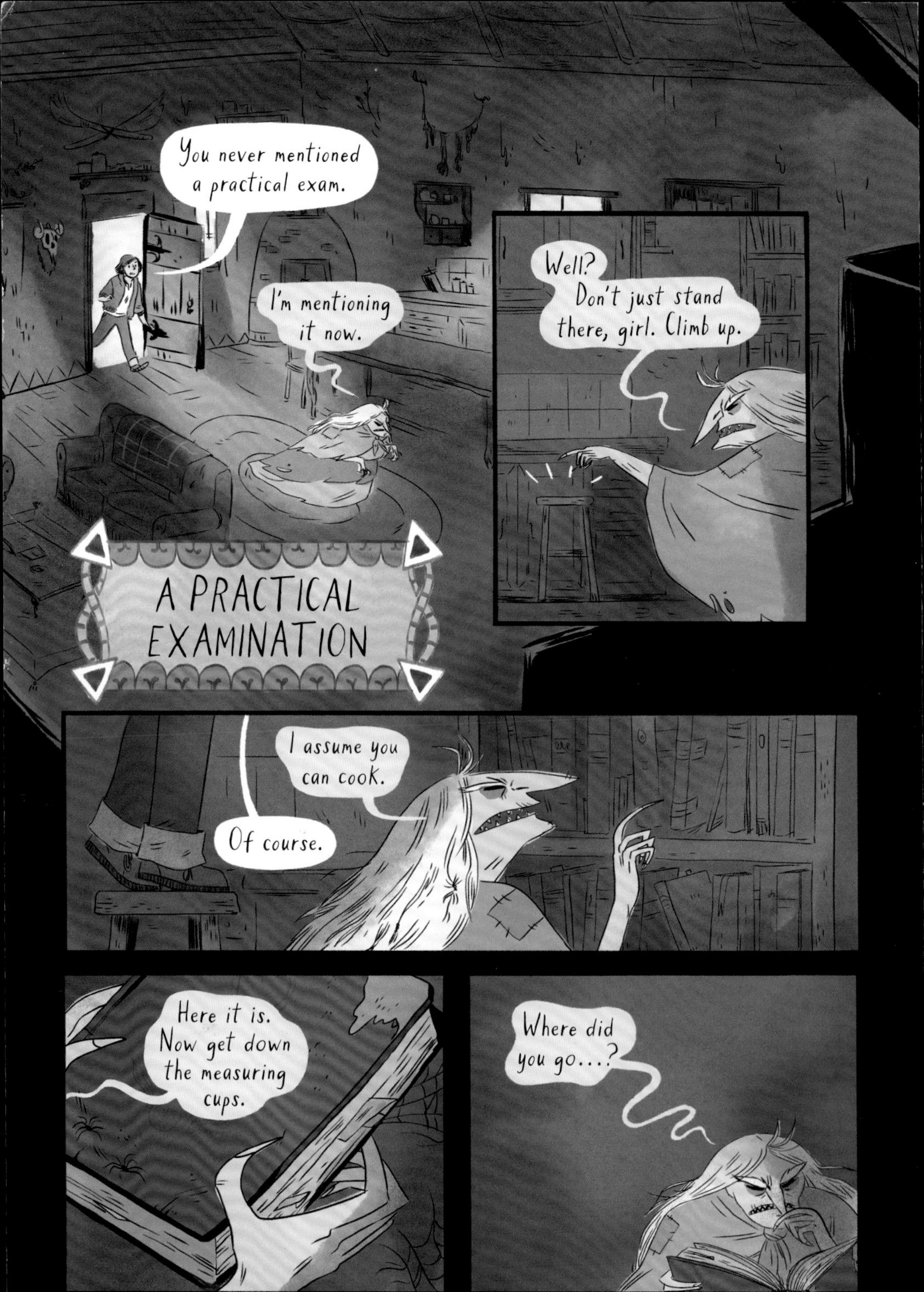
You never mentioned a practical exam.
I'm mentioning it now.
Well? Don't just stand there, girl. Climb up.
A PRACTICAL EXAMINATION
I assume you can cook.
Of course.
Here it is. Now get down the measuring cups.
Where did you go...?

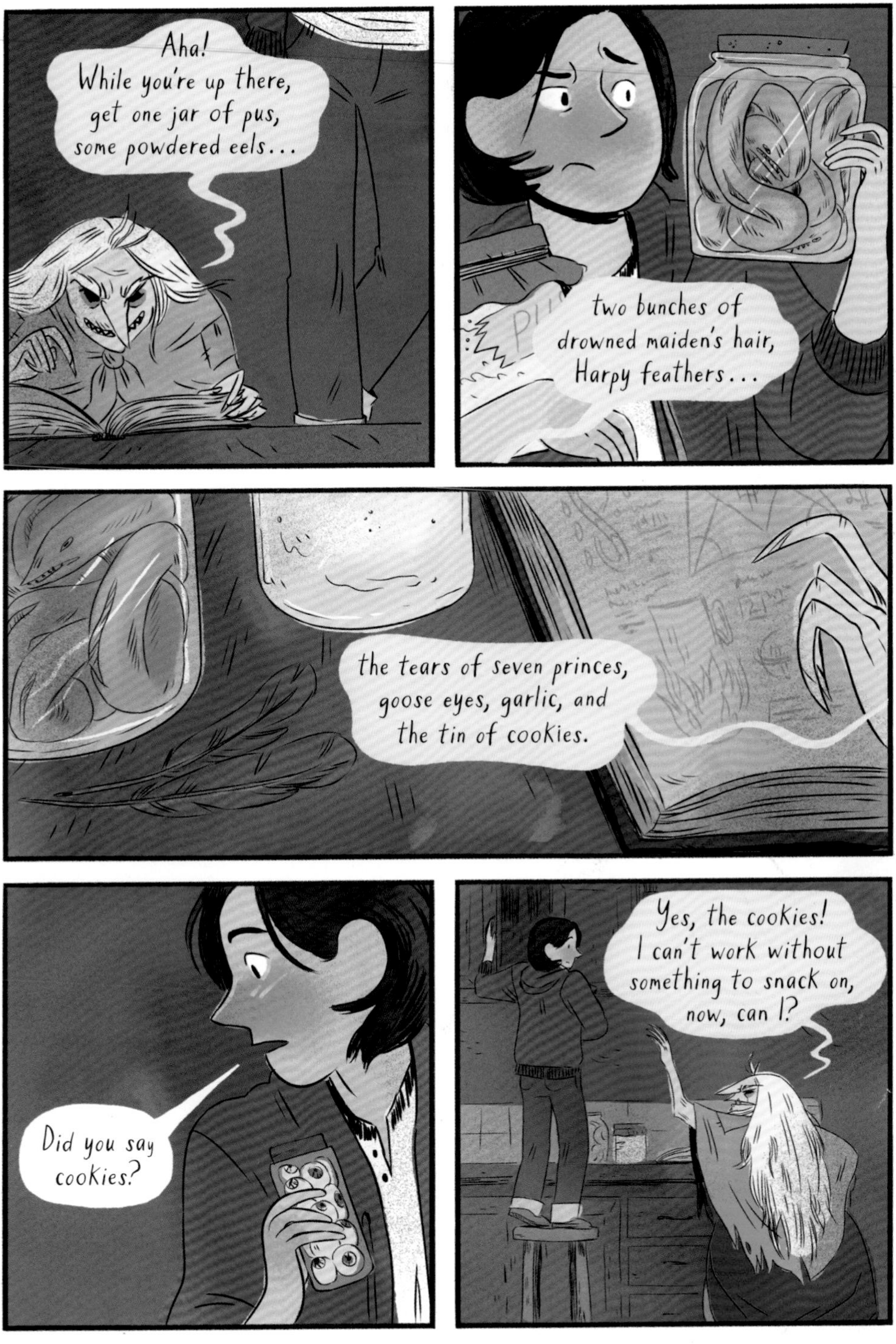
Aha! While you're up there, get one jar of pus, some powdered eels...
two bunches of drowned maiden's hair, Harpy feathers...
the tears of seven princes, goose eyes, garlic, and the tin of cookies.
Did you say cookies?
Yes, the cookies! I can't work without something to snack on, now, can I?

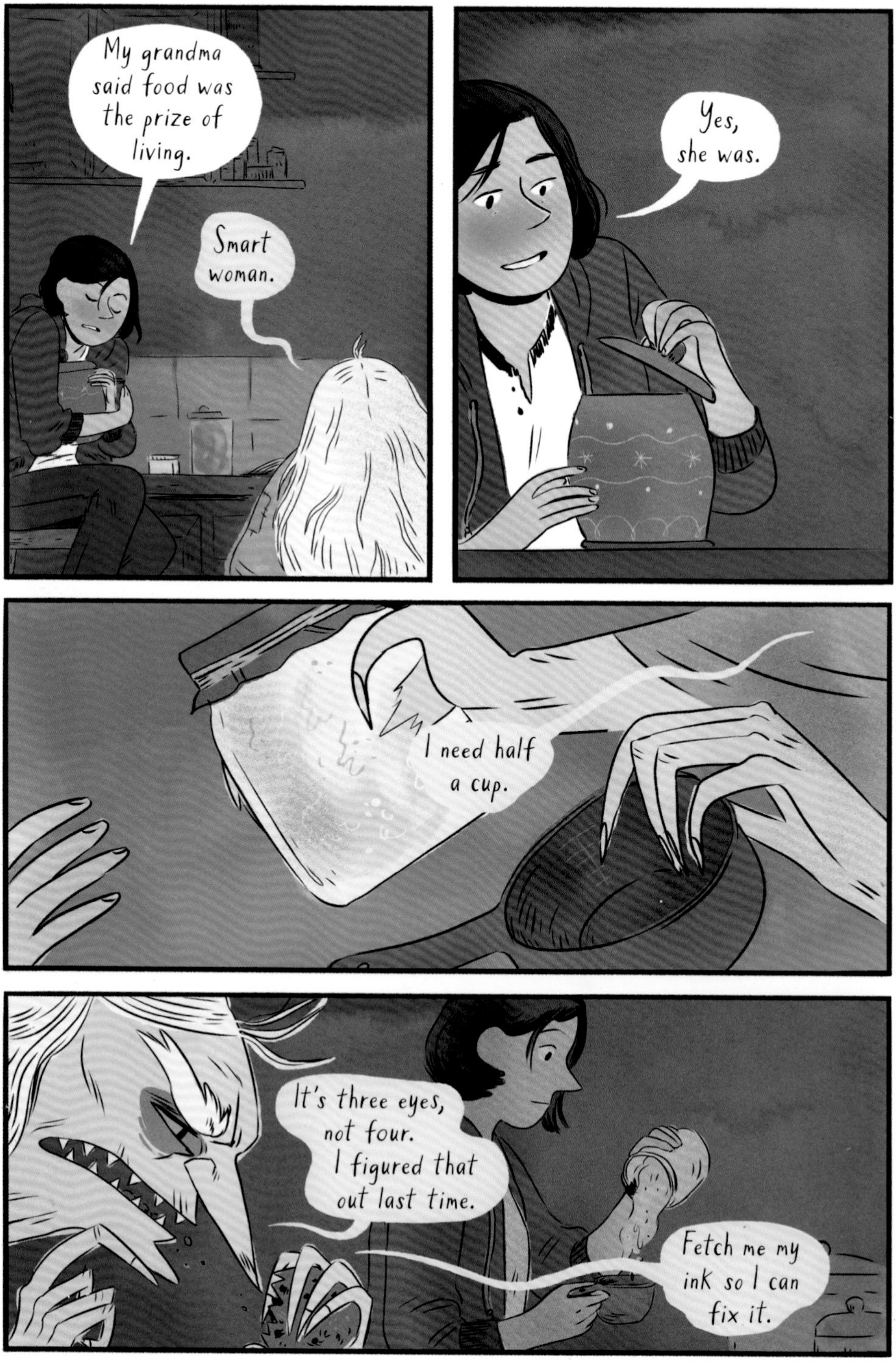
My grandma said food was the prize of living.
Smart woman.
Yes, she was.
I need half a cup.
It's three eyes, not four. I figured that out last time.
Fetch me my ink so I can fix it.

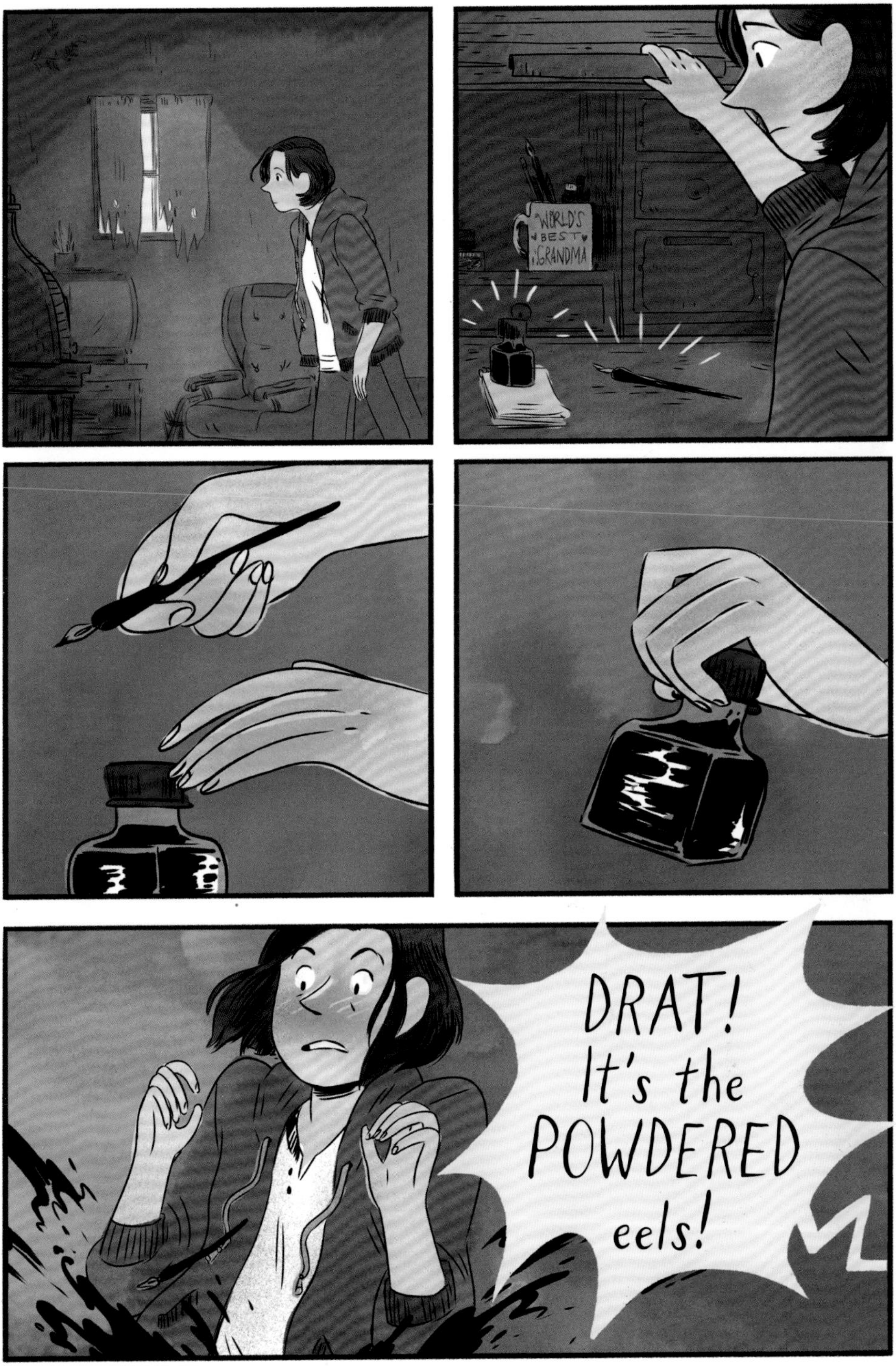
WORLD'S BEST GRANDMA
DRAT! It's the POWDERED eels!

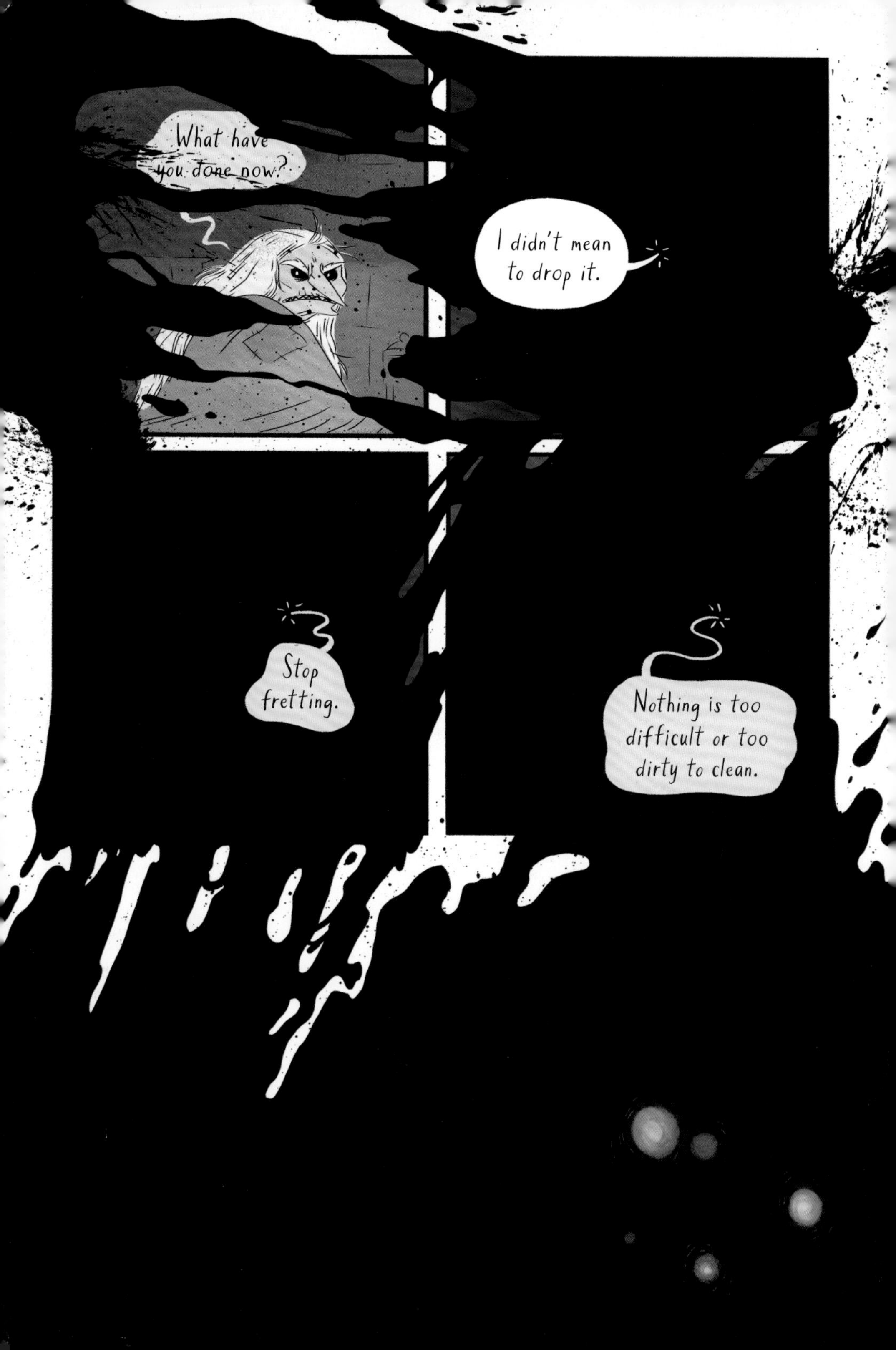
What have you done now?
I didn't mean to drop it.
Stop fretting.
Nothing is too difficult or too dirty to clean.

Aren't they beautiful, Grandma?

Yes. And I'm certain they're magical.

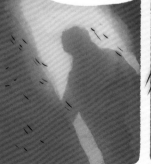

Masha, stay away from the bleeding hearts.

They're very delicate.

Those are the ones Mama planted, right?

Yes.

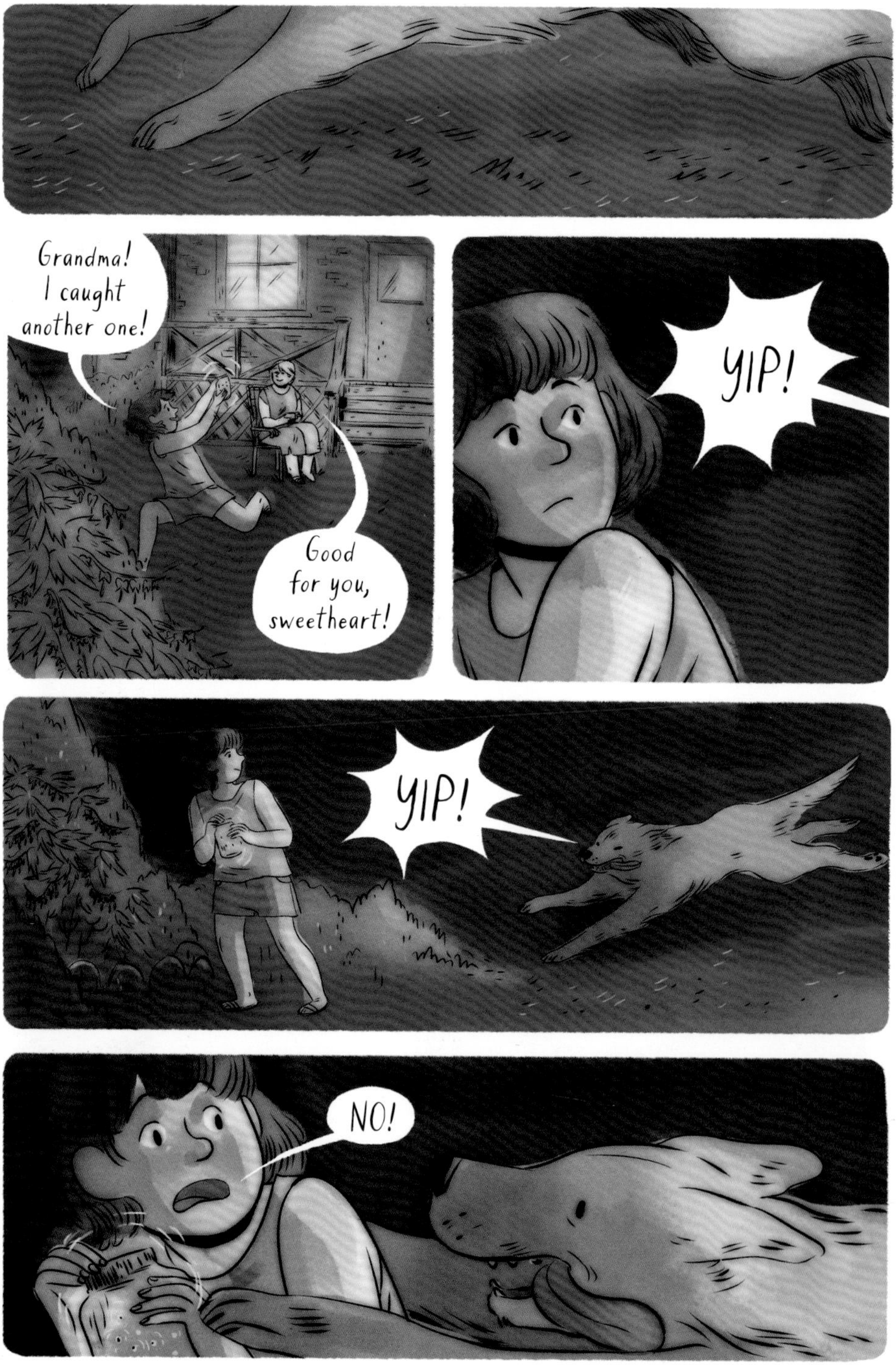
Grandma! I caught another one!
Good for you, sweetheart!
YIP!
YIP!
NO!

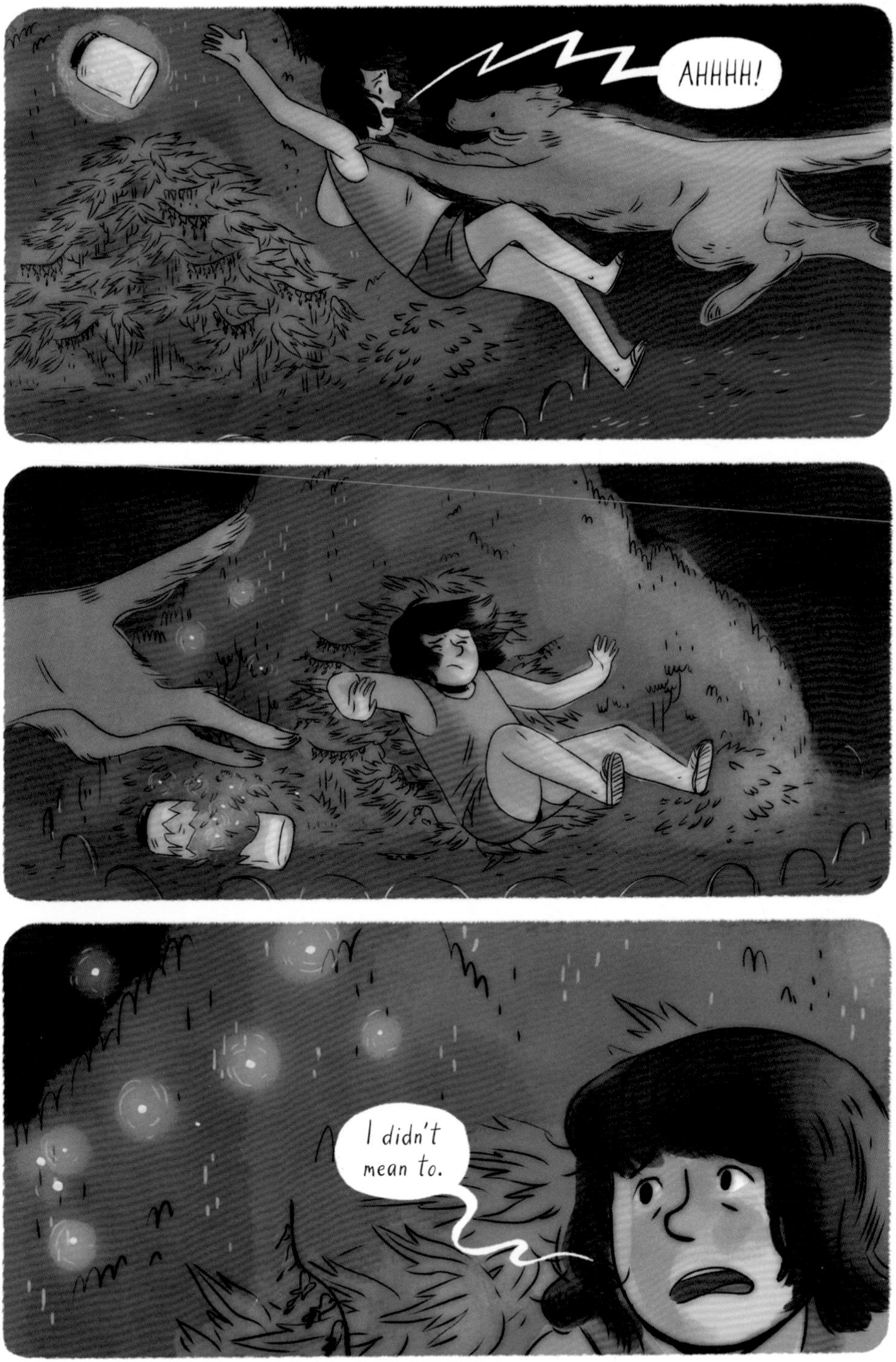
AHHHH!
I didn't mean to.

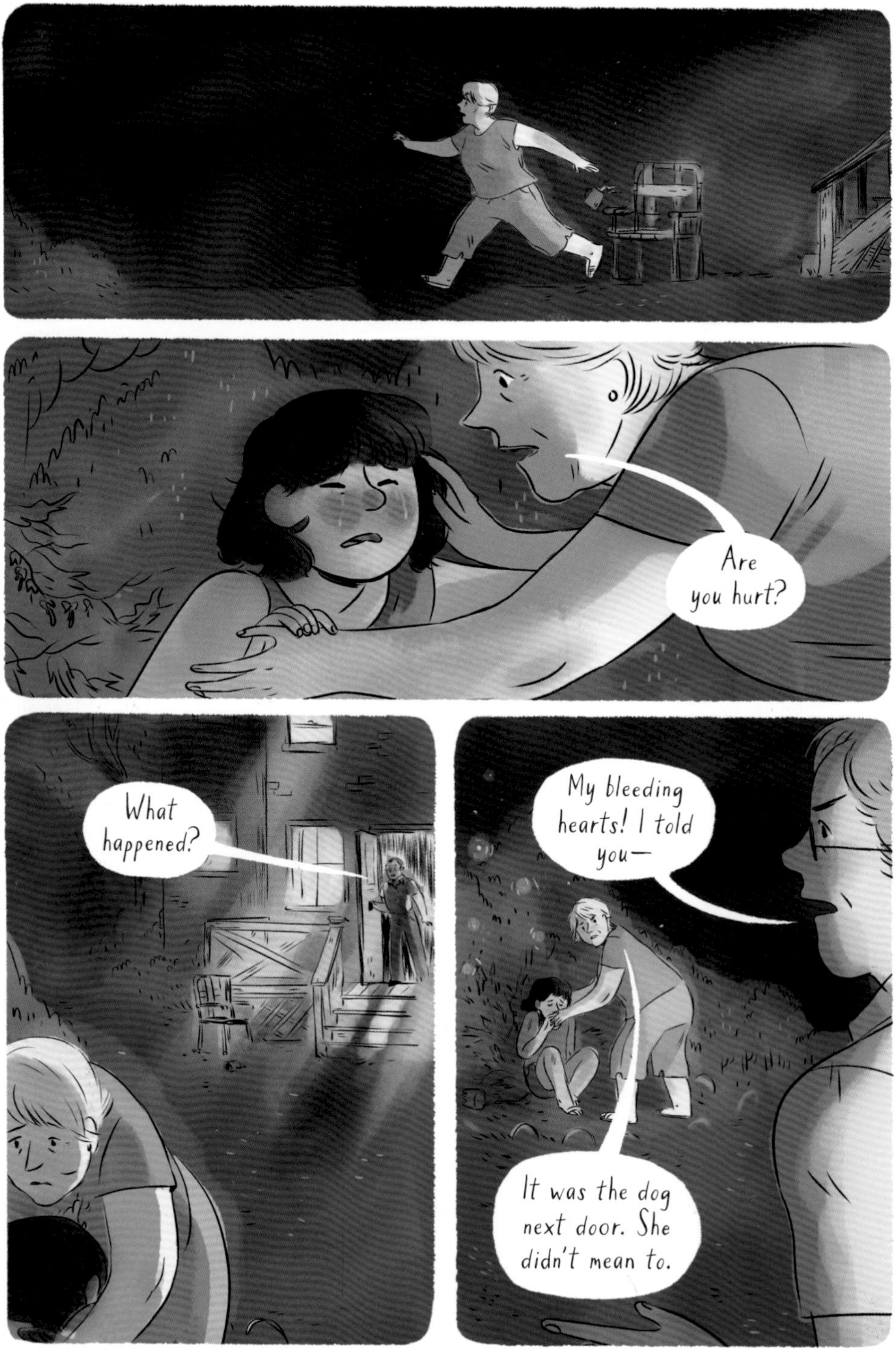
Are you hurt?
What happened?
My bleeding hearts! I told you—
It was the dog next door. She didn't mean to.

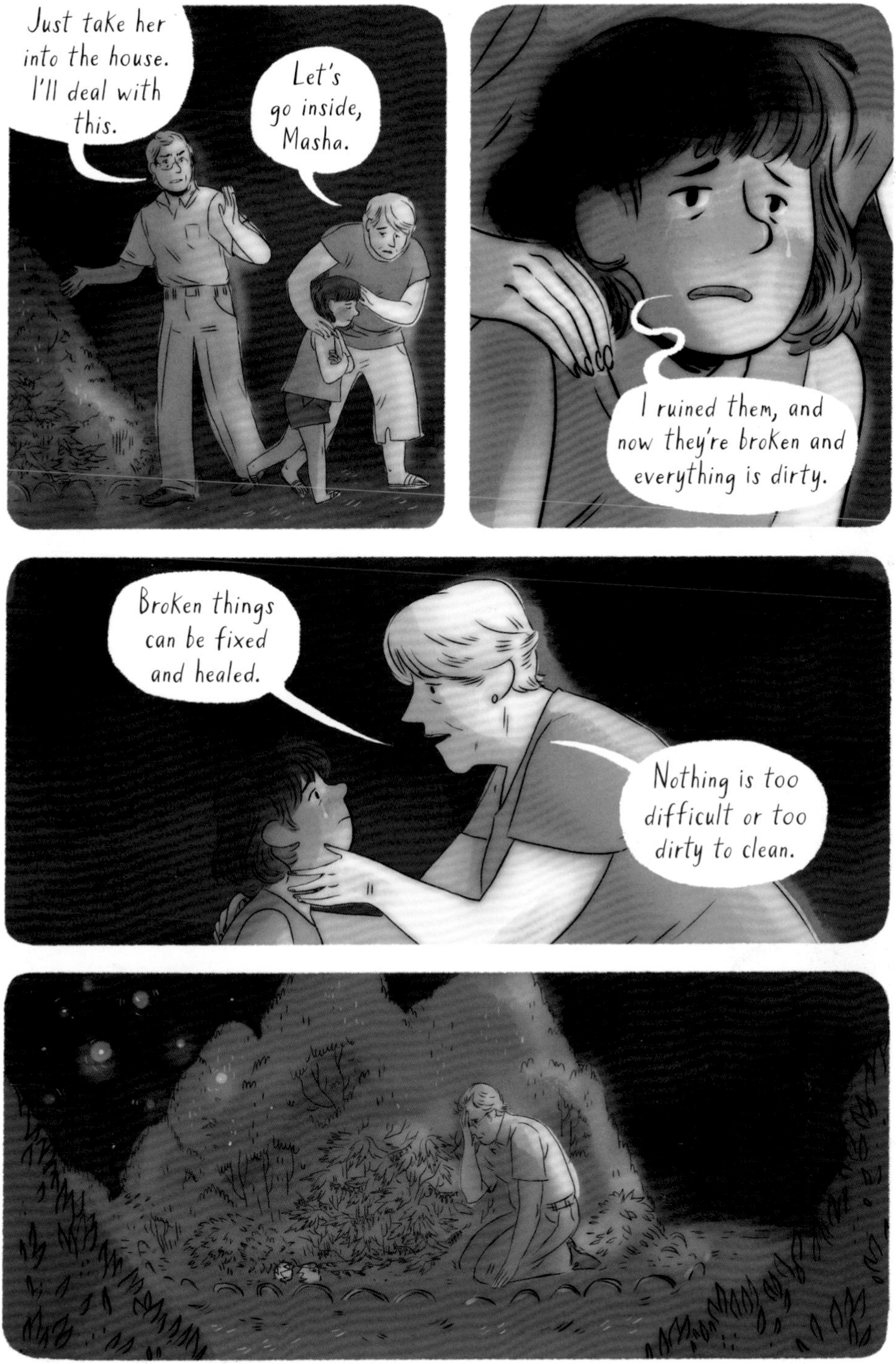

Just take her into the house. I'll deal with this.
Let's go inside, Masha.
I ruined them, and now they're broken and everything is dirty.
Broken things can be fixed and healed.
Nothing is too difficult or too dirty to clean.

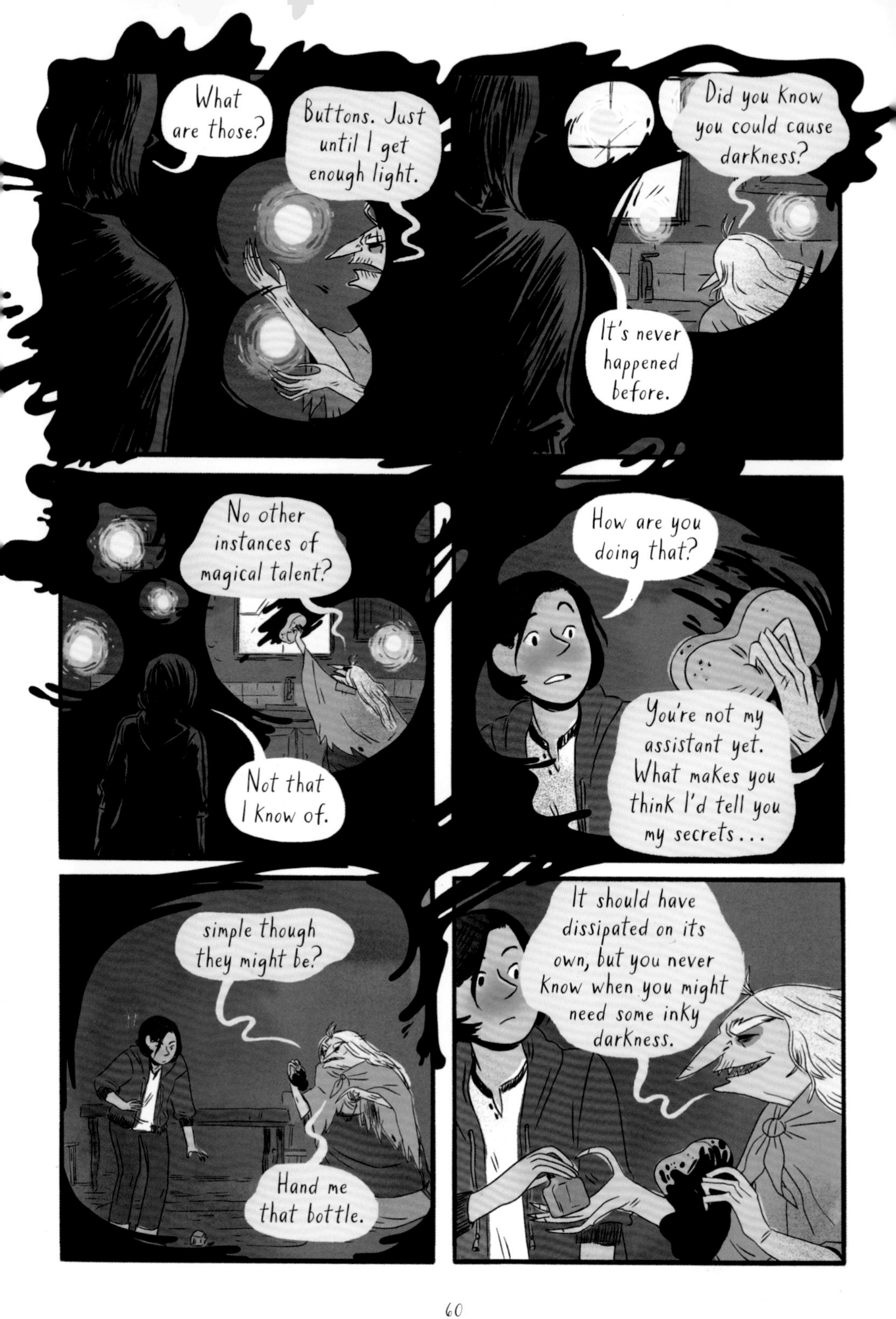
What are those?
Buttons. Just until I get enough light.
Did you know you could cause darkness?
It's never happened before.
No other instances of magical talent?
Not that I know of.
How are you doing that?
You're not my assistant yet. What makes you think I'd tell you my secrets . . .
simple though they might be?
Hand me that bottle.
It should have dissipated on its own, but you never know when you might need some inky darkness.

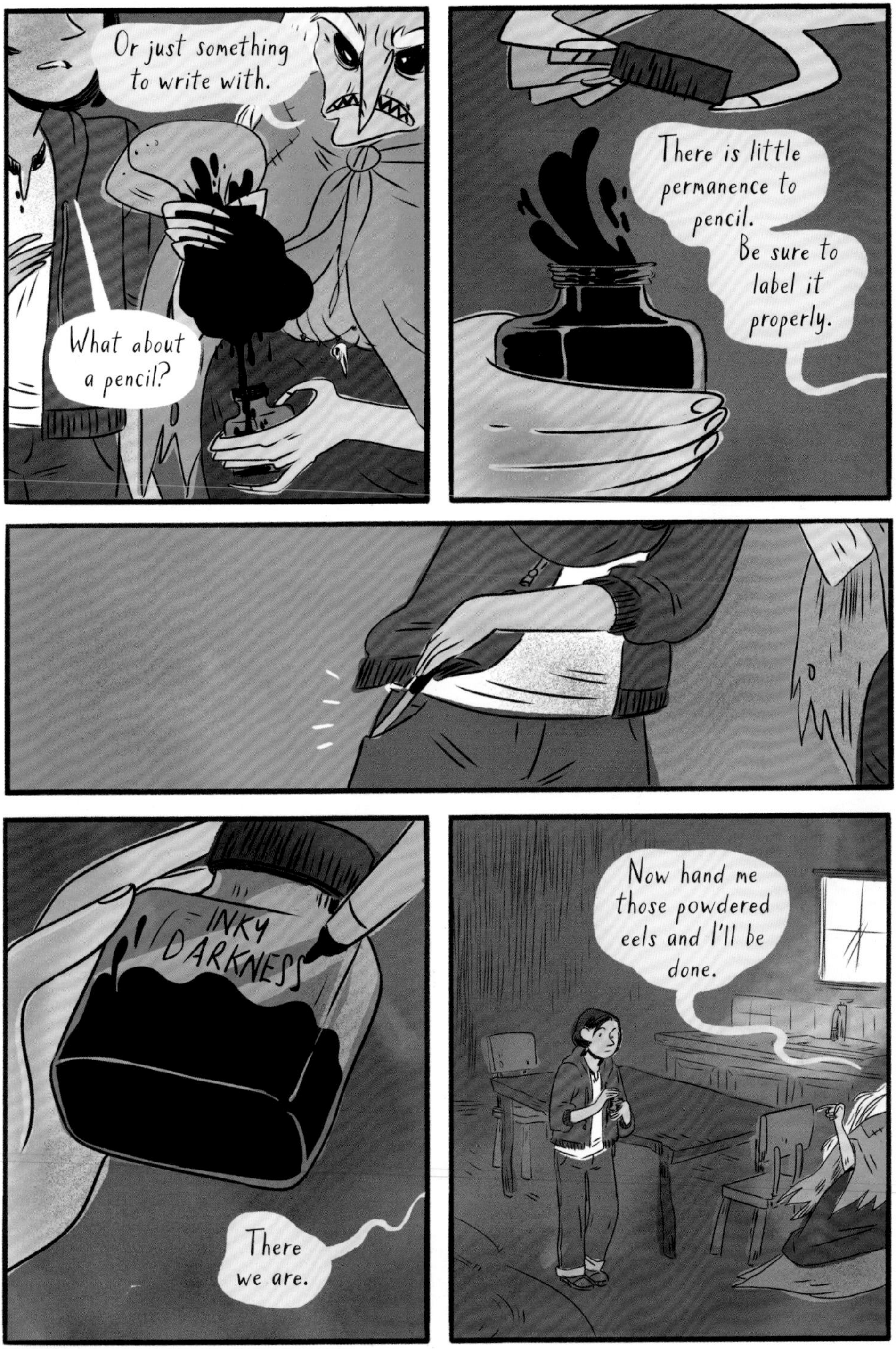
Or just something to write with.
What about a pencil?
There is little permanence to pencil.
Be sure to label it properly.
INKY DARKNESS
There we are.
Now hand me those powdered eels and I'll be done.

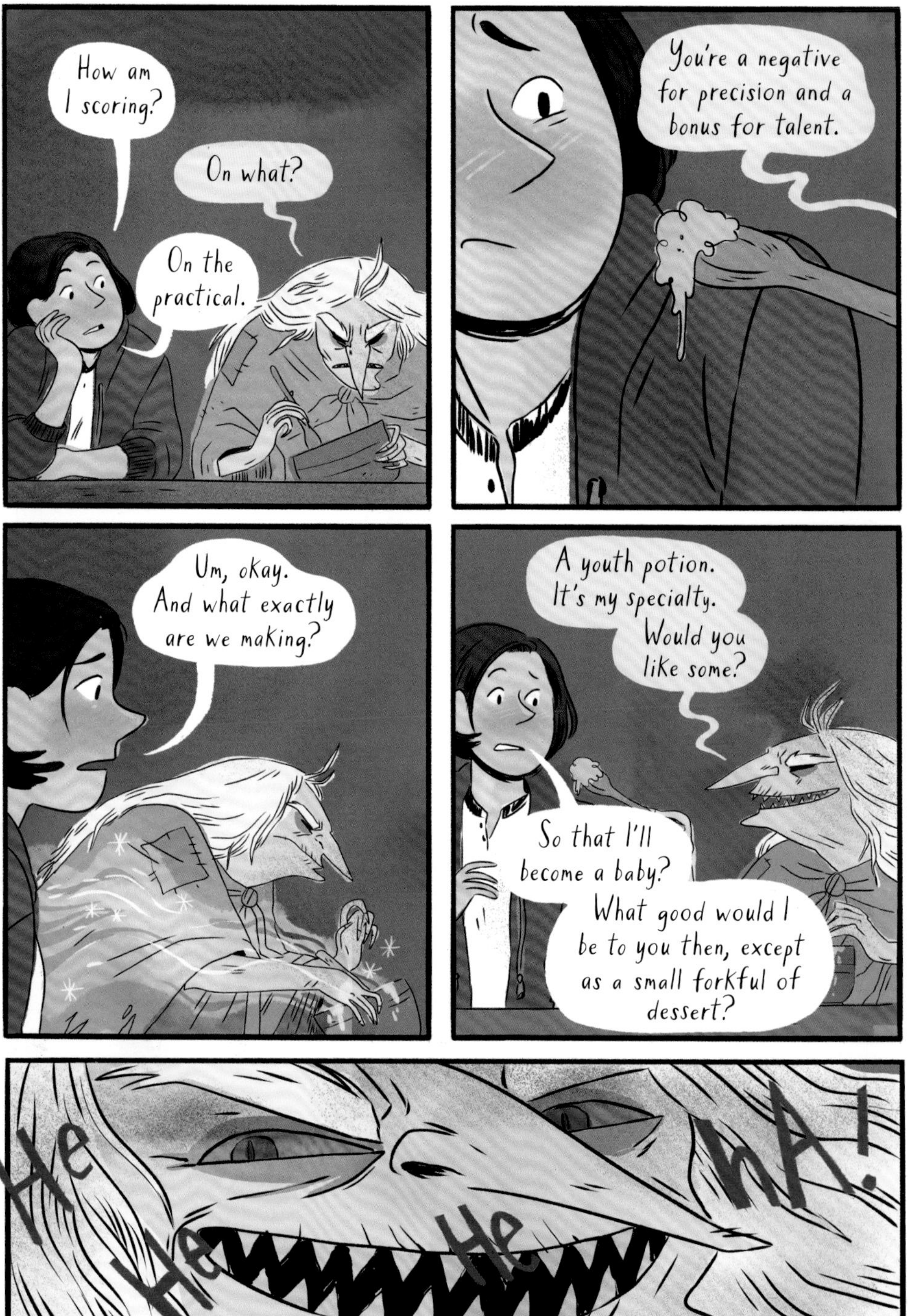
How am I scoring?
On what?
On the practical.
You're a negative for precision and a bonus for talent.
Um, okay. And what exactly are we making?
A youth potion. It's my specialty. Would you like some?
So that I'll become a baby?
What good would I be to you then, except as a small forkful of dessert?
He He He hA!

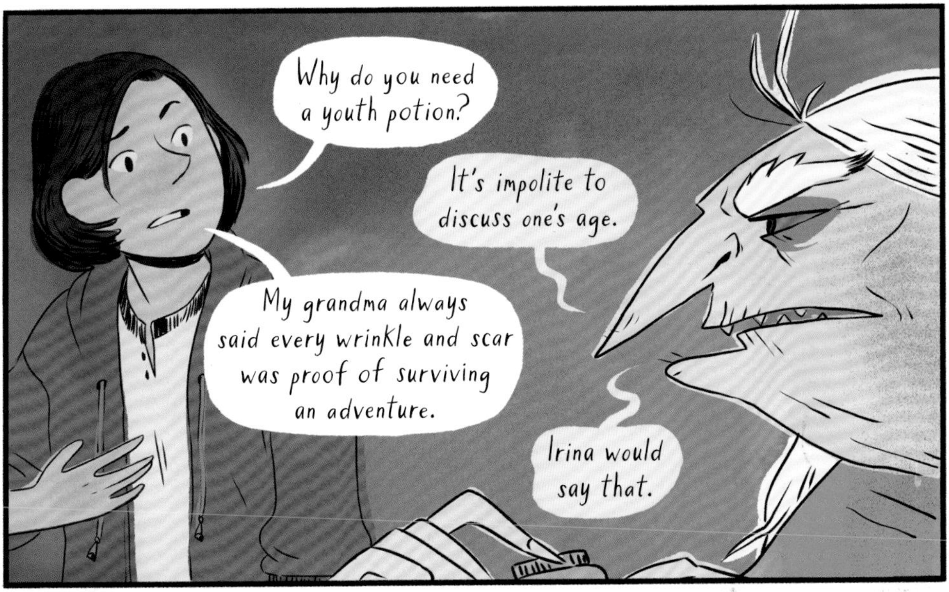
Why do you need a youth potion?
It's impolite to discuss one's age.
My grandma always said every wrinkle and scar was proof of surviving an adventure.
Irina would say that.

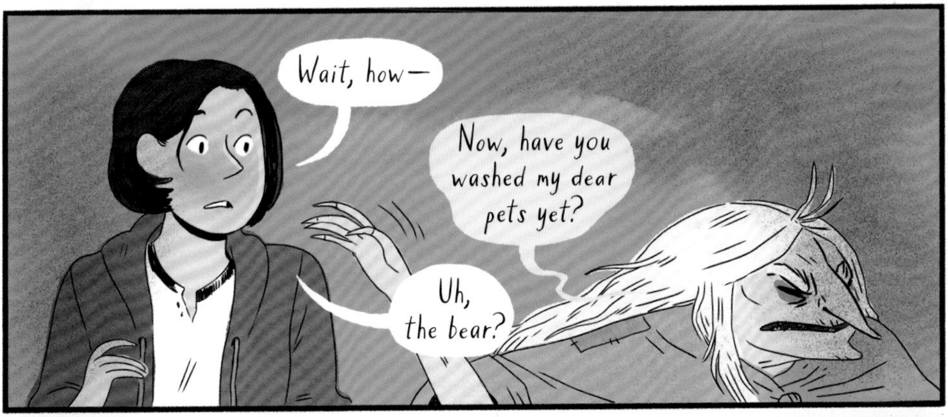
Wait, how—
Now, have you washed my dear pets yet?
Uh, the bear?

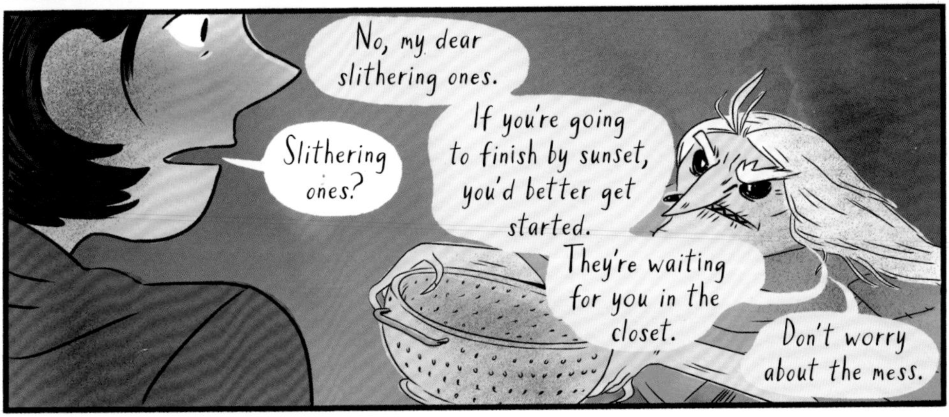
No, my dear slithering ones.
Slithering ones?
If you're going to finish by sunset, you'd better get started.
They're waiting for you in the closet.
Don't worry about the mess.

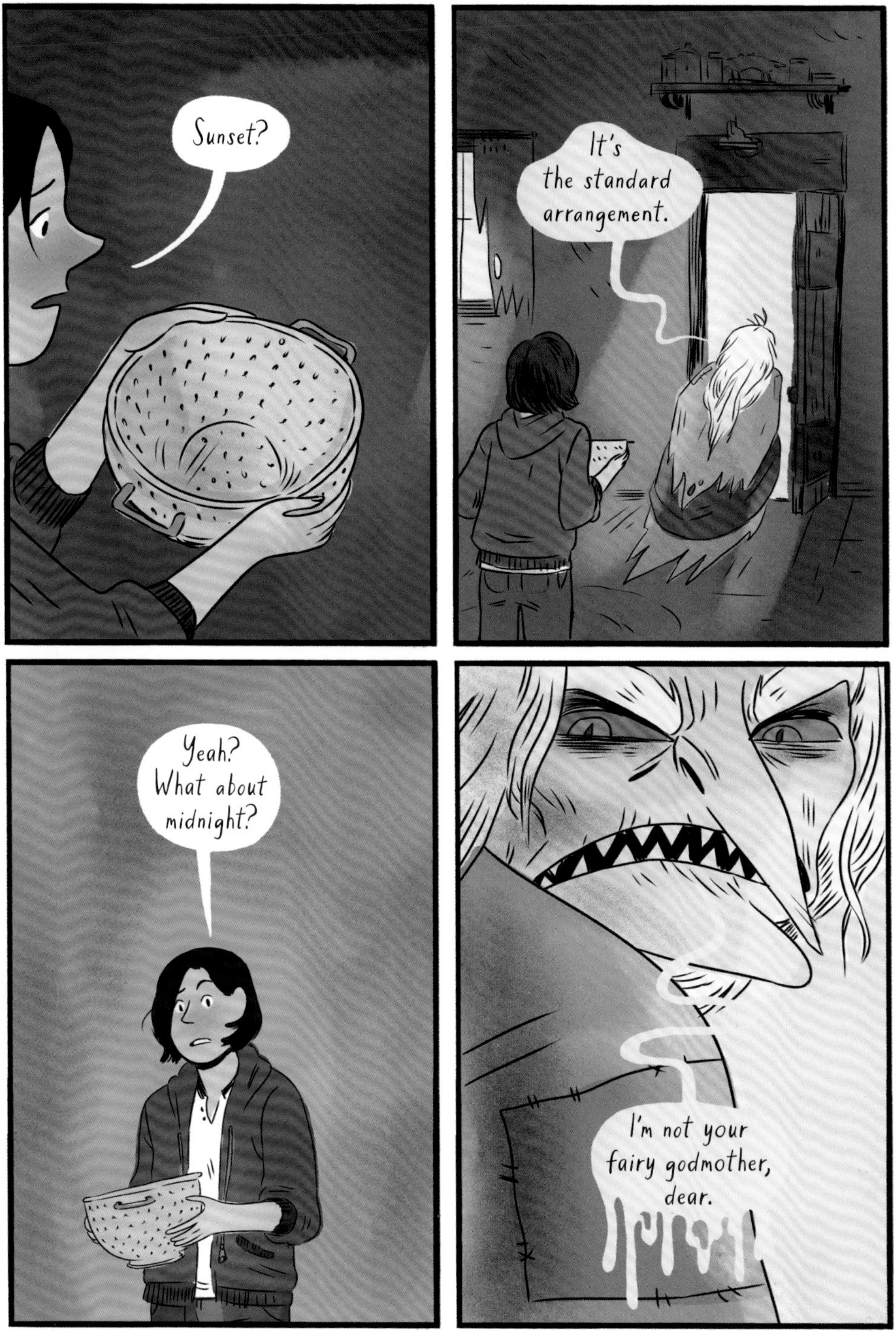
Sunset?
It's the standard arrangement.
Yeah? What about midnight?
I'm not your fairy godmother, dear.

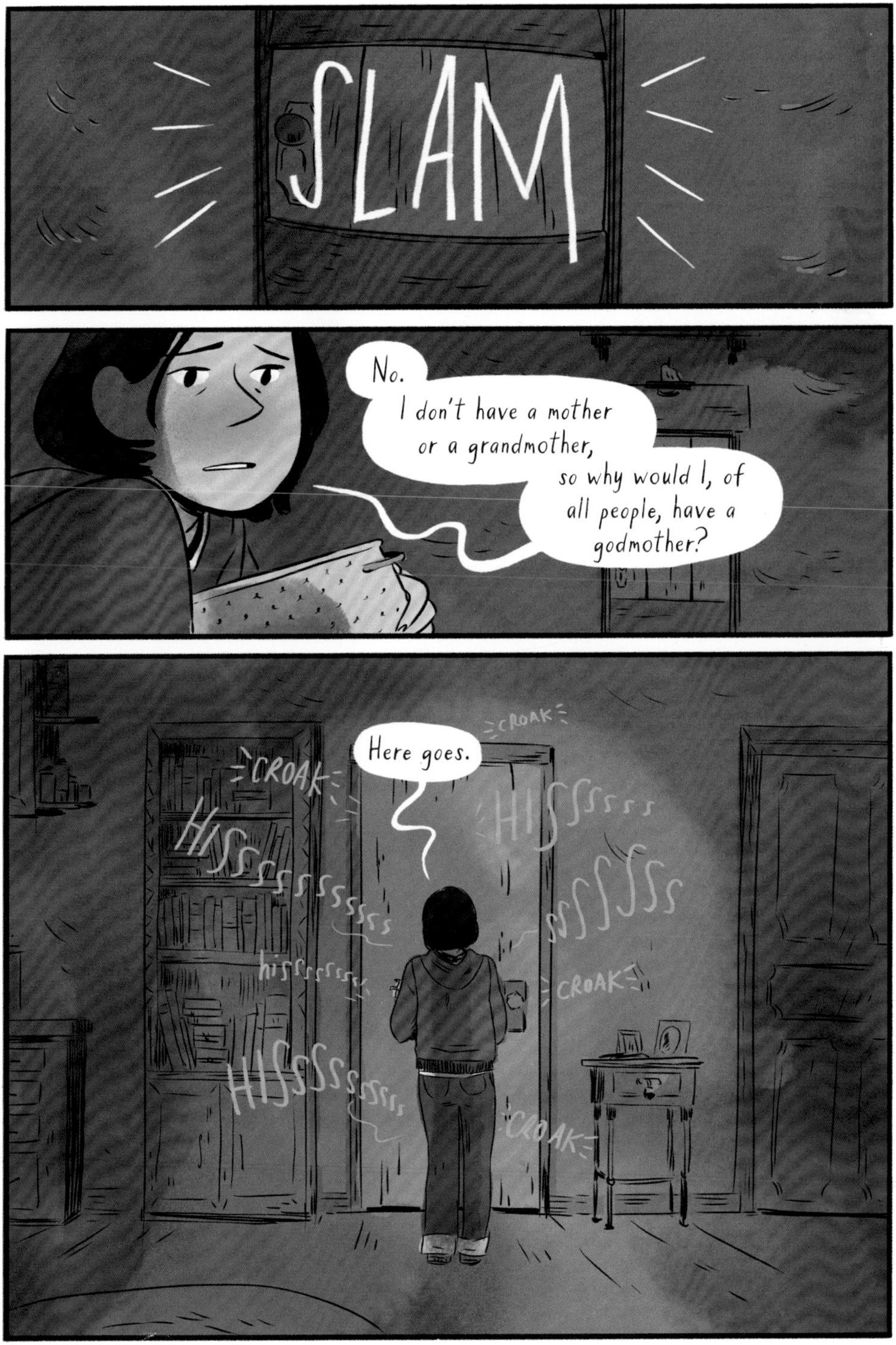
SLAM
No.
I don't have a mother or a grandmother,
so why would I, of all people, have a godmother?
Here goes.
CROAK
CROAK
HISSSSSSS
HISSSSSSSSSSSS
SSSSSSS
hissssssss
CROAK
HISSSSSSSSS
CROAK

THE SECOND TEST

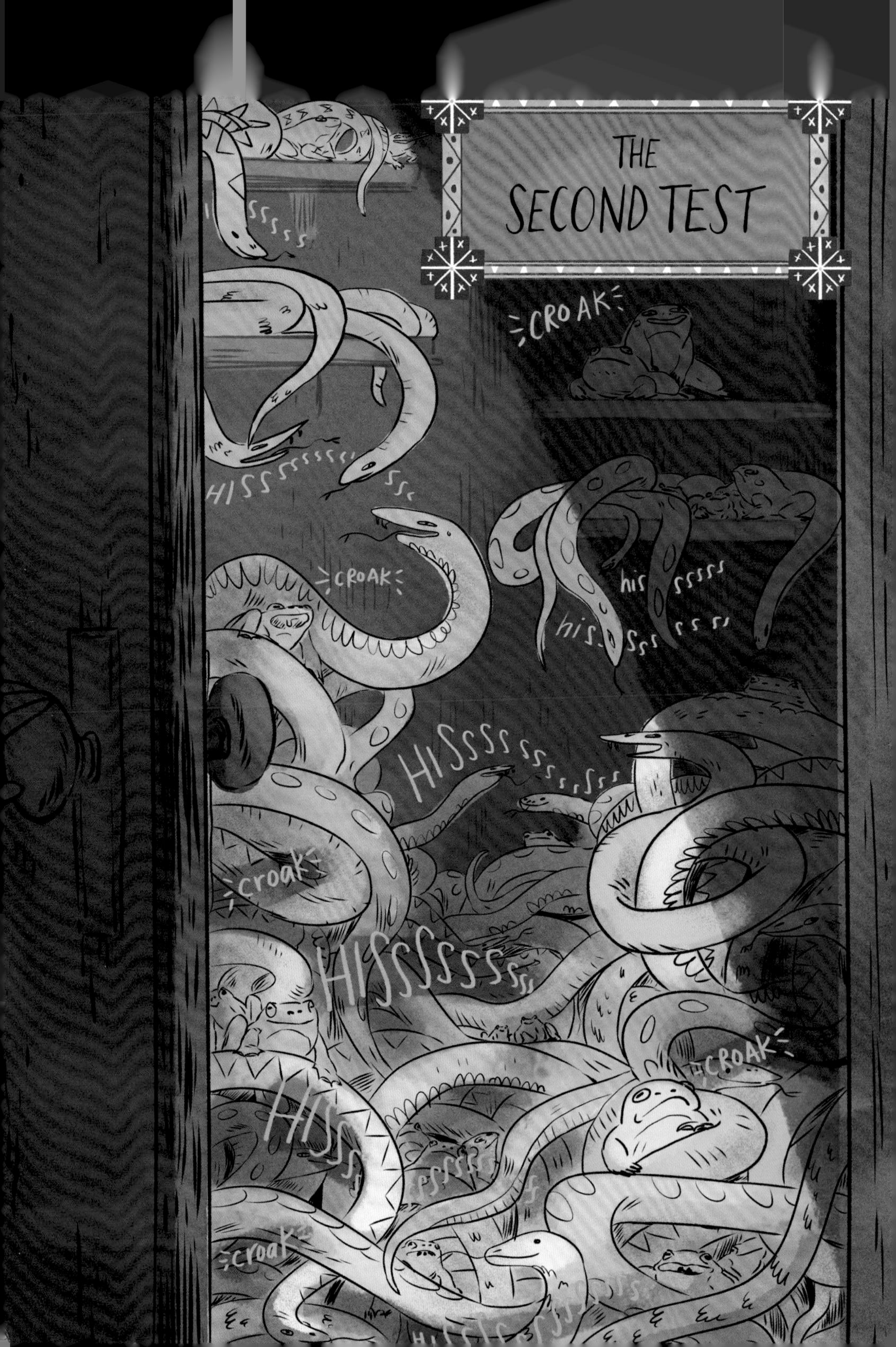
HISSSSSSSSSS
CROAK
CROAK
his
his
HISSSSSSSSSSSS
croak
HISSSSSSSSS
CROAK
HISSS
croak

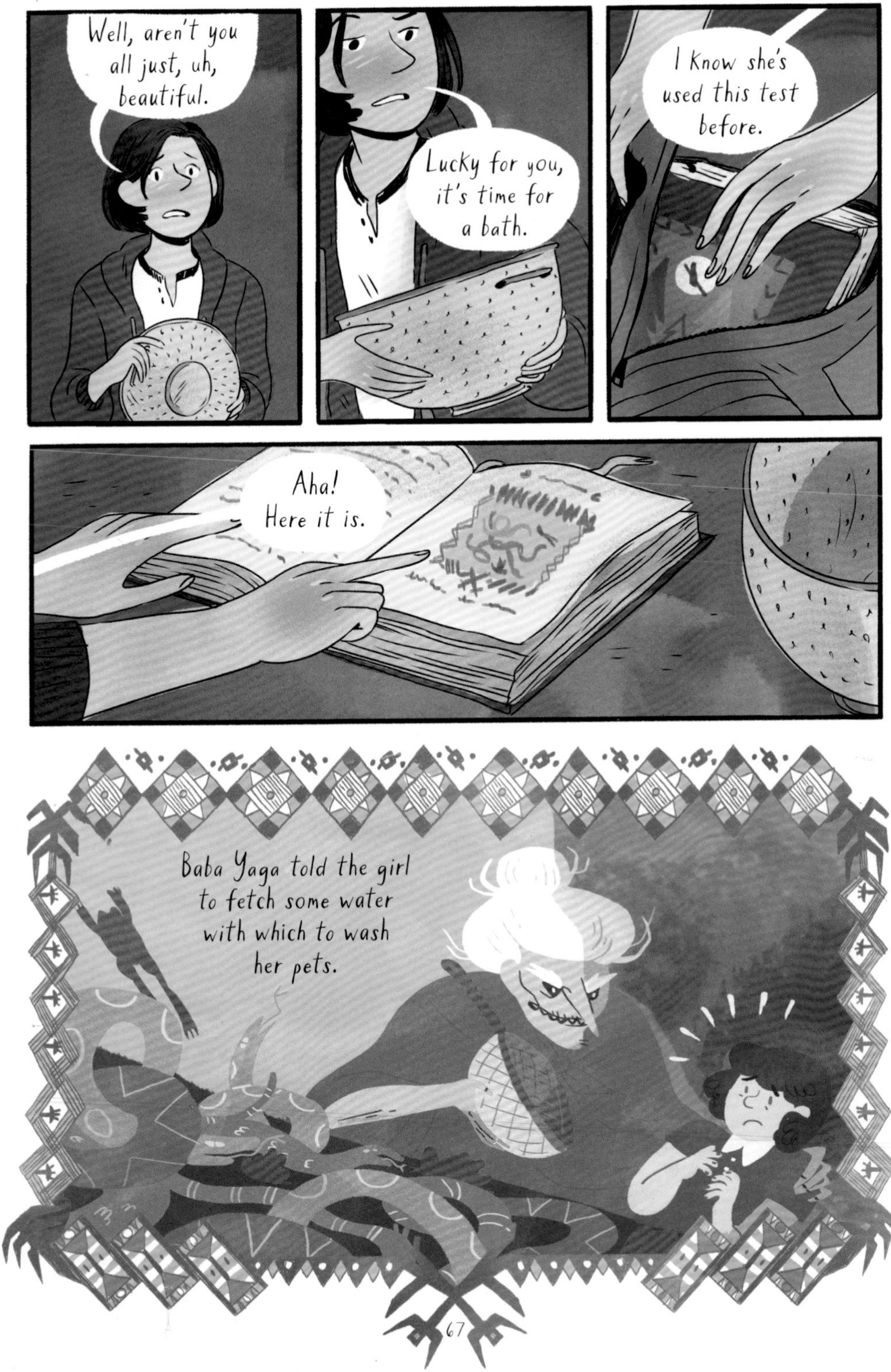
Well, aren't you all just, uh, beautiful.
Lucky for you, it's time for a bath.
I know she's used this test before.
Aha! Here it is.
Baba Yaga told the girl to fetch some water with which to wash her pets.

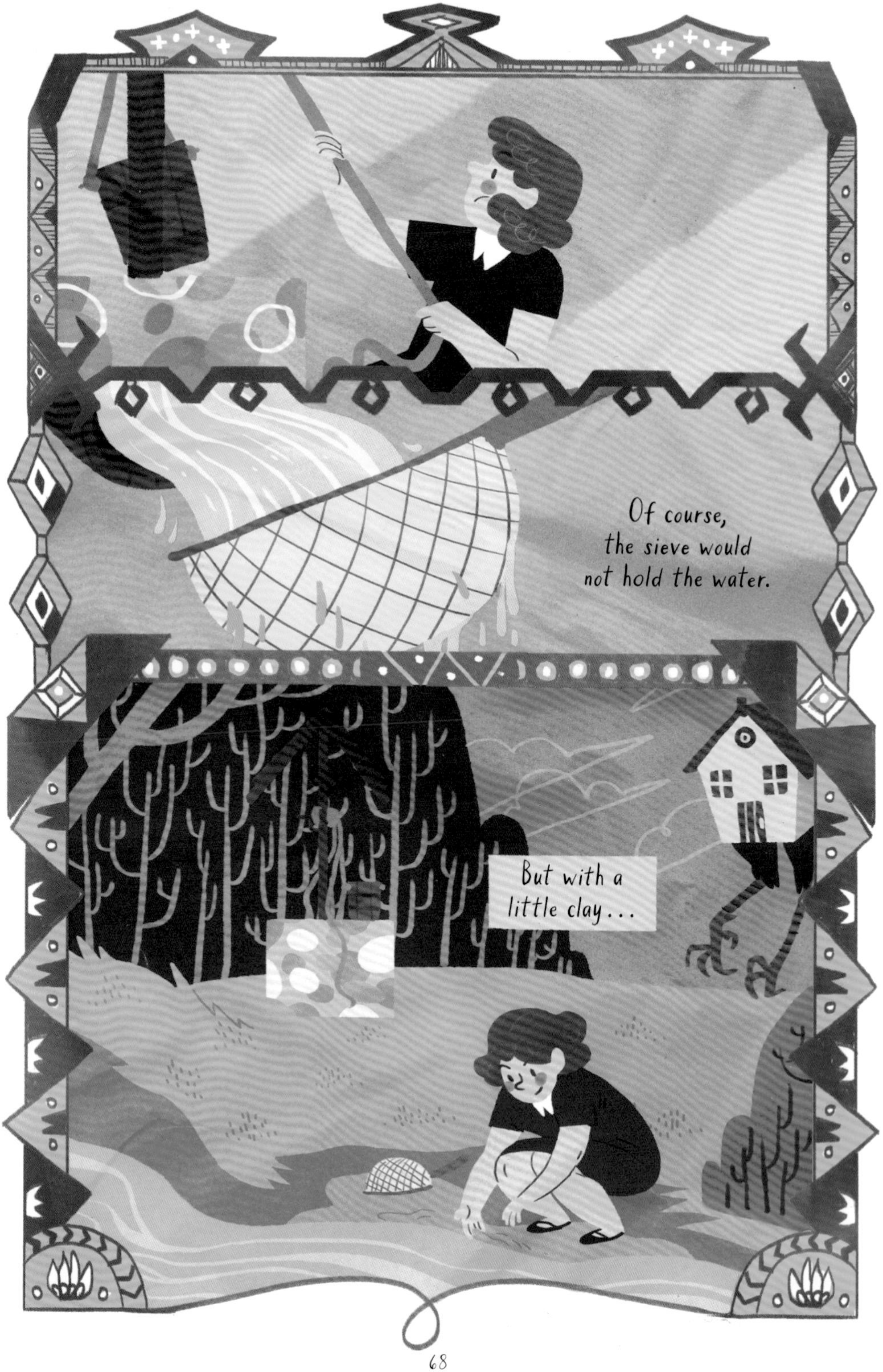
Of course,
the sieve would
not hold the water.
But with a
little clay . . .

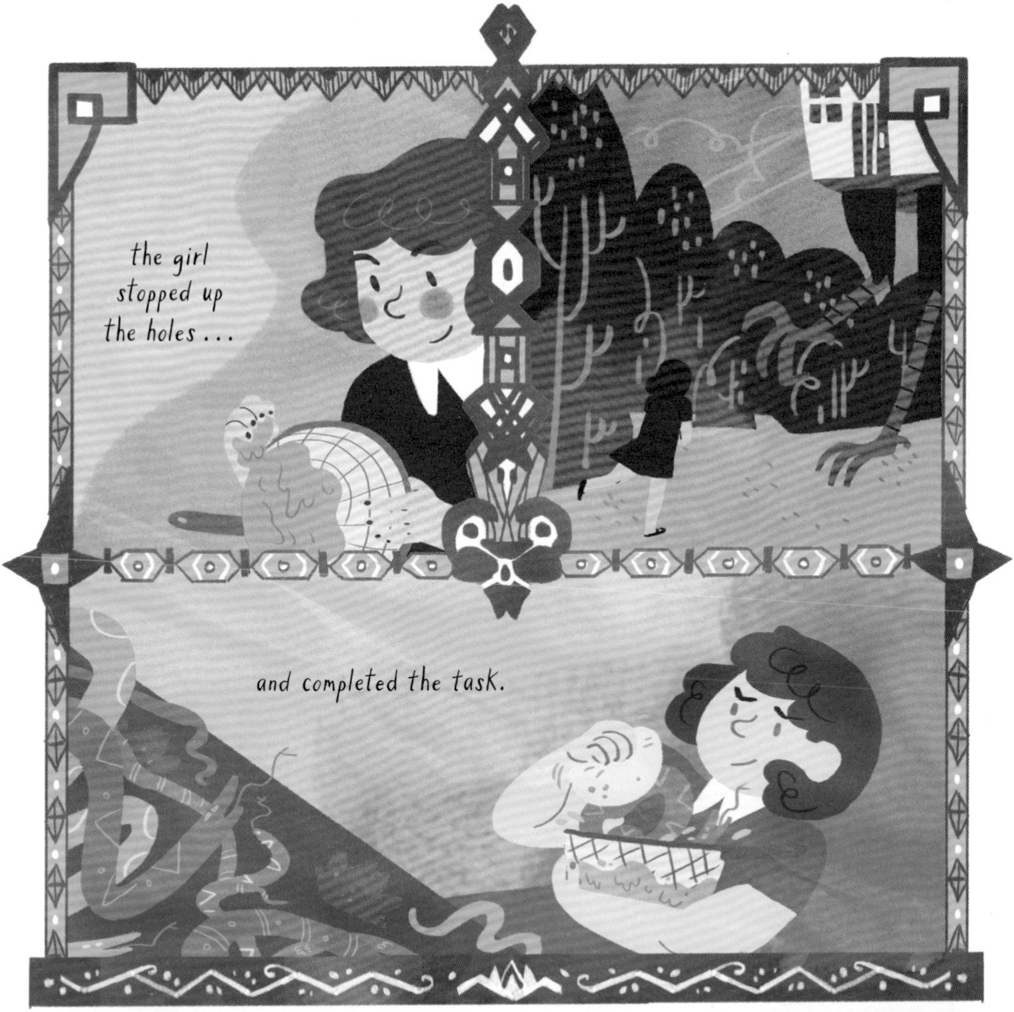
the girl stopped up the holes . . .
and completed the task.

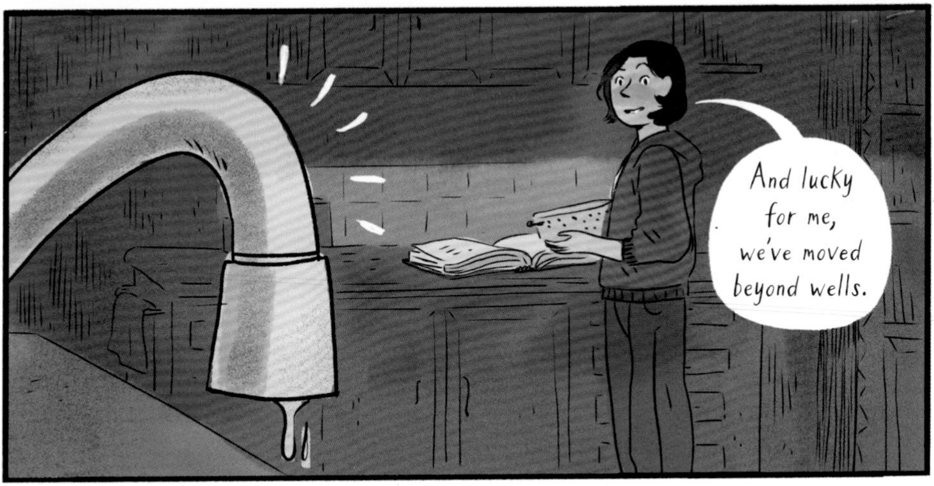
And lucky for me, we've moved beyond wells.

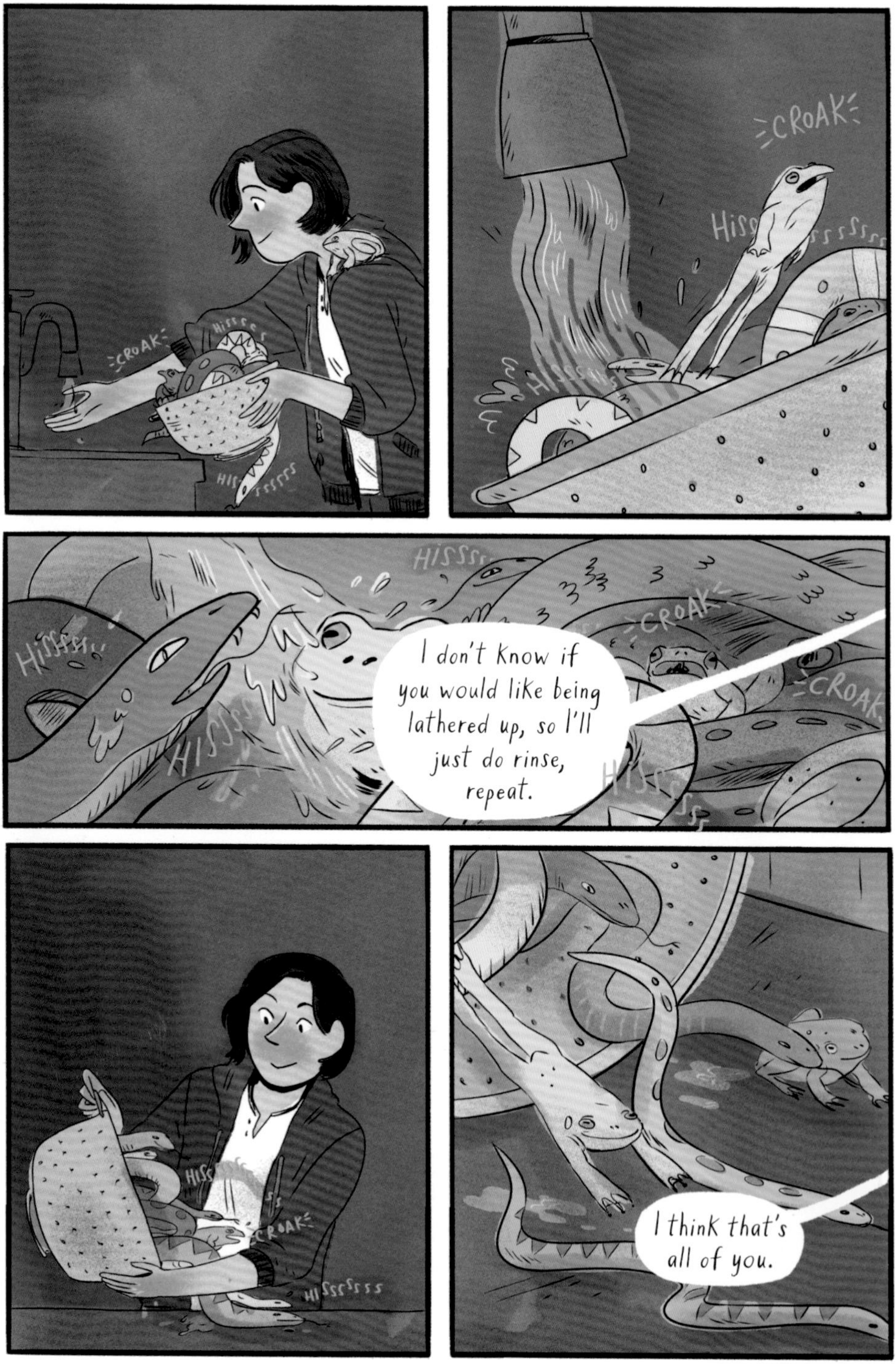
CROAK
HISSSS
HISSSSSSS
CROAK
HISS
HISSSS
HISSSS
CROAK
HISSSS
I don't know if you would like being lathered up, so I'll just do rinse, repeat.
CROAK
HISSSSSSS
CROAK
I think that's all of you.

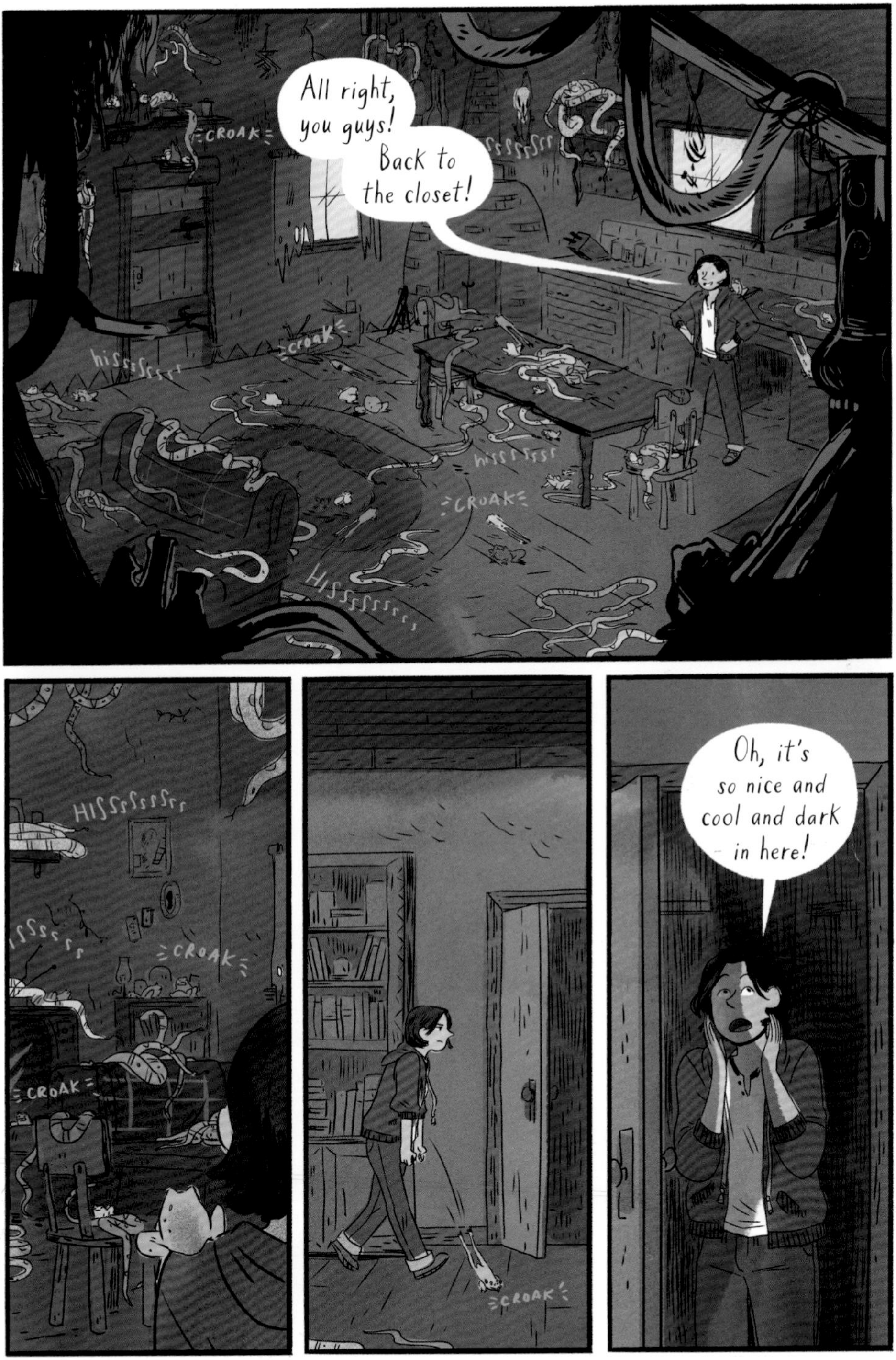
All right, you guys!
Back to the closet!
CROAK
SSSSSSSS
hisssSsss
CROAK
hissssss
CROAK
HISSSSSSSS
HISSSSSSS
ISSSSS
CROAK
CROAK
CROAK
Oh, it's so nice and cool and dark in here!

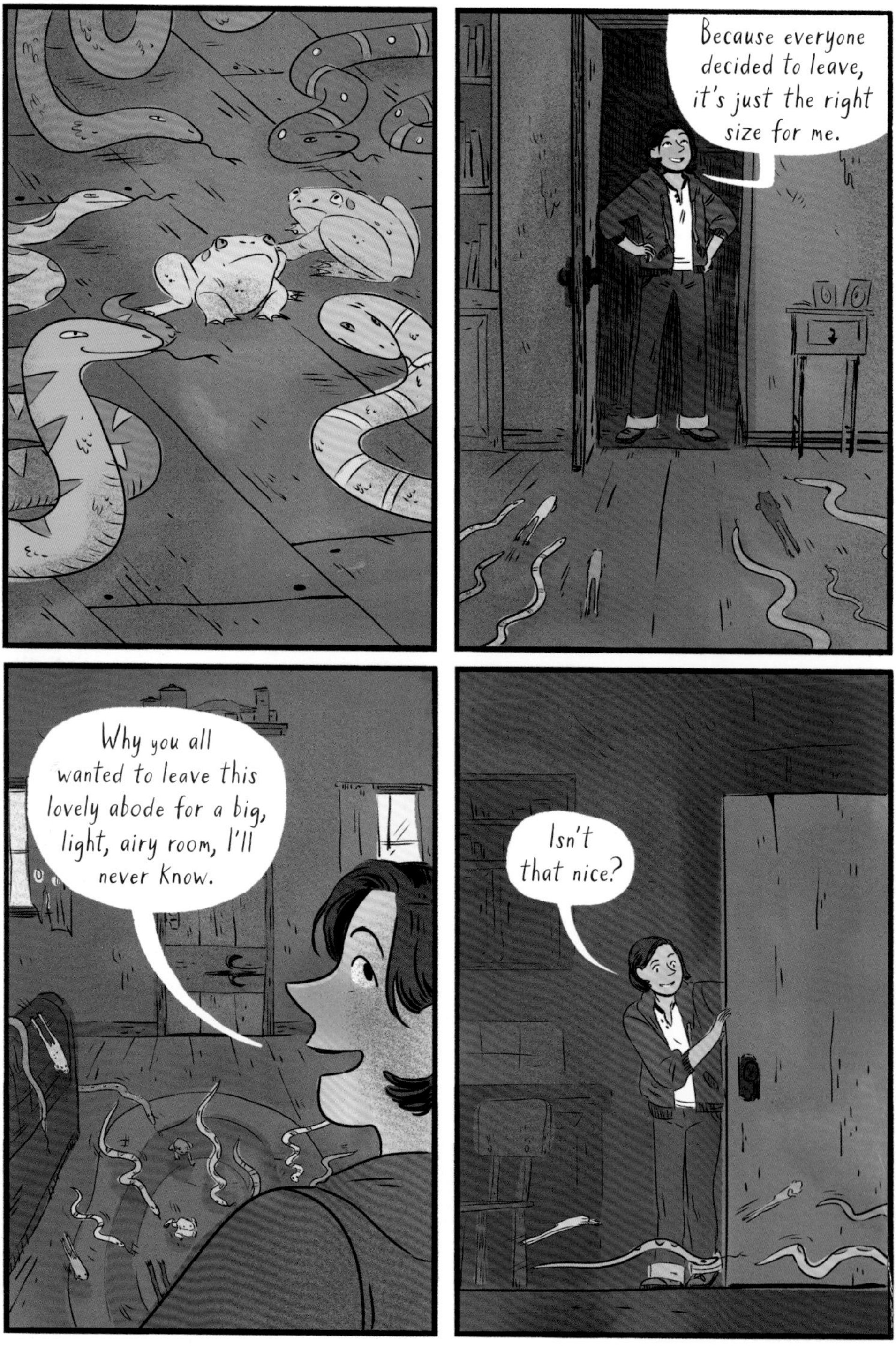
Because everyone decided to leave, it's just the right size for me.
Why you all wanted to leave this lovely abode for a big, light, airy room, I'll never Know.
Isn't that nice?

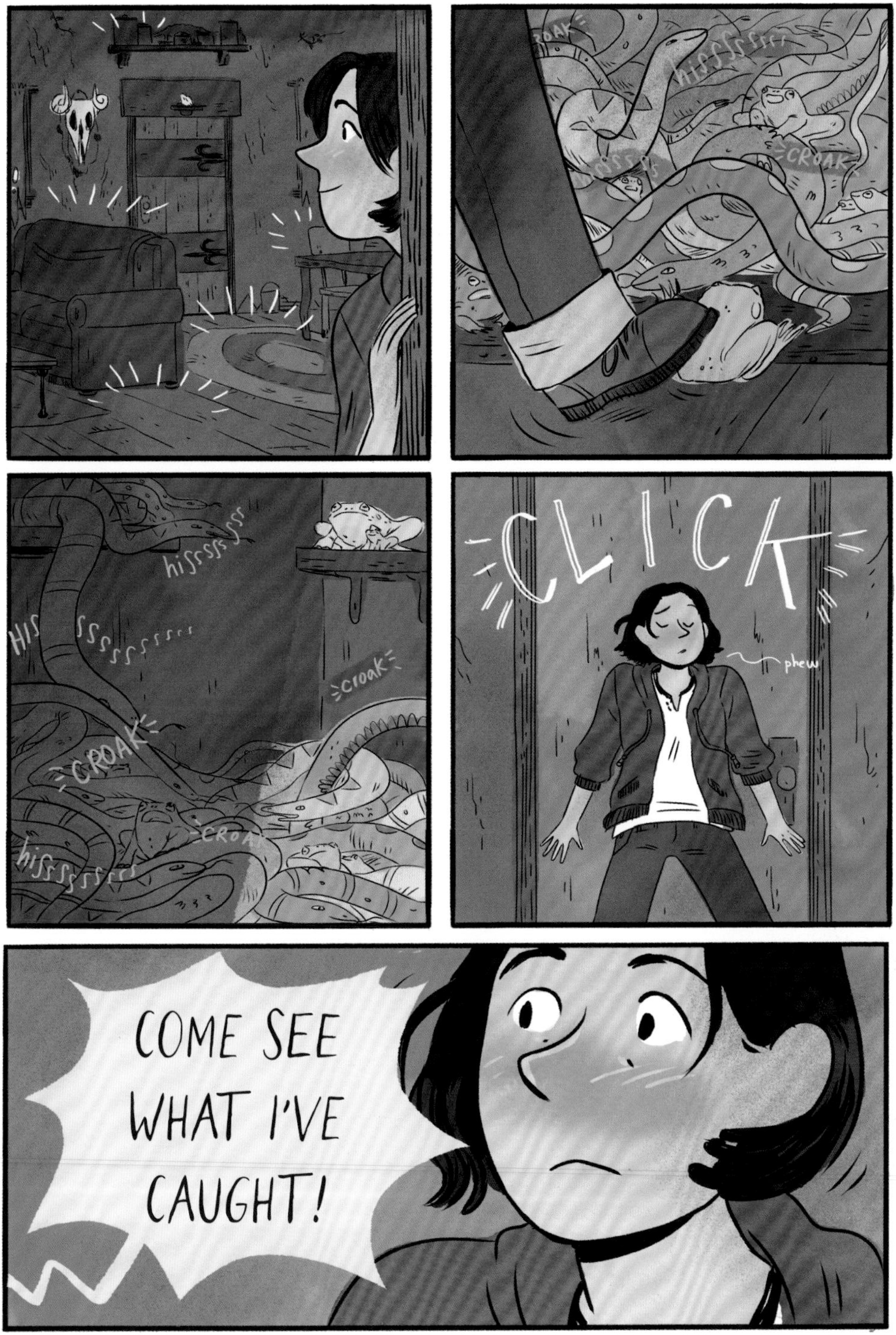
hissssss
CROAK
CROAK
hissssss
hisssss
HIS
sssssssss
croak
CROAK
CROAK
hisssssss
CLICK
phew
COME SEE WHAT I'VE CAUGHT!

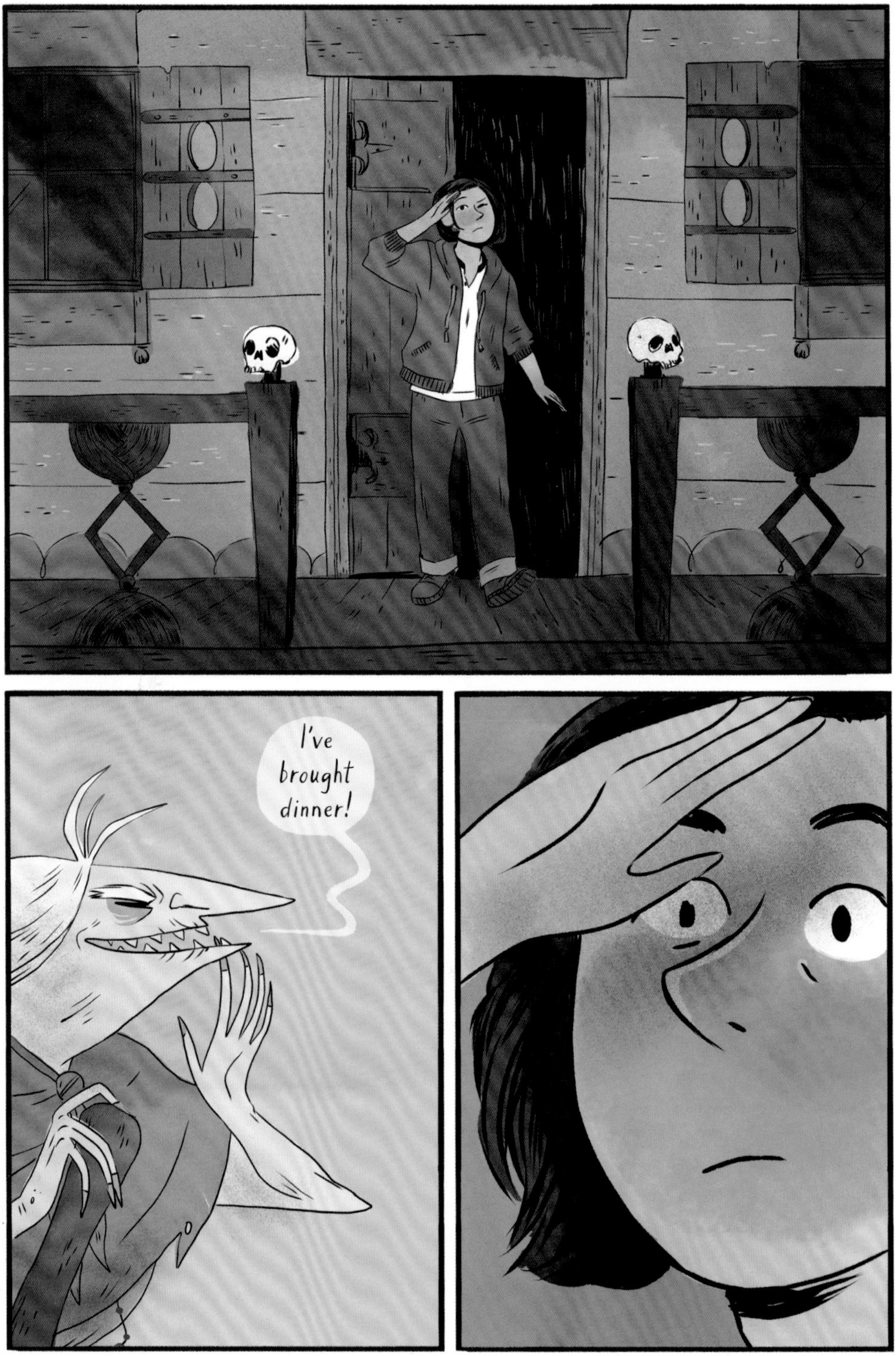
I've brought dinner!

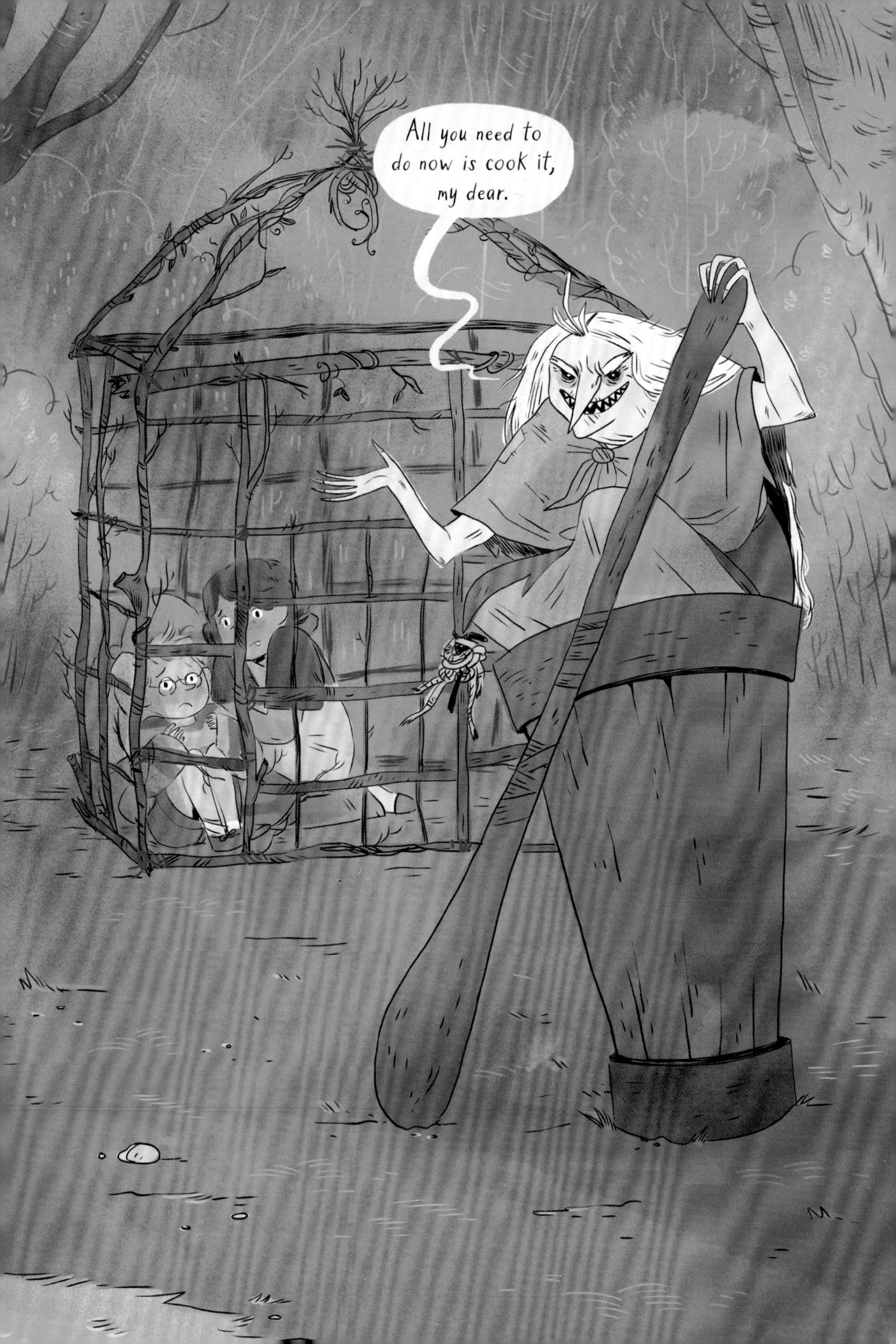
All you need to do now is cook it, my dear.

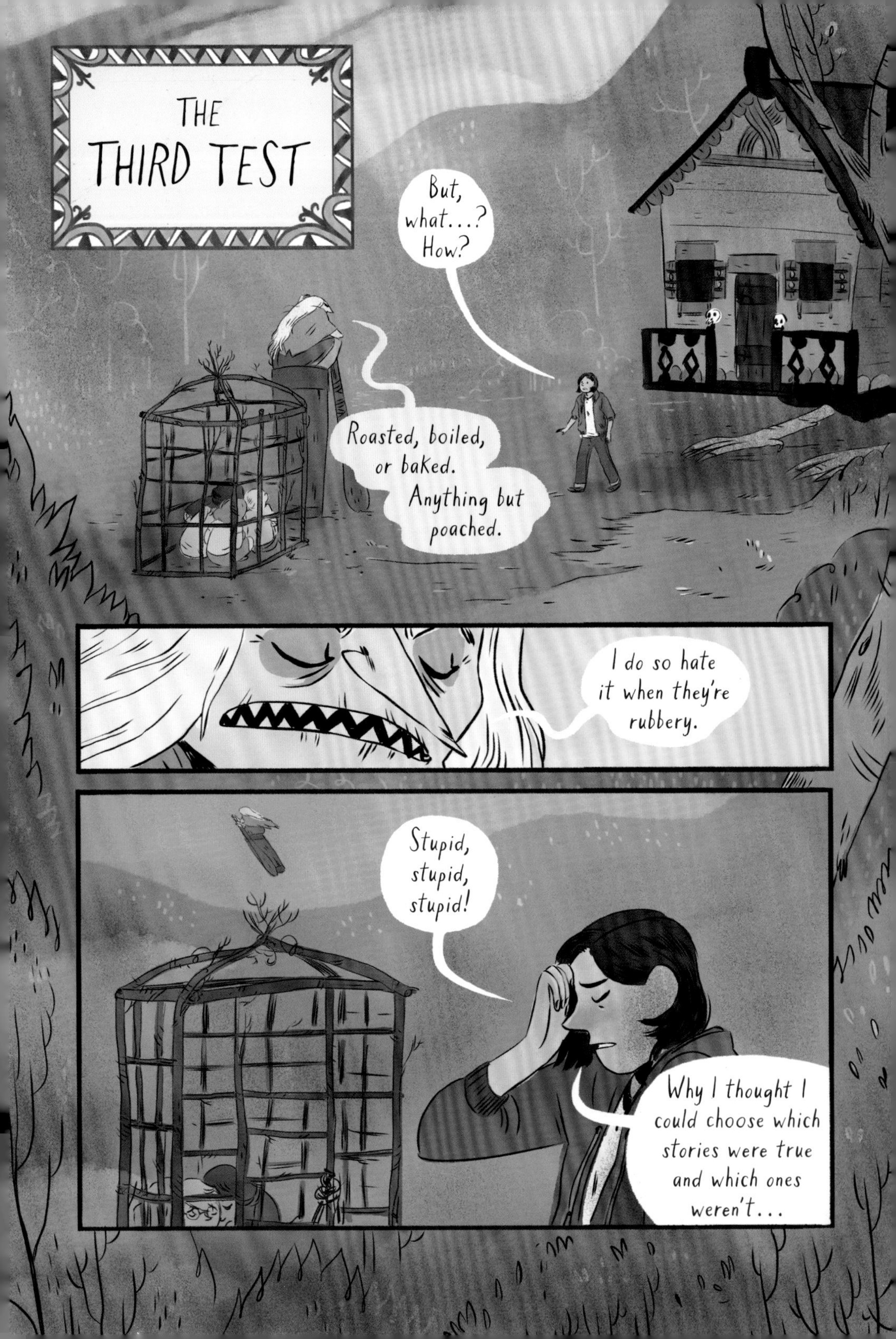
THE THIRD TEST
But, what...? How?
Roasted, boiled, or baked. Anything but poached.
I do so hate it when they're rubbery.
Stupid, stupid, stupid!
Why I thought I could choose which stories were true and which ones weren't...

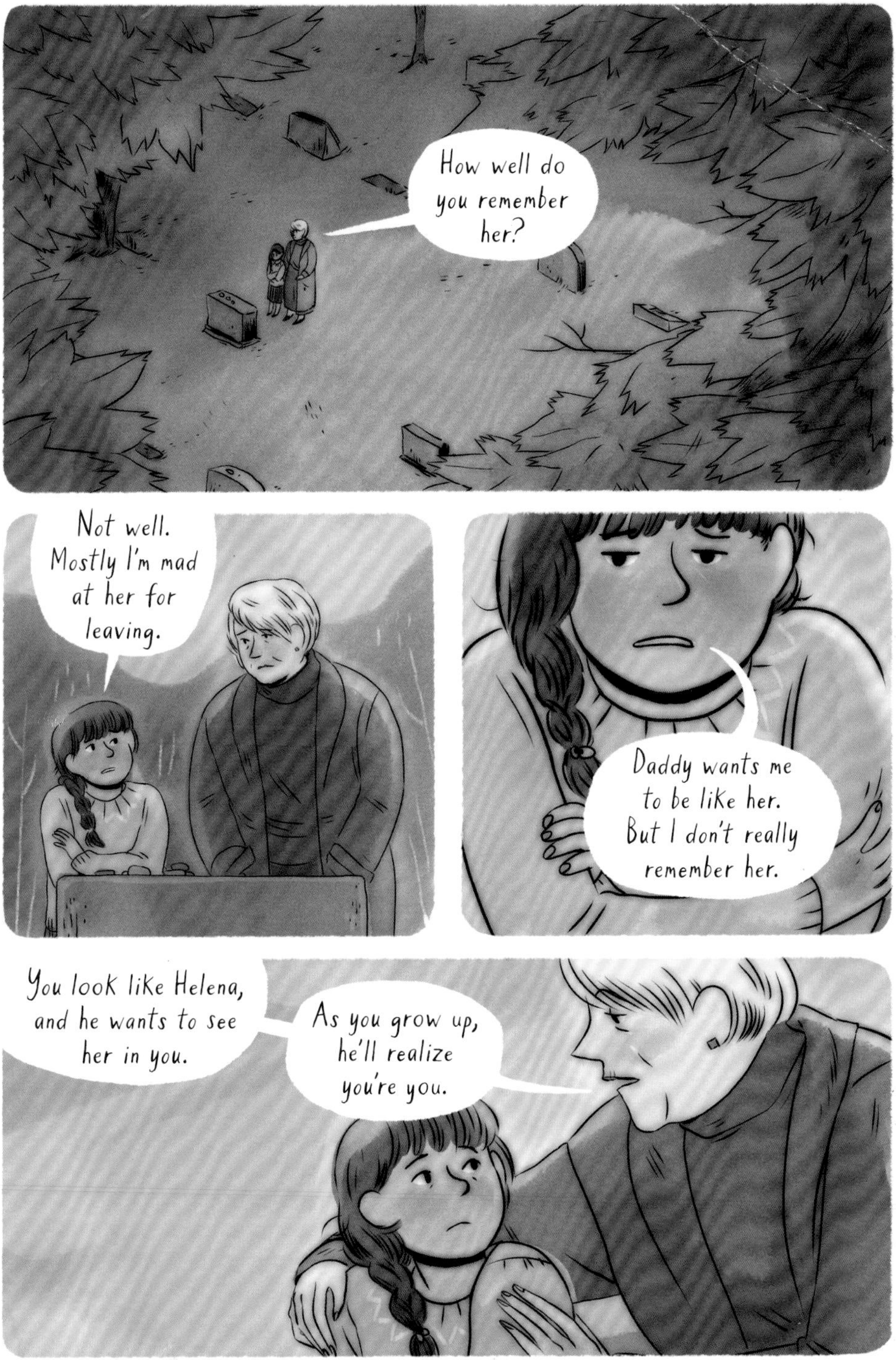
How well do you remember her?
Not well. Mostly I'm mad at her for leaving.
Daddy wants me to be like her. But I don't really remember her.
You look like Helena, and he wants to see her in you.
As you grow up, he'll realize you're you.

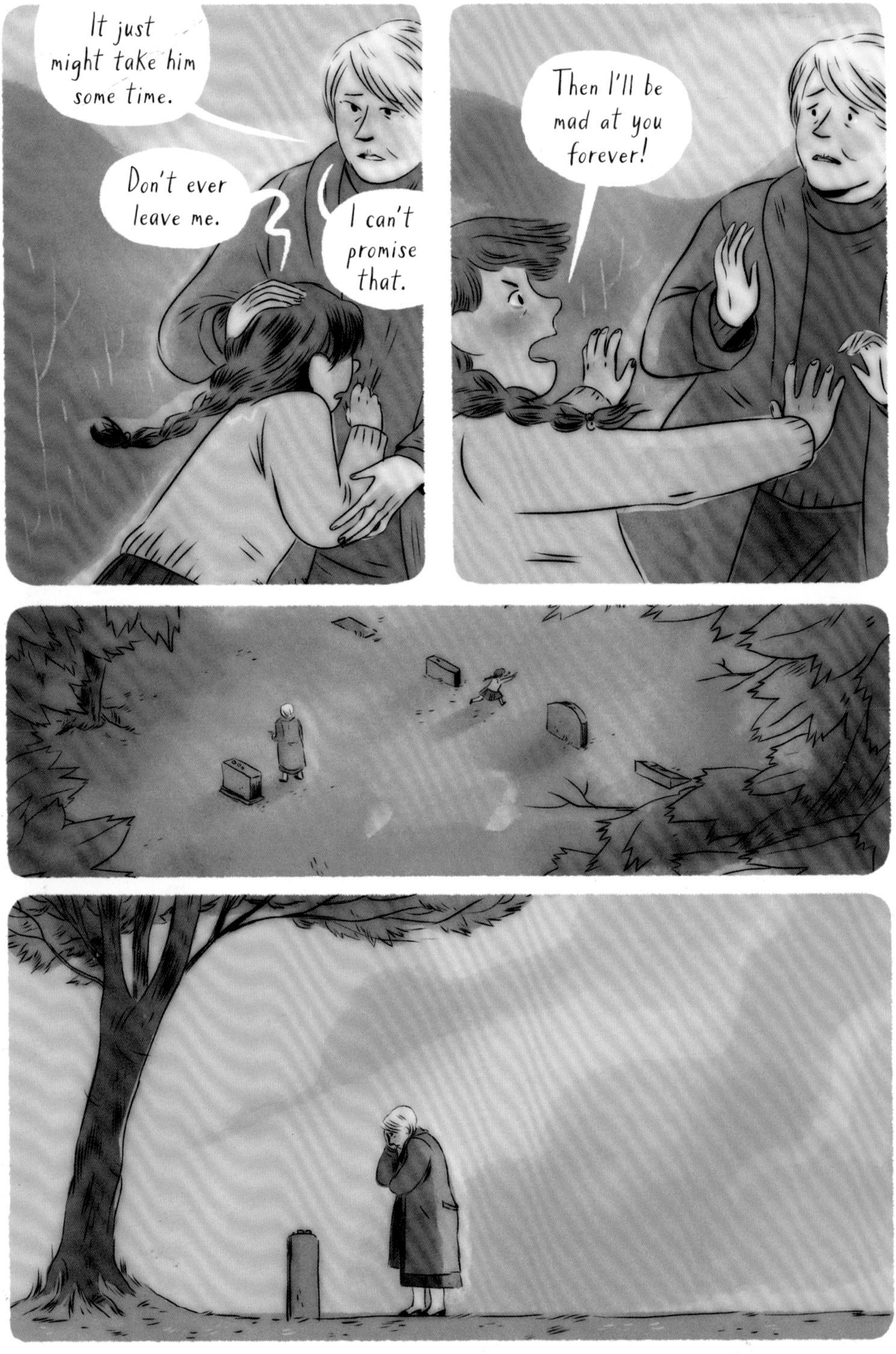
It just might take him some time.
Don't ever leave me.
I can't promise that.
Then I'll be mad at you forever!

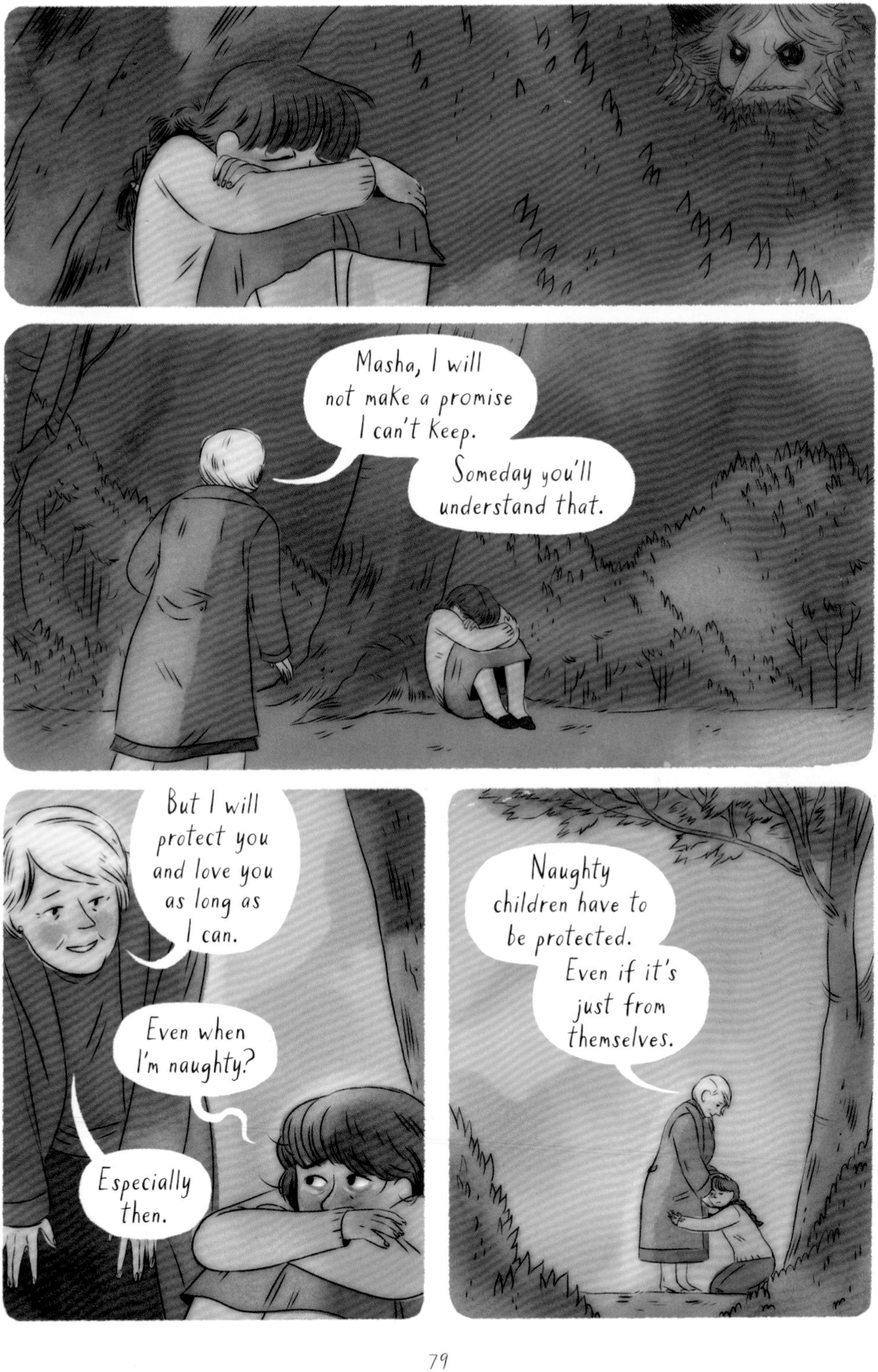
Masha, I will not make a promise I can't keep.
Someday you'll understand that.
But I will protect you and love you as long as I can.
Even when I'm naughty?
Especially then.
Naughty children have to be protected.
Even if it's just from themselves.

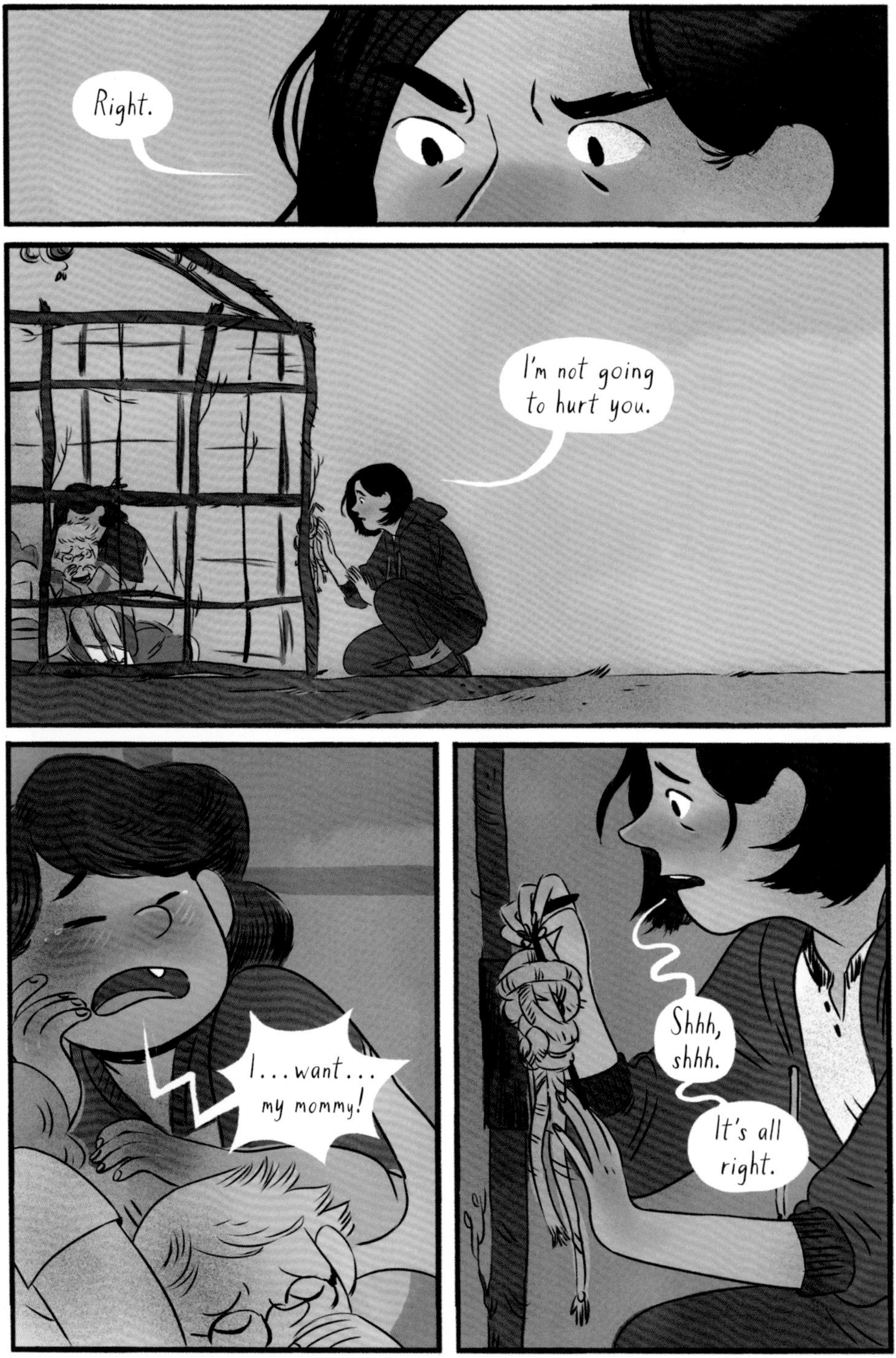
Right.
I'm not going to hurt you.
I...want... my mommy!
Shhh, shhh.
It's all right.

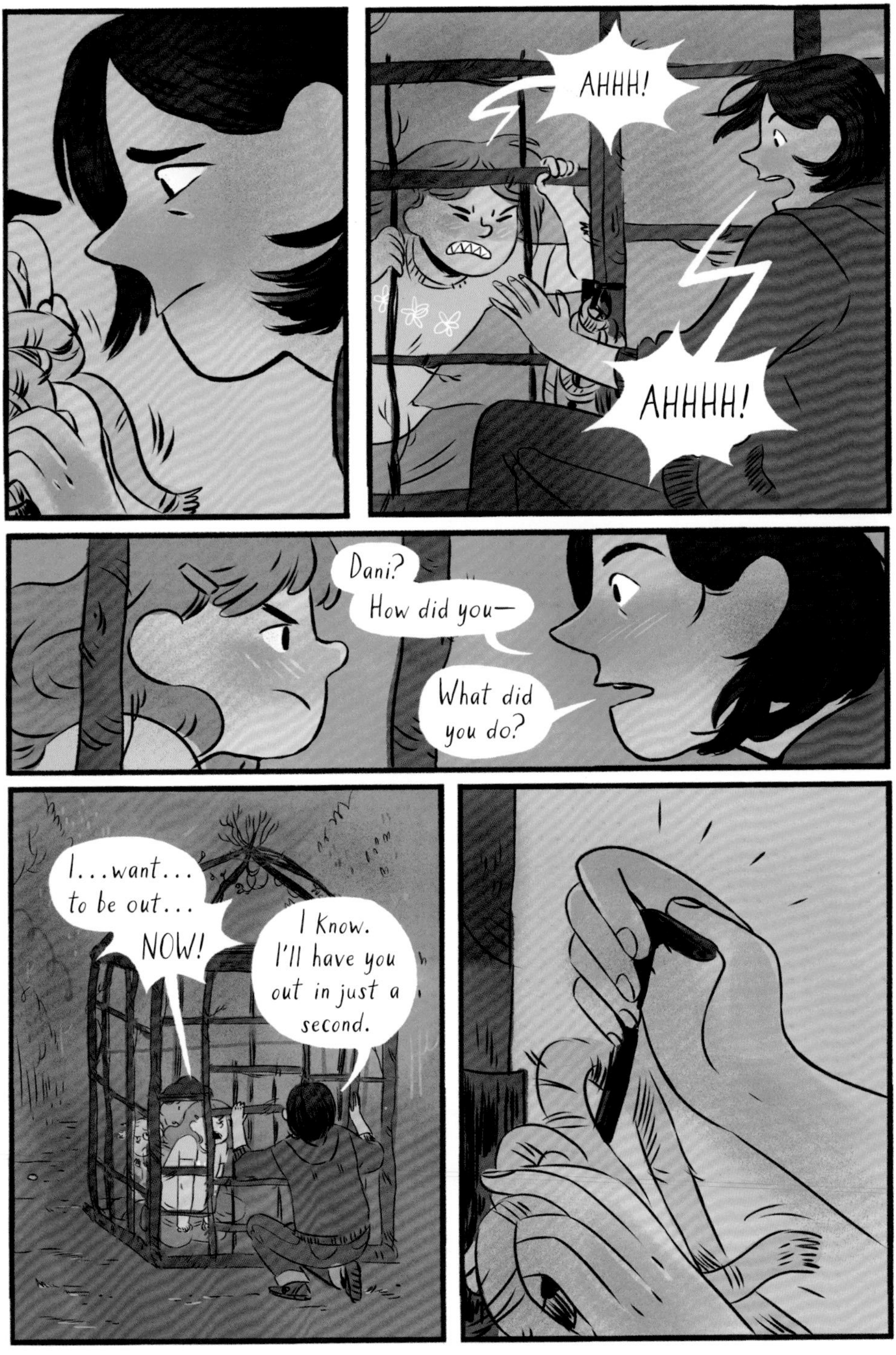
AHHH!
AHHHH!
Dani?
How did you—
What did you do?
I...want... to be out... NOW!
I know. I'll have you out in just a second.

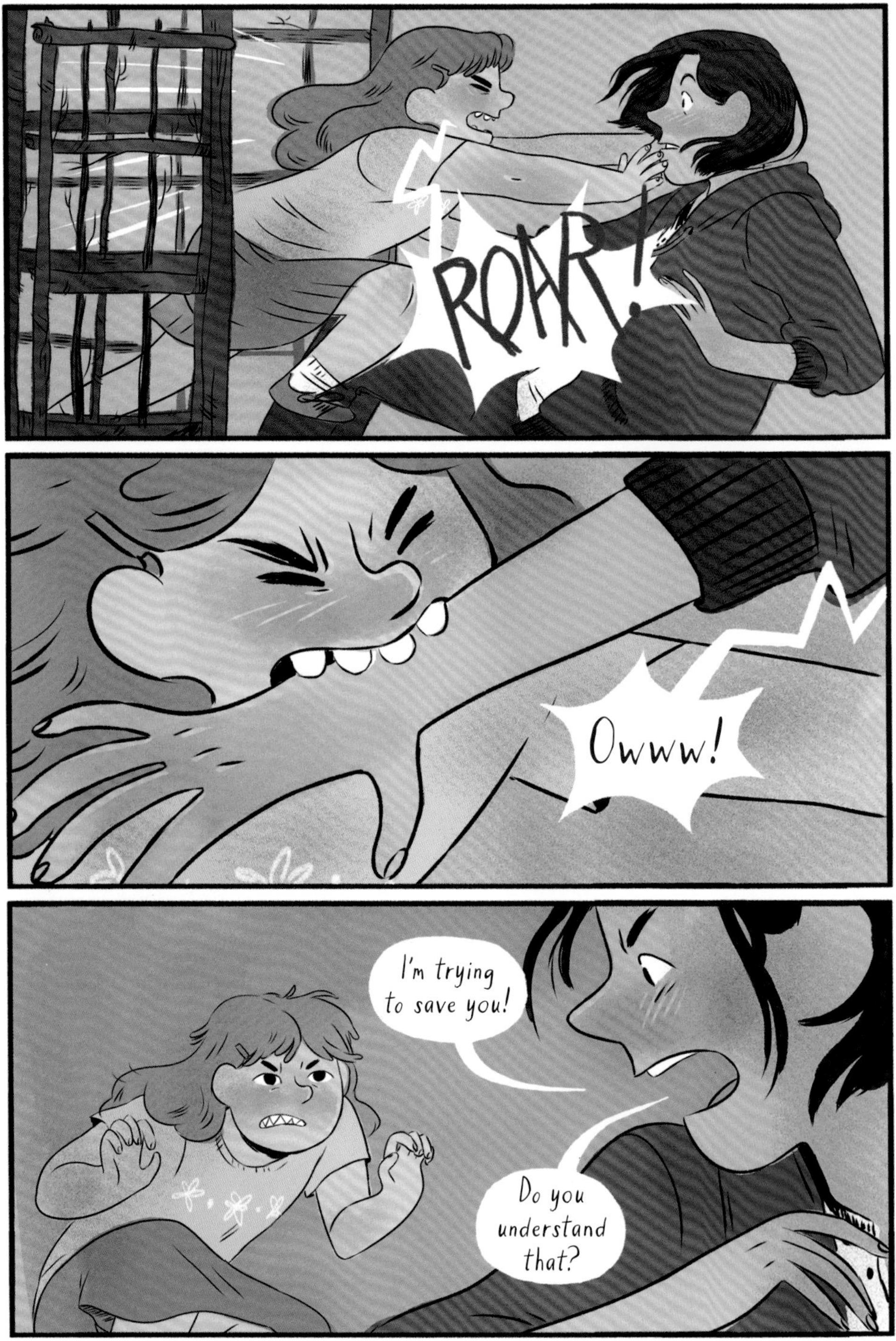
ROAR!
Owww!
I'm trying to save you!
Do you understand that?

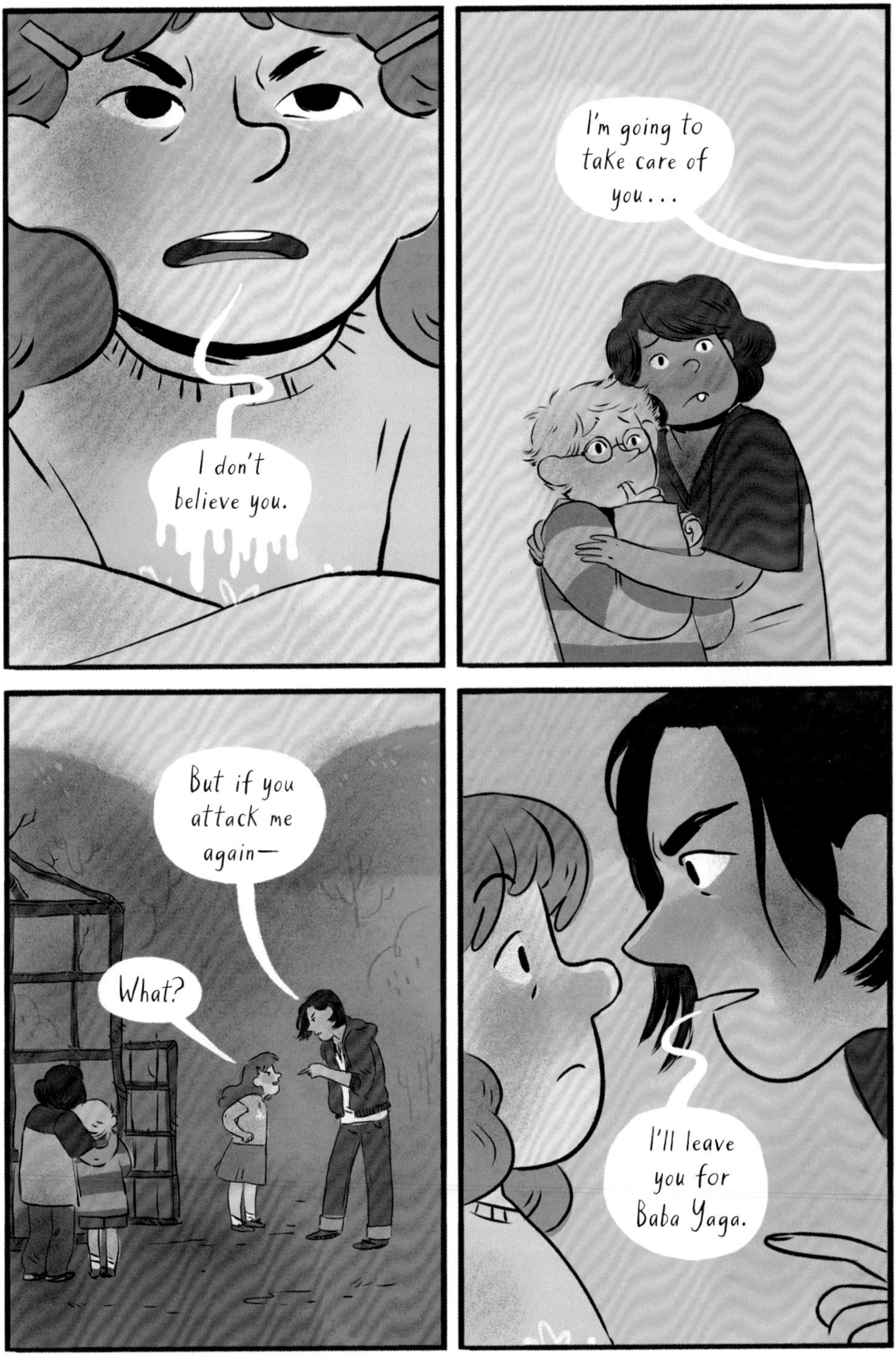
I don't believe you.
I'm going to take care of you...
But if you attack me again—
What?
I'll leave you for Baba Yaga.

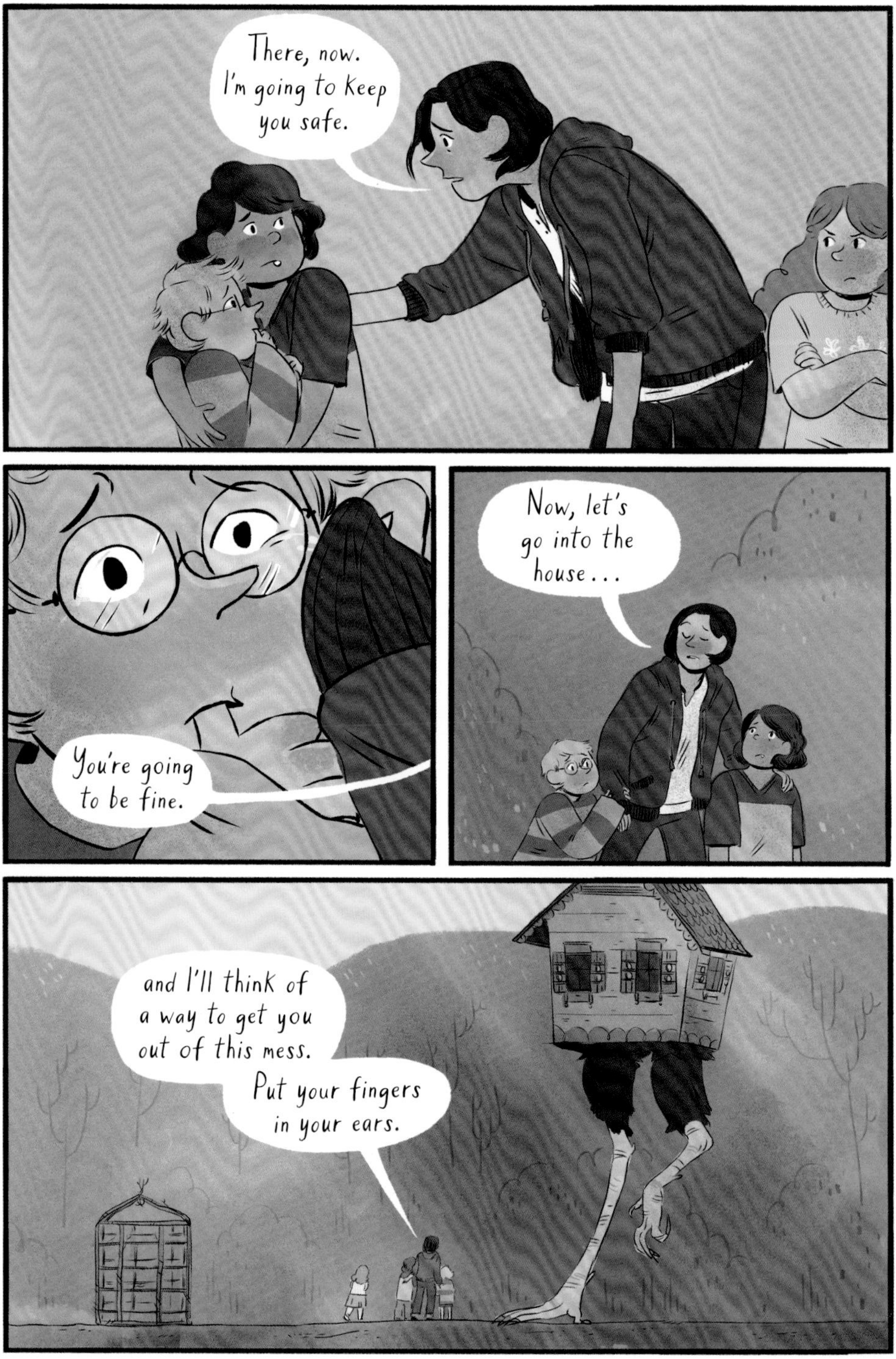
There, now. I'm going to keep you safe.
You're going to be fine.
Now, let's go into the house...
and I'll think of a way to get you out of this mess.
Put your fingers in your ears.

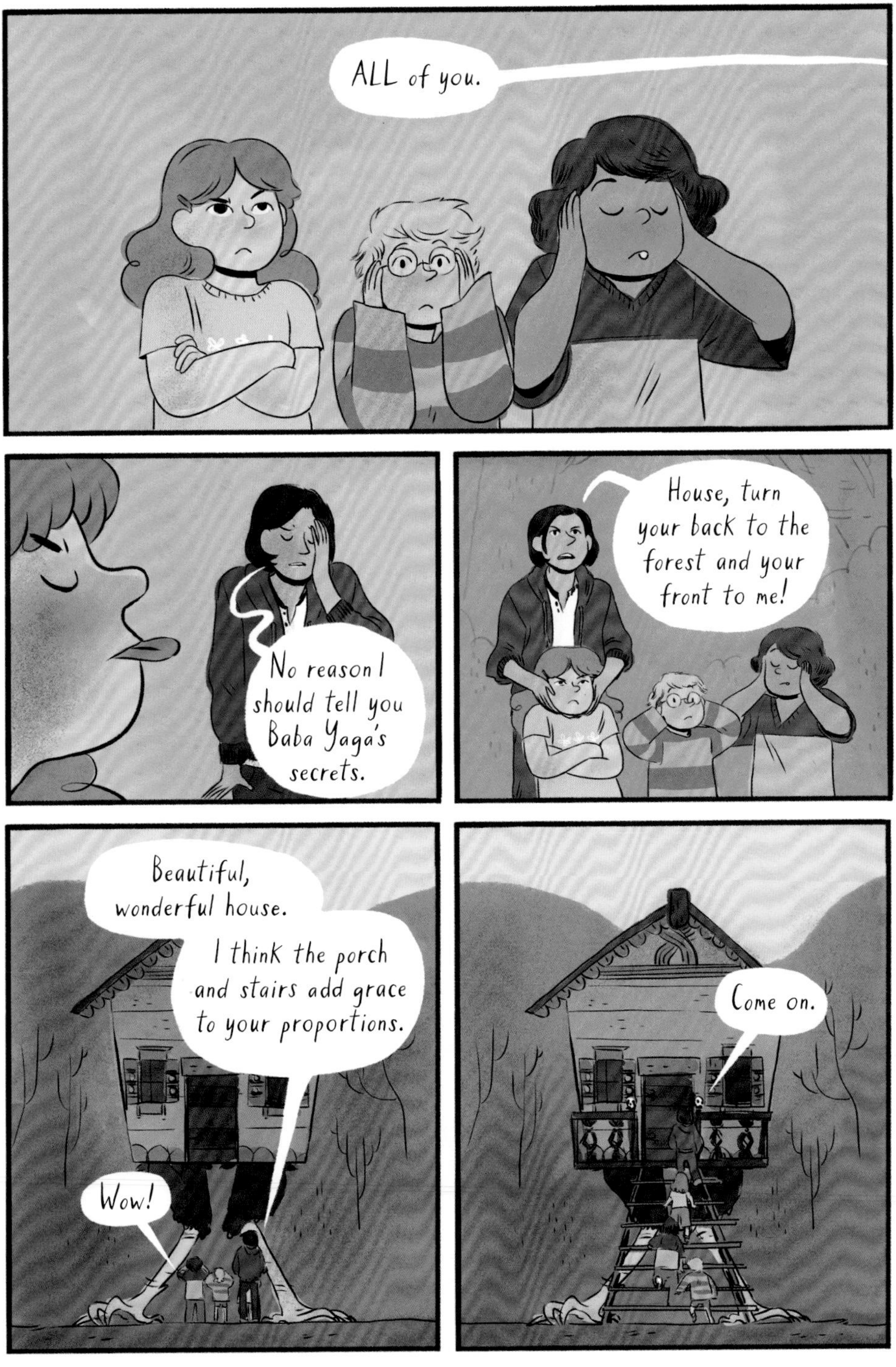
ALL of you.
No reason I should tell you Baba Yaga's secrets.
House, turn your back to the forest and your front to me!
Beautiful, wonderful house.
I think the porch and stairs add grace to your proportions.
Wow!
Come on.

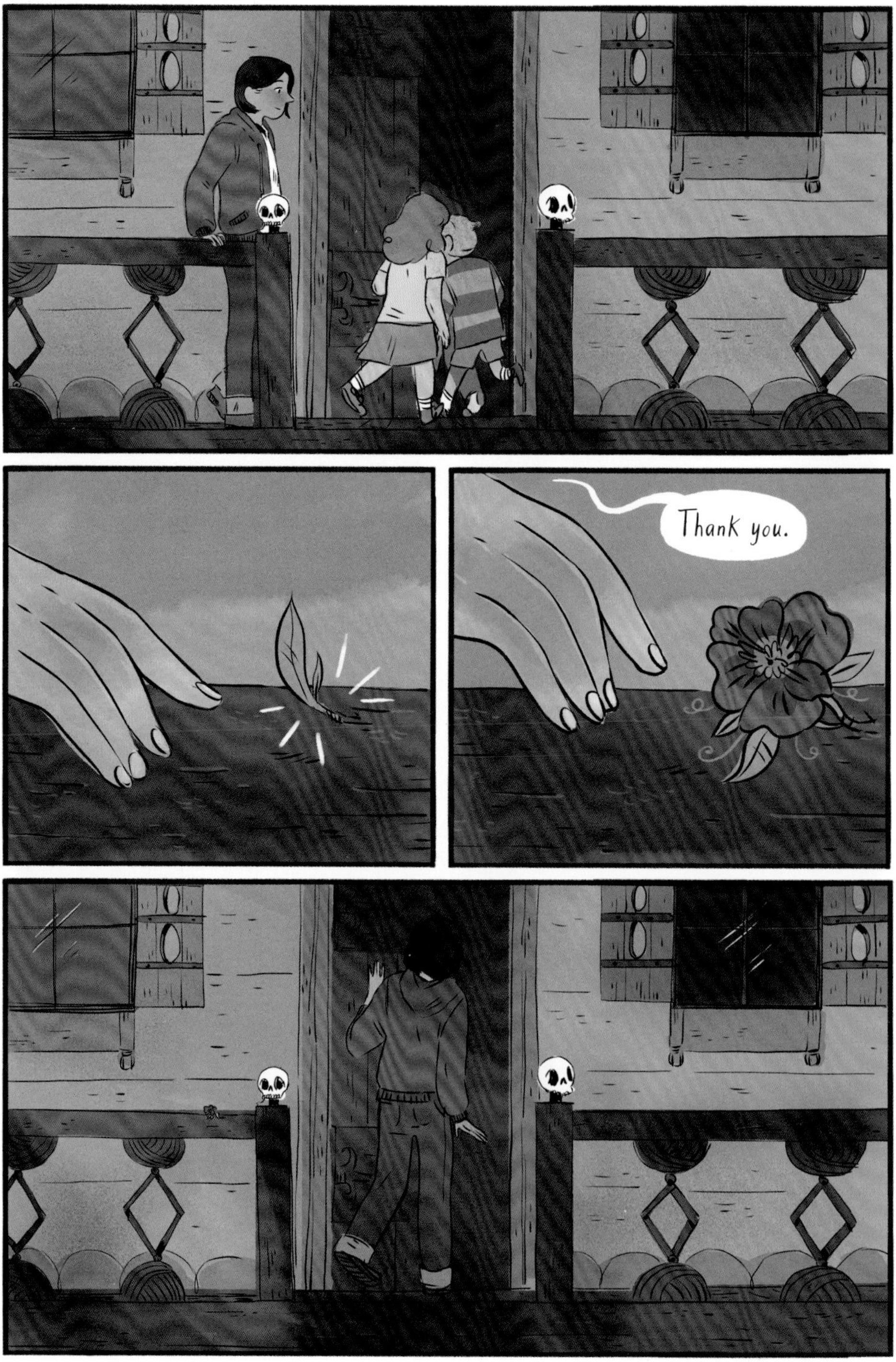
Thank you.

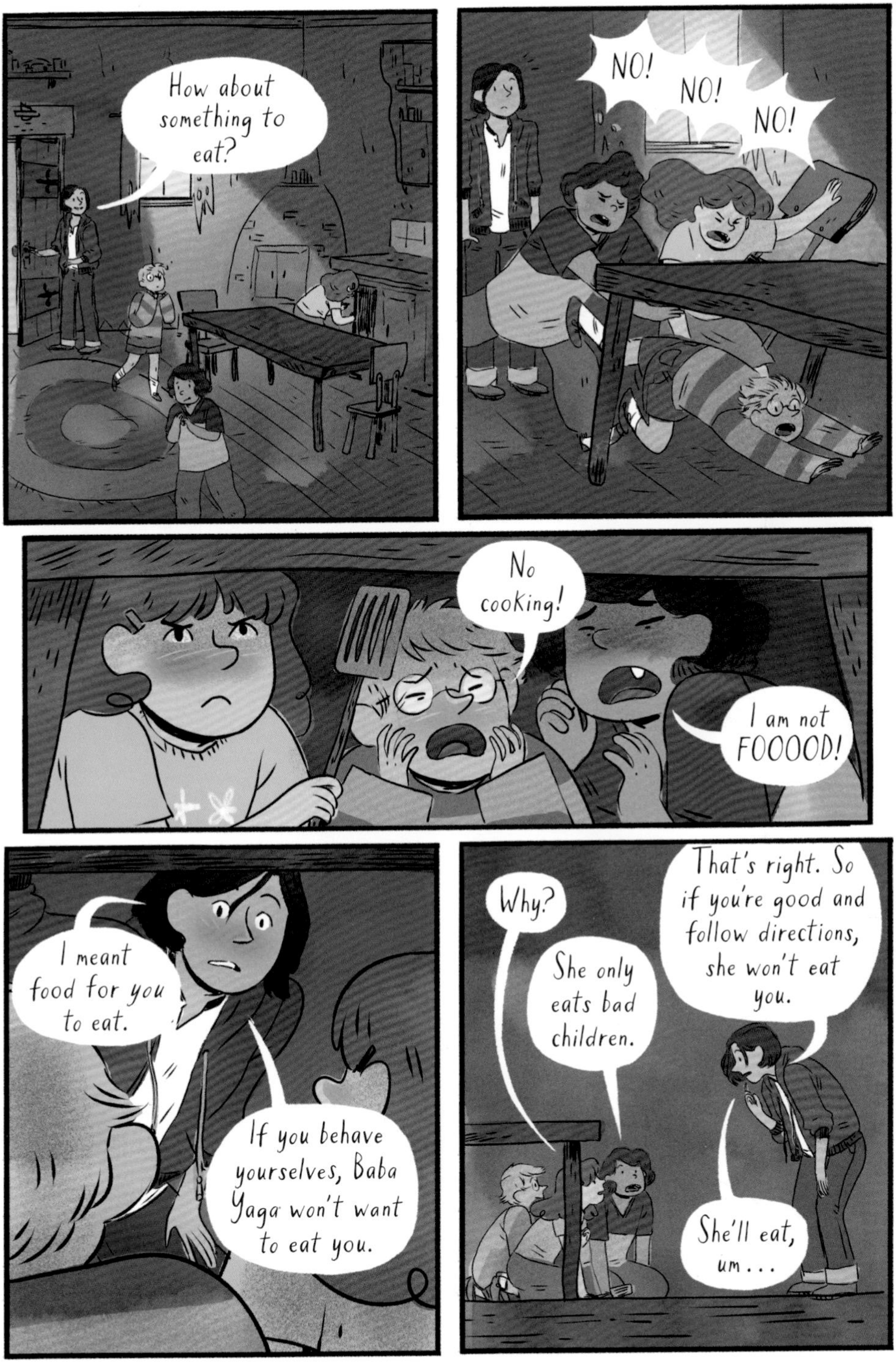
How about something to eat?
NO!
NO!
NO!
No cooking!
I am not FOOOOD!
I meant food for you to eat.
If you behave yourselves, Baba Yaga won't want to eat you.
Why?
She only eats bad children.
That's right. So if you're good and follow directions, she won't eat you.
She'll eat, um . . .

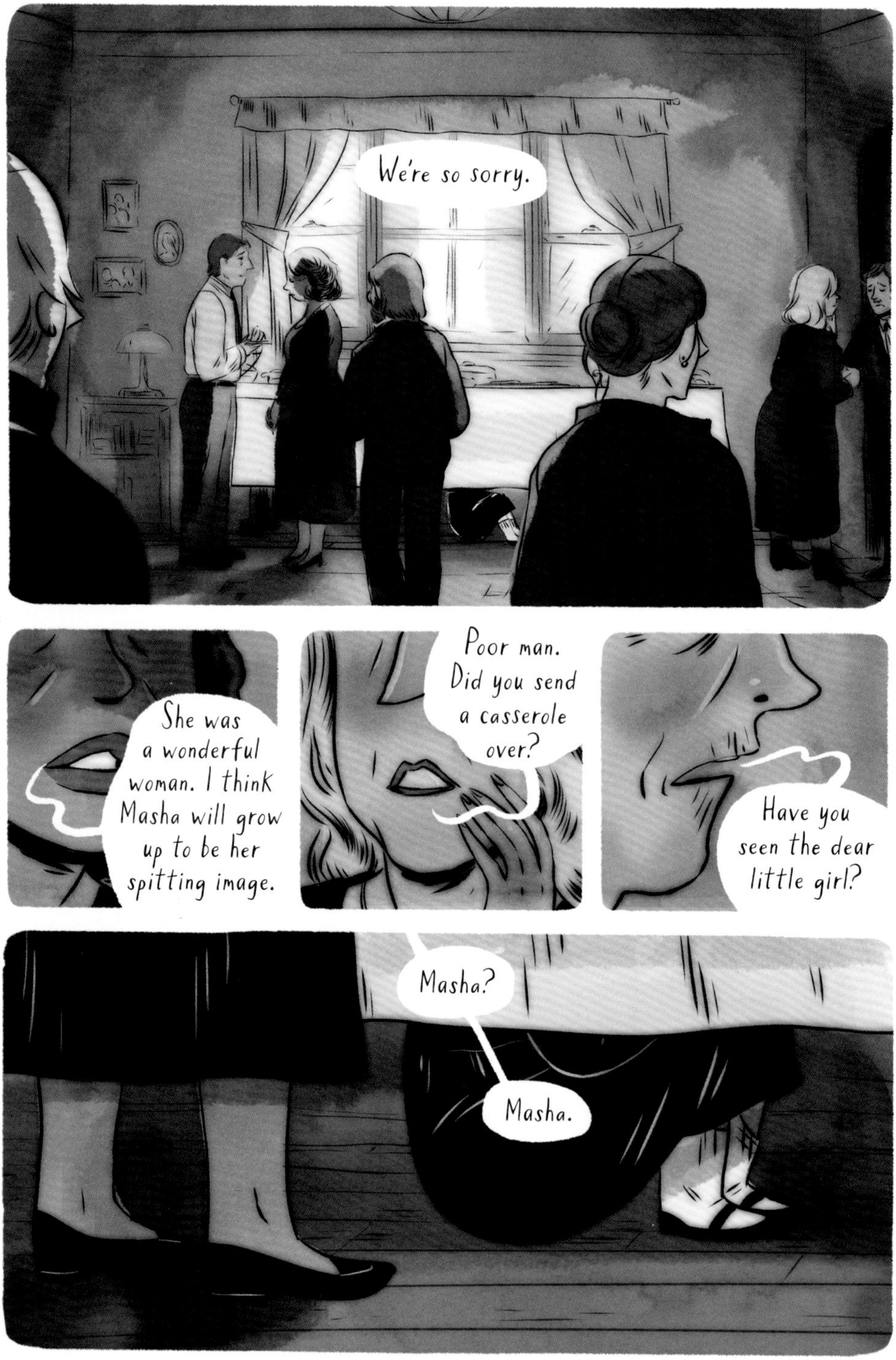
We're so sorry.
She was a wonderful woman. I think Masha will grow up to be her spitting image.
Poor man. Did you send a casserole over?
Have you seen the dear little girl?
Masha?
Masha.

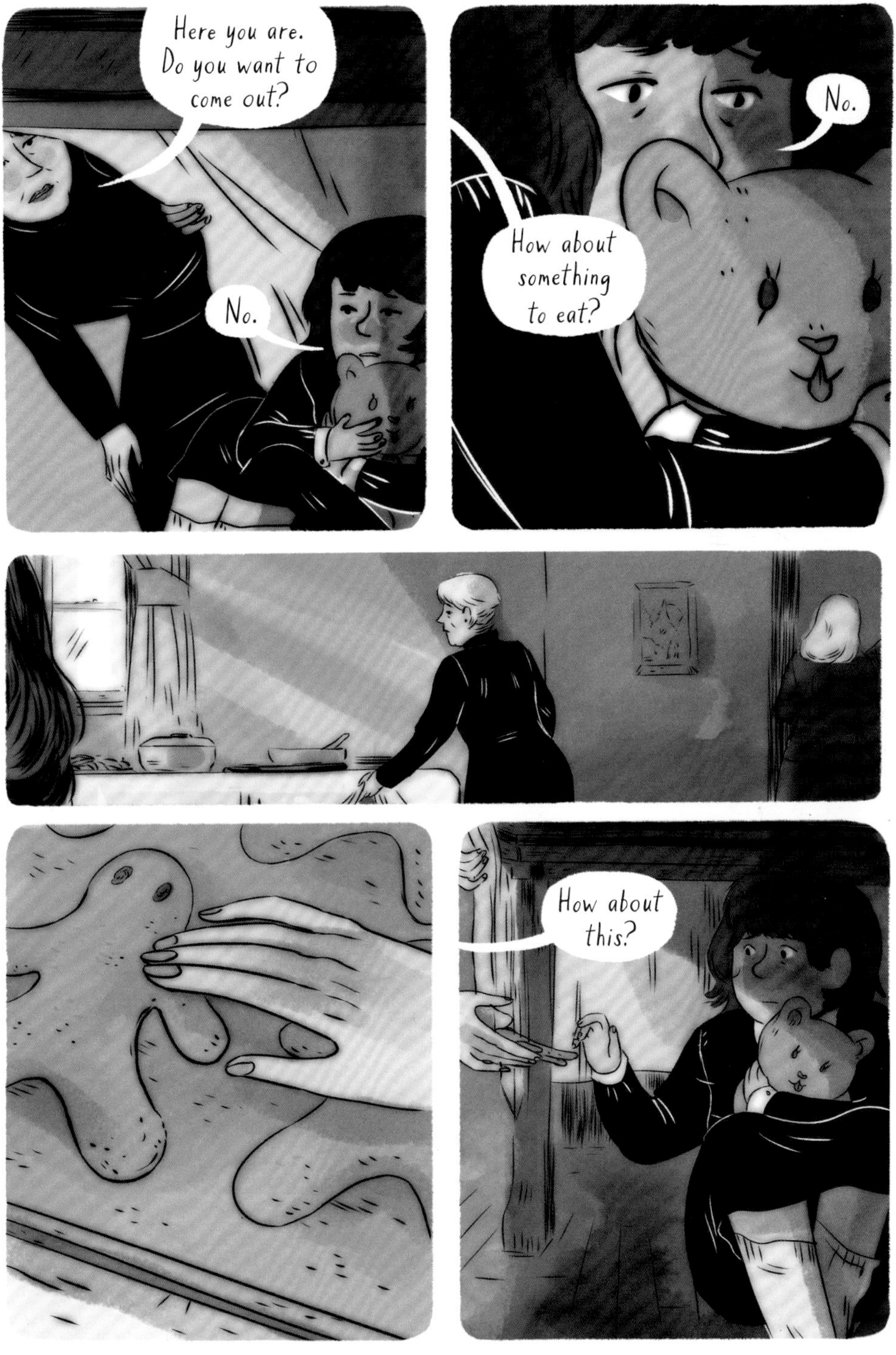
Here you are. Do you want to come out?
No.
No.
How about something to eat?
How about this?

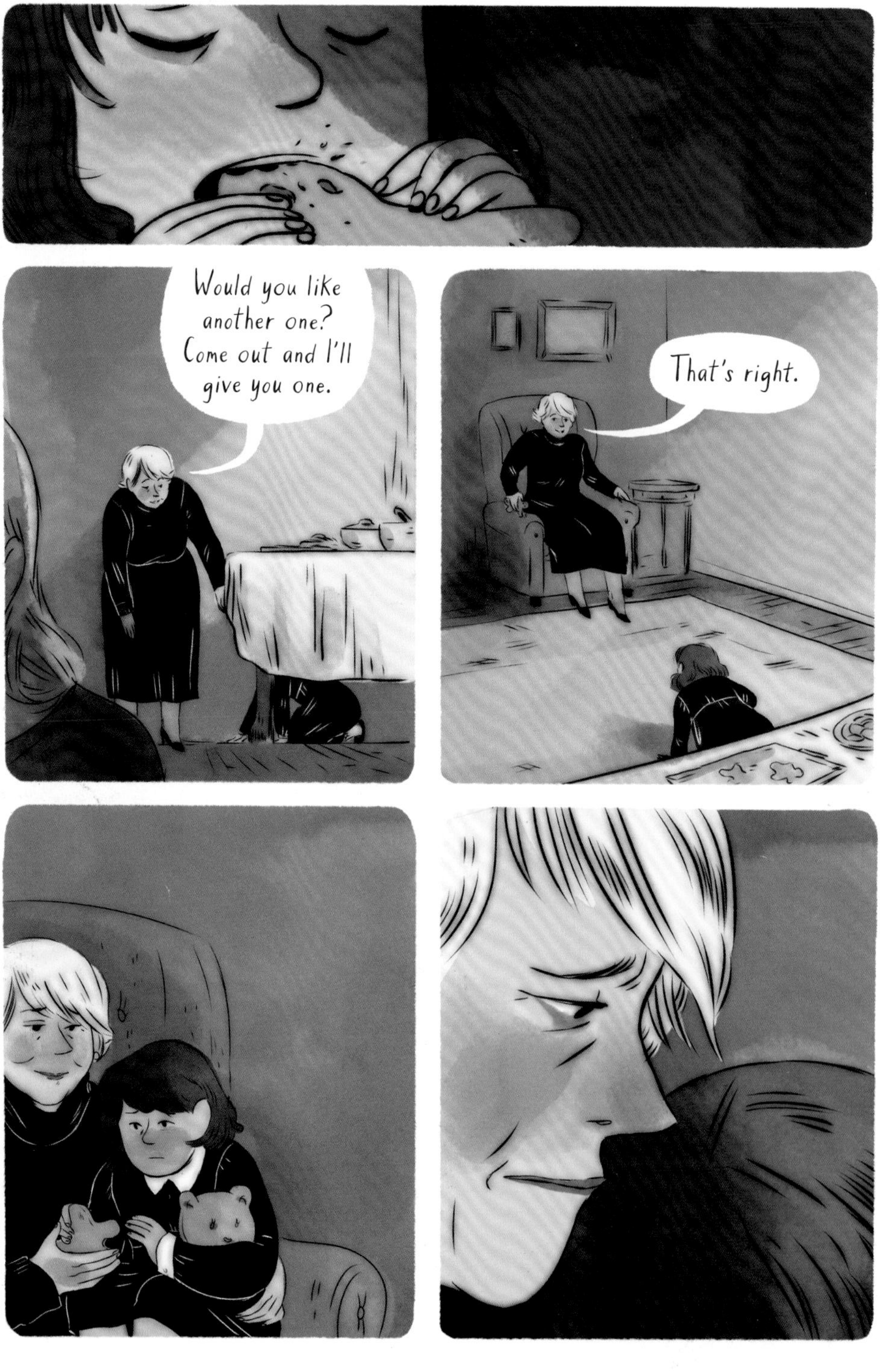
Would you like another one? Come out and I'll give you one.
That's right.

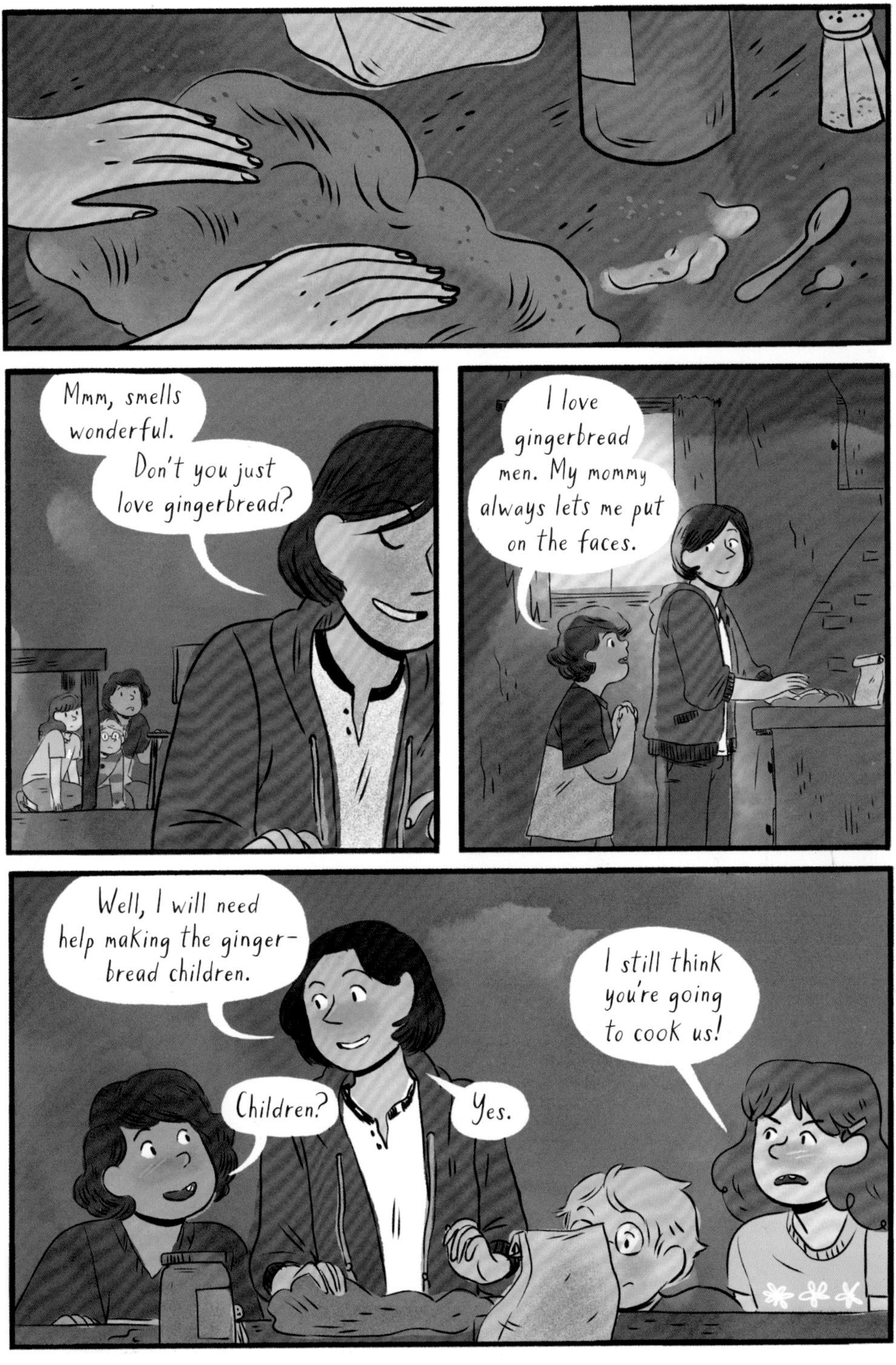
Mmm, smells wonderful.
Don't you just love gingerbread?
I love gingerbread men. My mommy always lets me put on the faces.
Well, I will need help making the ginger-bread children.
Children?
Yes.
I still think you're going to cook us!

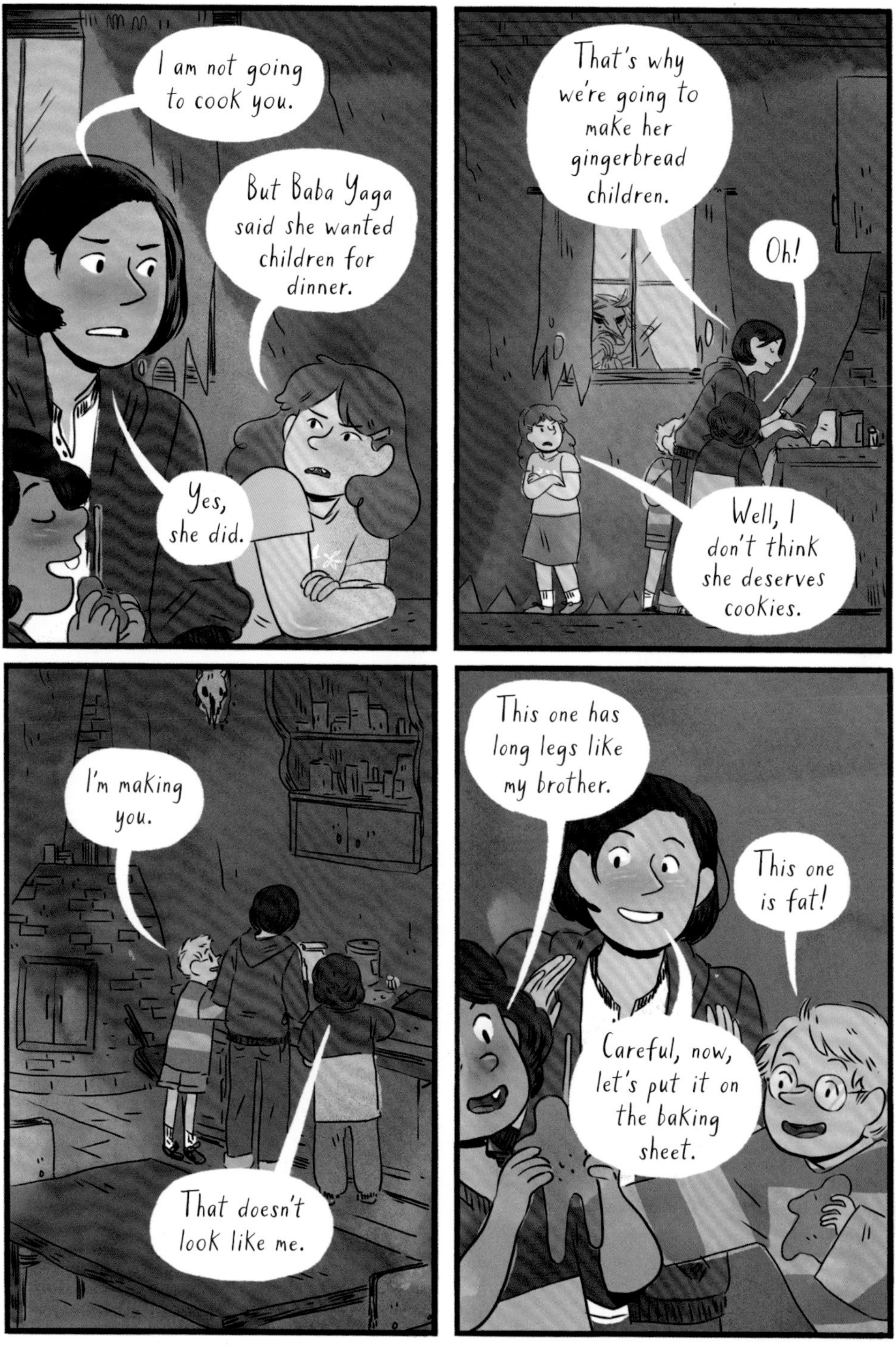
I am not going to cook you.
But Baba Yaga said she wanted children for dinner.
Yes, she did.
That's why we're going to make her gingerbread children.
Oh!
Well, I don't think she deserves cookies.
I'm making you.
That doesn't look like me.
This one has long legs like my brother.
This one is fat!
Careful, now, let's put it on the baking sheet.

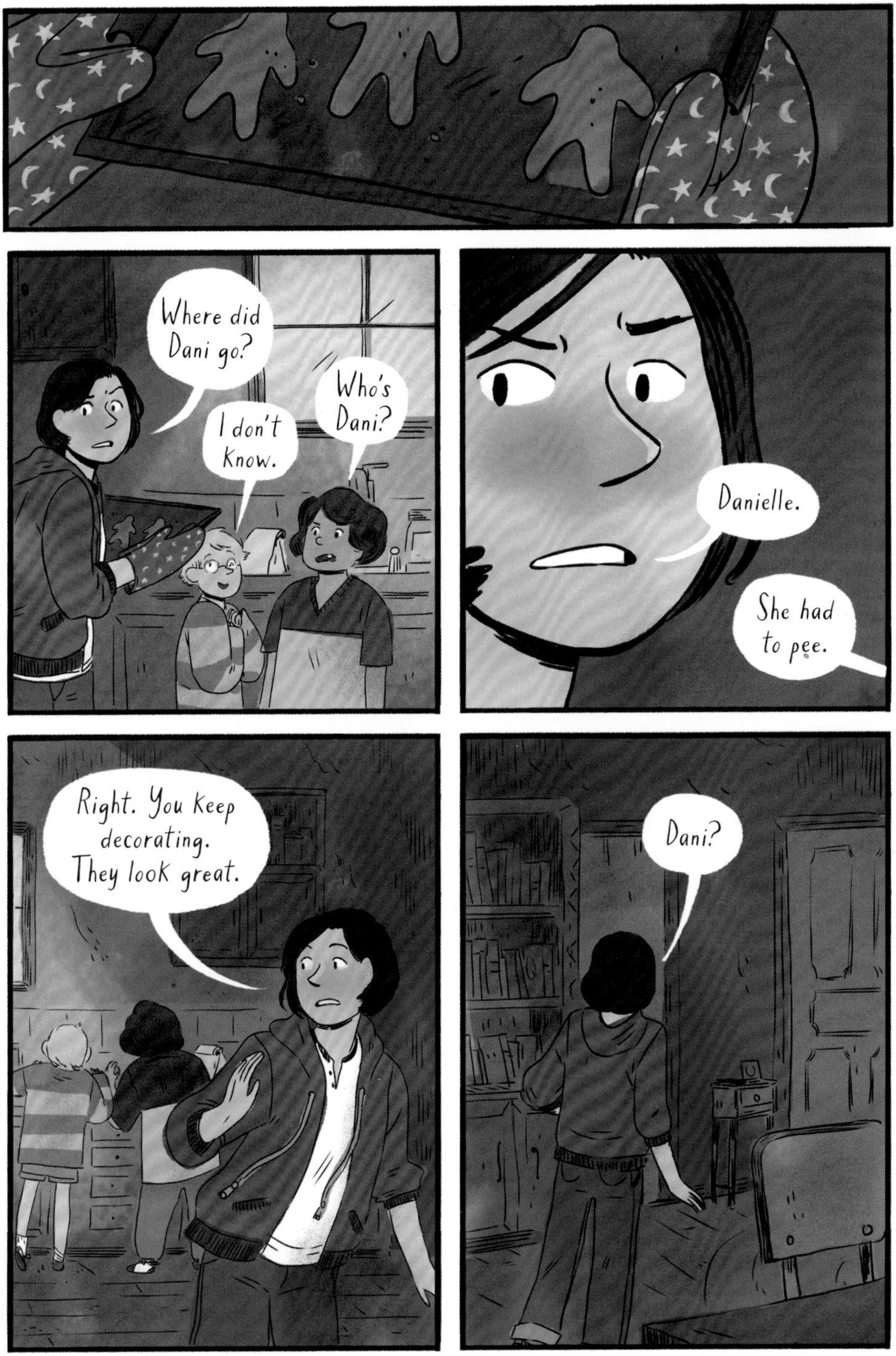
Where did Dani go?
I don't know.
Who's Dani?
Danielle.
She had to pee.
Right. You keep decorating. They look great.
Dani?

Dani? Are you done in there?
Yes . . . hee-hee-hee . . .
Do you need any help?
No!
Right.
There's a reason Baba Yaga brought you here.
Don't come in!

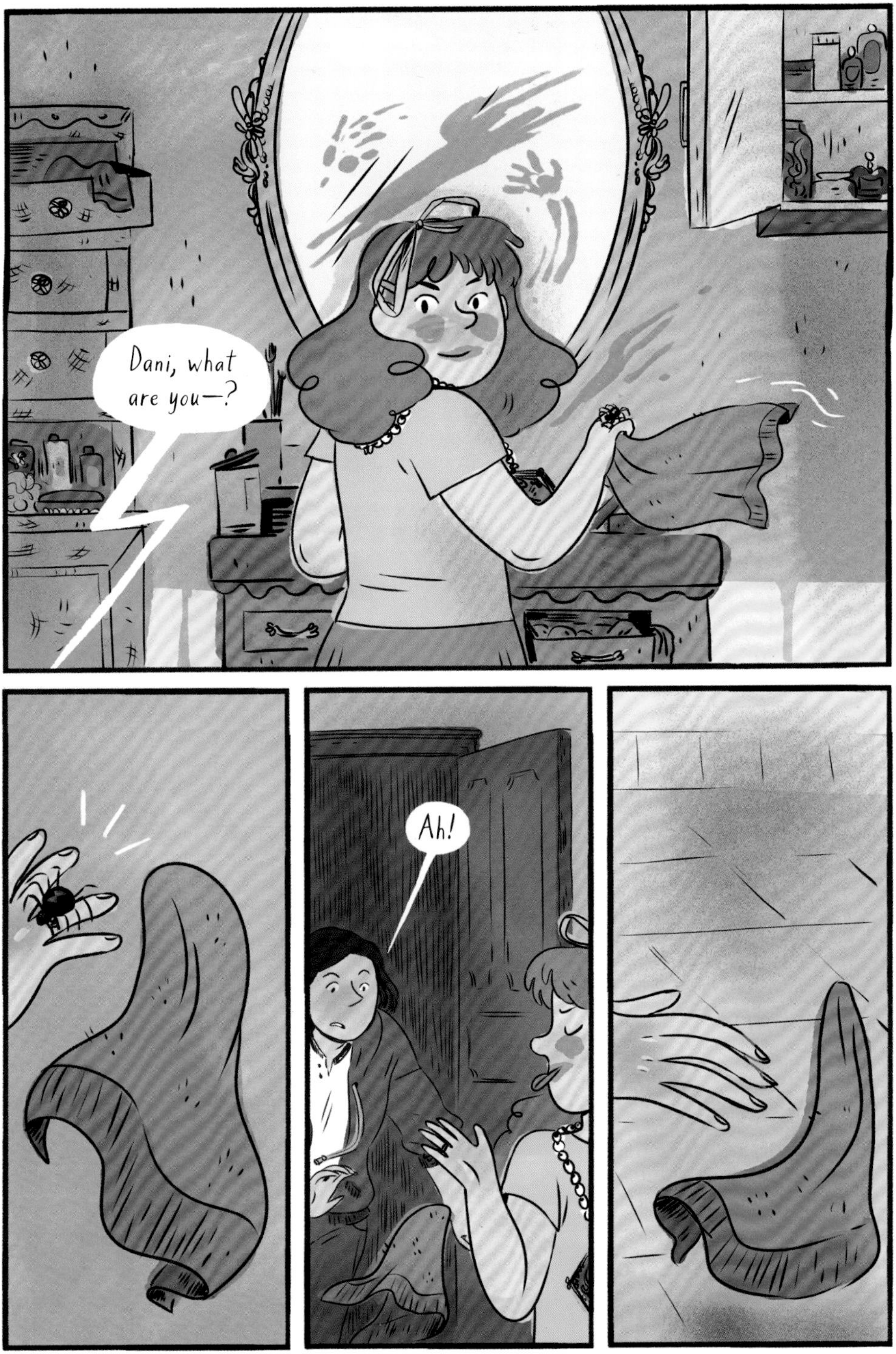
Dani, what are you—?
Ah!

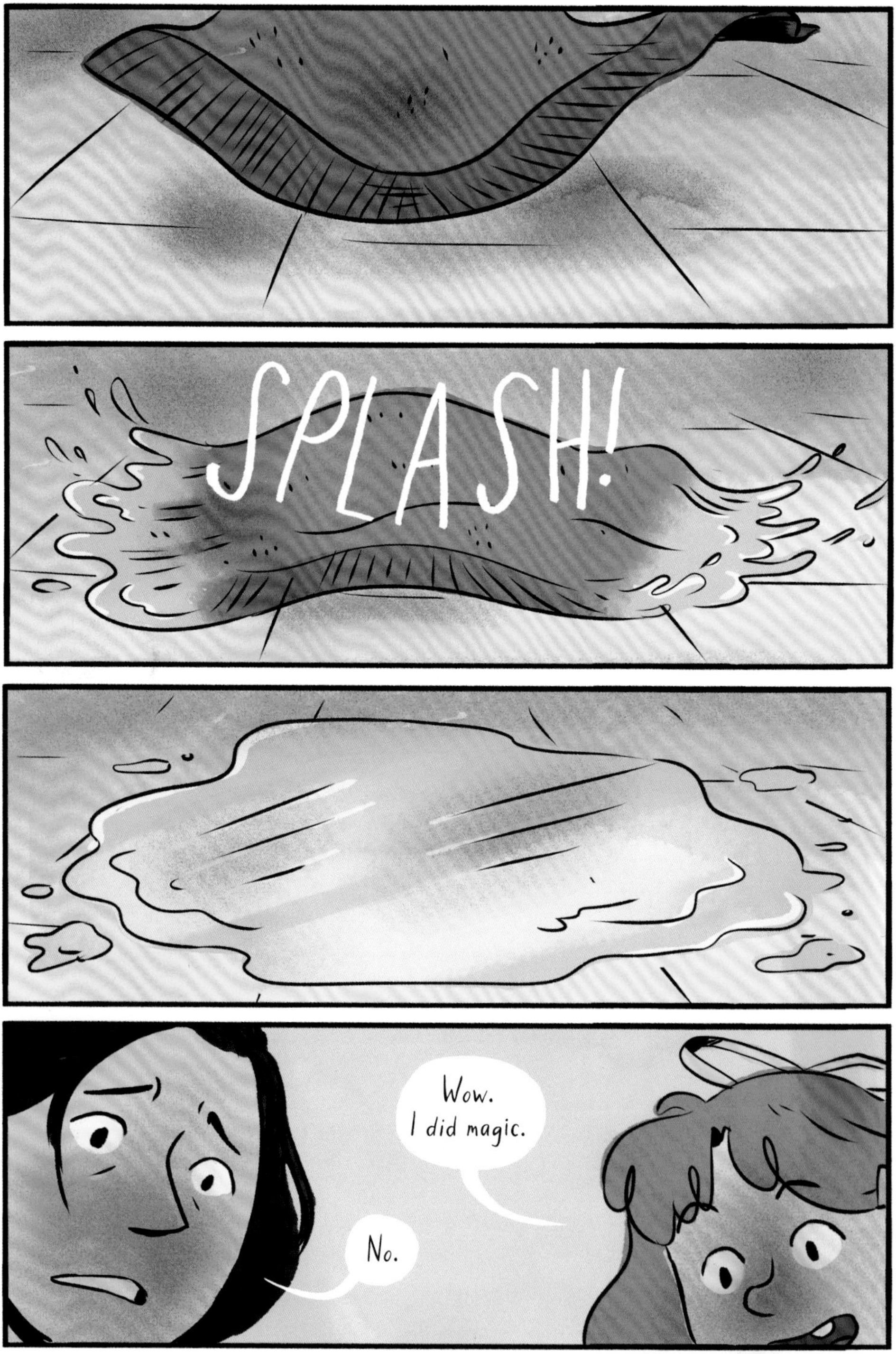
SPLASH!
Wow.
I did magic.
No.

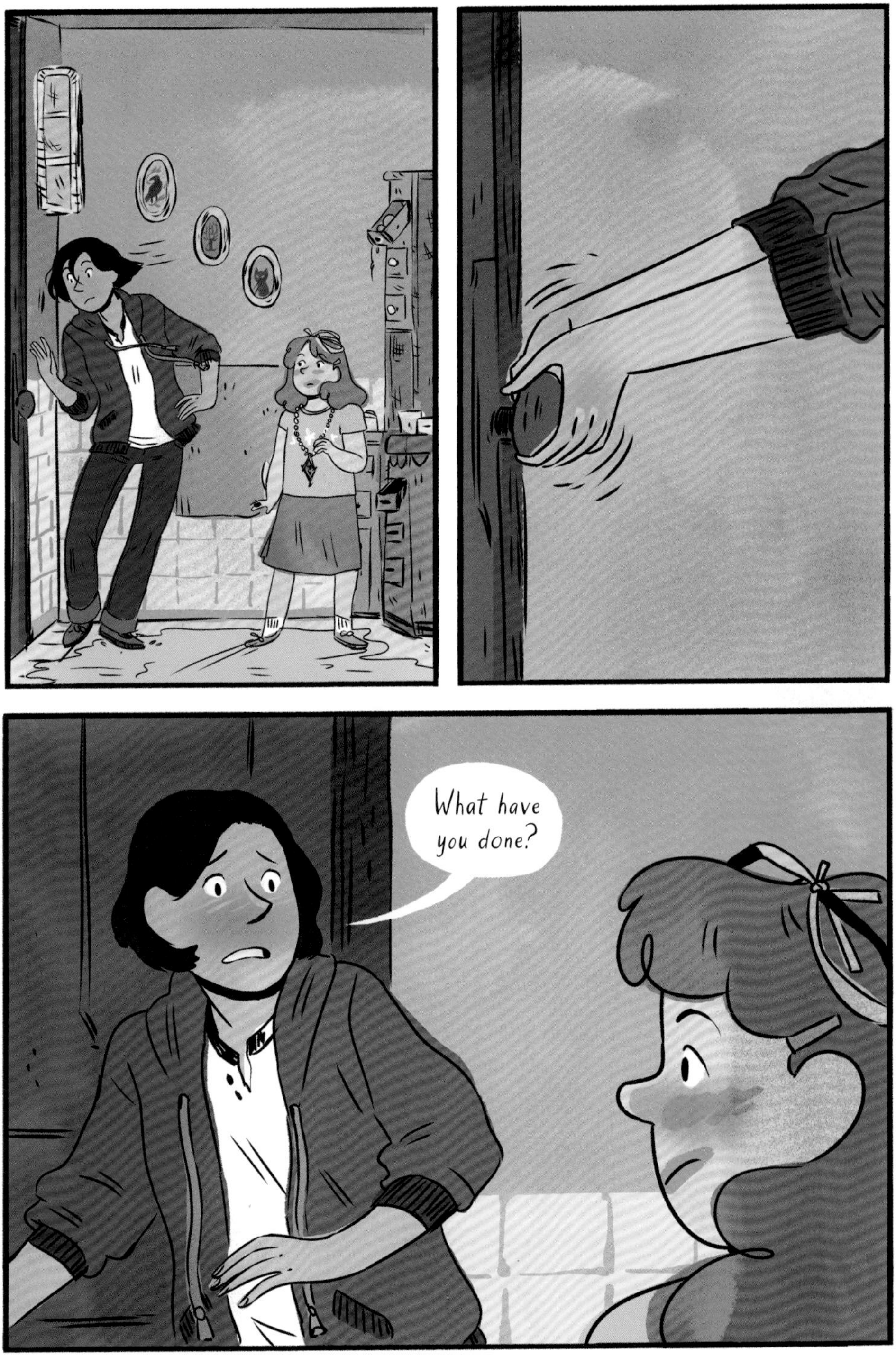
What have you done?

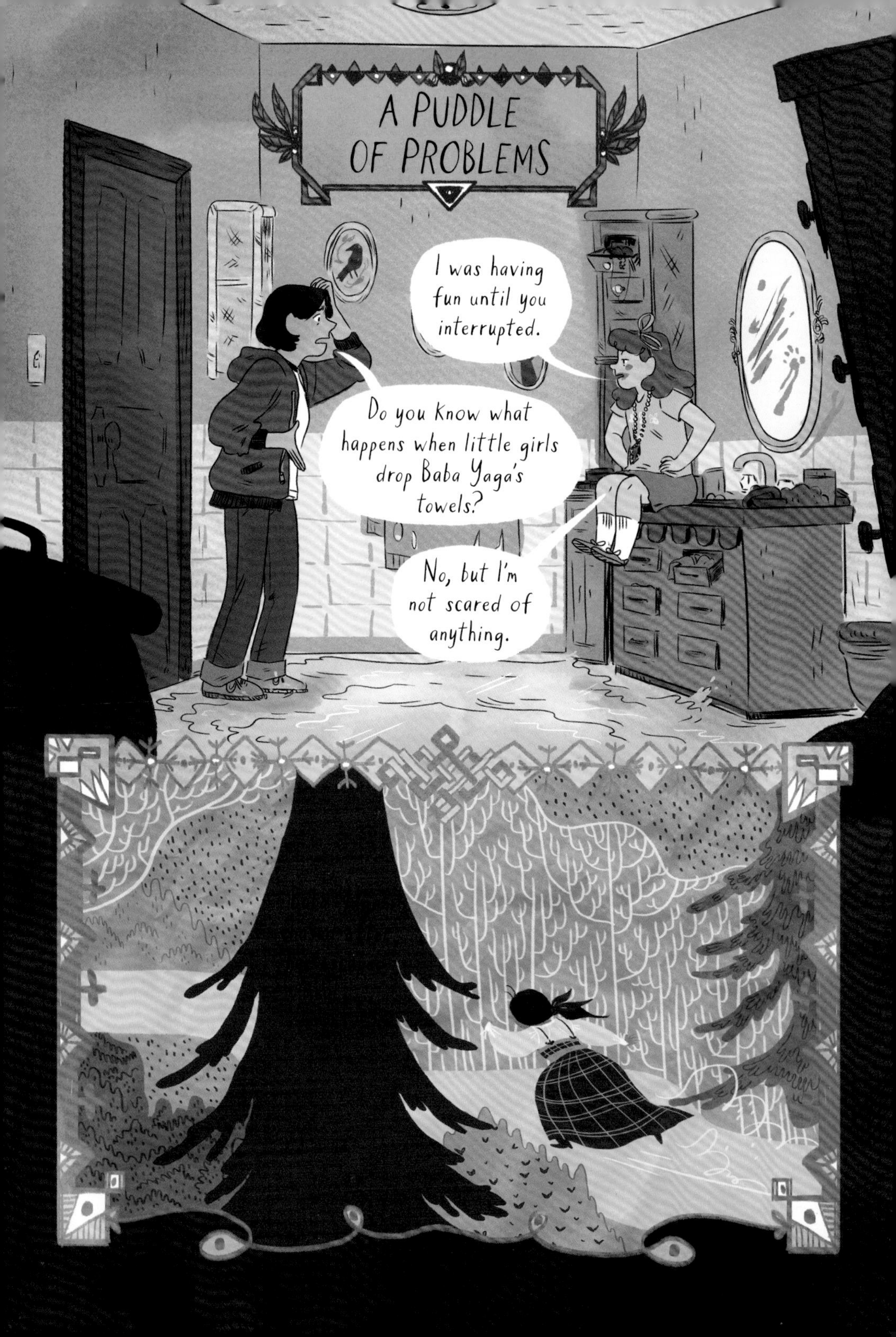
A PUDDLE OF PROBLEMS
Do you know what happens when little girls drop Baba Yaga's towels?
I was having fun until you interrupted.
No, but I'm not scared of anything.

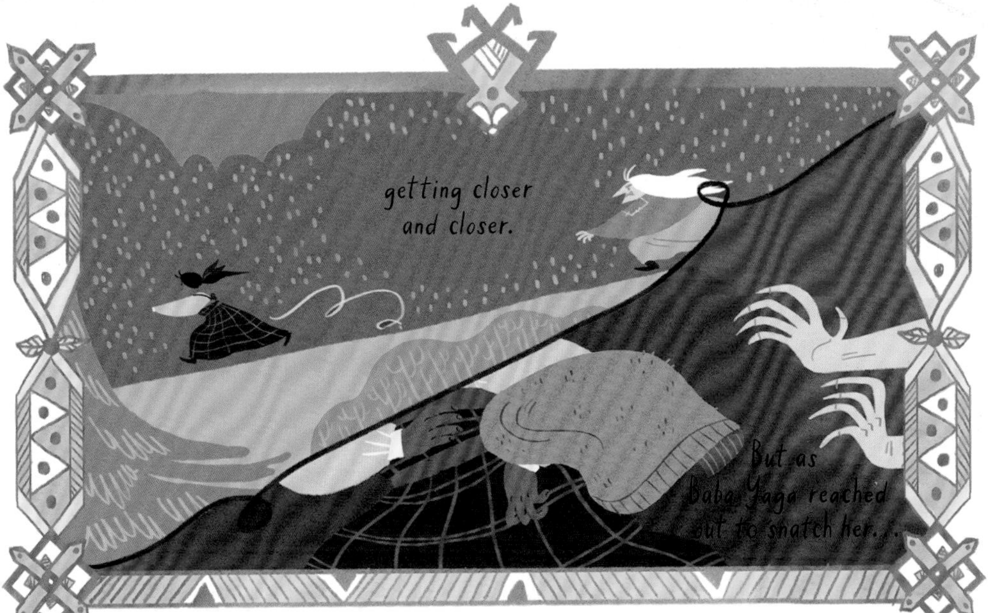
getting closer
and closer.
But as
Baba Yaga reached
out to snatch her. . .

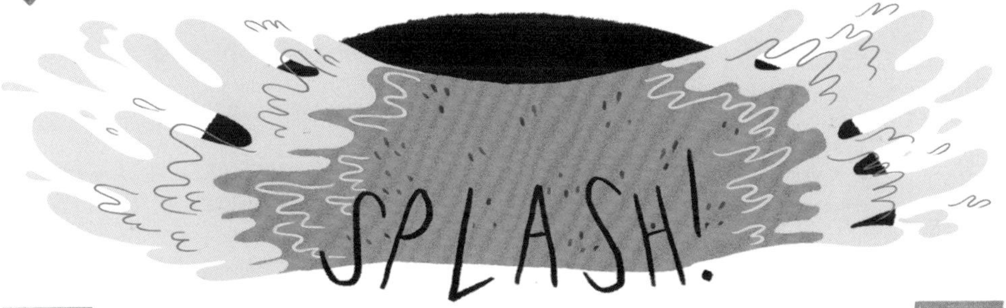
SPLASH!

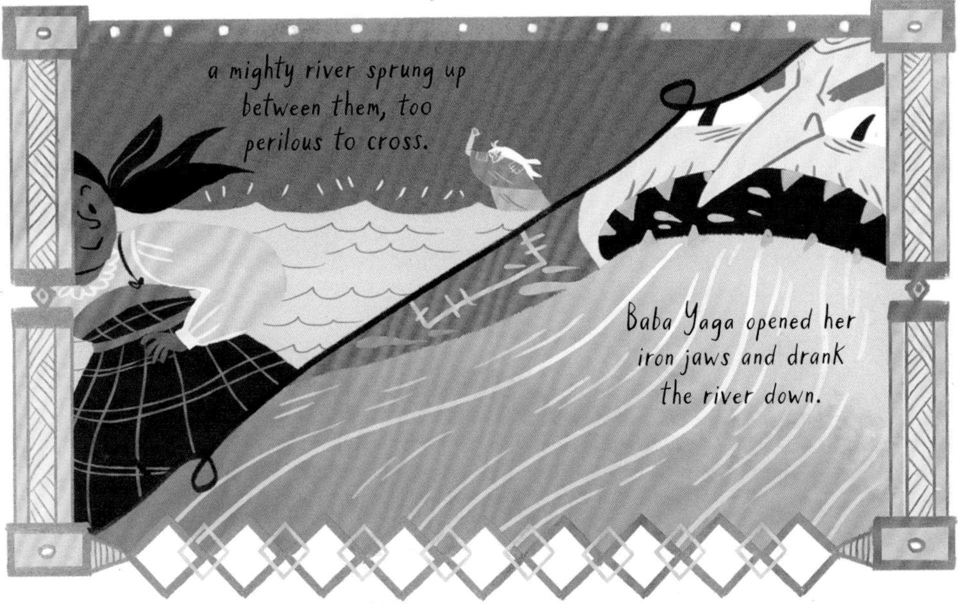
a mighty river sprung up
between them, too
perilous to cross.
Baba Yaga opened her
iron jaws and drank
the river down.

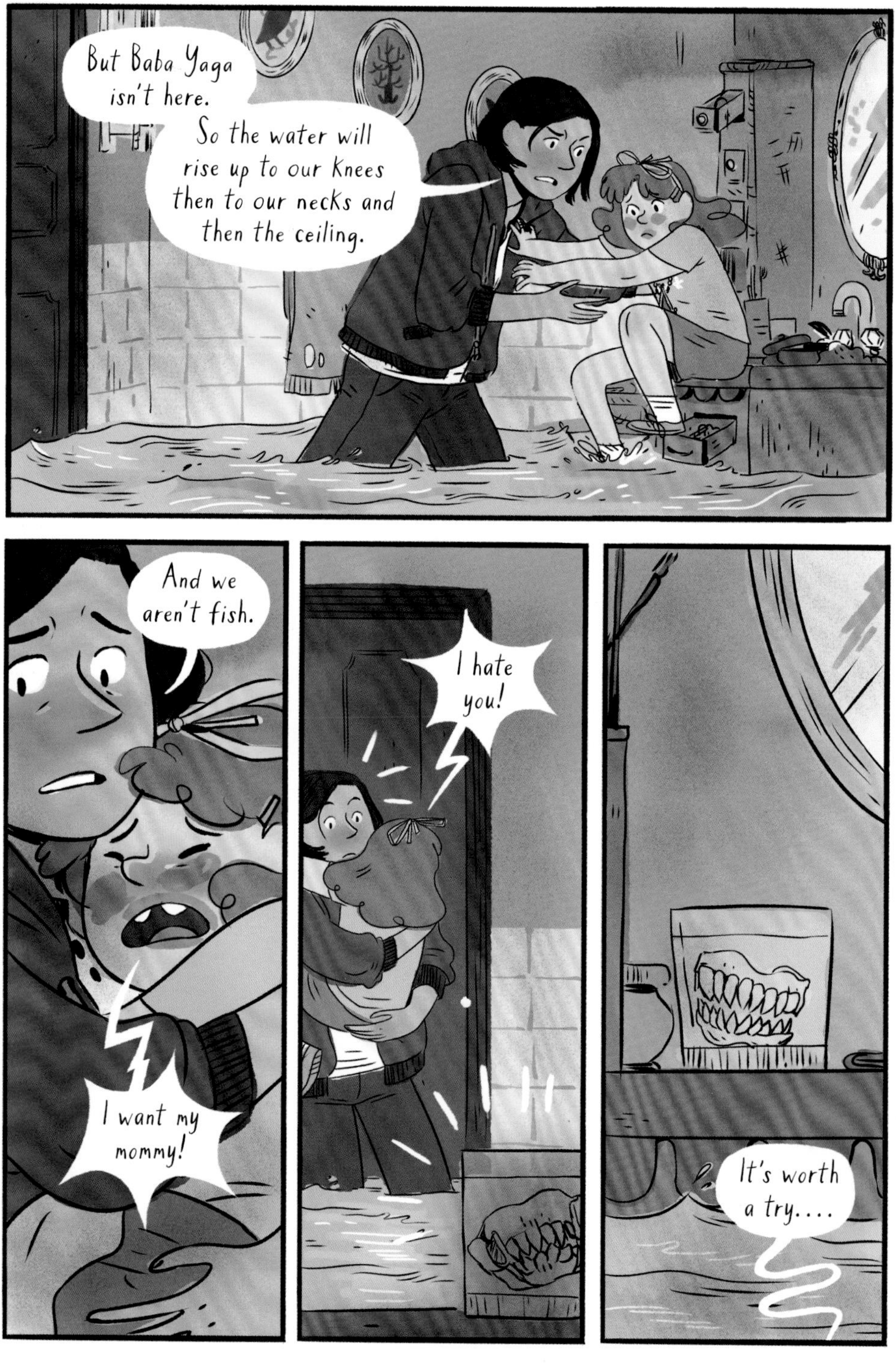

But Baba Yaga isn't here.
So the water will rise up to our knees then to our necks and then the ceiling.
And we aren't fish.
I want my mommy!
I hate you!
It's worth a try....

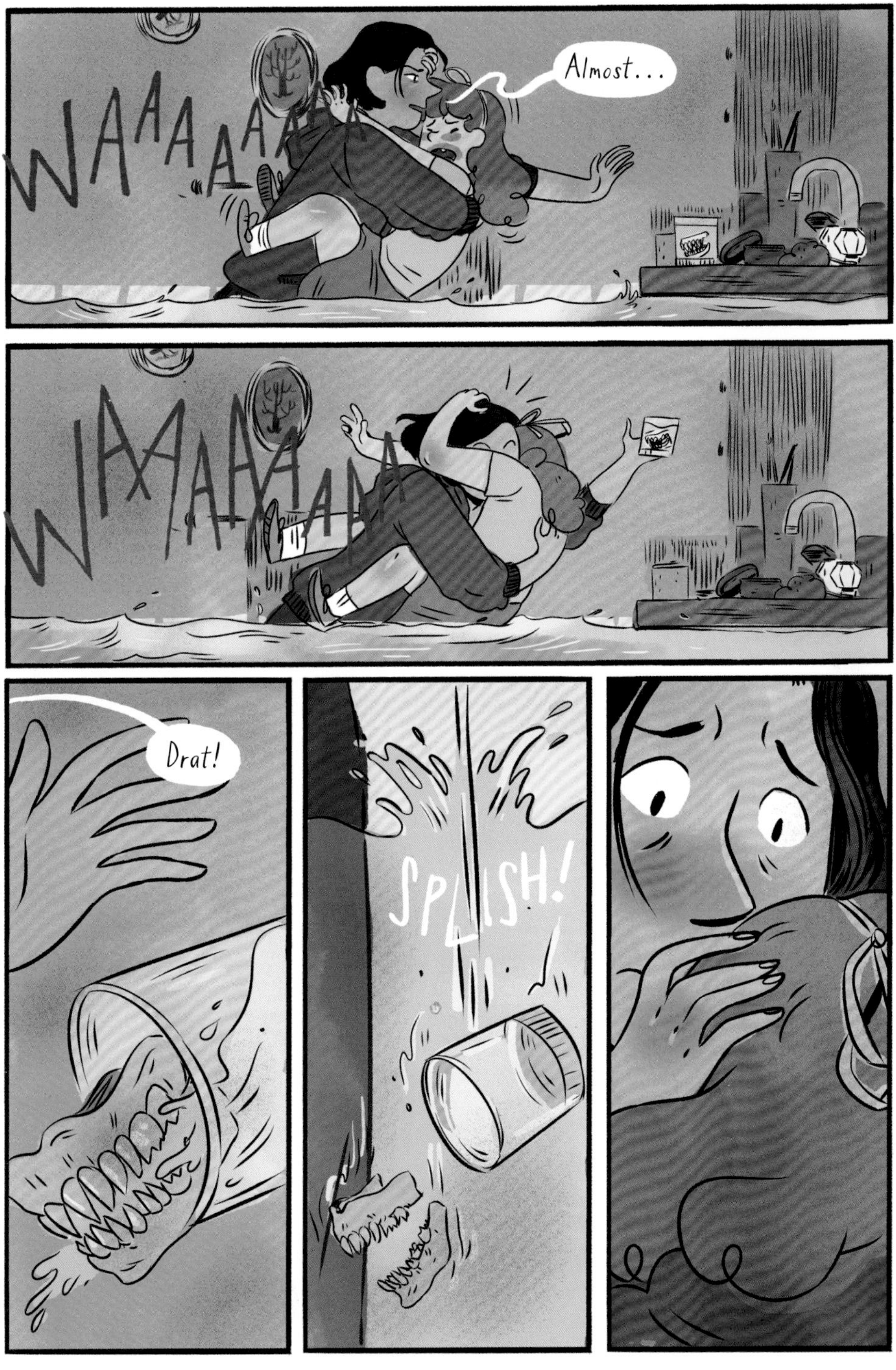
WAAAAAAAA
Almost...
WAAAAAAAA
Drat!
SPLISH!

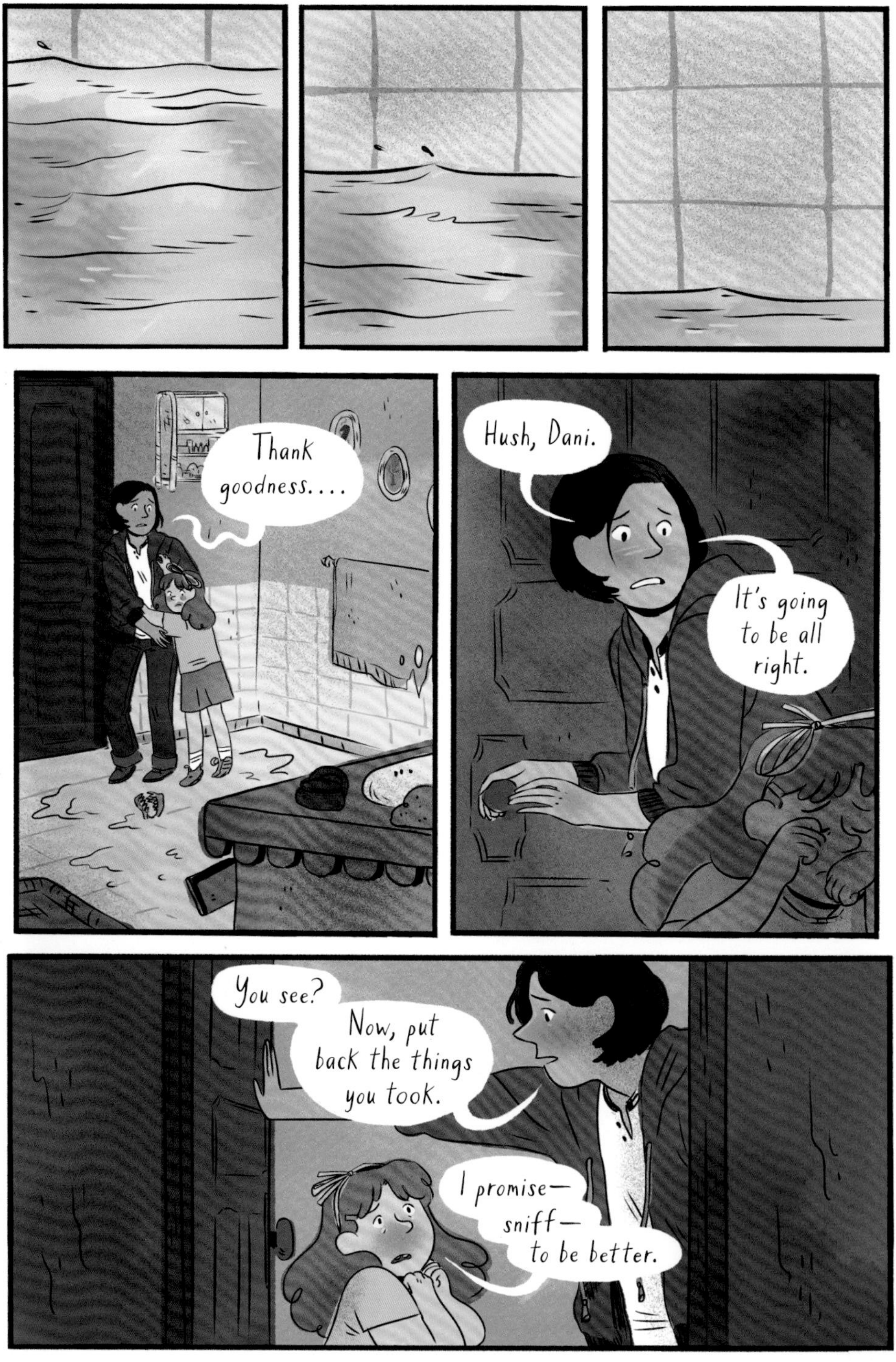
Thank goodness....
Hush, Dani.
It's going to be all right.
You see?
Now, put back the things you took.
I promise—
sniff—
to be better.

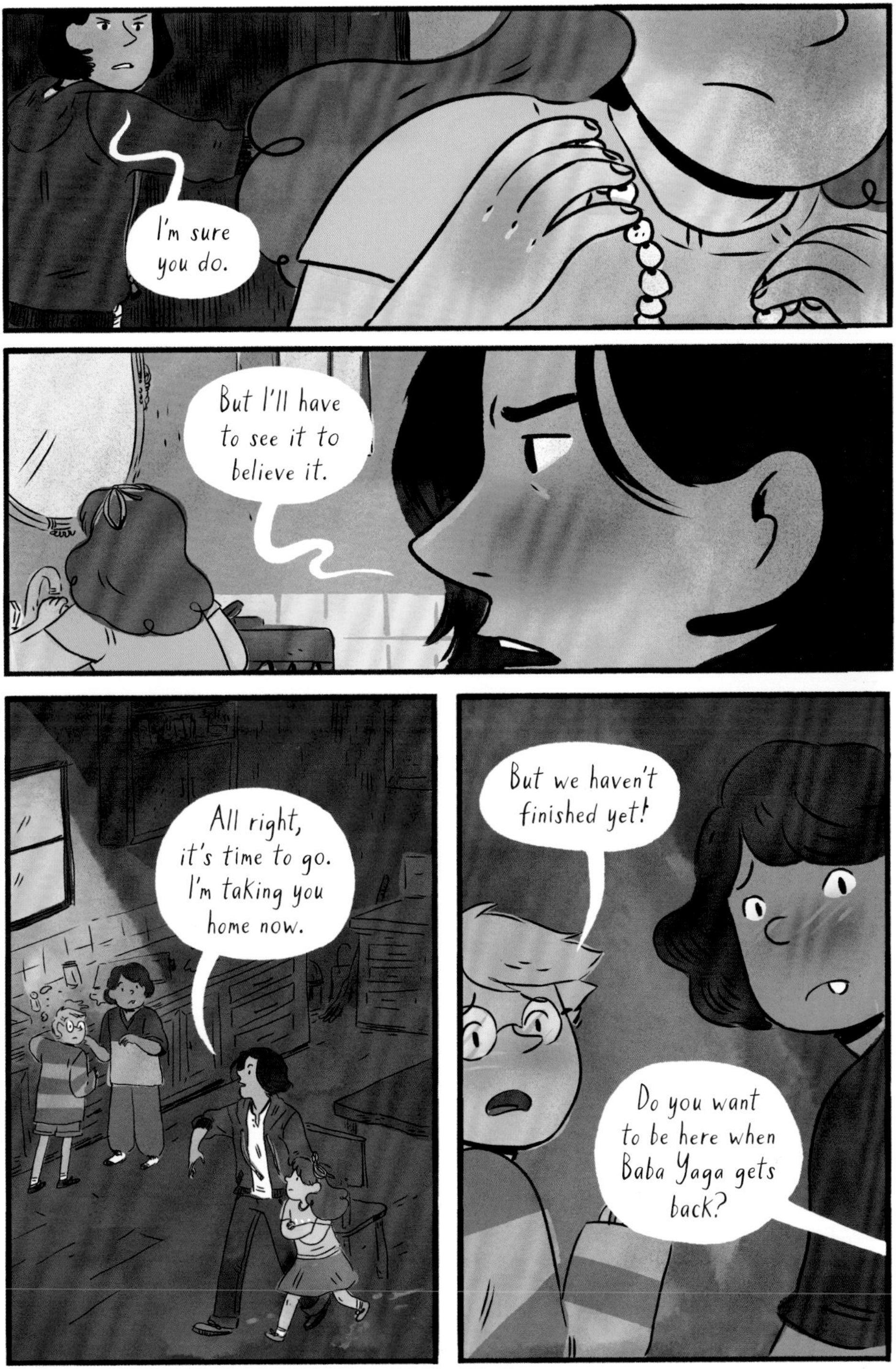
I'm sure you do.
But I'll have to see it to believe it.
All right, it's time to go. I'm taking you home now.
But we haven't finished yet!
Do you want to be here when Baba Yaga gets back?

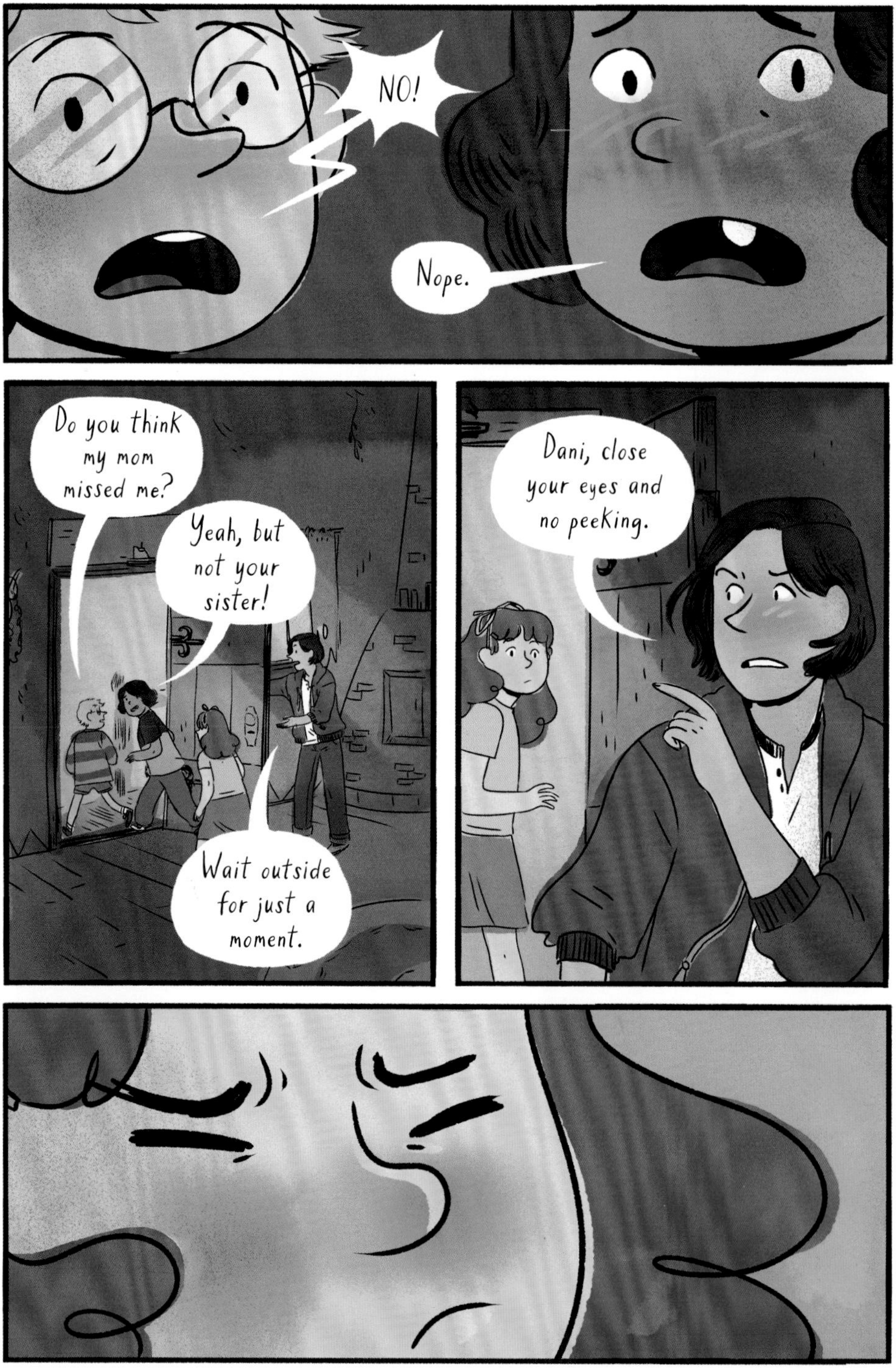
NO!
Nope.
Do you think my mom missed me?
Yeah, but not your sister!
Wait outside for just a moment.
Dani, close your eyes and no peeking.

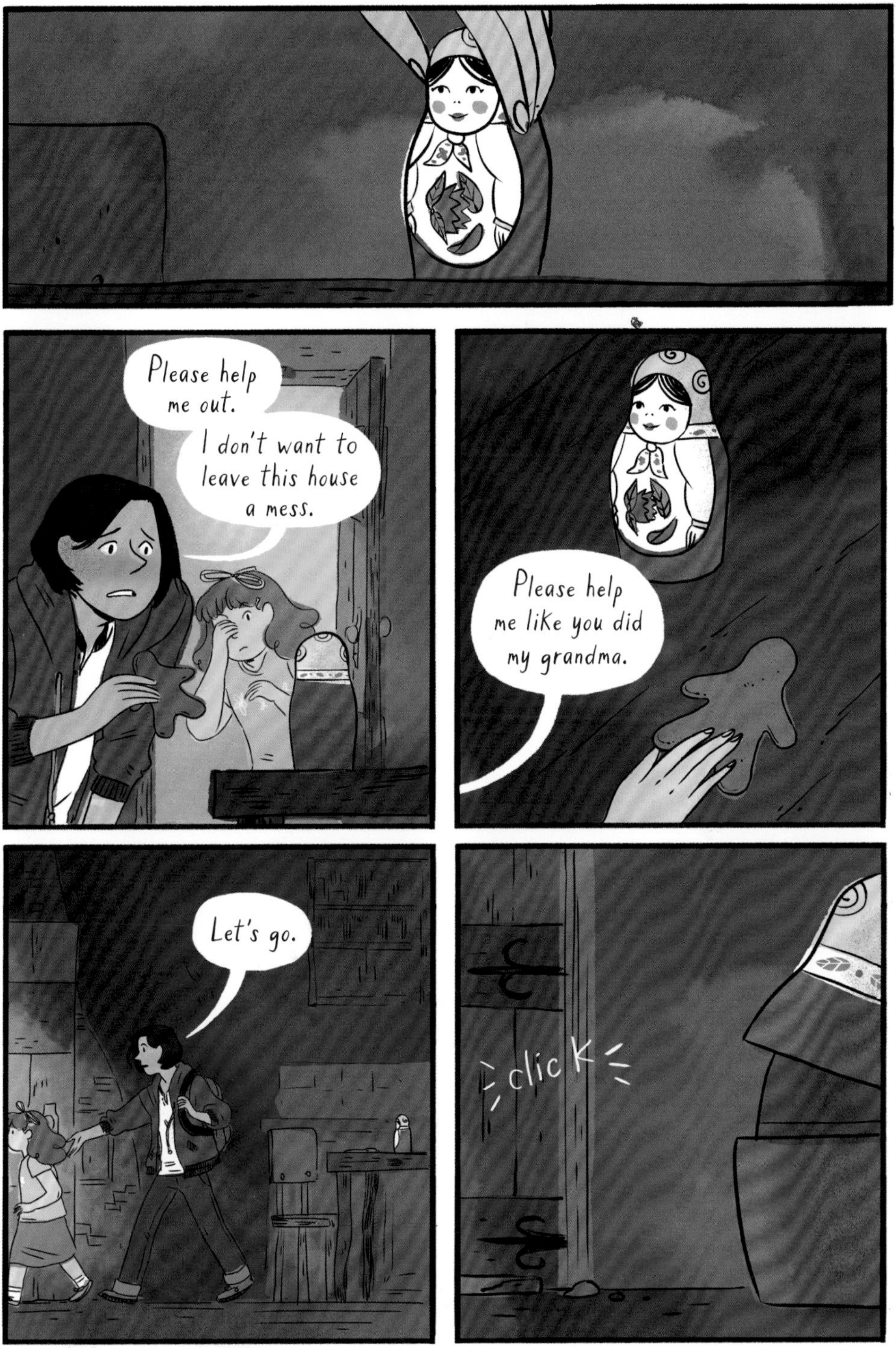
Please help me out.
I don't want to leave this house a mess.
Please help me like you did my grandma.
Let's go.
click

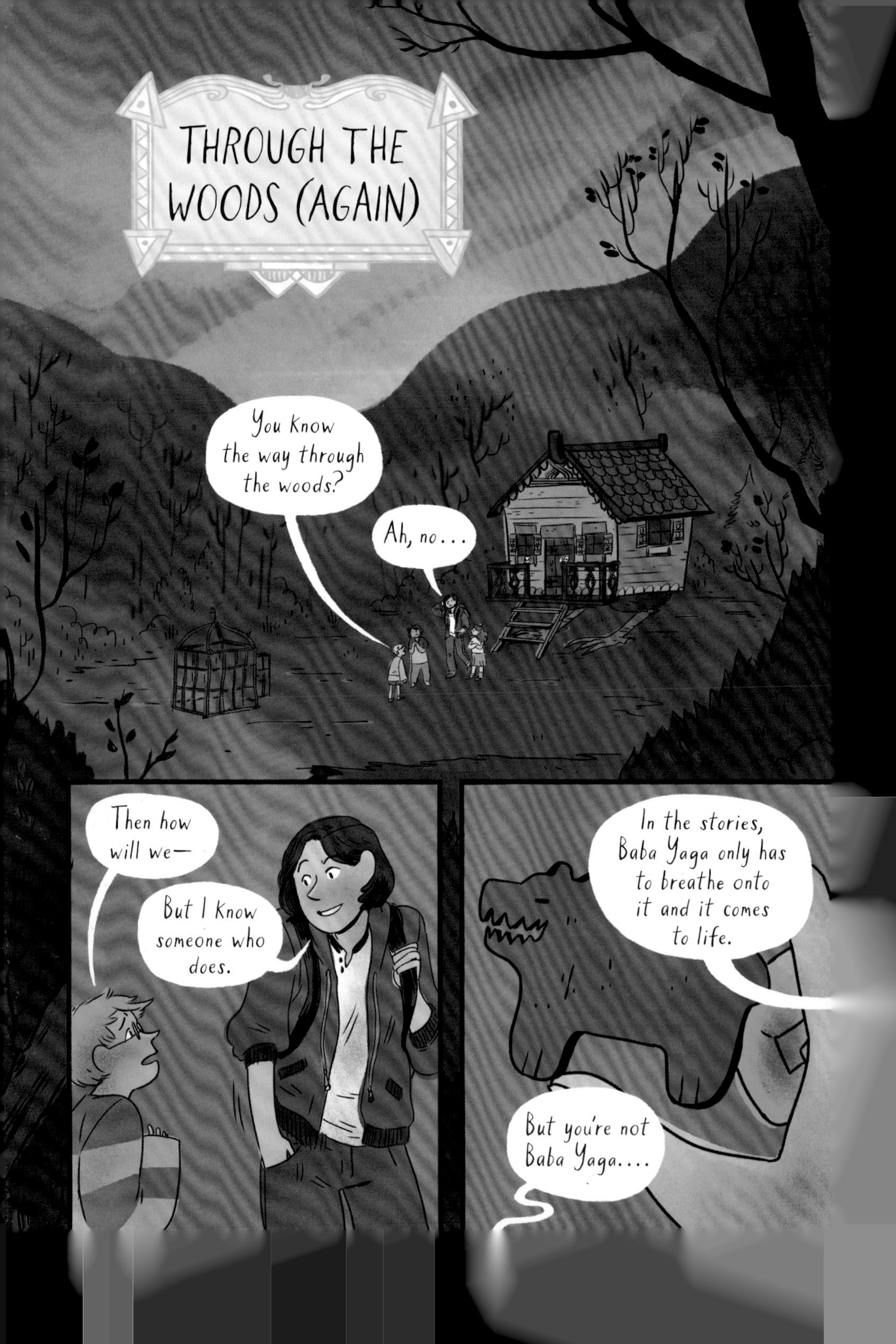
THROUGH THE WOODS (AGAIN)
You know the way through the woods?
Ah, no...
Then how will we—
But I know someone who does.
In the stories, Baba Yaga only has to breathe onto it and it comes to life.
But you're not Baba Yaga....

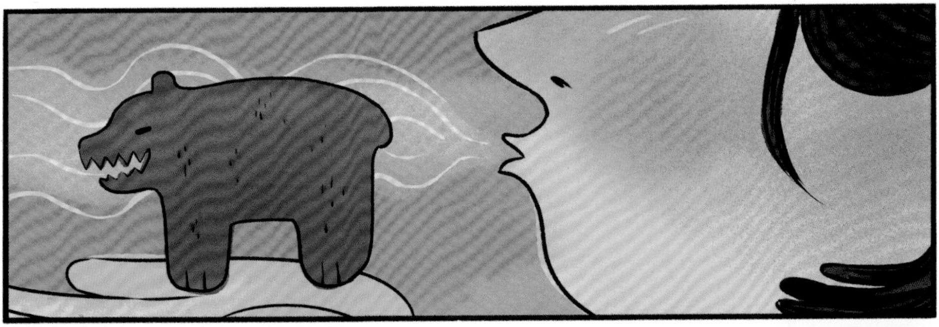

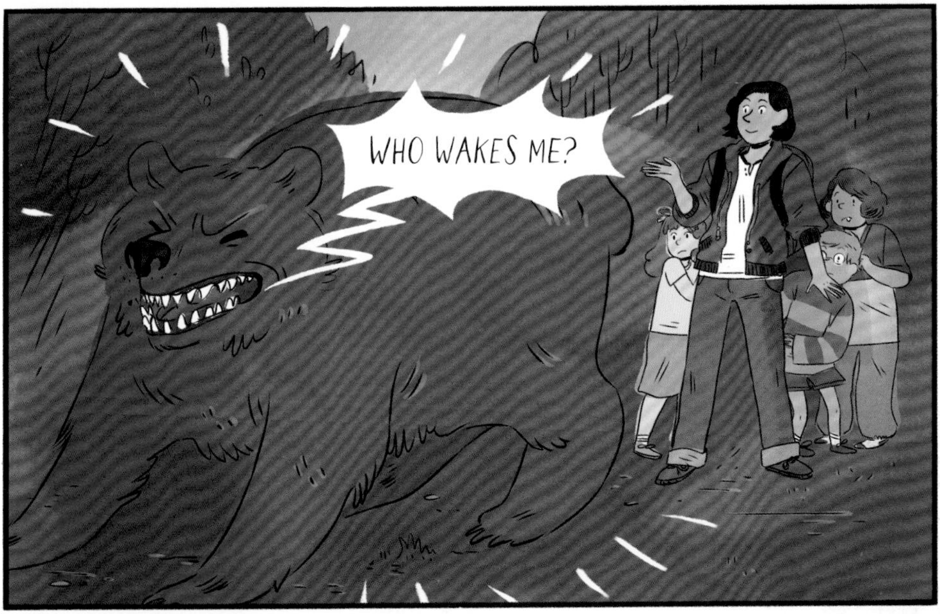
WHO WAKES ME?

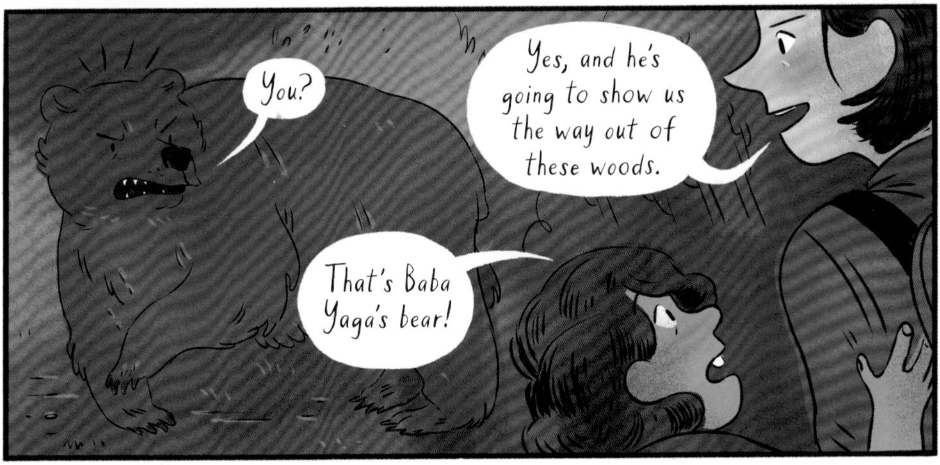
You?
Yes, and he's going to show us the way out of these woods.
That's Baba Yaga's bear!

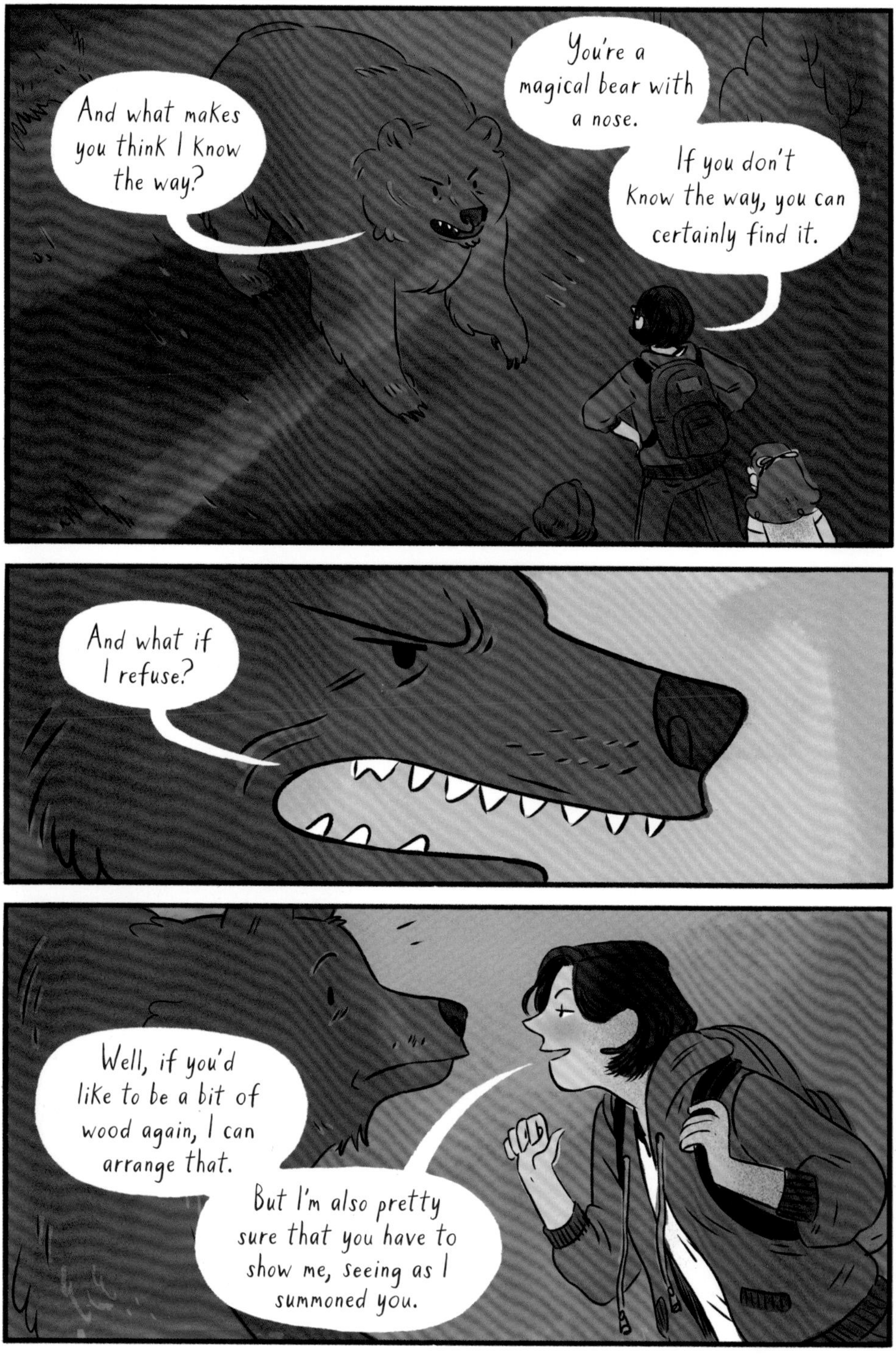
And what makes you think I know the way?
You're a magical bear with a nose.
If you don't know the way, you can certainly find it.
And what if I refuse?
Well, if you'd like to be a bit of wood again, I can arrange that.
But I'm also pretty sure that you have to show me, seeing as I summoned you.

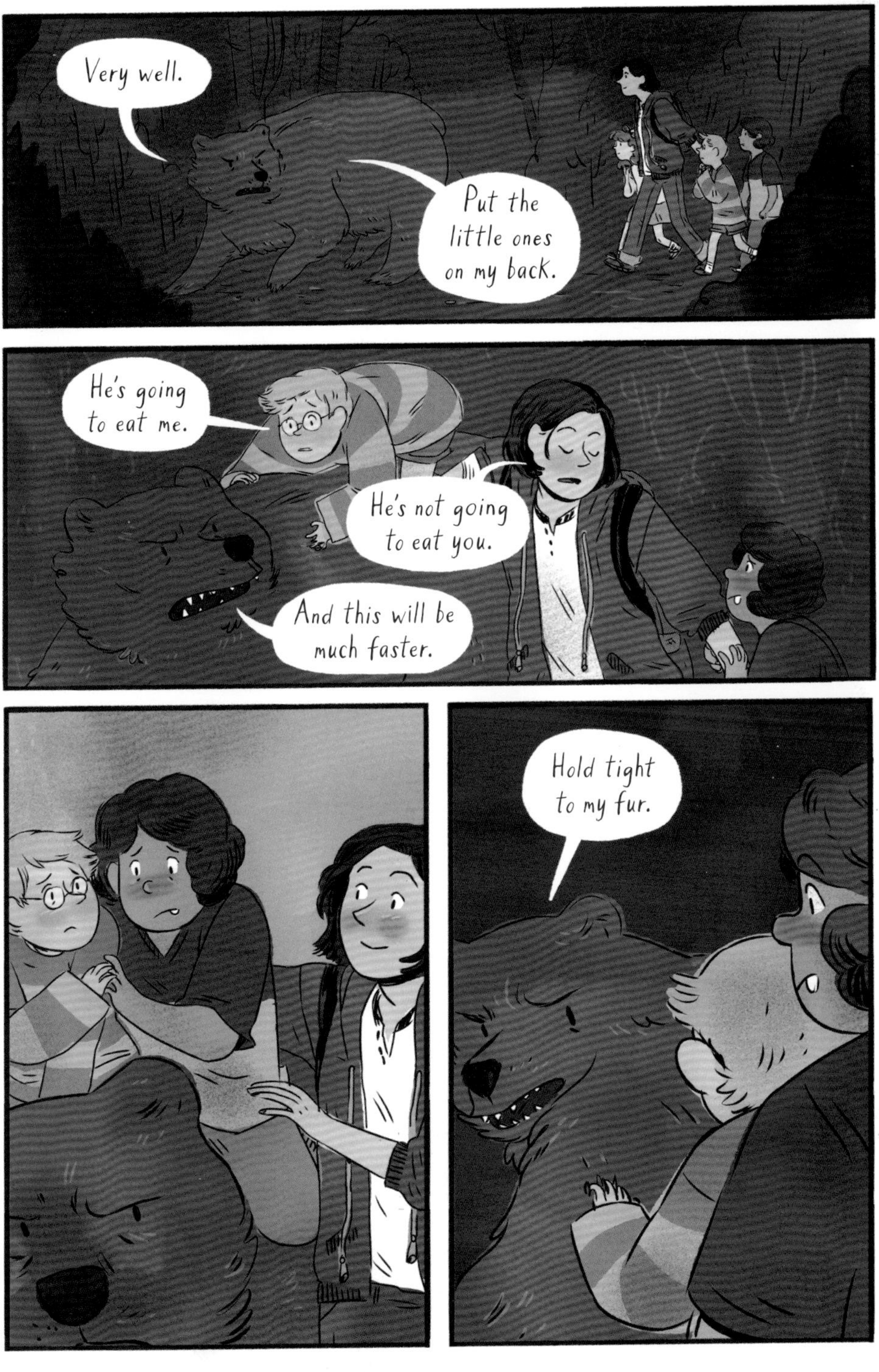
Very well.
Put the little ones on my back.
He's going to eat me.
He's not going to eat you.
And this will be much faster.
Hold tight to my fur.

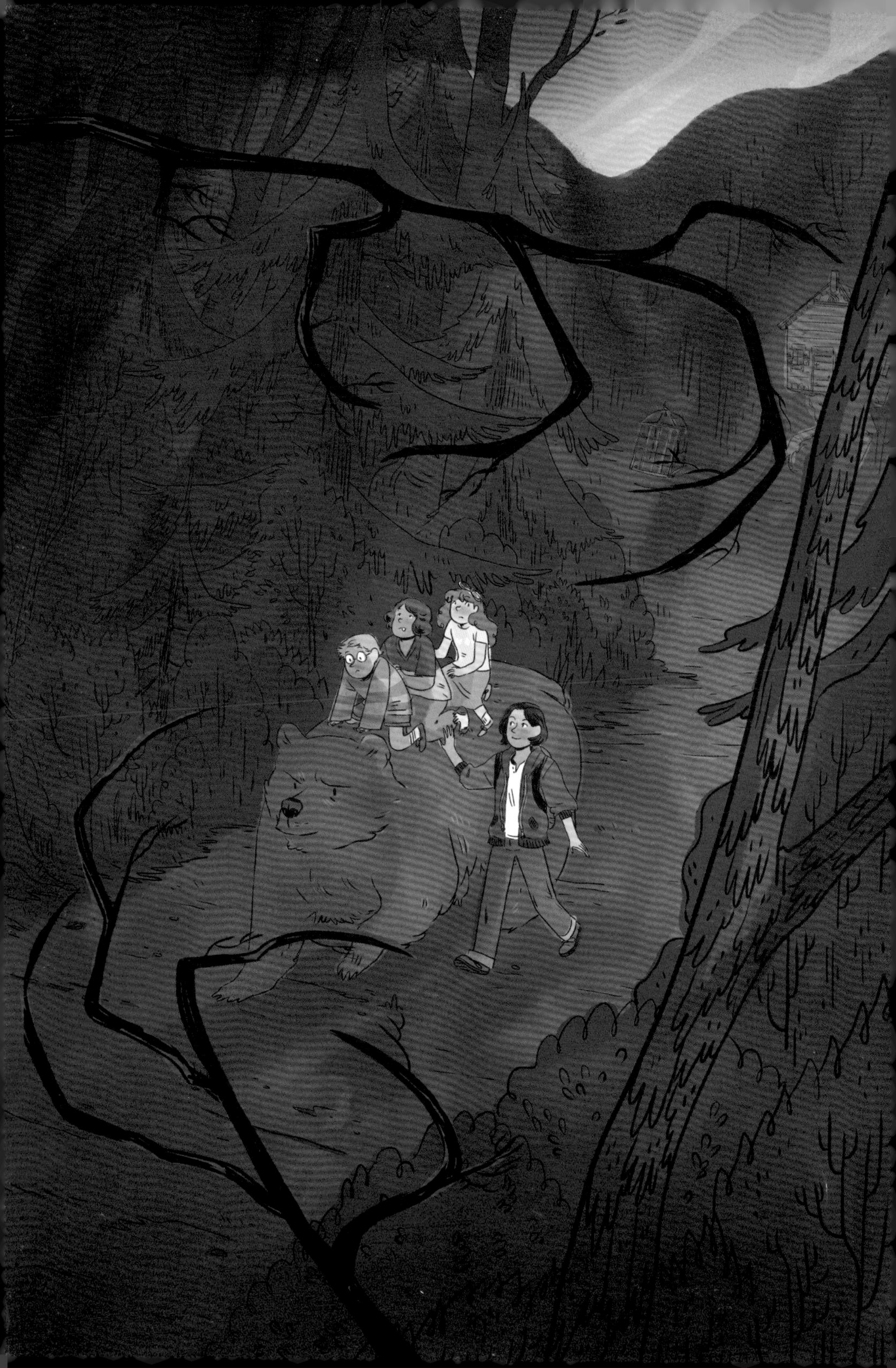

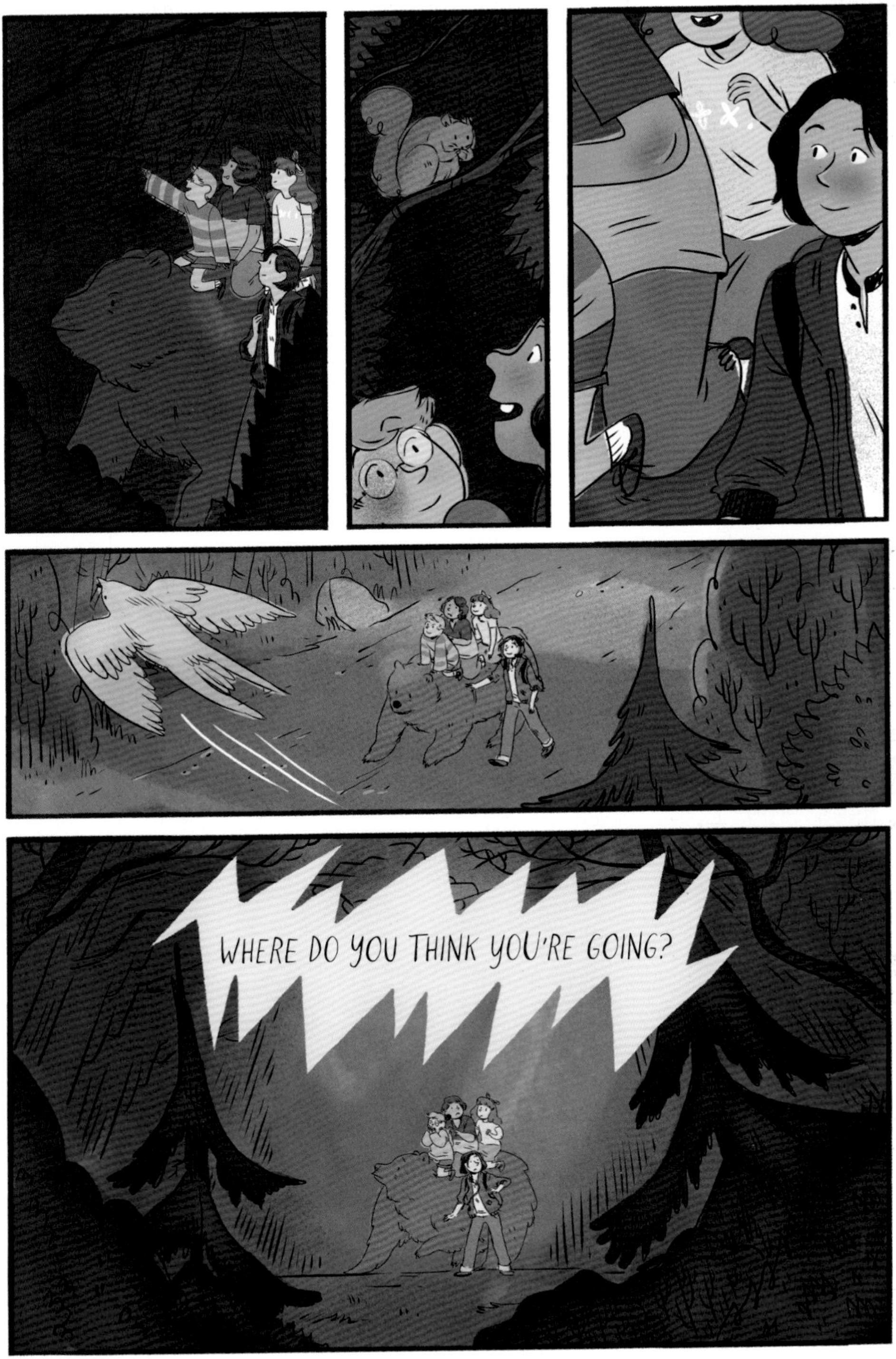
WHERE DO YOU THINK YOU'RE GOING?

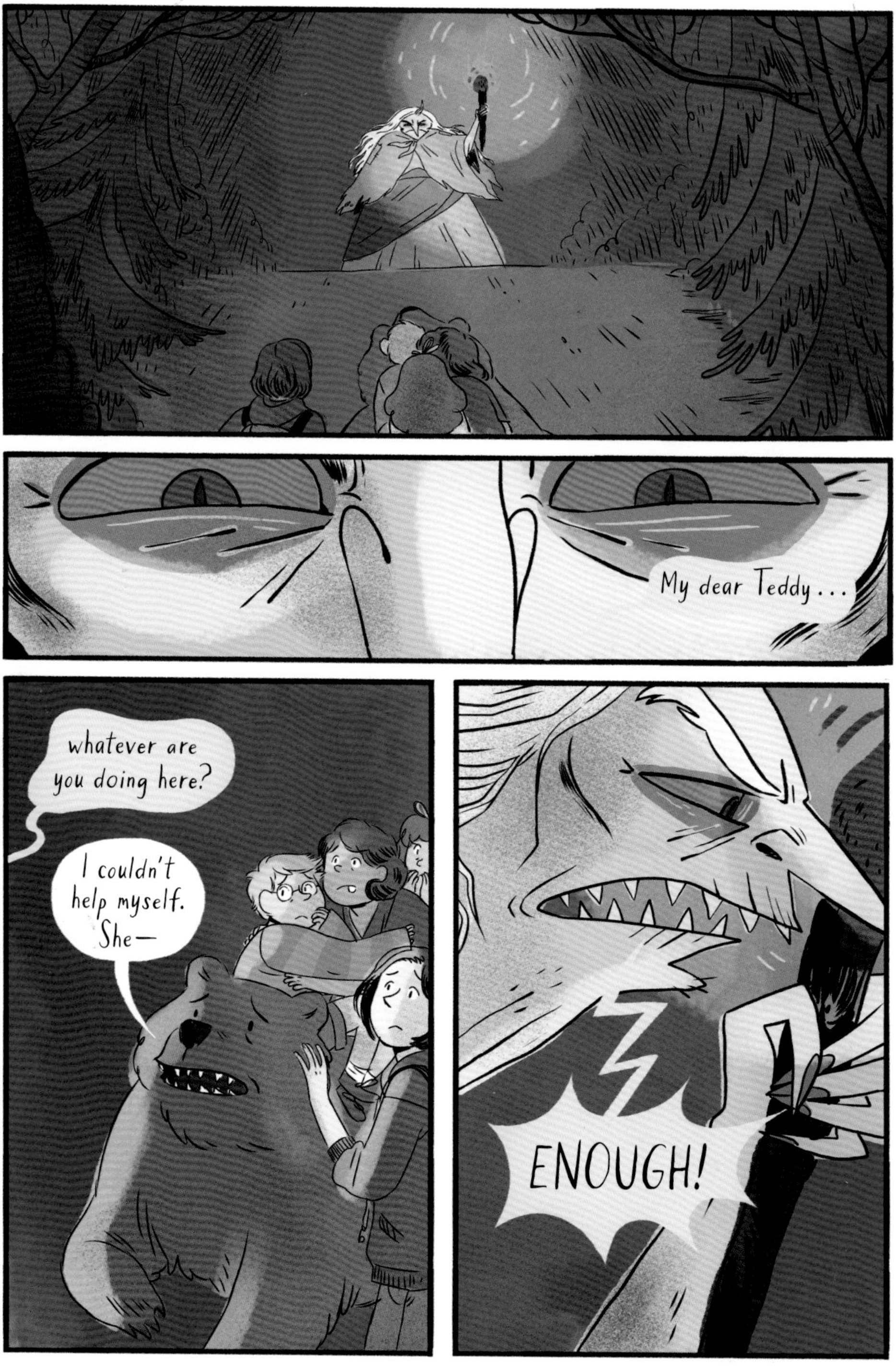
My dear Teddy . . .
whatever are you doing here?
I couldn't help myself. She—
ENOUGH!

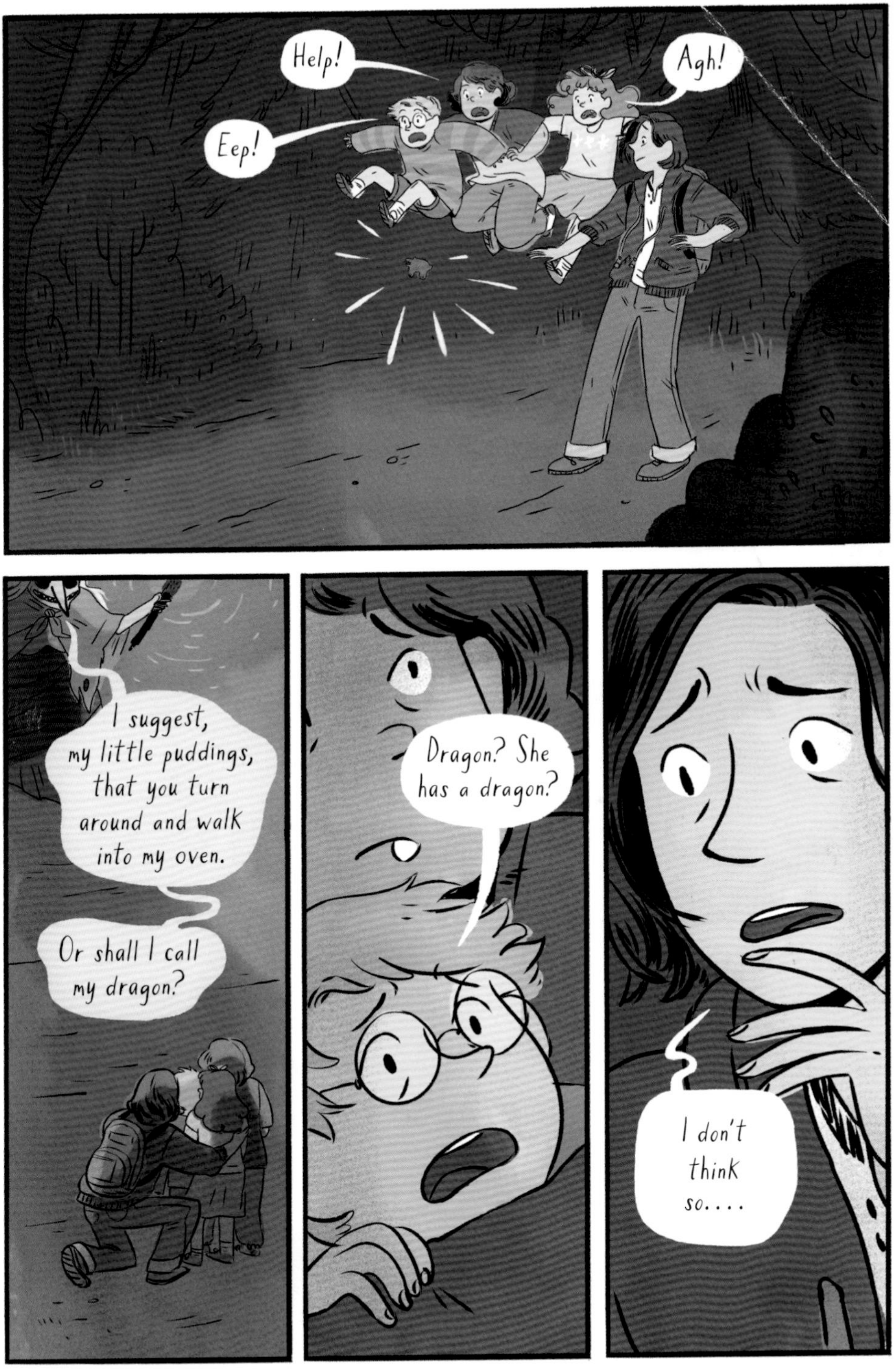
Help!
Eep!
Agh!
I suggest, my little puddings, that you turn around and walk into my oven.
Or shall I call my dragon?
Dragon? She has a dragon?
I don't think so. . . .

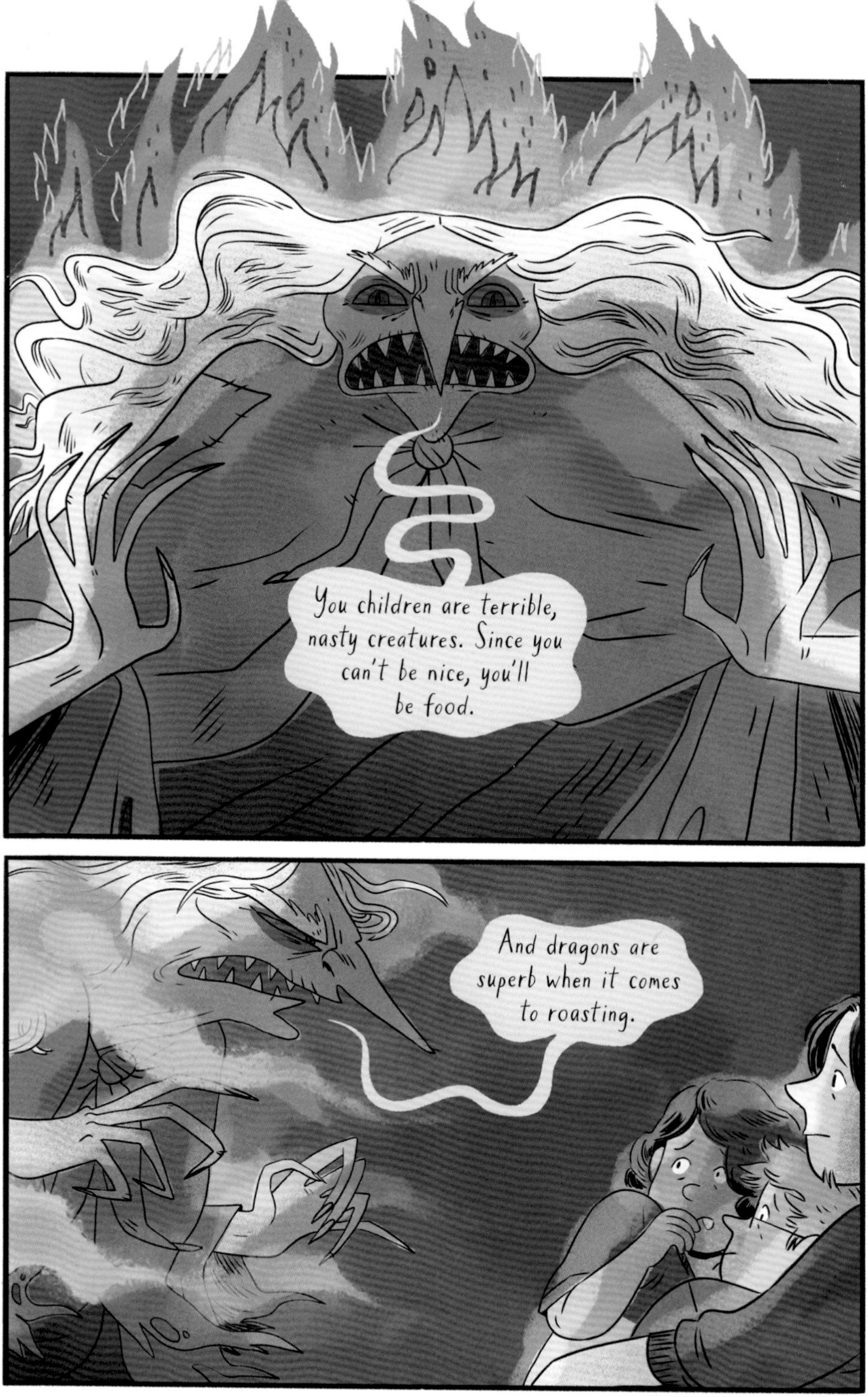
You children are terrible, nasty creatures. Since you can't be nice, you'll be food.
And dragons are superb when it comes to roasting.

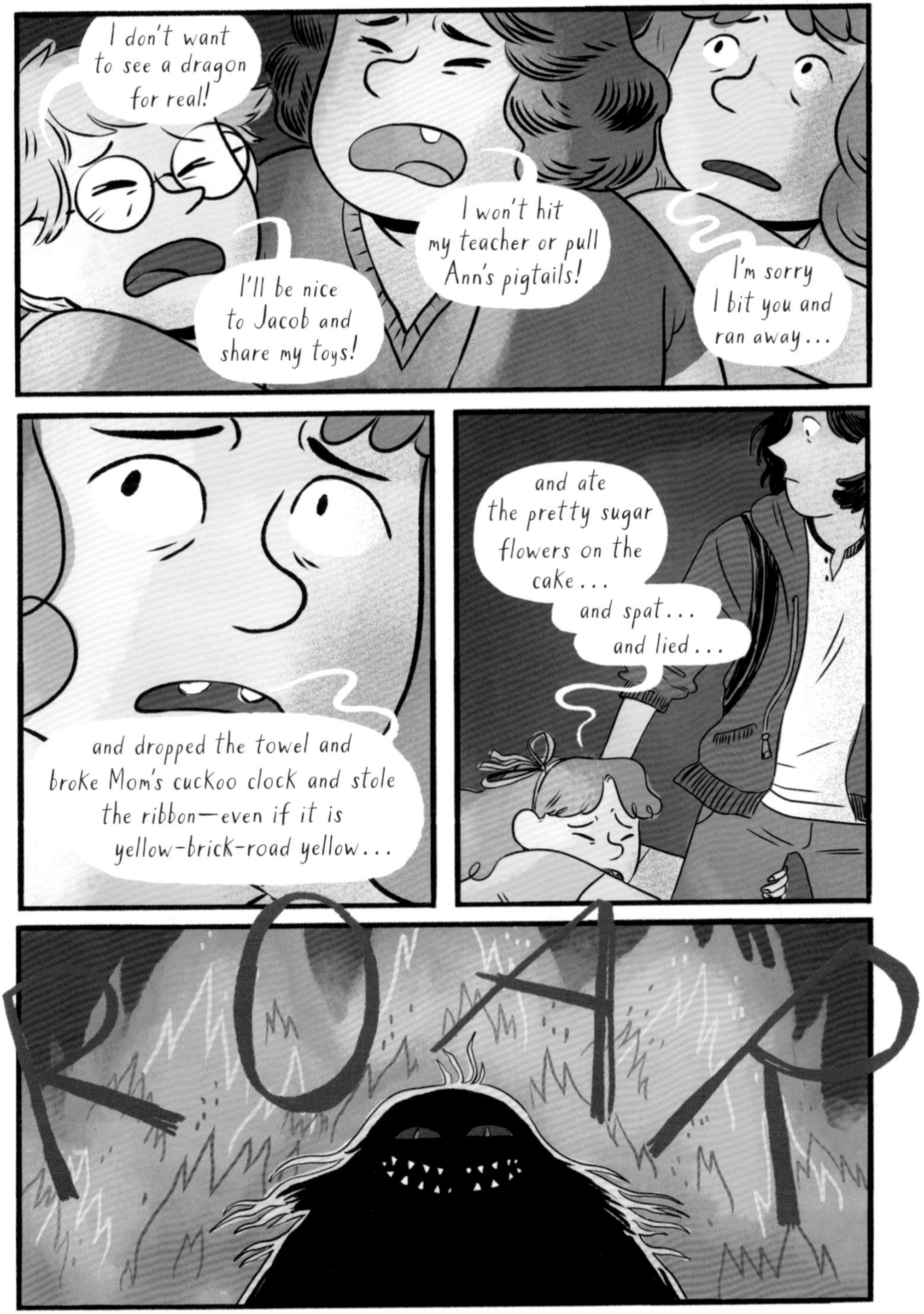
I don't want to see a dragon for real!
I'll be nice to Jacob and share my toys!
I won't hit my teacher or pull Ann's pigtails!
I'm sorry I bit you and ran away...
and dropped the towel and broke Mom's cuckoo clock and stole the ribbon—even if it is yellow-brick-road yellow...
and ate the pretty sugar flowers on the cake... and spat... and lied...
ROAR

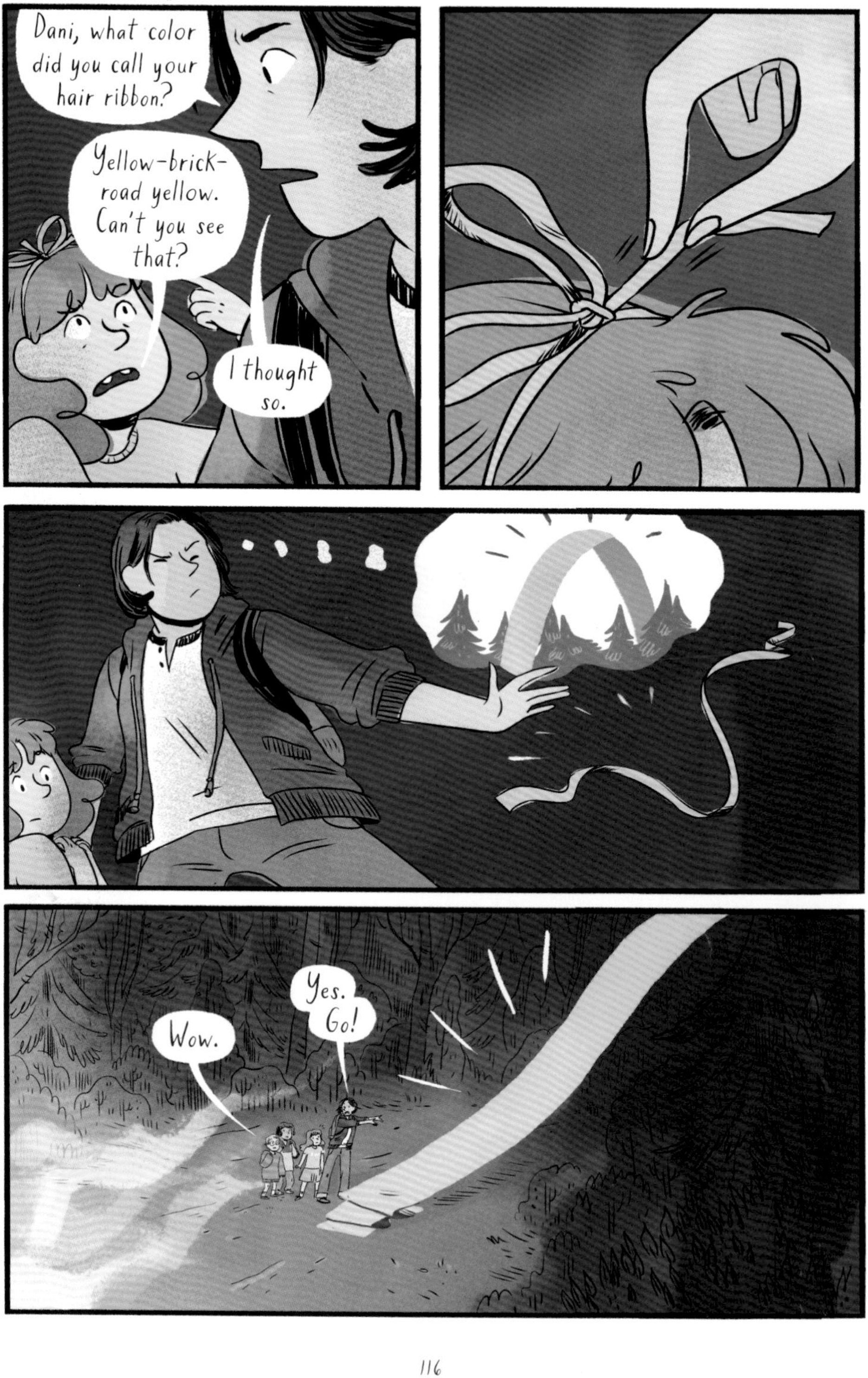
Dani, what color did you call your hair ribbon?
Yellow-brick-road yellow. Can't you see that?
I thought so.
Wow.
Yes. Go!

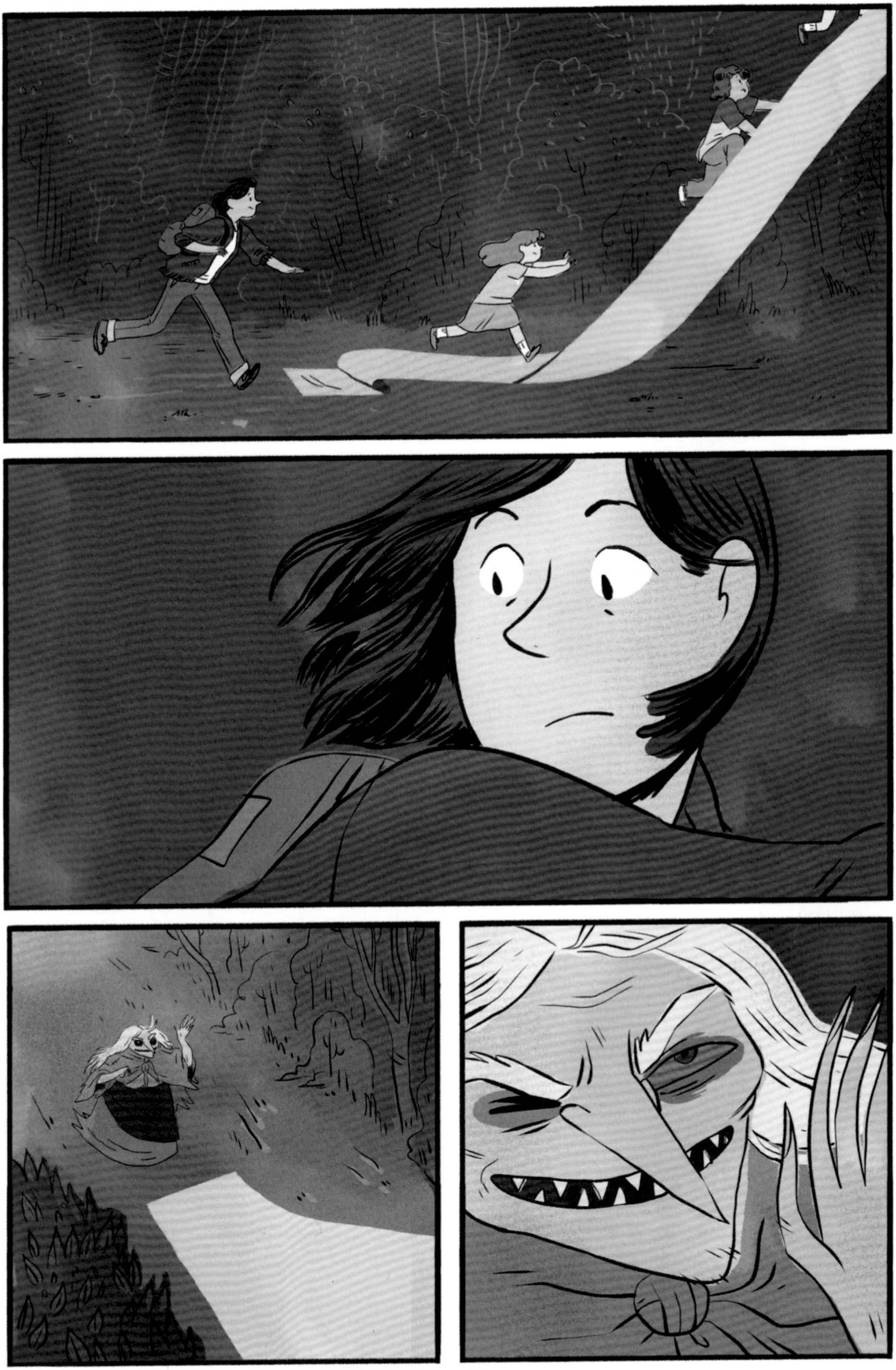

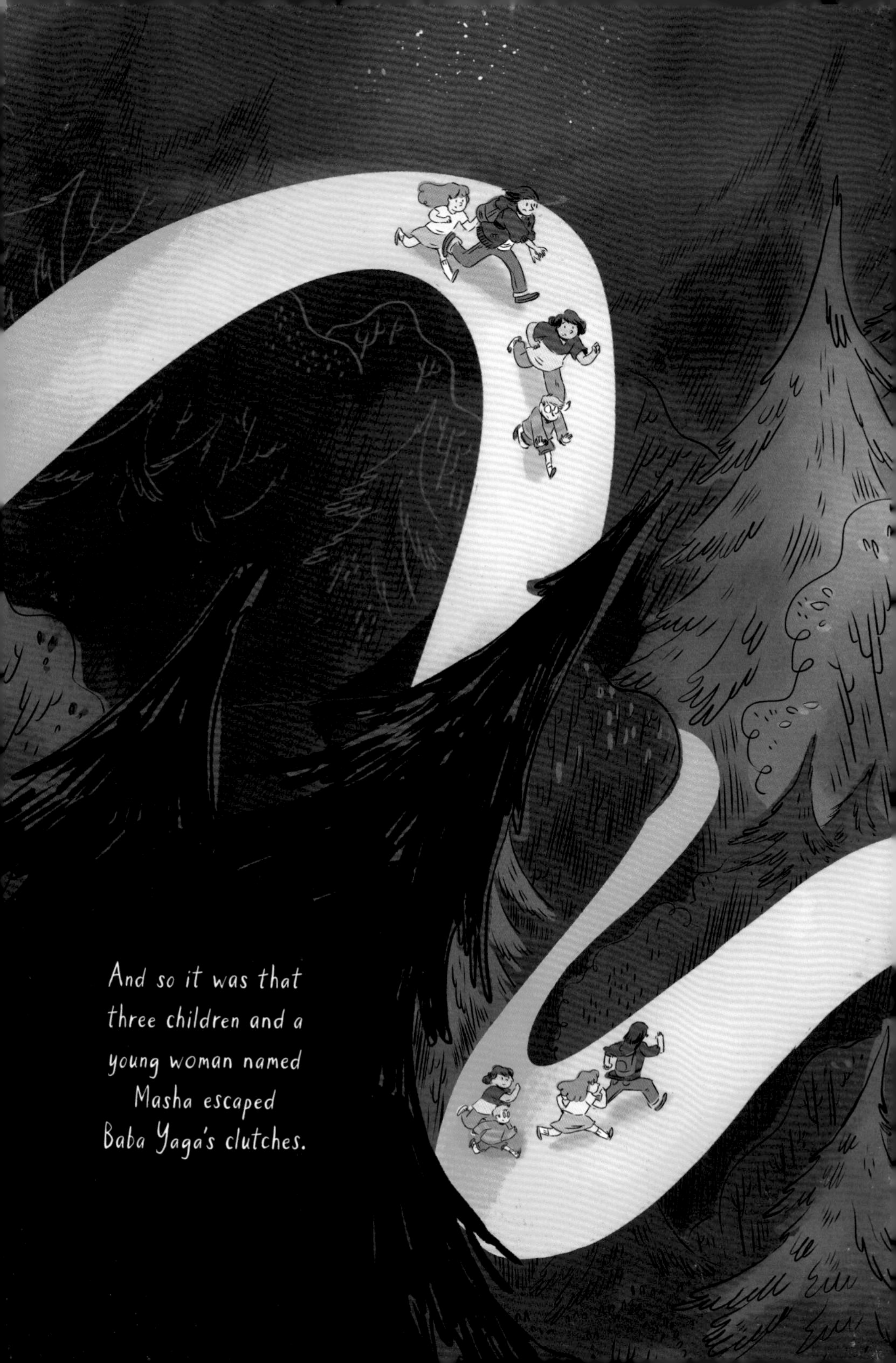
And so it was that three children and a young woman named Masha escaped Baba Yaga's clutches.

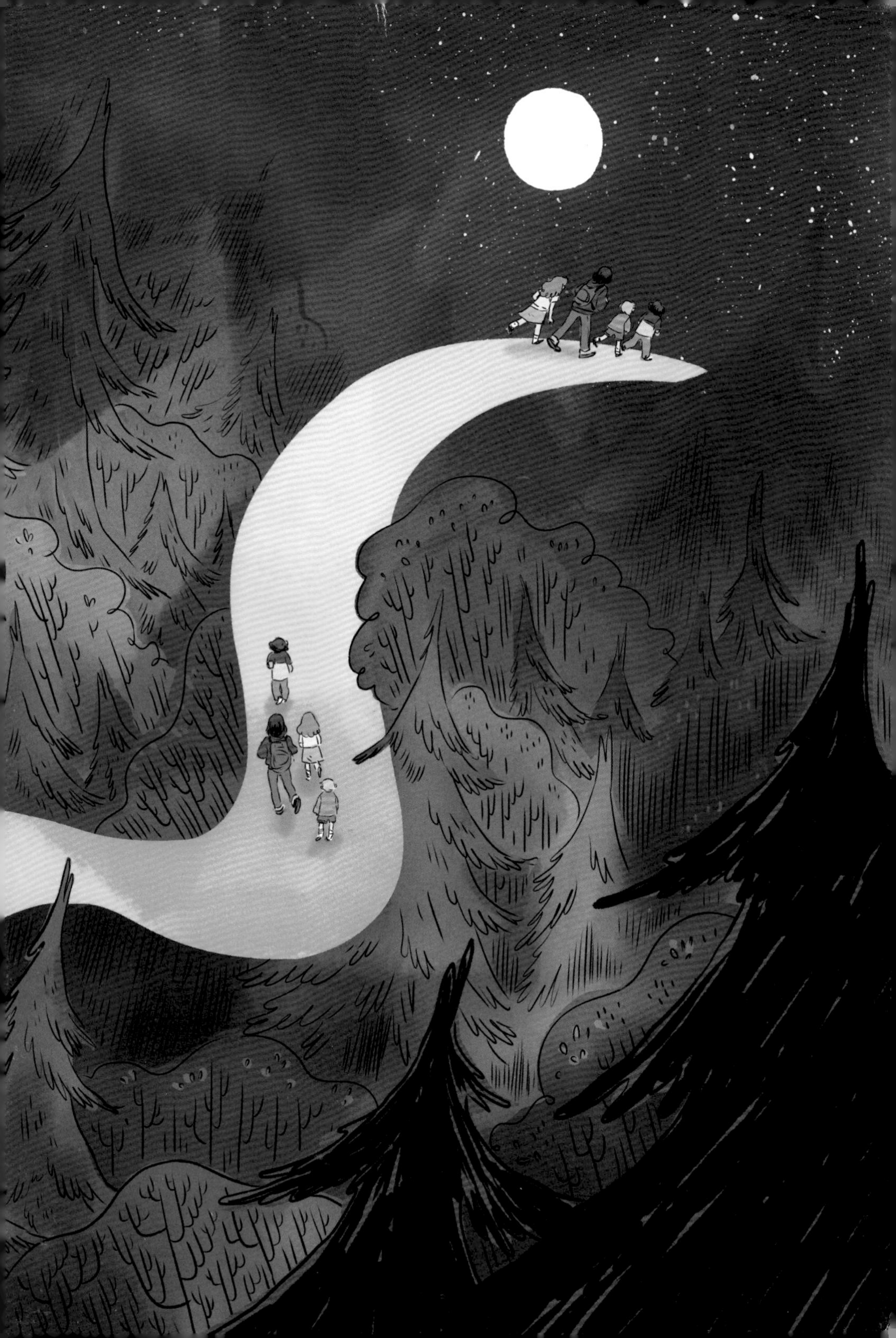

BACK WHERE WE BEGAN

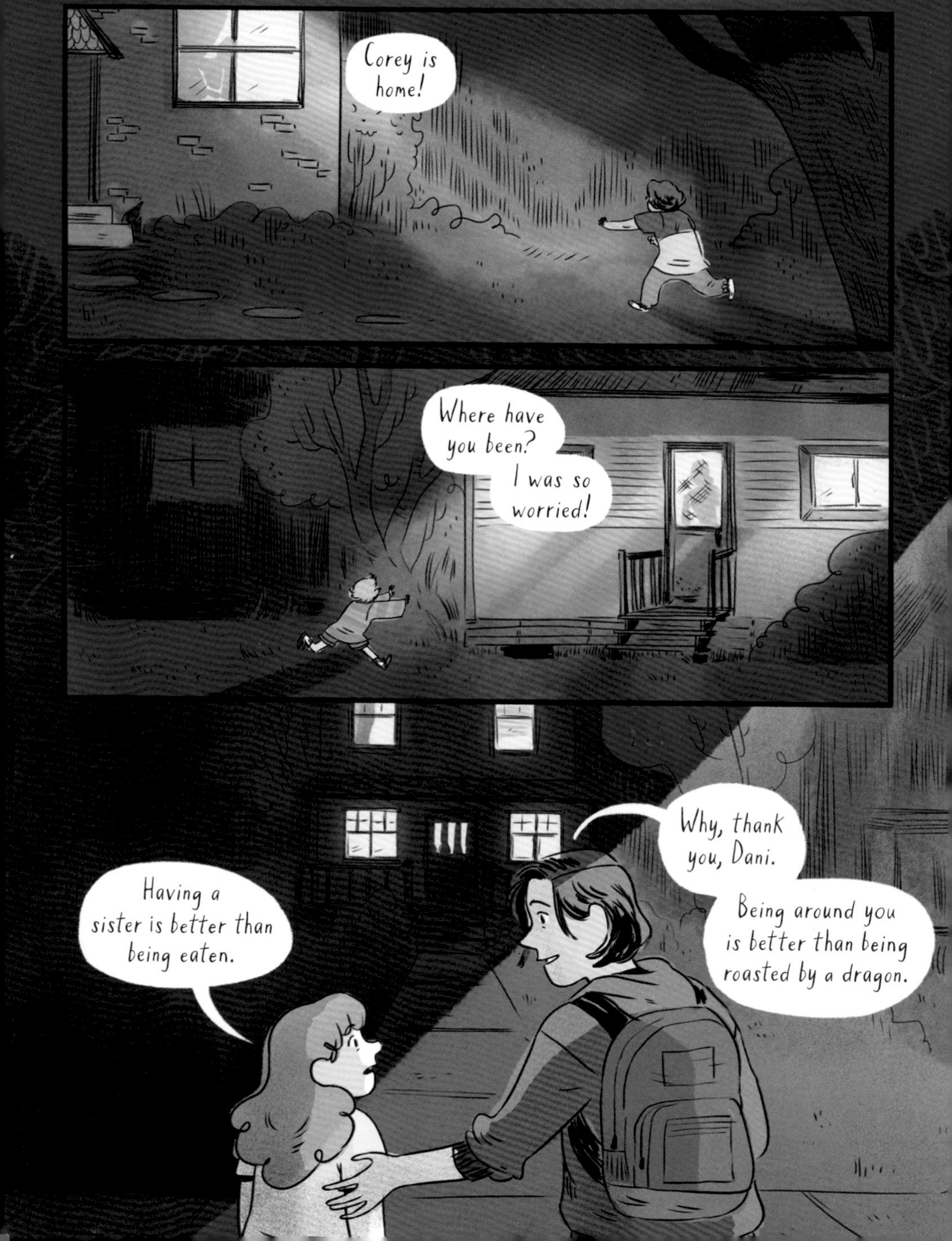

Corey is home!
Where have you been?
I was so worried!
Having a sister is better than being eaten.
Why, thank you, Dani.
Being around you is better than being roasted by a dragon.

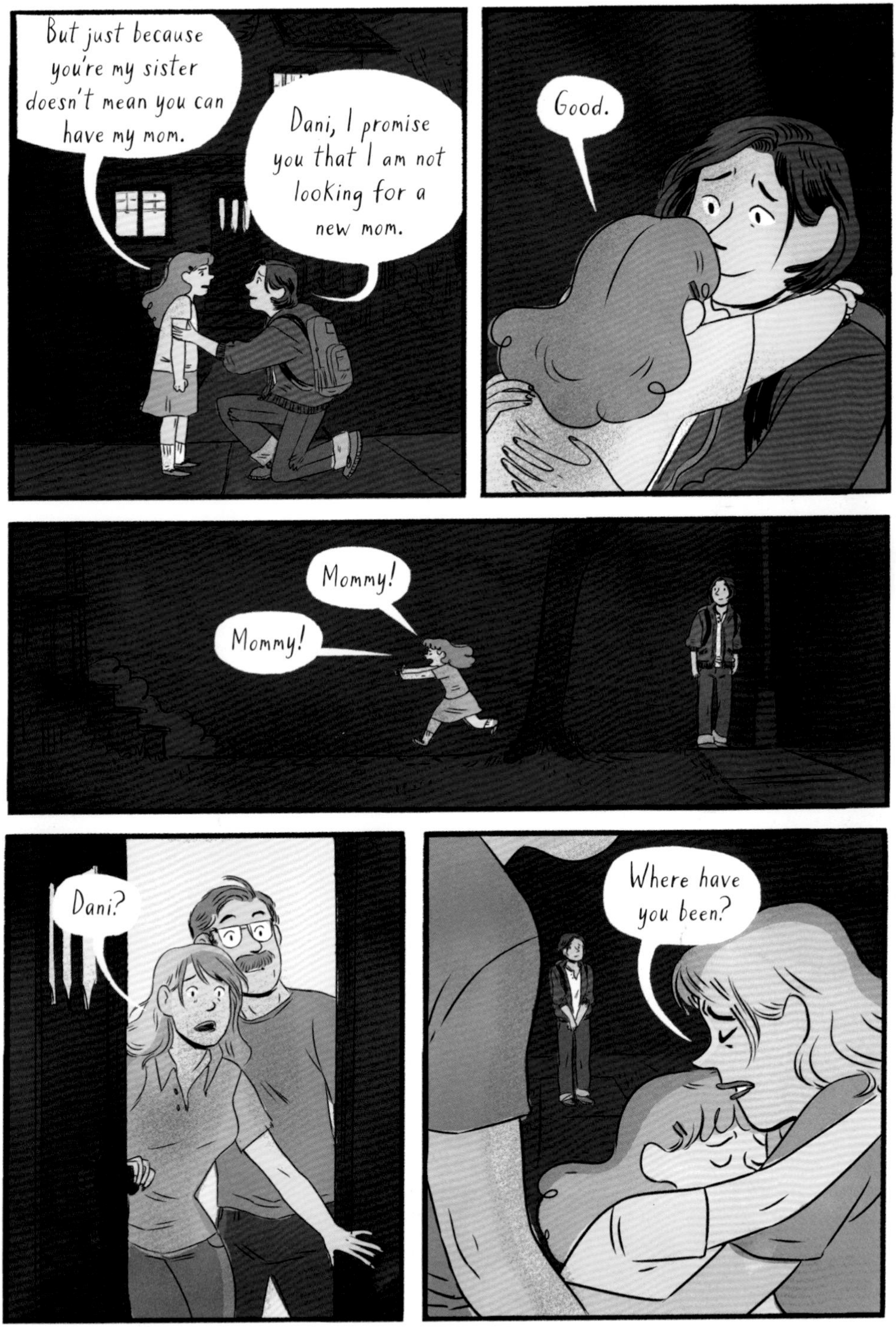

But just because you're my sister doesn't mean you can have my mom.
Dani, I promise you that I am not looking for a new mom.
Good.
Mommy!
Mommy!
Dani?
Where have you been?

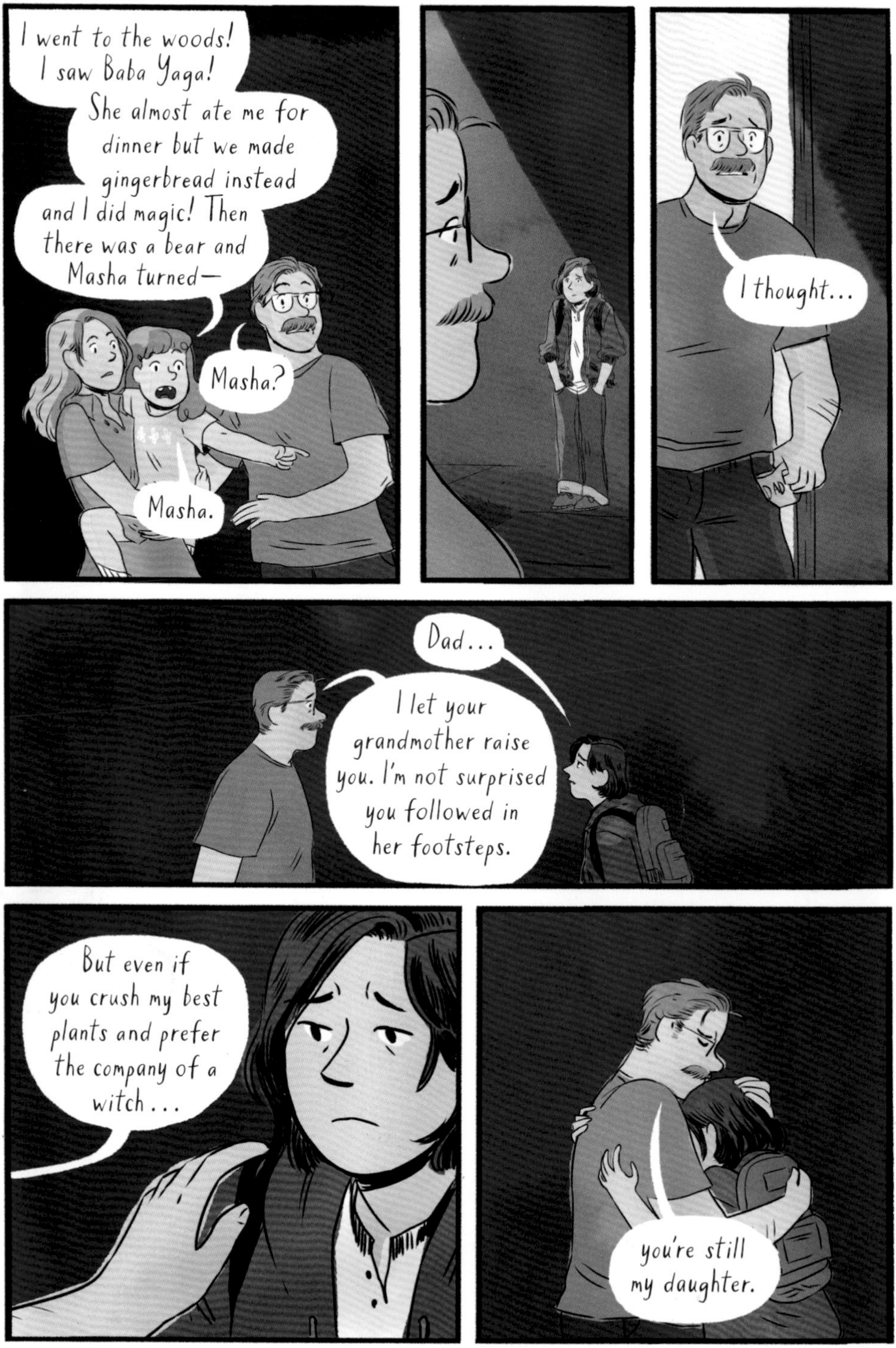
I went to the woods! I saw Baba Yaga!
She almost ate me for dinner but we made gingerbread instead
and I did magic! Then there was a bear and Masha turned—
Masha?
Masha.
I thought...
Dad...
I let your grandmother raise you. I'm not surprised you followed in her footsteps.
But even if you crush my best plants and prefer the company of a witch...
you're still my daughter.
DAD

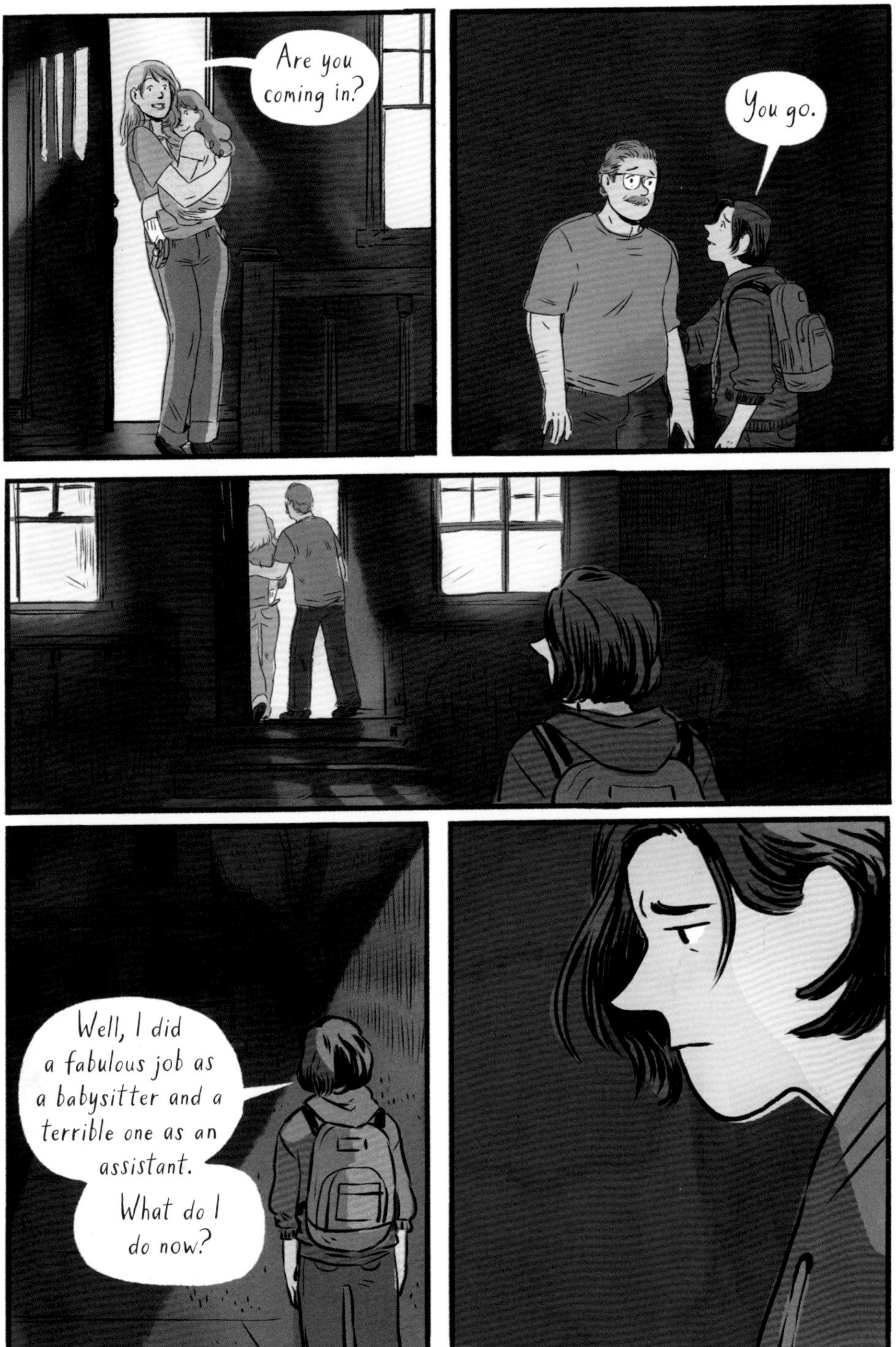
Are you coming in?
You go.
Well, I did a fabulous job as a babysitter and a terrible one as an assistant.
What do I do now?

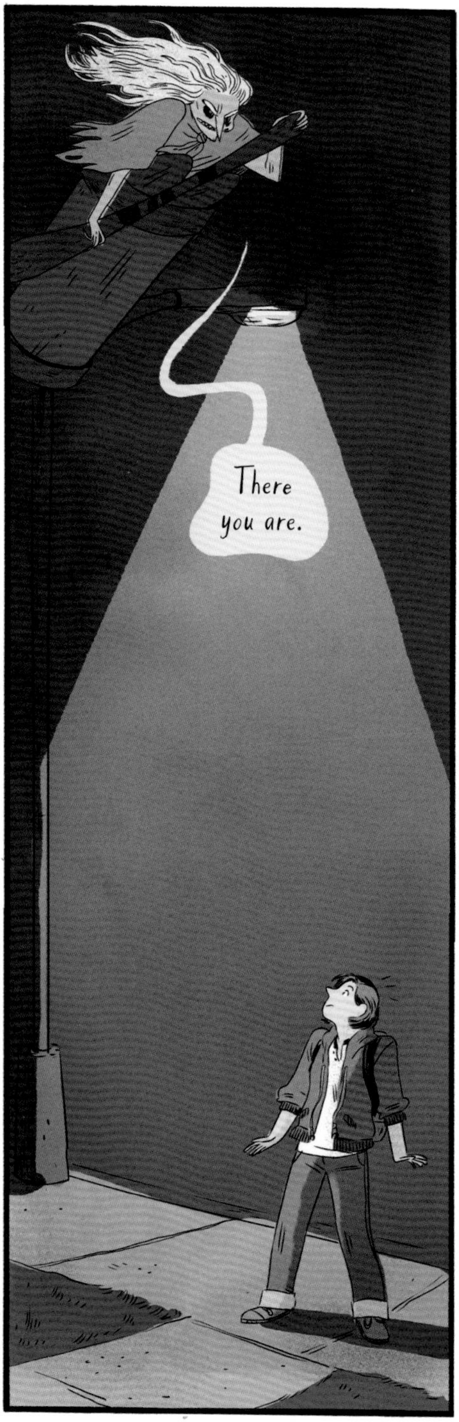
There you are.

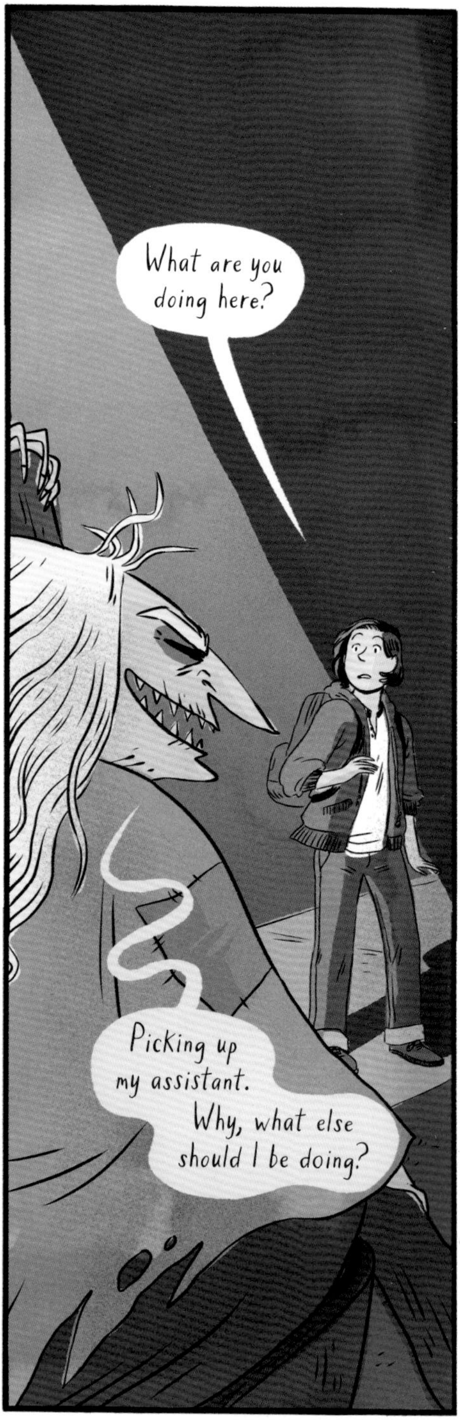
What are you doing here?
Picking up my assistant. Why, what else should I be doing?

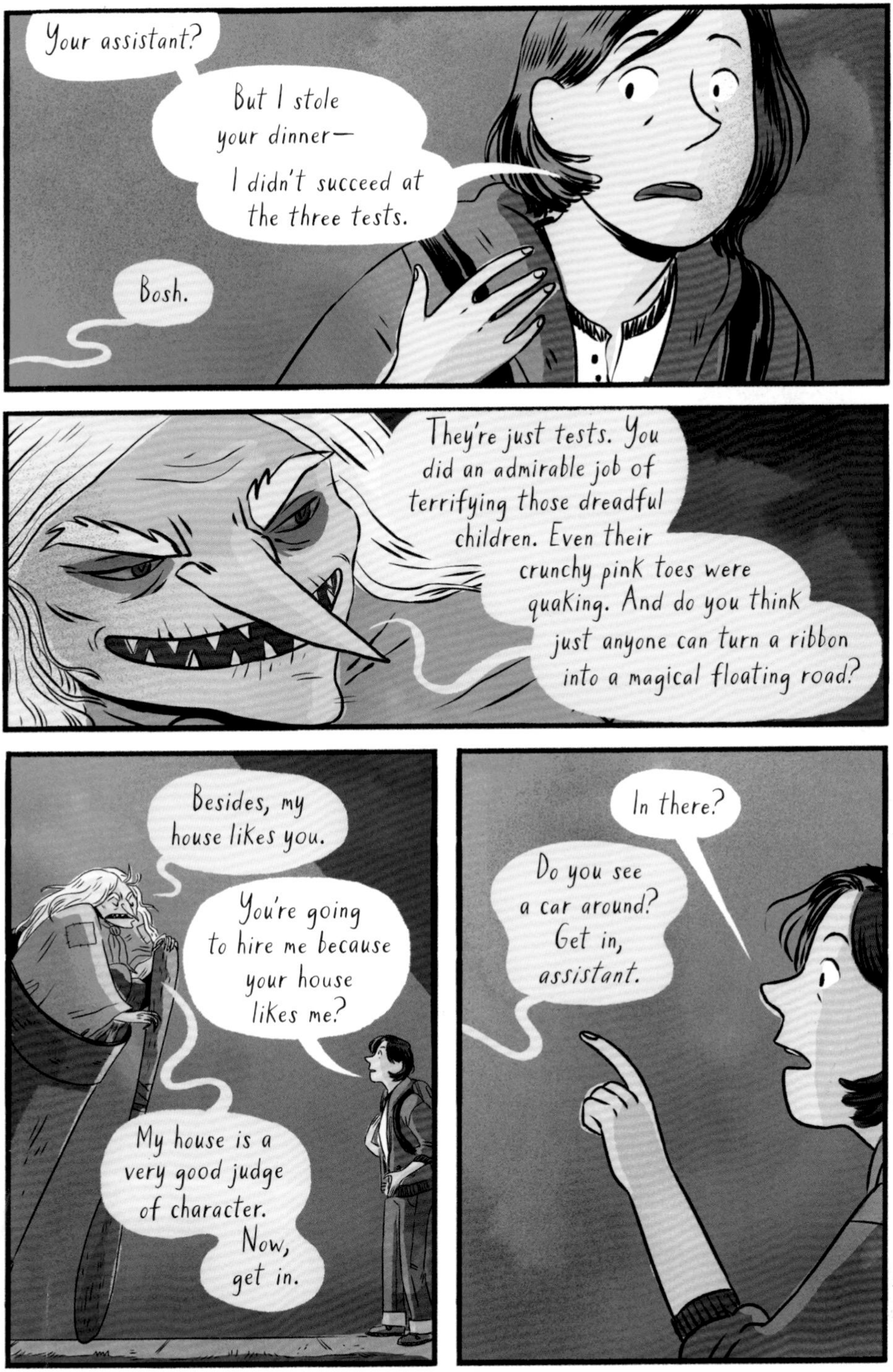

Your assistant?
But I stole your dinner—
I didn't succeed at the three tests.
Bosh.
They're just tests. You did an admirable job of terrifying those dreadful children. Even their crunchy pink toes were quaking. And do you think just anyone can turn a ribbon into a magical floating road?
Besides, my house likes you.
You're going to hire me because your house likes me?
My house is a very good judge of character.
Now, get in.
In there?
Do you see a car around? Get in, assistant.

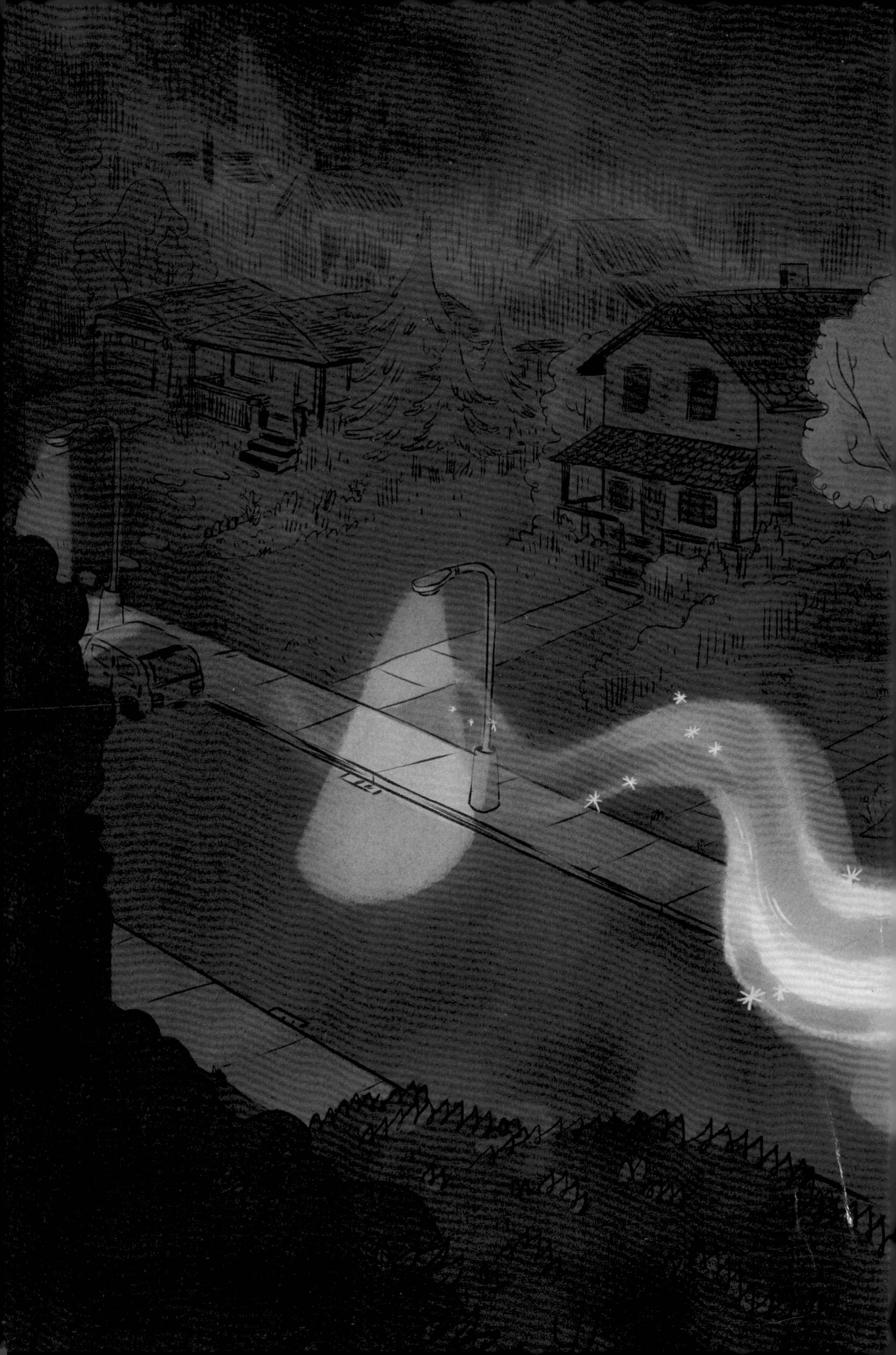

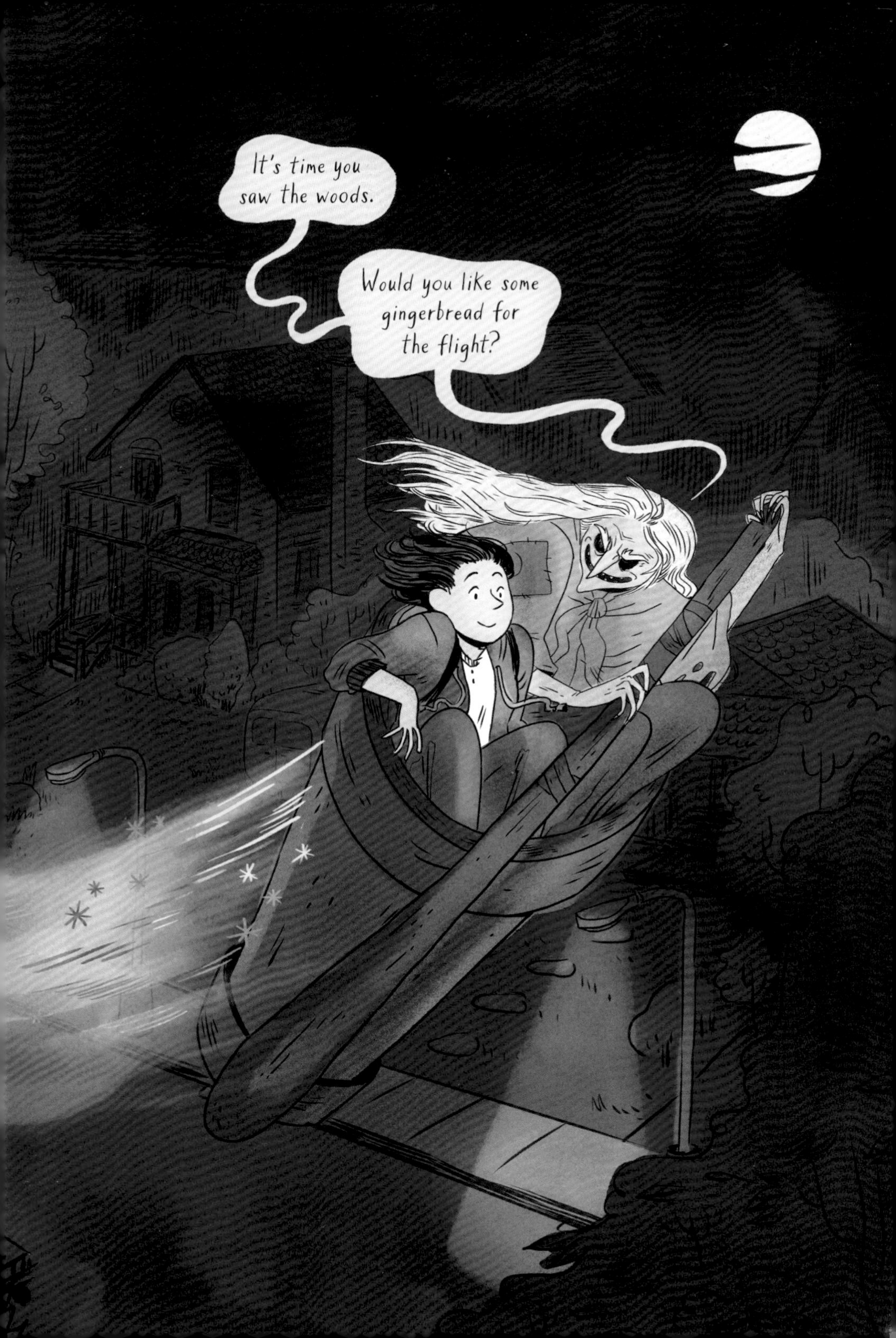
It's time you saw the woods.
Would you like some gingerbread for the flight?

Masha Sketches

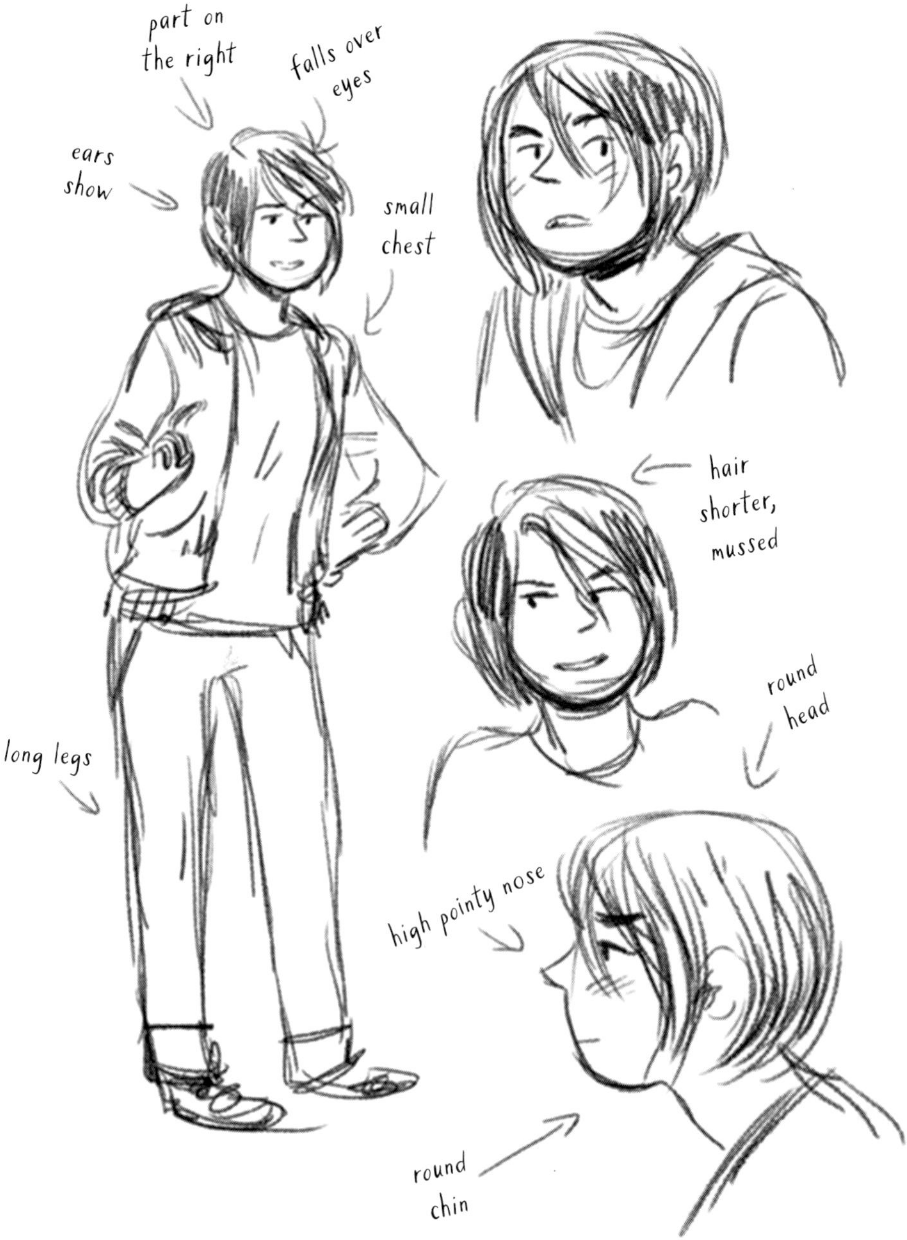

part on the right
falls over eyes
ears show
small chest
long legs
hair shorter, mussed
round head
high pointy nose
round chin

Grandma Sketches

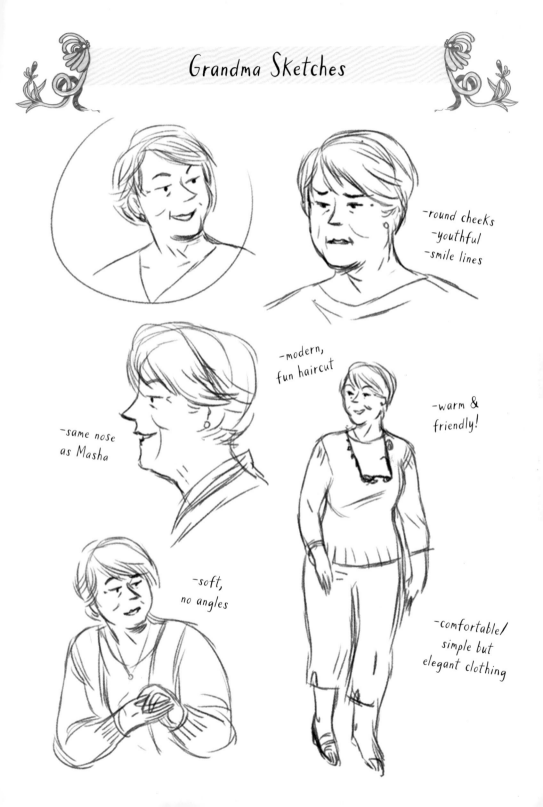

-round cheeks
-youthful
-smile lines

-modern, fun haircut

-warm & friendly!

-same nose as Masha

-soft, no angles

-comfortable/ simple but elegant clothing

Sketches of Baba Yaga's House

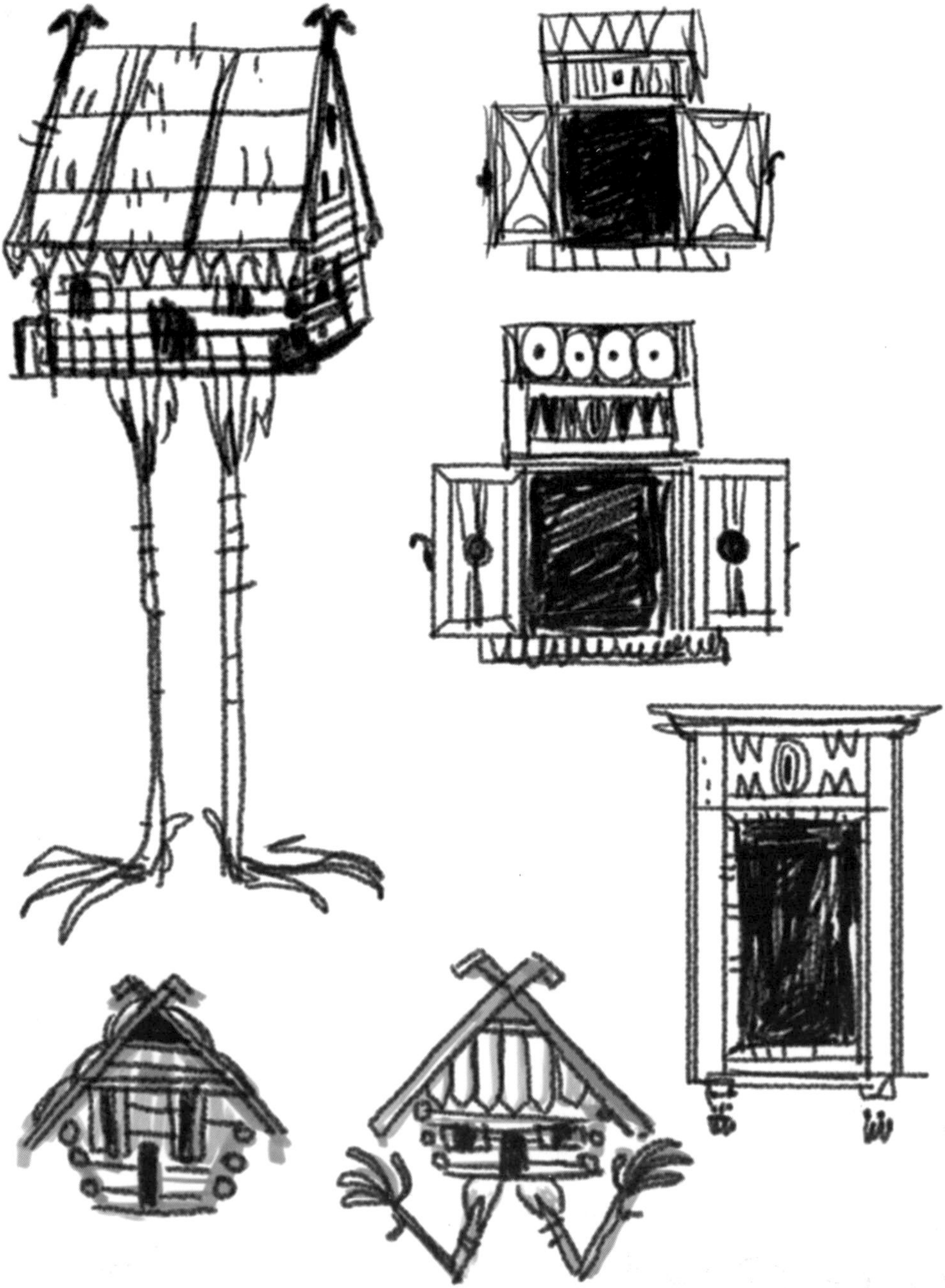

Baba Yaga Sketches

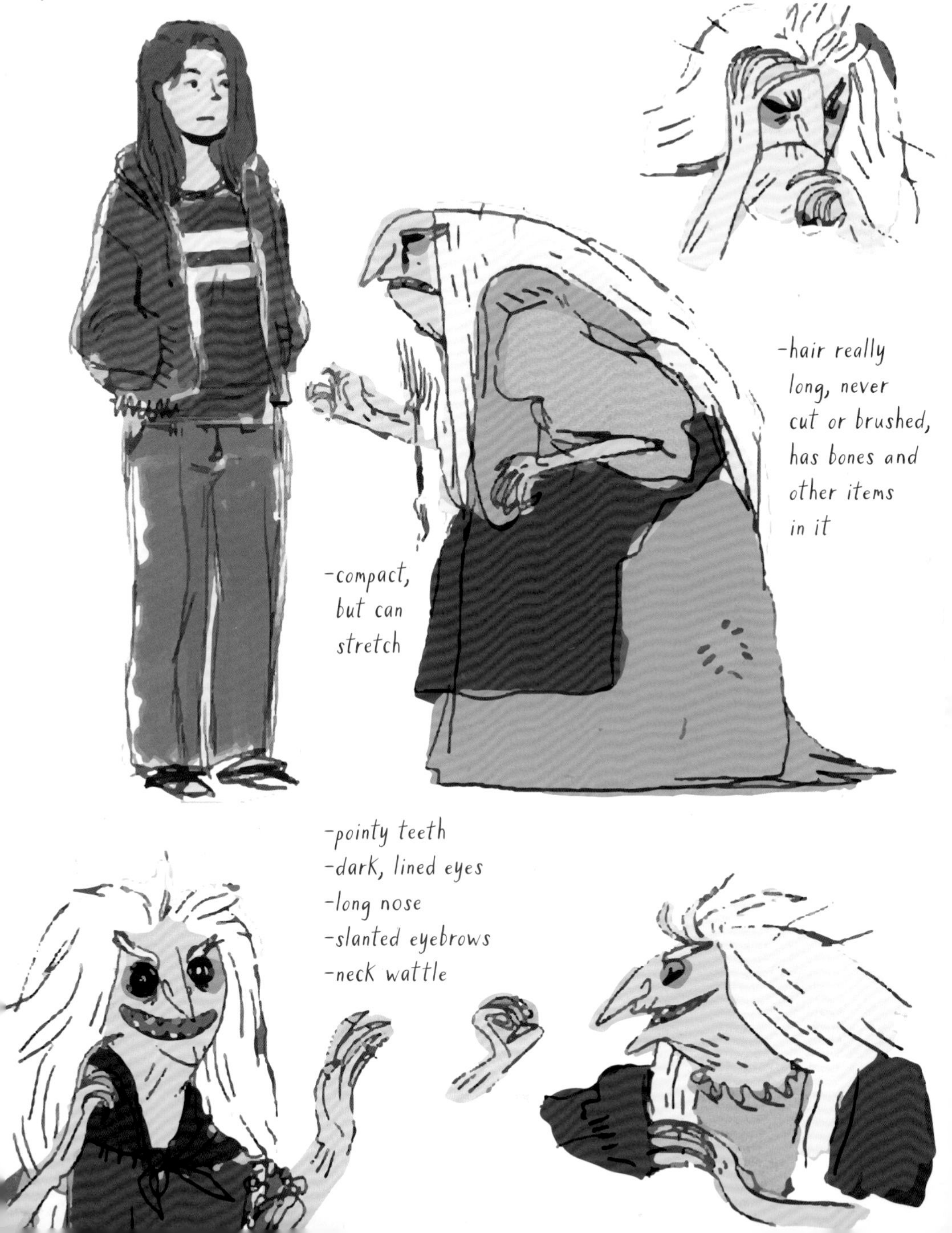
-hair really long, never cut or brushed, has bones and other items in it
-compact, but can stretch
-pointy teeth
-dark, lined eyes
-long nose
-slanted eyebrows
-neck wattle

For Grandma Lily, who has raised
generations of book lovers
M. M.

To my nephew, Liam
E. C.

Text copyright © 2015 by Marika McCoola
Illustrations copyright © 2015 by Emily Carroll

First edition 2015

Library of Congress Catalog Card Number 2014951398
ISBN 978-0-7636-6961-4

15 16 17 18 19 20 CCP 10 9 8 7 6 5 4 3 2

Printed in Shenzhen, Guangdong, China

This book was typeset in Emily Carroll.
The illustrations were created digitally.

Candlewick Press
99 Dover Street
Somerville, Massachusetts 02144

visit us at www.candlewick.com